"You've got a nerve!"

"Why should I feel guilty about you?" Olivia went on angrily. "You of all people? You're the one who should be ashamed of yourself. But not you—oh, no!" She gave a shrill laugh as she tried to jerk her chin away from his hand. *"You rat!* I can see that you're not known as the 'randy Vicomte' for nothing...!"

"How dare you say such things!" Raoul snarled.

"Get out!" she yelled as she twisted free of his embrace. "Go away and play games with your beloved Lucille—or Chantal, or whoever else you fancy at the moment, but leave me alone!"

Almost without realizing what she was doing, she put a hand toward a bowl, seized a lemon and threw it at him with all her strength. "I told you to get out!" she shouted as another lemon followed the first....

MARY LYONS

mended engagement

Harlequin Books

TORONTO • NEW YORK • LONDON
AMSTERDAM • PARIS • SYDNEY • HAMBURG
STOCKHOLM • ATHENS • TOKYO • MILAN

Harlequin Presents first edition June 1985
ISBN 0-373-10796-X

Original hardcover edition published in 1984
by Mills & Boon Limited
under the title *No Other Love*

Printed in U.S.A.

CHAPTER ONE

'But you promised to come to my wedding—you know you did!'

Olivia sighed, brushing a slim hand through her smooth length of thick chestnut hair, the brilliant colour of beechwoods in autumn. Really, her cousin Bridget was being totally unreasonable, as usual. It was absolutely typical of her to be telephoning from France in the middle of the day—the call must be costing her a fortune!

'Look, Bridget,' she said, with as much patience as she could muster, 'it's no good blaming me if there's an air traffic controller's strike, is it?'

'But you must come . . . you simply must! I mean, I've got to have *someone* from my family at the church, Olivia. Surely you can see that?'

'Of course I do,' she assured her cousin soothingly. 'But you must see that there isn't a damn thing I can do about it.'

'Rubbish! You must be able to get over here to Bordeaux!' Bridget's voice rose in frustration. 'It's only a case of crossing the English Channel, it's not the Atlantic Ocean for heaven's sake!'

Olivia's lips twisted in a wry grimace at the petulant tone in her cousin's voice, and with an effort she controlled the impulse to make an equally scathing retort. It didn't seem as if the past year, which Bridget had spent in Italy and France, had made her any easier to handle. Taking a deep breath, Olivia tried, once again, to explain the position.

'Okay, I'll go through it once more. Not only are the air traffic controllers here in Britain on strike, but it has spread to all their colleagues in Europe as well. So that means that no aeroplanes are flying across the Channel—or anywhere else for that matter. . . .'

'Yes, I know *that*—I'm not a complete idiot! But I was relying on you, Olivia. . . .'

'. . . So, my ticket for the flight from Heathrow to Bordeaux at the end of the week is absolutely useless,' Olivia continued, ignoring her cousin's interruption. 'What's more, I spent the whole of yesterday on the telephone to travel agents, British Rail, all the Channel ferry companies—and anyone else I could think of. Believe me, all trains, coaches, ferries and hovercrafts are fully booked, with waiting lists a mile long. There isn't a seat to be had for love or money, and considering that it's the middle of summer, I'm not surprised.'

'Surely there must be some way?' Bridget whined plaintively.

'Oh, sure. All I need is a few lessons in hang-gliding and I'll be right with you!' Olivia laughed ruefully. 'Come on, Bridget! Even you must be able to see that there is simply no way I can get over for your wedding. I'm really sorry, but there it is.'

'It—it's just not fair!' her cousin wailed.

'God give me strength!' Olivia muttered, putting her hand over the receiver and looking up as Sarah, her shop assistant, put her head around the office door.

'I'm sorry to bother you, Miss Harding,' Sarah said. 'Tim's gone with a client to the Oriental carpet warehouse, and Mr Anstruther from the Foreign Office is here to see you about the Embassy job in Moravia.'

Olivia had worked too hard to make a success of her interior decorating business to keep one of her most important and influential customers waiting. 'I'll be with him in a moment,' she told Sarah, before turning back to speak to her cousin. 'I'm sorry, Bridget, I'll have to go—it's business, I'm afraid. I'll be in touch with you again before the wedding, and I'm really sorry not to be able to be there in person. 'Bye.'

She stood up, leaning across her desk to replace the receiver, but not before she caught her cousin's plaintive wail: 'I'll think of something! You'll see—I'll think of something. . . .'

Later on in the afternoon as Olivia put the finishing touches to a decorative scheme for the interior of a mews house in Knightsbridge, she couldn't help smiling wryly at Bridget's refusal to accept the facts of life. How typical of her to insist on getting her own way against all the odds! Not that Olivia's widowed mother hadn't warned her, the last time she had gone down to Surrey to spend a weekend at her old home.

'Goodness knows that I've always felt sorry for the poor girl, although she won't thank you for making the effort, I'm afraid. Still, I agree that you must go over to France if you can, darling. She's always been such a "wild" girl, we must just offer up grateful thanks that she has decided to get married and settle down at last. However, she really ought to have at least one member of the family at her wedding, especially as the girl's marrying *a foreigner*!'

Olivia recalled how she had laughed at her mother's sniff of disapproval, before suddenly remembering her family's dismay when she had told them, five years ago, that she too was going to marry a Frenchman. Of course, that engagement to Raoul had been a very brief affair. . . .

Sitting now at her desk in the office at the back of the shop, she tried in vain to stop her mind from dwelling on the painful memories of the past. Images of herself and Raoul wandering contentedly hand in hand through the rustling, fallen leaves in Hyde Park; laughing as they had fed the ducks on the Serpentine before hurrying back through the falling dusk of the late afternoon to his apartment where, later, he had made love to her, teaching her and rousing her senses until her passion matched his. She had been happy then—deliriously, ecstatically happy; but she had paid a terrible price for such happiness. She had been so certain that Raoul loved her as she loved him. She had never realised that to him she was merely a temporary substitute for the girl he had really loved, and for whom he had discarded Olivia without a moment's hesitation, and with no word of explanation.

'Miss Harding . . .?'

Olivia had been so immersed in her thoughts that she hadn't heard Sarah come into the office, and looked up started out of her reverie.

'I'm—I'm leaving now, if that's all right. Do you want me to lock up and set the alarm?' the girl queried.

'No, I've still got some work to do down here, Sarah. You're off to the theatre tonight, aren't you? Who are you going with? Is it still Bruce?'

'Goodness, no!' her assistant giggled as she waved goodbye. 'That was last week. I'm going out with William now.'

'What it is to be young!' Olivia called after her in amusement, and then shrugged ruefully. If she didn't watch out she would soon be sounding like a sour old maid, whereas the truth was that she, herself, was only a little older than Sarah. Well, she might only be twenty-three, but there were times when she felt forty, and tonight was one of those times, Olivia thought as she put away her work and left the shop through a door at the back and mounted the stairs to her apartment.

Every time she entered the apartment, as now, she never ceased to be grateful to her grandfather for having bought the property in Sloane Street during the depression in the 1930s, and to her father for not having sold the shop and the two-floored apartment above when the family business had hit a bad patch just before his death. Specialising in the sale of high-quality reproduction furniture, the business had fallen on hard times when her father's heart condition had prevented him from taking the necessary interest in the shop.

Returning from that nightmare modelling trip to America, those five years ago, she had arrived to find her father stricken with a stroke, her mother totally preoccupied in nursing him, and the shop—on whose income the family relied—going to rack and ruin. How extraordinary, Olivia thought as she went to run herself a bath, that the few pieces of material she had run out to buy to drape over the dusty furniture, in an effort to try and make the window of the shop look more attractive, should have been the start of her interior design business: Harding Interiors. Customers entering the shop had been far more interested in the 'props' and the swathes of material draped so artistically, than in the pieces of furniture. By the time of her father's death a year later, the shop had changed dramatically and was producing a reasonable income on which she and her mother could live. Her order book was completely full for the next six months, and she had recently taken on her first full-time management assistant, Tim Newton. She employed Sarah in the shop to deal with the increasing passing, casual trade, since she also sold cushions, prints, lamps and other *objets d'art*.

Stepping out of the bath and towelling herself briskly, she couldn't help feeling a small glow of satisfaction. It had been hard work, of course, but now she could relax a little and admit that the business was a success. Not only had some of her interiors been featured in Vogue and Harper's and Queen, but she was in the happy position of not being able to accept all the commissions offered to her. The only drawback being that it left her with very little time for a social life, which conversely had been the great advantage of the business when she had first started, for it had meant that she had little or no time to think about Raoul. However, that wasn't the case nowadays, and she really must make her mind up about Ian Campbell, one way or another. . . .

Olivia glanced at the clock by her bedside and gave a small yelp of dismay. If she didn't stop daydreaming and dress quickly, she was going to be standing about half-nude when Ian arrived to take her out to dinner! She had quite enough trouble evading his questions about just when she was going to marry him and settle down, to want to give him any unnecessary encouragement.

Later on that evening she found herself gazing down at her steak with mounting dismay. 'I'm sorry, Ian. It—it looks simply delicious, but I just don't seem to feel hungry tonight, for some reason.'

Ian Campbell looked across the table at the fine, almost too slim figure of the girl, the shadows beneath her wide green eyes and the heavy weight of burnished chestnut hair as it brushed against her creamy skin.

'I'm not surprised!' he declared with a warm smile. 'Not only have you been working far too hard lately, but to have put up with all that nonsense from your cousin as well—it would be enough to make anyone feel exhausted! What you need is a good holiday.'

When they were driving back to her apartment, he returned to the subject again. 'You know, in some ways it is a pity that you can't go to your cousin's wedding,' he murmured, taking one hand from the steering wheel to cover hers where they lay in her lap. 'I think you ought to go away somewhere this August and have a good rest. You can come back refreshed, and then,' he squeezed her hands significantly, 'and then we can start making plans about the future. *Our* future, yes?'

Olivia returned the squeeze of his fingers, thankful at not having to give him an answer as his car drew up outside the shop.

'There's no need for you to come up with me,' she exclaimed as he came around to open her door and help her out of the car.

'Nonsense,' he smiled. 'I wouldn't dream of not escorting you to your front door.'

Slowly mounting the stairs beside Ian, she studied him covertly from beneath her dark eyelashes. Her mother had said she was crazy not to have said 'yes' when he had first proposed to her a year ago.

'Darling—he's perfect! A wealthy young solicitor; fair haired, good-looking and hard working. What more could a girl want, for heaven's sake?'

Mother's right, Olivia thought with an inward sigh as she fumbled in her evening bag for her key. What more could she possibly want? Ian was kind and gentle, he seemed to possess the patience of a saint as he waited for her to make up her mind about their marriage; and if his mild kisses failed to ignite her senses, well, that was more likely to be her fault than his. . . .

Her wayward, confused thoughts were interrupted by the shrill ringing of a telephone inside the apartment as she slid the key into the lock.

'You go and answer the phone while I'll make us some coffee,' Ian said firmly, disappearing down the passage to the kitchen.

With a shrug of resignation, Olivia went over and lifted the receiver. There was a loud crackling in her ears, followed by a distant roaring sound, but no trace of a human voice. 'Oh—for goodness sake,' she grumbled, replacing the receiver. Immediately she had done so, the phone rang again.

Barely controlling an impulse to swear loudly, she picked it up for the second time.

'. . . Hello . . . hello,' a faint voice broke through the crackling background.

'Bridget? Is that you?' Olivia shouted, half-recognising her cousin's voice.

'There's no need to shout!' Bridget's voice was suddenly very clear as the background atmospherics disappeared.

'Well, I had such trouble hearing you . . .'

'. . . I told you I'd solve the problem, didn't I?' Bridget's voice rang with unconcealed self-satisfaction and triumph. 'Well, I have—so there!'

'Solved what?'

'Oh—for heaven's sake, Olivia! I've arranged a way for you to travel to Bordeaux. It was quite simple, really. All I had to do was to. . .' Olivia's ears were suddenly filled with an angry crackling sound which made her flinch as Bridget's voice seemed to advance and retreat like pounding waves on a shore.

'. . . Henri . . . his uncle . . . staying in London. . . .'

'Bridget? Bridget—I can't hear you. Please speak very slowly, OK?' Olivia shouted in frustration as the humming and crackling continued unabated, relaxing to smile gratefully at Ian as he placed a cup of coffee on the table beside her.

'It's Bridget calling from France, and it's a perfectly dreadful line. I can't hear a thing—or hardly anything.'

'. . . Henri's uncle . . . Monsieur le Vicomte. . . .'

'Vicomte? What Vicomte . . .?'

'What's a Vicomte?' she turned aside to whisper to Ian. 'Is it the French version of a Viscount?' As Ian shrugged, she screwed up her face, trying to concentrate on the faint voice behind the atmospherics, which suddenly—as they had before—disappeared.

'. . . I mean it was such an obvious solution when you think about it, wasn't it? Henri's uncle will collect you at half-past two tomorrow afternoon. So all you have to do is to pack a case and Monsieur le Vicomte. . . .'

'Bridget! I can't possibly leave tomorrow. It just isn't possible! Bridget . . .? *Oh no!* The damn phone's dead! Of all the . . .!' Olivia slammed the receiver down in a fury.

'Oh, that's great—really great!' she exploded, jumping up and pacing about the room. 'You wouldn't believe it!' she turned to Ian. 'That imbecilic cousin of mine has asked her fiancé's uncle—some old Viscount—to call by and pick me up. Not at the end of the week, when I'd planned to fly over, but *tomorrow afternoon*, if you please. That girl is the absolute limit, she really is! I mean—how can I possibly leave tomorrow? It's ridiculous!'

'It isn't, you know.' Ian smiled gently at her as he

sipped his coffee. 'You were going at the end of the week anyway, weren't you? So, it's only four days earlier, that's all. You were telling me yesterday that nothing much happens in your business during August, since most of your customers are away from London. Your new assistant Tim Newton can easily cope with the jobs you have on hand, surely?'

'Yes, well . . .' she sighed. 'I suppose you're right. It's just—it's just that I hate having my hand forced.'

Ian put down his cup and stood up. 'It's time I went. I'm not going to bully you my dear, but I think you ought to pack your case and go off to France tomorrow. The holiday will do you good, you're looking much too thin and tired these days.' He bent down to deposit an affectionate kiss at the corner of her mouth.

Olivia touched his face tenderly before she turned away to open her flat door. 'I expect you're right, you usually are,' she admitted. 'However, I'm going to ring Bridget again tomorrow morning before I finally decide what to do.'

Locking the front door on Ian's departing figure, she rinsed through the coffee cups and then having cleansed her face and brushed her teeth, Olivia slipped on a lacy silk nightgown and sat down to brush her hair at the dressing table in her bedroom. The rhythmic strokes of the brush on her heavy curtain of shoulder-length thick, smooth and lustrous hair made her feel slightly calmer, and more able to take a rational view of Bridget's arrangements.

Her mother was right. Her cousin was indeed very wild, and thoroughly selfish, but when one looked at her background, Olivia didn't find it in her heart to blame her too much. Orphaned when she was only a small baby, her parent's having been killed in an air crash, Bridget had been claimed by her father's eldest sister and her husband, a dour childless couple. Olivia's parents had had her to stay as often as they could, but Bridget's childhood had been a gloomy one and when she had run away from home for the fifth time at the age of sixteen, the elderly couple had washed their hands of her.

Refusing all the offers of other members of her family to pay for a secretarial training, or some other gainful employment, Bridget had drifted from one casual job to another, working in disco's, pubs, cafes and even, as Olivia's mother had told her daughter in shocked tones, working as a hostess in a night club. Under the circumstances, Olivia could only be grateful that her mother had never set eyes on Bridget during her punk phase, when she would surely have fainted at the sight of her niece's hair standing stiffly on end, with one side of her head dyed green while the other was bright blue!

Following that period of rebellion, Bridget had apparently gone to Italy as an au pair. Olivia wasn't sure what had happened to terminate her cousin's employment with the Italian family, but she gathered from the occasional postcards that she received that Bridget had drifted up to France last September. There she had been able to earn good money by picking grapes in the Loire and the Médoc with the other students she had met on her travels. Olivia had heard no more, until she had received a phone call from her cousin a month ago, telling her that she was engaged to be married to someone called Henri Mercier, and asking Olivia to be present at the wedding.

Oh well, Olivia thought as she put down her brush

and moved across the room to climb into bed. She'd just have to sort everything out on the phone with Bridget in the morning. If her cousin thought that Olivia could just drop everything and dash off to France tomorrow, she was very much mistaken, and she'd have great pleasure in telling her so.

Unfortunately, Olivia couldn't get through to Bridget the next morning, and even when she gave up trying to dial direct and elicited the services of the operator, she had no better luck.

'I'm sorry, madam. I am reliably informed that sun spots are causing the interference,' she was informed by a smug, officious voice.

'Sun spots? What nonsense!' Olivia fumed. However, there seemed nothing she could do other than make arrangements for her departure that afternoon, before going back upstairs to the apartment to pack a suitcase.

As always, Ian had been right, she acknowledged ruefully to herself as she tried to decide what clothes she would need to take with her. Something special for the wedding itself, she mused, and then what? Apart from the sudden appearance of 'Monsieur le Vicomte' on to the scene—always providing that she had heard Bridget correctly in the first place—Olivia had not gained the impression that her cousin's fiancé was well off. Quite the reverse, in fact. Hadn't Bridget said something about Henri and his mother living in part of a house? Olivia hesitated for a moment and then decided to play safe by packing the simplest summer clothes she possessed, together with some extra accessories with which she could dress up the garments if the need arose.

Having sorted matters out to her satisfaction, she returned downstairs to the shop where, for some reason, they had their busiest morning for months. The telephone never seemed to stop ringing, the customers who came into the shop proving to be more exacting and demanding than usual. Olivia was glad to be able to escape upstairs for a late salad lunch, and was writing a note of instructions for her cleaning lady who came in twice a week, when the internal phone rang. It was Sarah, practically incoherent as she breathlessly stumbled over the message that a Frenchman was downstairs and asking for Miss Harding.

'Ask him to come up, please Sarah. Unless, of course, he's too elderly to manage the stairs,' she added, suddenly realising that Henri's uncle could be very ancient indeed.

'*Too elderly*. . .?' Sarah gasped incredulously. 'Really, Miss Harding, I—I don't think you quite realise. . . . Well, I mean to say . . .' she gave a nervous giggle. 'He's—er—the Vicomte's definitely able to. . . .'

Olivia sighed. 'OK, Sarah. I know it's been a busy day, but let's cool it, shall we? Just show the gentleman the way up to the apartment, and then why don't you go and have a quiet cup of coffee?'

Whatever could have come over the girl? Olivia shrugged, walking over to open her front door and catching her first glimpse of the tall, dark-haired man as he mounted the stairs.

Suddenly gasping, all the breath driven from her body by a shock-wave which rose up to hit her like a hard blow to the solar plexus, she clung tightly to the open door in a desperate attempt to prevent herself from falling. Recognition and fear welled up inside her like a sudden sickness as she felt her slim body beginning to shake as if in the fierce grip of a tropical fever.

'R-Raoul . . .?'

'Ah, Olivia. How very pleasant to see you again, especially after so many years, hmm?'

She felt as though she had strayed into a living nightmare as she registered the cool, faintly bored tones in the well-known voice. With glazed eyes she stared in bemused disbelief as the tall, elegant figure of the man who had caused her such heartache in the past, strode smoothly past her trembling form and entered the apartment.

Ten minutes later she was still having considerable difficulty in concentrating on what Raoul was saying. Clasping her hands tightly together in an effort to hide their trembling, she shook her head distractedly as she tried to force her dazed mind to function normally.

'I—I still don't understand what—what you're doing here. How can you be Henri Mercier's uncle? It—it isn't possible . . .' her voice trailed nervously away.

'*Mais oui*, it is entirely possible, my dear Olivia,' he drawled with cynical amusement. 'Henri is the son of my widowed sister, Hélène, who is ten years older than I. She and her son are, at the present time, residing in a wing of my château.' He raised his arm, glancing down at his gold watch. 'We do not have much time if we are to catch the ferry to Boulogne.'

'But—but Raoul, I can't possibly. . . . Surely you can see that it's quite out of the question for me to accompany you to France?'

'*Pourquoi?*' Raoul raised an autocratic dark eyebrow.

'Why? But—but surely it's obvious!' Olivia cursed inwardly as she felt her cheeks redden under his cool appraisal.

In the pool of silence which fell between them, she

looked again at the man to whom she had once been engaged.

Raoul de Varennes was all that she had tried to forget—and more. Tall, lean, dark and painfully attractive, his tanned skin was darkened further by the black hair which lay thick and smooth against his well-shaped head, sweeping down to curl over the edge of his collar. He was perhaps a little thinner than she remembered, and although he couldn't be more than thirty-five, there were several strands of silver among the dark hair at his temples. The steely blue eyes beneath their hooded lids were only part of his dark attraction. Set above an aquiline nose, they only hinted at the sensuality which was clearly evident in the curved line of his wide mouth.

Olivia took a shaking, unsteady breath as she tried desperately not to recall the broad-shouldered torso, the slim hips and the firm muscled thighs which lay beneath the light grey suit he was wearing with such ease and assurance.

Turning away to fiddle nervously with the pens and pencils on her open desk, she endeavoured to control the flushed, betraying quiver of awareness which scorched through her body. Oh yes, she told herself ruefully, she knew exactly what had 'come over' Sarah. How well she knew—and who better?—the devastating effect even one of his casual smiles could have on the female population. Women had obviously been standing in line for this man from the first day he put on long trousers—or even earlier, she thought grimly.

'Come, Olivia.' Raoul's calm, firm voice broke into her confused thoughts. 'There is little point in discussing what is, in effect, a *fait accompli*.' He gave her a cool smile. 'I agree that it is tiresome of my nephew, Henri, to wish to be married when he is so young; especially to that quite extraordinary young girl, Bridget. However, there is nothing that either of us can do, since the two young people are both over twenty-one.'

'That's—that's not what I meant at all!' she protested.

'*Ah bon.* Then, it would seem, the only question remaining is whether you intend to support a member of your family at her wedding . . .' he paused and shrugged. 'I can understand your reluctance, my dear Olivia. I must confess that the connection is not one that I would have wanted for Henri; your cousin Bridget is very much of the *petite bourgeoise*, is she not?'

I'm not your 'dear Olivia' she wanted to scream, gritting her teeth as Raoul's smile of cool disinterest flicked over her nervously trembling figure. 'My God! What a snob you've turned out to be,' she retorted curtly, grateful for the opportunity to be both genuinely scathing and also able to release some of the deep anger and hurt which was pounding in her head. 'Incidentally, just how long have you been so . . . er . . . "noble"?' she added caustically. 'Or is your title perhaps one of those handed out by Napoleon? They are very much looked down on in France, I understand.'

'My family is of the *ancien régime*, of course,' he snapped angrily, providing her with the considerable satisfaction of having managed to dent his cool self-possession. 'I inherited my title on the death of my great-uncle some four years ago, together with his estates. However,' he added dismissively, 'all that is by the way.'

'Well, it's certainly got nothing to do with me!'

Olivia gave a careless laugh, which even to her ears sounded slightly shrill and off-key.

'*Bien*,' Raoul murmured, hesitating for a moment as he studied her intently from beneath his heavy eyelids, before turning to walk slowly over to the window where he stood looking down into the street below. 'It is, of course, quite possible that you might feel—how shall I put it?—a little constraint, some uncertainty in your mind due to the small romance between us in the past. However, that was something which took place a very long time ago, *non*?'

Olivia looked at the thick dark hair curling down over his collar, the casual stance of his broad-shouldered figure as he continued to watch the traffic outside, while he talked calmly and dismissively about an affair which, it was quite clear, had never been of any major importance in his life.

'Ah, yes. So much has happened in the last five years, has it not? It would surely be foolish of us, Olivia, to let something that was merely nothing but a youthful—er—indiscretion, prevent you from accepting a lift from me to attend your cousin's wedding, hmm?'

Put like that, what could possibly be more reasonable or indeed a more sensible solution to her problem? How could she possibly refuse to accompany him to Bordeaux simply because they had once been engaged to be married? An engagement, it seemed, of which he had very little recollection.

If only she could be as cool, calm and unconcerned as Raoul. Maybe, if she had more time to think matters out, she would be able to find an alternative answer to her predicament? Unfortunately, it was clear that time was something she didn't have as Raoul pointedly looked again at his watch, waiting with impatient indifference for her answer.

There was no help for it, she realised gloomily. She'd have to accept his offer—if only because of Bridget. However irritating her cousin could be at times, Olivia really was in duty bound to attend her wedding—if at all possible. How could she refuse to go now, especially when she couldn't think of a good reason for not doing so . . .?

With a heavy sigh, she found herself reluctantly accepting Raoul's offer, and trying to stifle the waves of panic which swept through her body at the thought of being in close contact, for however short a time, with this man who had once meant so much to her.

Just over an hour later, seated beside Raoul as he drove his powerful, silver-grey Porsche down the hill into the busy seaport of Dover, Olivia could feel her head beginning to throb angrily as the accumulated tensions of the day began to take their toll. The panic had now settled down into a tight knot of almost sick apprehension, which lay like heavy lead deep in her stomach. Every instinct she possessed was overwhelmingly urging her to leave this car, and put as great a distance between herself and Raoul as she possibly could.

Her normally sparkling green eyes were cloudy and dull as she watched him skilfully negotiate the traffic and drive on to the ferry for Boulogne. Desperately, she tried to console herself with the thought that if Raoul could hardly remember their love affair, it was obviously going to make matters easier for them both during the trip, wasn't it? She turned to stare fixedly out of her window, furiously blinking away the moisture which was threatening to fill her eyes, and trying to ignore a large lump which seemed to have become stuck in her throat.

Parking the car in what seemed to be the bowels of

the ship, Raoul led her up to the main lounge. There, as the vessel left harbour, the noise and laughter of the holiday-makers rose in unison with their consumption of duty-free alcohol. Together with the heat and smoke, the lounge became almost unbearably claustrophobic, and suddenly not caring whether Raoul followed her or even if he had seen her go, she ran for escape up a stair-way and out into the fresh air of the top deck. Going over to lean against a rail, she gazed sightlessly out at the greeny-grey water as the ferry ploughed it's way across the Channel.

Maybe it was the hypnotic rhythm of the waves as they rolled past the ship, or the sheer emotional exhaustion of the past few hours, but there seemed little she could do to suppress the memories she had so resolutely buried five years ago. Memories which, since Raoul's dramatic reappearance in her life, now filled her mind to the exclusion of all else.

CHAPTER TWO

THE first time she had set eyes on Raoul de Varennes, Olivia had been nervously holding the reins of a thoroughbred racehorse and waiting patiently as Penny, the girl from *Bizarre* magazine, adjusted the full skirt of the ball dress that Olivia was modelling. Praying fervently that the highly strung animal would neither kick nor bite her, she looked across the courtyard at the two men talking to the photographer and his assistant. While she recognised the portly figure of the Newmarket trainer, whose stables were being used as a background to the afternoon's fashion shots, the man standing beside him was a complete stranger.

Olivia couldn't seem to tear her eyes away as she absorbed the man's hawk-like tanned face and the sensual appeal of his tall, broad-shouldered body, clad in a soft cashmere sweater over dark trousers closely moulded to his slim hips. Her gaze swept upwards, taking in his firm mouth and the high cheek bones, to meet a pair of steely blue eyes regarding her with a slow, almost insolent appraisal.

Nothing, in all her eighteen years, had prepared Olivia for the shock she experienced at the sheer animal magnetism projected by the stranger. Hairs tingled down the length of her spine and she almost staggered as her senses reeled under the assault of his forceful, raw masculinity.

'Yummy—isn't he?' Penny murmured with her mouth full of pins. 'That sexy chap over there is definitely what I call a gorgeous piece of male crumpet!' she added with a suggestive wink.

'*Penny!* For heaven's sake . . .!' Olivia hissed in an agony of embarrassment, the colour flushing her cheeks as she felt the man's eyes slide over her figure; a scrutiny of scorching intensity that seemed to strip away the satin dress to lay bare the soft flesh beneath.

'Oh, he's French, so I don't suppose that he'll have understood a word I've said—unfortunately!' The girl from the magazine grinned as she bent down to adjust and pin a fold in the couture dress. 'And how you can be such a prude, especially after some months in the business, I'll never know!'

Olivia was well aware that compared to many of the people in the fashion industry, she was lamentably ignorant and inexperienced. Leaving her convent boarding school at the age of sixteen, she had followed her mother's advice and joined her best friend, Anna, at a Cordon Bleu cookery school which like her convent had been buried deep in the English countryside.

Anna's mother was a well-known actress and it was she who had insisted on taking Olivia to a modelling agency when she had completed her cookery course, claiming that the young girl was far too beautiful to remain hidden in a kitchen. Not that Olivia was enamoured with her own looks; longing to possess the softly rounded curves of many of her friends rather than what she thought of as her own gawky, thin and far too tall figure.

To her amazement the head of the model agency had enthused over her five feet nine inches, and what was referred to as 'a delicate slenderness and unconscious grace of movement'. Reacting with a giggle to such fulsome compliments, Olivia had been totally bewildered and was still apt to feel breathless at the speed of resulting events. 'The face of the year' a national newspaper had claimed in banner headlines on a double-page spread, and she had been kept working almost continuously ever since. For the last month the world-famous photographer, Ashley Warne, had insisted on using her for much of his fashion work, and although she was convinced it couldn't last, she found herself enjoying her new profession even if it wasn't as glamorous as she had supposed. Most of her life seemed to be spent standing still for long boring stretches of time—as now—while adjustments were made to the clothes being photographed.

'There, that should please Ashley,' Penny muttered, standing back to check her handiwork. 'Let's hope he wraps this session up soon. It's getting colder and the light will be going any minute.'

Olivia shivered slightly as the cool breeze of the October afternoon ruffled the horse's mane and sent a flurry of fallen leaves skidding across the worn cobbles of the stable courtyard.

'OK, darling. One more time,' Ashley Warne called out. 'That's lovely . . . great. A big smile . . . super . . . lovely. Look back over your shoulder—and again, darling. Lovely . . . fantastic. . . .'

As the familiar, encouraging murmurs flowed over her head, Olivia was almost painfully aware of the tall stranger. He was now surveying her with a fierce intensity that was not only making her blush furiously, but causing her pulses to race almost as though they were out of control. For one heart-stopping moment she closed her eyes, feeling quite faint as an unexpectedly strange, nervous thrill of excitement and apprehension spiralled through her body.

She turned away, trying to hide her blushing cheeks as

she struggled for composure. Taking a deep breath, she glanced back through her eyelashes at the group around Ashley, thanking her lucky stars that they didn't seem to have noticed anything. The last thing she wanted was for the famous photographer to think that she wasn't capable of ignoring background distractions. He had seemed pleased enough with her work so far, but it would only need a small doubt about her professionalism for him to ask her agency to send him another model. God knows, there were hundreds of young hopeful girls who would have given their eye teeth for a chance to be photographed by Ashley Warne.

'OK, that's it,' Ashley was agreeing reluctantly as his camera assistant showed him the reading on the light meter. 'Thanks for your help, Penny. And as for you, Olivia, kindly remember that I want to see you bright-eyed and bushy-tailed on Monday morning. The "Riccardi Girl" isn't supposed to have bags under her eyes—so no late nights this weekend!'

'You must be joking!' she grinned, almost laughing aloud at the thought of doing anything so ridiculous as to jeopardise her first, really big chance in the modelling world.

Studiously ignoring the man, who was still staring fixedly in her direction, she followed Penny out of the courtyard.

'Well! That guy *certainly* fancies you—some people have all the luck!' Penny sighed enviously as they entered the small office which had been provided for Olivia to change in and out of the clothes being photographed for *Bizarre* magazine.

'Oh—for goodness sake!' Olivia's response was muffled as she swept the dress up over her head and handed it to the other girl. 'He's probably just interested in the horses,' she added dismissively.

'Oh, yeah!'

Ignoring Penny's hoot of derisive laughter, Olivia bent down to slip on a tight, pale grey polo-necked sweater and slim black cords which she tucked into knee-high, black leather boots.

'Honestly, if it's a choice between you and that horse—I'll bet anything you like that it's your "form" that Frenchman's interested in!' Penny's giggles were so infectious that Olivia found herself grinning sheepishly in response.

'Very funny! Anyway, what makes you so sure that he's French?'

'I only heard him speak a few words to the owner of the stables, but it was quite enough to get hold of his sexy, French accent. He's apparently got some horses in training up here, which makes him rich as well as scrummy! It costs a fortune to keep a racehorse nowadays. My boyfriend likes to go racing, and he says. . . .'

Olivia let the words wash over her, brushing the long length of her burnished chestnut hair as she tried to sort out her chaotic thoughts. During the past six months, she had become used to being stared at, especially when on location, as today. She couldn't understand, therefore, why the tall Frenchman's obvious preoccupation with herself should make her feel so incredibly nervous and self-conscious. Even thinking about him now was causing her to feel most peculiar.

'By the way,' Penny's voice cut into her thoughts. 'Do I gather from what Ashley's just said, that you've landed the Riccardi contract?'

'Yes, I only heard this morning. I—I still can't really believe it!'

'I'm not surprised! Half the models in London must have auditioned to be the "Riccardi Girl". Well done!'

'Honestly, I had no idea it was so sought after,' Olivia confessed. 'My agent just handed me an address and told me to go along to the office in Mayfair as fast as I could. It was absolutely pouring with rain ... you've no idea how ghastly I looked when I went in to meet all those Italians!'

'It's a good idea, cocktails which are already mixed and ready to pour. I hear their advertising agency are going to be spending millions on the promotion.' Penny smiled quizzically. 'And I can see exactly why they chose you, even if you can't. I hope you realise that your face is going to become one of the best known in Europe?'

'No—I ...' Olivia shrugged. 'It's all happened so fast that I haven't really taken it in yet,' she confided.

'Didn't Lucille audition for the contract? I don't suppose that she's going to be exactly thrilled to hear you've got the job?'

Olivia felt worried for a moment at the thought of competing against the girl with whom she shared an apartment, and then as she recalled Lucille's full diary, she relaxed.

'Lucille's far too busy,' she explained. 'She's working in the Caribbean at the moment and then she's due to go to New York for at least a month. I'm certain that she won't mind one way or another.'

'I expect you're right,' Penny replied in a neutral voice. Olivia, then, had been too inexperienced to realise Lucille's burning ambition and what it could lead to. It never occurred to her to watch out for fireworks from the fiery, temperamental French girl.

'I think that's everything,' Penny commented five minutes later as she finished packing up the clothes that Olivia had been modelling. 'How are you going to get back to London? I'm off to my parent's home in

Norfolk and Ashley and his assistant are spending the weekend in Cambridge.'

'It's absolutely no problem, I can easily catch a train,' Olivia assured her.

However, as they rejoined the others, it appeared that Ashley Warne had been busy on her behalf.

'I've just been having a word with this gentleman,' he announced, nodding towards the Frenchman. 'He says that he's driving straight back to London and will be happy to give you a lift.'

'Oh, no! I mean—there's really no need to bother . . .' Olivia protested breathlessly.

'It is no bother—no bother at all, *mademoiselle*.' The Frenchman's voice, husky and faintly amused, made her feel both excited and terrified at one and the same time.

Trying to ignore the wide grin on Penny's face, Olivia glanced swiftly up at the foreigner, only to be thrown into increased confusion by a cynical, sardonic glint in the steely blue eyes regarding her so intently.

She shrugged as nonchalantly as she could, realising that to refuse would only make her appear ridiculous. She might find the Frenchman particularly disturbing, but she wasn't prepared to let her colleagues guess that fact.

A few minutes later it had all been settled and she found herself being issued into a low red sports car and on her way to London.

The silence in the car seemed to last for eternity, and the longer it lasted, the harder it seemed to find something to say. She hunted feverishly through her mind for some polite conversation which would help to ease the situation.

'The weather, perhaps? Hmm?'

'I—I beg your pardon?' Olivia frowned, glancing swiftly sideways at the Frenchman.

'I understand,' he continued, his mouth twitching in silent humour as he stared through the windscreen, concentrating on the road ahead, 'I understand that when the British do not know what to talk about, they discuss the weather. It was only a suggestion, of course. Perhaps you can think of a more amusing topic, hmm?'

'How did you guess? I mean. . . .' She glanced up startled, meeting such a warm, infectious grin that she found herself smiling nervously in return. 'Well, you must admit that it is awkward. I—I don't even know your name or—or anything about you.'

'That is a matter that is easily remedied. My name is Raoul de Varennes, I am thirty years of age, and I can assure you, my dear *mademoiselle*, that I am very, very respectable. For some months I have been here, in your country, studying the retail wine trade with Messrs Abercrombie and Hall. You have perhaps heard of the company, yes?'

Olivia nodded. Even she, who drank very little, knew the name of the famous wine shipping firm.

'*Ah, bon!* It is very necessary that I should establish my credibility, since not only do I think that I have fallen in love with you, but I would also very much like to take you out to dinner tonight.'

'But—but you can't!' she gasped, her heart pounding with a strange excitement.

'*Pourquoi?* Do you have another date this evening?' he queried coolly.

'No—no I haven't. But—but that wasn't what I m-meant. I m-mean. . . .' Stammering and blushing, she laid her head back on the luxuriously upholstered seat. She must—she simply must pull herself together quickly. Even if he hadn't said what—what she thought he'd said, the warm smell of the leather seats and the elusive, masculine aroma of his aftershave was affecting her already dazed senses in a thoroughly disastrous manner.

'So, you have no date for tonight and are free to join me for dinner, yes?'

'But I didn't say that,' she protested. 'Besides, you don't even know my name or—or anything about me.'

'*Mais oui!* I know that your name is Olivia Harding, that you are eighteen years of age and that I find you ravishingly beautiful. What more is there to say?'

Olivia found herself reduced to silence, her heart pounding like a sledgehammer. No one had ever talked like that to her before, and she wasn't sure how the game—if it was a game?—should be played. Most of the women this man knew would be as sophisticated and cool as himself. They would know how to conduct the sort of witty, smart conversation, full of sexual innuendos and amusing *double entendres* that was well outside her own experience.

Before she became too swamped with nervous uncertainty, he began to talk slowly and calmly about the differences he had noticed between the life he led in France and that in Britain. Describing some of the amusing mistakes he had made with both the language and the British way of life, he made her smile so much, that by the time they reached London she felt far more relaxed and at ease.

'You must forgive me for teasing you, *ma petite*,' he said with a smile as he brought the car to a halt outside her apartment. 'Nevertheless, I very much hope that you will indeed join me for dinner tonight, at eight, hmm?'

He had taken her blushing confusion for assent, and with a warm smile driven off down the road.

Olivia was not prepared to admit, even to herself,

exactly why she felt so nervous as she prepared for her date with Raoul that evening. However, when he arrived looking so incredibly suave and elegant in his dinner suit, she was glad she had taken trouble with her own appearance. The gleam of appreciation in his eyes as they swept over the burnished sheen of her long hair to rest on the brief, low-cut bodice of her green silk dress, made her legs tremble as he smoothly escorted her down to his car.

Raoul had booked a table in a small, intimate restaurant where, as he told Olivia, he had ordered a meal which he hoped would please her; an aim in which he succeeded. He had been charming, friendly and apart from the occasional blush she couldn't control when she felt his eyes lingering on the soft curves of her figure, his conduct had been impeccable.

Driving back after their meal together, Olivia felt her stomach clench in nervous alarm as they arrived outside the building which housed the apartment she shared with Lucille. In the past she had dated quite a few boys, and when those evenings had ended with a goodnight kiss, Olivia had found the experience less than earth shaking. Lately, living here in London, her good looks and the lure of the fashionable modelling world had attracted many men to her side; none of whom had particularly interested her. Moreover, the demands of her job had ensured that her available free time was more likely to be spent washing her hair and getting a good night's sleep, than in kicking up her heels in nightclubs or dating devastatingly attractive men like Raoul. Such men, as she had gathered from her new friends among the modelling fraternity, found virgins gauche and boring, preferring girls who 'knew the score'.

Not for the first time, Olivia felt a fierce longing to

be an experienced woman of the world. If only she had
the sexual sophistication of Lucille, for instance, who
picked and discarded lovers as the mood took her.
Maybe if she had some practical sexual knowledge to
fall back on, she wouldn't be feeling quite so nervous
as she sat beside a man who, it was clear to even her
innocent eyes, knew all there was to know about the
female sex.

However, she need not have worried. Raoul had
merely escorted her to the front door and with a smile
raised her hand to his lips before running back down
the steps to his car and roaring away into the night.

How could she have been so naive as to have been
upset by the remarks he had made on the journey back
from Newmarket? As she undressed in her bedroom
later that evening, Olivia almost groaned at her
ignorance in over-reacting in such a gauche manner to
what had obviously only been meant as an amusing
conversational gambit. Her last depressing thought,
before she fell asleep, was that Raoul must have been
thoroughly bored by her lack of sophistication, and it
was extremely unlikely that he would want to see her
again.

However, if Raoul was suffering from boredom, he
managed to hide the fact very well during the
following week as he claimed every spare minute of
her time.

'What about your business?' she asked in some
confusion one afternoon as having finished a photographic session, she once again found him waiting for
her outside Ashley Warne's studio. 'Shouldn't you be
at work?'

'You must have forgotten that I told you I am
having a few day's holiday?' he replied blandly, taking
her case and issuing her into his red sports car.

'Where are we going?' she asked, peering apprehensively out of the window. It had been a lovely, warm autumn morning, but now it looked like rain. 'I'm simply not wearing the right clothes!' Olivia gestured ruefully to her hip-hugging jeans and the thin silky blouse which emphasised the rounded swell of her breasts.

'There is no need for you to worry, *ma petite*, you look perfect,' he assured her with a warm glance from beneath his heavy lids as he drove swiftly through the busy streets.

Glancing furtively at his arrogant profile, she found herself wishing that he would stop calling her '*ma petite*' in that disturbingly caressing tone of voice. In the first place, while at five foot nine inches she was still much shorter than Raoul's tall figure, *petite* was hardly the right adjective. And in the second place. . . . She sighed unhappily. It was laughable really, she supposed, but when she looked back on her nervous apprehension as to whether Raoul would kiss her goodnight, that first evening he had taken her out, she felt more like weeping with frustration.

He had insisted on seeing her every day during the last week, and during that time Raoul had never done any more than kiss her hand. The intensity of her longing for him to press his mouth to her lips, to be roughly crushed within his embrace, was becoming almost more than she could bear. She seemed to be filled with strange inexplicable desires, which not only increasingly racked her body, but also shocked her innocent mind. Was this what writers and poets meant by love? This wild, breathless excitement, a bitter-sweet longing which seemed to turn her limbs to water whenever she thought about Raoul; let alone found herself sitting so closely beside him as she was at the moment.

So, what was wrong with her? she asked herself for the hundredth time. Raoul seemed to want her company—demanded it, in fact. And yet, when they were together, he treated her with a cool charm which left her feeling baffled and frustrated.

'*Voilà!* You can see there is no problem with your clothes. We will just go for a walk, yes?' Raoul's voice broke into her chaotic thoughts as she looked up to see that they had come to a halt in Hyde Park.

They spent some time wandering slowly along the paths, their feet scrunching over the fallen, rustling leaves, before going over to feed the ducks on the Serpentine. Olivia was laughing so much as she watched a duck having a tug of war with one of Raoul's shoelaces, that she failed to notice the sky darkening ominously overhead. Moments later, her fears about her scanty attire were borne out as the heavens opened, and they were forced to run back to the car through a heavy downpour which left her soaked to the skin.

She laughingly protested at his concern, but after a quick glance at her drenched, shivering figure, Raoul insisted on taking her to the penthouse apartment he leased just the other side of the park.

She was given no opportunity to look over the huge apartment, which she had never visited before, as he hustled her across the large hall and into a luxurious bathroom. Impatiently ordering her to take off her wet clothes, place them on the hot radiator and then to have a warm bath, he turned to leave the room.

'Honestly! Anyone would think I was dying of pneumonia, instead of just being a bit wet,' she grumbled, wishing with all her heart that he wouldn't keep treating her as if she was made of delicate porcelain. His only reply was a short bark of laughter as the door closed behind him.

With a rueful shrug, Olivia sprinkled bath oil liberally on to the water and soaked in the scented depths of the large bath for well over an hour, relishing the luxury of the heavy gold taps and the ornately carved mirrors reflecting the soft glow of the crystal lights. A luxury which was far outside her limited experience. Emerging from the bath, she wrapped herself in a white towelling robe she found on the back of the bathroom door, and made her way into what she assumed was the lounge, her bare feet moving silently over the thickly piled carpet.

Ignoring the softness of the silk drapes, the smooth leather chairs and the polished rosewood furniture, her eyes were drawn irresistibly to Raoul who was sitting at a desk with his back to her at the other end of the vast room. Her heart seemed to leap in her body as an unbearable longing surged through her limbs. Her body trembled as she fought an overwhelming urge to run and put her arms about his neck, and tell him. . . . Tell him what? It was almost a relief to acknowledge the simple truth to herself, at last: that she had fallen deeply and irreversibly in love with Raoul. Only, how could she? How could she tell this man that she was desperate for love of him, when they had only met a week ago and he had never even so much as kissed her?

The small sigh which escaped her lips alerted him to her presence. Turning to look at the girl in the doorway, his hooded gaze swept over the glorious chestnut hair pinned up on top of her head, her long legs revealed by the short robe whose belt tightly clasped her slim waist.

Olivia almost flinched as just for a second it seemed as if his face tightened into a harsh bitterness, before she saw that she must have been mistaken. With his normal cool smile, he rose from his chair and went over to a drinks tray set on a table in the corner of the room.

'My dear Olivia!' he drawled lightly. 'If my friends could see you now, they would undoubtedly accuse me of cradle snatching! You look more like fourteen than eighteen years of age in that ridiculous robe. Would you like a drink?'

She could only nod dumbly, unable to find her voice. Her mouth seemed suddenly dry and her body was rocked by a wave of sensuality which left her shaken and appalled. It could only be—*it must be*—the unnatural freedom of her naked form beneath the dressing gown, but she had an almost insane desire to feel the cool touch of his hands on her heated body. Taking a deep breath, she moved over to look out of the huge window at the panoramic view of London. She could feel beads of perspiration breaking out on her forehead as she fought to control her trembling figure. What on earth was happening to her?

'Sit down and make yourself comfortable.'

Raoul's voice seemed to come from somewhere far off as she tried to pull herself together, staggering over to one of the deep leather sofas on legs that felt as if they were made of jelly.

'Are you feeling warmer after your bath?' he asked as he came over to sit down beside her on the sofa.

Olivia nodded, trying to achieve a cool smile as he handed her a large whisky and soda.

'Careful, *chérie!*' he cautioned, reaching forward to steady the drink in her wildly trembling hands. Olivia gave a cry of dismay as she felt the glass slip from her shaking fingers, and in lunging forward to save it she found herself in his arms. Time seemed to stand still for a moment as his eyes blazed down into hers, his face only inches from her own.

'*Oh, mon Dieu!*' She heard his husky murmur, and then the hard pressure of his mouth sought the parted trembling sweetness of her lips, all coherent thought obliterated as he crushed her firmly to his chest. Her heightened senses relayed to her the aromatic tang of his cologne, the warmth of his body beneath the thin silk shirt, the heavy pounding of his heart. Her arms seemed to be acting of their own volition as they slid about his neck, her fingers burying themselves convulsively in his dark hair as her whole body melted against him with feverish desire.

Raoul raised his head, his breathing as ragged and unsteady as her own and an expression in his eyes that made her gasp with a tremulous, aching excitement.

'Olivia!' he muttered hoarsely. '*Mais non!* We must stop. You are so young, so innocent. . . .' She could see a vein beating wildly at his temple and felt his body tremble violently against hers as he fought for control.

'Please . . . please kiss me again, Raoul,' she whispered, her senses reeling out of control as she leant against him with an innocent provocation that produced an answering deep groan. His arms closed convulsively about her slim body, her lips parting beneath his with a small moan of satisfaction as she felt the involuntary shudder that ran through him at the yielding warmth of her body.

A sudden spasm of fright leapt inside her as she felt his hands slip inside the open towelling robe to stroke the supple contours of her bare back, but it was a fear which gave way to an ever-widening tide of erotic pleasure at his cool touch on her skin. Even as she gasped at the explicit sexuality of his fingers moving to cover her breasts with urgent possession, she knew that this was what she wanted; what she had always instinctively wanted from the first moment they had met. Almost mindlessly, Olivia lay back in his arms as his mouth left hers to trail down her neck with scorching intensity, his lips moving hungrily over the curve of one creamy breast before returning to possess her lips in a kiss of devastating sensuality.

Aeons of time seemed to pass when at last, with what seemed to be a superhuman effort, Raoul managed to tear his lips away. *'Mon Dieu! Non—non!'* he breathed thickly, gazing down at the soft, trembling figure in his arms. 'My darling—*ma chérie*—you can have no idea of what you are doing!'

'I—I want you to make love to me,' she whispered huskily, her arms reaching up to him once more.

'Olivia!' he groaned as he gently caught her hands and held them tightly in his own. 'I, too—I also wish that it were possible. My God! From the first moment that I saw you, I have thought of nothing else but teaching you to make love. It—it has been driving me crazy!'

'I—I didn't realise . . .' she gasped as his words lit a flame of trembling excitement that scorched through her body.

'No,' he sighed deeply. 'You did not, and that is why this is wrong.' His mouth came down to silence her instinctive protest. *'Ma petite,* you must understand that you are so young and so very innocent—so untouched. It would be wrong, almost criminal of me to take advantage of your innocence.'

'But—but I love you!' she cried, not understanding how he could be rejecting her, when he obviously wanted her every bit as much as she desired him.

'Love? Don't you realise that I am twelve years older than you? What can you know of love at your age?' he ground out harshly. 'Go and get dressed, and then I will take you home.' His voice was almost savage as he rose, pushing a hand roughly through his hair as he stalked over to look out of the window.

His change of mood frightened her, driving the colour from her face. Tears filled her eyes and splashed weakly down her cheeks as she clutched the robe closely to her body and fled from the room.

The atmosphere was thick with constraint as they drove back to her apartment in silence. Olivia's head throbbed with misery and unhappiness, her cheeks burning with mortification as she slowly realised that Raoul had only been interested in her in a physical sense, and even that desire had been curbed by her virginity. As for her declaration of love—his sharp reaction to her words had very clearly demonstrated that her feelings were not reciprocated.

Raoul curtly insisted on seeing her to the door of her apartment, and it was only as her trembling fingers hunted for her key that she realised her tote bag, containing her make-up and the accessories which she always carried with her as the tools of her trade, was still in the back of his car. He told her to let herself into the apartment while he went down to fetch her bag.

Entering the apartment she was surprised to see that the lights were on, and going into the lounge she saw the slim, svelte dark figure of her friend Lucille, who had obviously just arrived back from the Caribbean.

'You look brown,' she said gazing at the older girl's tanned face. 'Did you have a good time?'

'Not half as good a time as *you*, I understand!' Lucille snapped. 'Did you really think that you could keep it a secret from me?'

'A—a secret? I—I don't understand?' Olivia looked at her in bemusement as she registered the fact that her friend was furiously angry.

'"I don't understand"!' Lucille mimicked harshly. *'Mon Dieu!* When I think of all that I have done for you! Oh, what a viper I have nourished in my bosom—what an evil snake in the grass!' The French girl's voice was heavy with venom, her arms gesticulating wildly as with a twisted, scowling expression on her face she marched rapidly back and forth across the room.

'C'est scandaleux! You have stolen my contract. It was mine—*à moi!'* she screamed with rage.

'Contract?' Olivia's dazed, weary mind tried to comprehend what she was saying. 'Do—do you mean the Riccardi contract?'

'Of course! It was promised to me—*positivement!* And now, what do I find on my return?' Lucille ground her teeth in fury. 'I find that all my oh-so-good friends are laughing at me. They tell me that my contract has been stolen by a little milk-sop—a little Miss Nobody—to whom I gave shelter, and who has now knifed me in the back!'

'But Lucille. . . . I never—Oh. . .!' Olivia's head rocked as she reeled back from the French girl's angry slap on her face.

Feeling so shattered by the blow, and stunned by the unexpected tirade which had broken about her head, it was some moments before Olivia realised that Lucille had stopped yelling, and was staring open-mouthed at the door as if she had seen a ghost. Spinning around, Olivia saw that Raoul had entered the room; although just how long he had been standing there she had no idea.

'Raoul! What are you doing here?' Lucille demanded breathlessly. 'I had no idea that you were in London, *chéri.'*

Olivia watched in astonishment as a simpering pout

ousted the angry expression on Lucille's face. It appeared that she and Raoul knew each other, she realised, feeling almost sick as she noted the greedy, sensual hunger on the French girl's face as she smiled up at Raoul.

Ignoring Lucille, he strode swiftly across the room to place an arm about Olivia's trembling figure. He gently turned her face towards him, his mouth growing taut and grim as he surveyed the livid red mark on her cheek.

'Will you never learn to curb that vile temper of yours, Lucille?' His voice was cold, his glare of icy contempt clearly shaking the French girl.

'Ah, Raoul . . .' Lucille purred huskily, lifting one slim shoulder in a nonchalant shrug. 'I was just a little cross—you know how it is.'

'I heard quite enough to know *exactly* how it is,' he ground out angrily, turning back to gently smooth the hair from Olivia's brow. 'Never mind, darling, the mark will soon fade.'

'"*Darling*"?' Lucille's eyes narrowed dangerously, flicking rapidly over Olivia and Raoul, her face whitening with shock as she noticed for the first time Raoul's protective arms about the trembling girl.

'What are you doing with this—this *ingénue*? Surely you have not been reduced to robbing cradles for your pleasure?' she mocked savagely. 'However, I suppose that little slut. . . .'

'Be silent!' Raoul's face was white with anger and outrage. 'How dare you use such words about someone who ...' he paused for a second, '. . . someone who is about to become my wife. I would have a care as to what you say in future,' he warned through gritted teeth.

Olivia's eyes widened, her heart spinning with joy

and happiness. Raoul wanted to marry her! Despite the scene in his apartment, he did love her after all! She felt almost faint at the wild surge of rapture which flared through her body.

'*Your wife?* You are intending to marry that—that girl?' Lucille shrieked with rage. 'But—but you can't! What about us, Raoul?'

Her words shook Olivia, but Raoul brushed them aside with a cool shrug. 'Us? What about us, Lucille?'

'But it was always understood. . . .'

'I understand nothing, other than the fact that you, I am told, have had many lovers since you came to England, hmm?' he retorted curtly. 'As far as I am concerned, any arrangement between our families is null and void.'

Lucille promptly lost what little control she had retained, screaming at the top of her voice in a stream of French which Olivia was only too thankful she could not understand. Raoul waited, his face an icy mask of disdain, until Lucille at last fell silent.

'You have finished? That is good. Come, Olivia, I will not allow you to stay in this place a minute longer.' He walked over to the door and held it open, beckoning imperiously to her to follow him.

'You little fool!' Lucille called after her departing figure. 'Do you think that you will be able to make him happy, let alone keep him by your side? How long do you think it will be before he leaves you for someone else? Believe me, he will take your heart and break it into little pieces. Remember what I have said, Olivia, when you are weeping your heart out for your faithless lover—remember what I have said!'

'*Remember what I have said. . . .*' The words spat out with such venom those five years ago, now beat a savage tattoo through Olivia's brain, echoing the rhythm of the ship's engines as she gazed blindly out at the English Channel. If only she had taken notice of Lucille's prophetic words, maybe the shattering heartbreak she had suffered only two months later, might in some way have been avoided. . . .

A sudden alteration in the throbbing background noise broke through her dark memories and alerted her to their imminent arrival at Boulogne. Raising her head she saw the tall, commanding figure of Raoul walking across the deck towards her. For five long years she had tried to forget this man who had so blighted her life. She had been so certain as the years went by that she had at last broken free of his spell. So why did she now feel this frightened apprehension, a deep numbing fear of what lay ahead?

CHAPTER THREE

LYING back in her seat, Olivia tried to relax her rigidly tense body against the soft, black leather upholstery. She would, under any normal circumstances, have been interested in the passing scenery, but her mind now seemed empty and utterly exhausted by emotional strain. With dull, apathetic eyes she gazed up at the old walled town of Boulogne, swiftly left behind as the silver-grey Porsche forged its way past sand dunes and small pine forests and on towards the open farmlands of upper Normandy.

'I regret that we were forced to arrive in France so far north.' Raoul's cool voice broke into the constrained, oppressive silence within the car. 'However,' he shrugged his broad shoulders, 'due to the air traffic controller's strike, I had to take any channel crossing that I could find.'

Olivia, whose body seemed filled with a hard lump of apprehensive despair, could only manage an indistinct murmur in reply to his words. Exactly where they landed in France seemed totally unimportant, quite irrelevant beside the numbing fact that she was going to be trapped within this man's orbit for the next two weeks. Raoul had mentioned something about a château, hadn't he? He couldn't possibly be expecting her to stay there, so perhaps she would be able to find a room in a hotel when they reached Bordeaux?

With an unhappy sigh, she closed her eyes against the rays of the late afternoon sun as they slanted in through the windscreen. It was no good. She was far too tired to make any concrete plans to avoid Raoul's presence—the effort required being more than her weary brain could manage.

Sunk in misery, she missed the quick turn of Raoul's head, the searchingly intense glance from behind dark sunglasses as he observed the strain of the past hours reflected in her pale cheeks. With a grim tightening of his lips, he swung the vehicle off the auto-route and on down a side road.

Some minutes later, Olivia was jolted from her mindless reverie as she felt the car slide to a stop. Opening her eyes she looked about her in bewilderment. They appeared to have arrived in a small town, the car parked in a square with a tinkling fountain, surrounded by elegant, tranquil, eighteenth-century houses.

'What—I mean where. . .?'

'Montreuil,' Raoul answered crisply, getting out of the car and coming around to open her door. 'You are clearly in need of refreshment,' he added, bending down to help her alight.

'There's no need . . .' she muttered as Raoul placed a firm hand on her elbow to lead her across the pavement and beneath the striped awnings of a small restaurant. Sitting her down at a table, he went over to the bar and returned with a glass which he placed before her.

'Oh, I can't! I simply can't possibly—not at this time of day,' she sighed wearily, gazing into the amber depths of a large brandy.

'But yes, you must!' he insisted. 'You are not looking at all well, Olivia. So drink it up, and you will soon find that you feel much better, truly.'

The unexpectedly warm concern in his voice

produced a heavy aching pain in her chest. Staring blindly down at the red-and-white checked tablecloth, she fought to control the weak tears which threatened to fall at any minute.

'*Bien!*' he murmured, watching as she put out a shaking hand for the glass and slowly raised it to her lips. 'I must now make a telephone call, but I expect to see that you have drunk all the cognac by the time I return, hmm?'

Her green eyes followed his tall, lithe figure, which disappeared into the dark recess behind the bar as she cautiously sipped the strong liquor. By the time she had emptied half the glass, Olivia was ruefully admitting to herself that Raoul had been right. The fiery liquid surging through her veins was indeed helping to alleviate the overwhelming self-pity and nervous apprehension which had filled her mind, to the exclusion of all else, since Raoul's sudden reappearance. Feeling slightly stronger, she leaned back in her chair and looked around the small restaurant, empty apart from two workmen who were talking earnestly together by the bar. Her glance swept over the simple furnishings and bare walls, her eyes widening in startled dismay as they came to rest on the tattered, faded remains of a Riccardi poster.

Involuntarily, she gulped down the rest of the cognac, gasping both from the burning explosion in her stomach and from the sudden, unexpected shock of seeing herself again after so many years. She couldn't seem to tear her eyes away from the face smiling so radiantly out at the world. It was almost as if the model was a complete stranger, some unknown girl whose dewy skin and sparkling eyes seemed to be proclaiming only too clearly that she was deeply in love. In love with life—and with the man now using the telephone behind the bar.

What on earth had she done to deserve this? By what malign twist of fate had she been brought here to face her past happiness and joy? Olivia could only sit staring at the poster in stunned bemusement as the years rolled away, and she was once again a young girl in the throes of her first and only love affair. . . .

A light touch on her shoulder recalled her from the past, back to the realisation of her present predicament.

'*Plus ça change, plus c'est la même chose!*' Raoul murmured as he helped her to her feet, his eyes following hers to the poster on the wall.

'I'm—I'm well aware that I've changed!' she snapped bitterly as he led her trembling figure from the restaurant. It might have been the effect of the cognac, or the sudden shock she had just sustained, but her feet seemed to miss a step on the pavement. A moment later her stumbling, weary body was firmly clasped within Raoul's arms, her cheek resting against the soft wool of his jacket and her nostrils filled with the well-remembered, evocative scent of his Antaeus aftershave.

'You have a very uncertain grasp of the French language, my dear Olivia!' Raoul murmured quietly as she gazed up into his face in bewildered confusion. '"The more things appear to change, the more they in fact remain the same", is a literal translation of what I have just said—not at all what you thought, hmm?'

'No, I . . .' Olivia raised an unsteady hand to brush back the heavy sweep of chestnut hair from her face. She could feel her cheeks flushing beneath the glinting, steely blue eyes which skimmed over her figure with cool appraisal, before he released her and walked over to open the passenger door of the car.

'We have some way to travel, so I suggest that you

close your eyes and try to sleep,' he said as the engine fired, and they smoothly accelerated away from the town and back to join the auto-route.

That's easier said than done, she thought gloomily, only too well aware that her senses were strung up to fever pitch after having been so tightly clasped in Raoul's arms—the living reality behind so many of her despairing dreams of the last few years. Watching his lean brown fingers select and place a cassette in the stereo player, she leant back in her seat and closed her eyes as the soothing strains of Debussy's *L'Après-midi d'un Faune* filled the car.

Darkness had almost fallen when she felt herself being gently shaken awake. 'Come, Olivia! It is time to rouse yourself. As you can see, we have arrived.'

Blinking rapidly and still feeling drugged from her sleep, she looked about her in bewilderment. 'This— this isn't your château, surely?' she muttered, gazing up at a large, old timbered house covered with rambling roses. Soft light spilled forth invitingly from the open windows, behind which she could see figures passing to and fro, the muted sounds of conversation and laughter fill the night air.

'*Mais, non!*' Raoul laughed dryly. 'It would seem that your knowledge of geography is on a par with that of the French language! Alas, we have a long way to go before we reach the Médoc, and I have therefore decided that we shall spend the night here at the Lion d'Or.'

'But, I didn't—didn't realise. . . .'

'My dear girl, it is late and I am tired and hungry. So, I imagine, are you, hmm? There is absolutely no need for you to worry, you will be quite—er—safe, you know!' he added sardonically.

Olivia was thankful for the dim light which hid her

blushing confusion. He was right—her knowledge of France was abysmal. Why on earth she hadn't realised that they would have to spend a night on the road, she couldn't for the life of her imagine.

'You must, of course, please yourself,' Raoul drawled silkily as she remained nervously silent in her seat. 'Do, by all means, spend the night out here if you wish! As for myself, I intend to relax in comfort.'

The interior light of the car came on as he opened his door, Olivia gritting her teeth in frustration. She could plainly see his eyes, gleaming with unconcealed mockery above lips which twitched in silent humour. *The damn man was laughing at her!*

Nervous apprehension swiftly gave way to smouldering, impotent fury as she realised that she had no choice but to accompany Raoul. Casting a cold glare of acute dislike at the amused expression on his face as he helped her from the car, she allowed him to guide her stiff, resentful figure towards the main door of the hotel.

Some twenty minutes later, Olivia sank down on to the comfortable bed and looked around at her unexpectedly luxurious surroundings. She must have been given one of the best rooms of the hotel, she thought, as she viewed the pale rose-coloured moiré silk drapes over the windows, matching the quilted bedspread on which she was sitting. A deep piled cream carpet covered the floor, while small antique chairs and tables graced the elegant room.

She couldn't have decorated it better herself, she realised, getting up with a small sigh to go over to where the uniformed porter had placed her suitcase. Their arrival had clearly been expected—was that the reason for the phone call in Montreuil? Raoul had been greeted with obsequious attention and many mutterings of: '*Bon soir, Monsieur le Vicomte*' as the various members of the hotel staff had hurried out to bring in their luggage, before conducting them to their allotted rooms.

Removing her nightdress and dressing gown, she stared down at her packed clothes trying to decide what to wear for dinner. This was obviously a very smart hotel and if she was going to have to face a meal with Raoul, she would need all the self-confidence she could muster. Coming to a decision at last, she hung the dress up in the large wardrobe before going through into the en suite bathroom.

Olivia was just about to get into the bath when she heard a knock on a door. Slipping into her dressing gown, she re-entered the room to find Raoul framed in a doorway she hadn't noticed before; one which clearly connected her bedroom and his.

'What—what are you doing here?' she demanded breathlessly.

'You forgot your handbag.' He held it up before lightly tossing it on to the bed. 'I thought that you women never forgot such an important appendage?'

'Well, it only goes to show that with all your experience of women, even *you* can sometimes be wrong!' she retorted bleakly, infuriated by his sardonic grin.

'Tsk—tsk!' He clicked his tongue, smiling with heavy cynicism as he viewed the flashing sparks of anger in her green eyes. 'You must calm down, *ma petite*! Surely you can see that the key to this door is on your side of the room? There is no need for this—er—over-reaction, hmm?'

'Why you—you. . .!' Olivia gasped with fury, unable to think of any words rude enough with which to express her rage at his arrogant and totally unwarranted, snide remarks. And then, when she at last found her voice, it was too late, as the door clicked shut behind his retreating figure, leaving only the sound of his mocking laugh to ring in her ears.

She was still feeling angry and upset as she slipped into her dress and went to sit down at the dressing table. Looking at her flushed cheeks in the mirror, she grimaced with irritation and self-disgust. Raoul was right. She was over-reacting to a situation which, while it was none of her making, was nevertheless one fraught with difficulties. It was understandable that she had been confused by the turn and speed of events that day, but she wasn't still eighteen, no longer the young, unsophisticated girl who had fallen so deeply in love with Raoul. She was a successful business-woman of twenty-three, and there was no need for her to just respond blindly to whatever pin-pricks he might devise, was there? If Raoul could manage to be cool, calm and collected about their disastrous reunion, she really must strive to be equally impassive—whatever the provocation!

Leaning forward to apply her lipstick, she paused with her hand in mid-air. Just why—why was Raoul being so dismissively cool, when by rights he was the one who should be troubled by his behaviour towards her in the past? Since it was he who had discarded her without a moments hesitation, surely he might have had the grace to look even slightly disconcerted, when he had marched into her apartment back in London. But he hadn't—far from it! Raoul hadn't shown even an ounce of surprise at their renewed association, and certainly not the slightest glimmer of remorse. The bloody man! she ground her teeth angrily as she finished applying her make-up. It was obvious that he was a hardened roué, nothing but a debauchee who wandered happily through life, breaking one girl's heart after another!

Her thoughts were interrupted by a knock on the door which led out into the hotel corridor. Swiftly practising a cool, sophisticated smile which belied the turmoil churning inside her body, she rose to gather up her evening purse and went over to open the door.

'I didn't like to enter your room, just in case I—er—disturbed you again!' Raoul drawled mockingly as he lounged casually against the door-frame. His hooded eyes flicked over her slim figure dressed in deep amber silk, echoing the rich colour of her hair. The bodice was cut low and tightly moulded to her slim waist, before breaking out into a skirt of soft, unpressed pleats.

'You always looked ravishing, my dear Olivia, and I can see that tonight is no exception!' he murmured with appreciation, his gaze lingering on the gentle thrust of her breasts.

His words washed over her almost unheard; all her good resolutions of the past half hour seeming to disappear as she absorbed his tall body, clothed in a dinner suit that emphasised his broad shoulders and the long length of his legs. Oh Lord! she thought miserably, feeling sick as a hard knot of desire clenched tightly in the pit of her stomach. Gazing at the white shirt which contrasted so starkly against his tanned, handsome face, she couldn't prevent herself from acknowledging that he was still the most devastatingly attractive man she had ever known.

Taking a deep breath to steady herself, Olivia walked beside Raoul down the red-carpeted corridor. 'If—if I seemed upset, it was—er—only because I was tired from the journey.' She assumed a casual smile as she airily waved away any suggestion that she had been disturbed by the scene in the bedroom. 'Far more important, *chéri*, is the fact that I'm starving—absolutely ravenous in fact!'

Smiling brilliantly into his face, Olivia was pleased to note his puzzled frown as he registered the faintly sarcastic emphasis she had placed on the uncalled-for endearment. However, he merely contented himself with dryly assuring her that the hotel's *menu gastronomique* was second to none.

Throughout the delicious dinner she kept up a stream of insouciant, bright chatter, Raoul responding equally smoothly, despite the almost wary glances he bestowed on her from time to time. It wasn't until they were being served coffee, and Olivia was congratulating herself on the success of her newly assumed personality, that he delivered a body blow which completely destroyed all her euphoria.

'Tell me—have you always lived in your—er—château?' she enquired with saccharine sweetness. 'I don't think I can remember you referring to it in the past; but then, as you so rightly pointed out, it's so easy to forget one's "youthful indiscretions", isn't it?'

His lips tightened, his eyes narrowing and momentarily darkening as her shot clearly struck home. 'Until the death of my great-uncle, I lived mainly in Paris. It was only when I inherited his estates four year's ago that my wife and I moved into the château.'

'Your—your *wife. . .*?'

Raoul lifted a dark eyebrow. 'My dear Olivia,' he purred softly, 'surely you knew of my marriage?'

Olivia's head pounded and throbbed as if she had been hit very hard by a blunt instrument, and she could feel the blood draining away from her face as she fought to control her trembling hands. Of course she should have known! How incredibly foolish—how crassly stupid of her not to have realised that such an attractive man was bound to be married. He'd proposed to *her*, hadn't he? And although he'd skipped out of that engagement fast enough, it sounded as if he'd married very soon afterwards—and who else but to Lucille? Oh God! what a fool she'd been!

Rigid with shock, Olivia felt as if she was standing outside her own body, watching as she calmly placed her napkin down on the table, and equally calmly rose to her feet. 'I'm sure you'll understand if I ask you to excuse me, Raoul,' she murmured blankly. 'It's been a long day and I'm very—very tired. . . .' She didn't wait to hear his response as she turned blindly away, and on legs which moved stiffly like those of a marionette, walked slowly across the dining room and away up the stairs.

On reaching her bedroom, Olivia stripped off her clothes like an automaton, climbing into bed and turning off the light to lie wide awake, staring up into the darkness above her head. Gradually, as the hours ticked slowly by, her frozen numbed mind began to absorb the reality of Raoul's words: he was married and had been for some time—almost certainly very soon after he had jilted her. It seemed ridiculous that it should make any difference, after all this time. But like a victim of frostbite, as her chilled, numbed body slowly relaxed in the warmth of the bed, so she was filled with almost unbearable pain. Pain as fresh now, in high summer, as on that December so long ago. Restlessly tossing and turning, the memories she had thought so deeply buried rose again like ghosts from the past to haunt her; just as Lucille's taunting voice had warned her of the danger of getting involved with Raoul.

However, she had been too much in love to listen,

too overwhelmed to give a thought to the future as he drove her back to his apartment, following the cataclysmic scene with Lucille. She had still been shaking with reaction from the French girl's blow, too confused by her flatmate's anger to consider that she herself was now homeless. All she could think about, the only consideration which filled her mind, was that Raoul did love her after all, and had openly declared his intention of marrying her.

On their arrival at his apartment, she had been further confused by Raoul issuing her into a guest bedroom, and kissing her on the forehead as he bade her goodnight. She had thought that now they were unofficially engaged, he would at least lose any compunctions he had about making love to her; not understanding how he could leave her alone, in a strange bedroom, on this of all nights. She hadn't been able to sleep, feeling so lonely and apprehensive about the future, that she had finally screwed up her courage and tiptoed through to his room finding him every bit as wide awake as she herself had been.

'*Ah non*, my darling,' he had whispered as she had slipped in between the sheets. 'We should wait until we are married.'

Driven by a force she couldn't control, Olivia pressed her warm, slim figure against his naked form, provoking a deep, helpless groan as his arms tightened involuntarily about her. Lost in their mutual passion, despite the raging excitement of his kisses and caressing hands, he had shown restraint and infinite tenderness as he gently led her inexperienced body from one delight to another; raising Olivia to heights of ultimate ecstasy, such as she could never have imagined possible.

In the days that followed, with Raoul's avowals of

love and devotion filling her whole existence, she had been nonplussed by his determination that she should have her own apartment.

'For heaven's sakes! Why can't I stay with you? I—I don't want a place like this, all on my own,' she had exclaimed helplessly as he insisted on showing her around an apartment in Knightsbridge.

'It is not proper—it is not suitable that a young girl should live with a man, even if they are to marry,' he had replied firmly, and despite her objections, he had persuaded her to lease the apartment for a few months. 'After which, *chérie*, we will be married, *oui*?' he had whispered softly, kissing away all her protests.

'You're nothing but a raving hypocrite!' she teased him as they lay in her new bedroom, late one afternoon, satiated from making love.

'Of course!' he laughed. 'But that is the way of the world, *non*?'

'Well, it's certainly not my world. All the girls I know are quite open about where and with whom they sleep.'

'Nevertheless, *ma petite*, I do not think my family, or your mama and papa, would be pleased to know that their young daughter was behaving in such a way?'

'Well . . .' she grinned ruefully. 'You could be right.' She had wanted to tell her parents the exciting news of her engagement, but she had been forced to set it all down in a letter, since they were on a cruise to the Canary Islands hoping to improve her father's frail health.

'Besides which, my darling girl, I have to leave London very soon on a visit to California.'

'*Oh no!*'

'Alas yes. It has been arranged for some time that I should visit the vineyards in the Napa Valley. My great-uncle is very old, and it is his wish that I should inherit his estates and, most importantly, the Château Cheval Noir vineyard. It is therefore essential that I meet and talk to as many *vignerons* as possible, so that I prepare myself to take over the family business, you understand?'

'Yes, I—I suppose so,' she sighed heavily. 'You won't be away for too long, will you?'

'Only one month, *chérie*, I promise. I will return in mid-December to see your parents and formally ask them for your hand in marriage. I must also ask their permission to take you to France for Christmas—for you must also meet my family. We can maybe be married in my family chapel, yes?'

'Oh yes, my darling Raoul!' she breathed huskily.

'*Ah bon!* So you see why it would not have been a good idea to leave you all alone in my apartment, and in the meantime we have two more weeks together.'

'Is that all!' Olivia shrieked in half-mocking dismay. 'Well, don't just lie there—do something!'

'Like this. . .?' he murmured, his mouth coming down on hers with a fierce possessiveness, which left no room for anything, other than the complete consumation of their love for each other.

Olivia had been unbearably lonely while Raoul was away in America, living for his letters and resolutely burying herself in work, chiefly with Ashley Warne to fulfil the Riccardi contract. She had never heard another word from Lucille, who was apparently modelling in New York.

On the date of Raoul's return, Ashley had ruefully laughed and sent her home after only a few hours' work. 'You're no good to me today, Olivia, and in fact I think I've got enough shots now to keep those Italians happy.'

'You mean, we've actually finished the contract?' she asked, hurriedly getting dressed in her own clothes.

'Yep. I'm off to America myself next week, although how I'm expected to find any fashion models who will be sufficiently sober during the Christmas festivities, beats me! I wish you'd come over and pose for my new assignment, the money's simply fabulous!'

'You'll find someone,' she laughed, sweeping her accessories into her tote bag. 'Is Cecil going with you?' she asked, referring to Ashley's assistant, whose relationship with his good-looking employer was the subject of some speculation.

'Absolutely, darling—how could I possibly manage without him?' Ashley grinned as he opened the door of his studio. 'Have a wonderful time with your handsome fiancé, and a very Happy Christmas if I don't see you before I go.'

'Thank you for everything,' she murmured, bestowing a kiss on his cheek before flying down the stairs in a feverish hurry to get back to her apartment.

Raoul had told her in his last letter that he wasn't sure what flight he would be able to get, and so there was no point in meeting him at Heathrow airport. He had assured her that he would ring her, just as soon as he arrived back at his apartment.

Olivia sat by the phone all the rest of that day and well into the night, the instrument remaining obstinately silent. Sleeping fitfully, she rang Raoul's apartment the next morning, gaining no reply. By the late afternoon she had become seriously worried, enough to phone the airport to see if any planes from America had been delayed, and secretly fearing that she would be told of some disaster. However, there had been no mid-air collision, and she was informed that, somewhat unusually for the time of year, all estimated times of arrival had been adhered to.

Telephoning Raoul's apartment yet again, she was delighted to get an engaged signal, her relief turning to frustrated puzzlement as three hour's later she was still getting the same tone. Although it was nearly midnight, she decided that any action was better than the gnawing uncertainty she had felt all day, and half an hour later she was pushing the doorbell of Raoul's apartment.

There seemed to be a long delay before she could hear a chain being released and the door slowly began to open. 'For heaven's sake, darling. I've been so worried, I. . . .' Her voice trailed away as she found herself gazing, not into Raoul's handsome face, but that of . . . *Lucille*!

'What—what are you doing here?' Olivia whispered hoarsely, her startled eyes widening with shock as she saw that Lucille was wearing nothing but a diaphanous nightgown.

Lucille didn't reply, merely shrugging her shoulders, her thin red lips stretching into a malicious smile as someone called her name from the depths of the apartment.

Olivia stood rooted to the spot as again the person called, only stronger and more querulously this time: 'Lucille! Tell whoever's there to go away. . . .'

Recognising Raoul's voice, Olivia gave a gasp of pain and tried to enter the apartment, only to find her way effectively barred by Lucille's outstretched arm across the doorway.

'I'm coming, Raoul darling!' the French girl called over her shoulder, before turning back to Olivia. 'Can't you see that we're . . . er . . . busy? That he doesn't want you any more? Oh yes,' she laughed malevolently. 'I knew he would become bored with you and your lack of sophistication. Now, go away you silly little girl, and perhaps you won't make such a fool of yourself next time? Believe me, *c'est fini*! Your affair, it's all finished!' Lucille hissed as she shut the door firmly in Olivia's face.

Olivia never managed to recall in detail exactly how she got back to her own apartment, or what she did during the next week. Shutting herself away, seeking darkness and shelter like a wounded animal, only one episode shone out with painful clarity: the phone call from Lucille, passing on Raoul's demand that Olivia should return the diamond and sapphire ring which they had chosen together. That cruel request, delivered with heartless glee by Lucille, had broken through the blank numbness of her mind, producing a storm of tears and leaving her with a deep, burning resentment that Raoul hadn't been man enough to tell her, to her face, that he wished to terminate their engagement.

After telephoning her parents to tell them that her forthcoming marriage was off, and that she intended to spend Christmas alone, she might well have remained in the apartment for weeks, if she hadn't received a call from Ashley Warne in New York.

'Olivia? Thank God I've managed to get hold of you. I don't know what your plans are—but cancel them and come over here immediately!'

'What on earth are you talking about?' she muttered apathetically.

'You won't believe it—the stupid girl I'd chosen to model all that fabulous jewellery, was in a pile-up on the freeway yesterday. She's in intensive care and I'm in the soup—everyone's out of town for heaven's sake!'

'Oh, I can't, I. . . .'

'Oh yes you can! Just tell you fiancé that it's all in a good cause. With the amount of money the client is paying, you won't have to work for months!'

'I—we—the marriage is off. . . .' she murmured haltingly.

'Oh Lord—I'm sorry, love. What you need is a change of scene. Get your skates on and fly out here as soon as possible—like yesterday! I'll have a ticket waiting for you at the airport, and I'm staying at the St Regis hotel, so I'll book you a room immediately and we'll have a jolly Christmas together. OK?'

'Well, I. . . .'

'Good girl—I knew I could count on you. 'Bye.'

Now, as she looked back over the years, Olivia thought that in many ways that modelling assignment had saved her sanity, despite the horrendous strain under which she had faced the arc lights and the long hours. She would have had to take up the reins of her life again, somehow, and Ashley's phone call and his insistence that she join him in America, had merely accelerated the process. Having to take over her father's shop on her return had kept her almost too busy to think of anything other than business, and her forced withdrawal from the world of fashion photography had come as a welcome relief.

Only once in her life had she experienced the hell that men and women could create for one another, and that had been at Raoul's instigation. She must make sure that there never was a second time, because she doubted that she was capable of surviving such a horrendous, traumatic experience ever again. . . .

As the pale fingers of dawn lit the sky, something woke her up from a restless sleep. Her face and pillow were damp with tears, and as she lay staring into the unfamiliar darkness, she realised that the sounds which had awoken her had been her own desperate sobbing. She hadn't cried such miserably helpless tears like that since. . . . Not since her life had been so irrevocably shattered that Christmas long ago.

CHAPTER FOUR

SITTING in front of her dressing table the next morning, Olivia sighed, realising that despite her skilful use of make-up, there was no way she could completely disguise the dark shadows beneath her eyes. With a wry grimace at her reflection, she reminded herself of the photographic models' golden rule: that a good night's sleep was a necessary prerequisite for a fresh looking face the next morning.

Paradoxically, despite the tired exhaustion and lethargy resulting from such a restless night, Olivia found that she now felt more tranquil, more at peace with herself and her troubled feelings for Raoul. The resurrection of her deeply buried memories seemed to have acted as some sort of catharsis; releasing all her repressed emotions, and leaving her with a calmer acceptance of the difficult situation in which she found herself.

Well, somewhat calmer anyway, she told herself as she went down to breakfast. Although she had been dreading the thought of having to face Raoul again, so soon after the news of his marriage last night, there was nothing she could do to evade the inevitable confrontation. As she had slipped into a pair of navy-blue slacks, topped by a blue and white check shirt, mad thoughts of somehow escaping from the hotel flitted across her mind. But where to go and how to get there, had proved to be unanswerable questions. Raoul had taken possession of her passport at Dover, and presumably had used it last night for their registration at this hotel. He wasn't likely to hand it over without her giving him a good, valid reason for doing so, was he? The thought of having to concoct some far-fetched story seemed beyond her at the moment. Even if she did manage to think of something, there was bound to be an argument somewhere along the line, and she *really* couldn't face anything like that this morning. Besides, there was Bridget's wedding to consider. Having come this far, Olivia couldn't just run away without some explanation. Apart from anything else, it would be admitting not only to herself, but also to Raoul, that she felt more for him than just the brief memory of an old friendship.

Slowly descending the stairs, Olivia wasn't sure what she really felt for Raoul. Looking across the dining room at his tanned, aristocratic profile, she knew, with an absolute certainty, that she didn't want to delve into her complicated, emotional response to the man now sipping his coffee as he perused the newspaper in front of him.

Taking a deep breath, she forced herself to walk slowly and casually over to the table, Raoul looking up at her approach and folding up his copy of *Le Figaro* as he rose to hold out a chair. She felt suddenly breathless as her eyes took in his dark hair, glistening damply as if he'd just had a shower, and his tall figure clothed in beige linen slacks with a matching short-sleeved silk shirt, open at the neck.

'*Bonjour*, Olivia. You are looking very lovely this morning,' he murmured.

On the contrary, I look dreadful! she wanted to snap, alarmed to find just how swiftly her nervous, antagonistic feelings towards him reasserted themselves once more. So much for the new cool, calm and collected Olivia! she thought grimly, turning with relief to give her order to a hovering waiter.

'Only coffee?' Raoul queried as she began to fill her cup from a silver jug. 'Are you sure you won't have a *brioche*? We have a long journey ahead of us, today.'

Olivia shuddered. 'No, I—I really can't face anything more than coffee in the morning.'

'Ah, yes, I remember now,' he replied smoothly.

Well, if so, it's clearly the only damn thing he does remember! she told herself, outwardly ignoring his words as she welcomed the warmth and comfort of real coffee made from freshly roasted beans.

'What time will we reach your château?' she asked, her controlled, even voice breaking into the long silence between them.

'I am not certain,' he shrugged. 'My car was not performing well for the last few miles, last night. I must call at a garage along our route, just to have the engine checked over, you understand.'

'I hope we aren't too delayed. I mean—I'd like to see my cousin as soon as possible,' she warned him. Really, if it had been anyone else, she might have suspected that old gag about running out of petrol!

'You look as though something has amused you, Olivia?' he drawled, refilling their cups from the tall silver jug.

'No—quite the reverse,' she replied shortly, burying her nose in the rising steam of her coffee. What on earth could have brought such an extraordinary thought into her mind? As if he could possibly have had any idea of. . . . It was all too ridiculous! It must be due to the softer expression on his face this morning, compared to the cold, bland exterior he had presented yesterday. His tone of voice was warmer too, not nearly so harsh and abrasive. However, in the present circumstances, her instinctive, momentary impression that he was seeking to spend more time in her company, was not only foolish, but *definitely* not applicable to the relationship between herself and Raoul!

Three quarters of an hour later they were on the road, driving along quiet lanes as Raoul explained that he was cutting across country from one auto-route to another. Olivia had found some sunglasses in her suitcase, which helped guard her eyes against the brilliant morning sunshine. However, she soon pushed them up on top of her chestnut hair as her eyes savoured the brilliant colours of the countryside. Passing lush emerald meadows and pastures containing sheep and cattle, they drove on through countless tiny villages and small forests of beech, oak and pines; crossing swiftly flowing streams and wide, placid rivers as they continued in a south-westerly direction towards the Brittany coast.

'The countryside is lovely—so green and fresh even in the midst of summer!' she exclaimed, so enchanted from the scenic view from the car that she had forgotten, for the last hour or two, her ambivalent feelings for the man beside her.

Raoul took his eyes off the road to give her a brief, warm smile. 'Ah, yes. This part of my country is not so well known, and at this time of year is looking particularly beautiful, mostly due to all the rain we had in early July.'

'I'm surprised that you had bad weather here,' she said idly. 'In England we had a hot July—for a change!'

'It was a very serious matter for the grapes. We were lucky in the Médoc, but I fear the thunderstorms and hail have caused much damage to some of my friends' vineyards in Burgundy.'

'Is the weather so important for making wine?'

'Absolutely vital!' he assured her. 'A freak hailstorm, for instance, can devastate the vines of an estate or an entire commune, and in a bad year that means no vintage.'

'What happens if you don't have a—a vintage?' Olivia queried, becoming interested in a subject she knew nothing about.

Raoul smiled grimly. 'Financial disaster! To put the matter simply: first of all, the area of vines in current production on my estate is approximately seventy hectares—about a hundred and seventy-three of your English acres. On average we produce about twenty thousand cases of wine each year, and the selling price of the best wine, Château Cheval Noir, 1961, is roughly £70 per bottle. On top of which . . .'

'. . . OK, OK!' She turned to smile at him. 'I get the general picture, although my mental arithmetic isn't good enough to work it all out.'

'It is much better not to!' he agreed with feeling. 'However, other than one or two late frosts, we ourselves have been very lucky this year, thank God!'

'Do you—er—do you enjoy your life as a wine-maker?'

'But yes, of course! *"Vigneron"* is the correct word, by the way; we must improve your French while you are over here with us, Olivia!' He cast her a sideways, amused grin. 'It is possible that I could have become a *rentier*, someone who lives off inherited wealth, but that I feel is no life for a man, and certainly not for me.'

Olivia stared blindly out of her car window. 'We'? 'Us'? If he thought she was going to meekly sit down and take French lessons from his wife, he was in for a big surprise! It seemed as if a cloud had come over the brilliant blue sky, obliterating the relaxed atmosphere which had existed between them during the past hour, and causing her to shiver despite the heat of the day.

'We are now driving into Vitre.' Raoul's voice cut into her disturbed thoughts. She looked up to see that the Porsche was winding its way through old streets, filled with ancient timbered and slate-fronted houses in a remarkably good state of preservation.

'It's almost as if we had returned in time to the Middle Ages,' she murmured appreciatively.

'Yes, it is charming,' he agreed as he stopped the car beside the pavement, leaving the engine running and turning to release her seat belt. 'Now,' he smiled, 'I am going to drop you here for a short while. Order yourself a coffee or whatever you wish in that café over there, and I will return just as soon as I have had a mechanic look over the car.'

'I—I don't need your money,' she snapped, suddenly nervous at finding his body so disturbingly close to hers as he leant over to thrust some notes into her hand.

'I am not buying *you*, Olivia! Merely a cup of coffee, hmm?' he drawled sardonically as she got out.

She watched as the vehicle drove away, and then walked diffidently over to the café. Later, as she sat outside at one of the small tables, sipping her coffee and watching the local inhabitants going about their business, she castigated herself for being so unnecessarily rude to Raoul. There wasn't any need for her to have been so prickly about letting him pay for a simple *café au lait*—especially when she still had to settle up with him for the cost of the hotel last night. Honestly, she told herself, smoothing a distracted hand over her hair, you've got to calm down—you really have!

Olivia was still giving herself good advice when Raoul returned half an hour later. 'Is the car all right?' she asked, seating herself once more beside him.

Waiting while she snapped on her seat-belt, he throttled away from the curb nodding towards a red light glowing on the dashboard. 'As you can see, the central warning light has come on, which indicates that there is some malfunction of the engine. The mechanic couldn't find anything specifically wrong, but he thinks it may be something to do with the *différentiel* or maybe *la bôite de vitesses*—the gear box.'

Olivia, who wasn't in the slightest bit mechanically minded, tried to look as though she knew what he was talking about. 'Will—will it prevent us from reaching your château? I mean—is the car likely to break down completely?'

'Oh no,' he assured her. 'But I'm afraid that we must not travel too fast, and it seems only fair to warn you that we may well have to spend another night on the road.'

Glancing swiftly at him through her eyelashes, Olivia could detect nothing in his bland expression as he concentrated on driving out of the town. She decided that she must have imagined the faint, very faint hint of amusement in his cool voice, as they wound their way through the countryside once again. Leaning back in her seat, she tried to close her eyes against the sight of his tanned, muscular arms, and the long, slim brown fingers gripping the wheel. It must be because she was feeling tired from her sleepless night, but she seemed to be becoming increasingly and disturbingly aware of his strongly powerful male presence.

'Now, we will stop here for lunch,' Raoul announced some time later. Jerked from her self-absorption, she saw that he had drawn into a small parking area, with heavy wooden tables and benches set out under trees by a grassy meadow bank.

'We are fortunate, such places are normally full of tourists at this time of year,' he announced as he brought the car to a stop.

'Lunch? But I don't see. . . .' Olivia looked around her in puzzlement.

'I asked the hotel to prepare us a picnic lunch,' he answered smoothly, going around to the back of the vehicle and opening the boot. 'I take it you have no objection?'

Olivia laughed. 'Hardly! I've only just realised how hungry I am. I think a picnic is a great idea, and especially in such a lovely place as this.' She got out of the car, stretching herself and admiring the beauty of her surroundings. Blushing slightly as she saw Raoul's eyes flick over her breasts which were thrown into prominence by her action, she went quickly over to the wooden table to help him unpack the wicker hamper.

'You—you call that a picnic?' she queried in amazement. 'I'd call it a banquet!' Her eyes grew wide as she gazed down at the snowy white linen napkins, which lay folded neatly on top of porcelain plates bearing a gold-painted crest. But it was the food which made her gasp with pleasure. Small pots of pâté de foie gras, topped by tiny flecks of black truffle covered with aspic, were placed next to slivers of chicken breasts folded inside crisp lettuce leaves; cold lobster in its shell and a salad niçoise curved around a large chunk of camembert. Olivia's nose twitched at the warm, fresh smell of the accompanying crusty rolls, and the newly baked small tarts filled with crème pâtiesserie, on which nestled wild strawberries. She watched bemused as Raoul lifted a bottle of wine from a cool bag, his brown fingers deftly applying the corkscrew provided as he quickly removed the cork.

'Heavens!' she breathed ecstatically. 'I haven't seen anything so delicious for—well, for simply ages!'

Raoul gave a dismissive shrug. 'It is only a small *déjeuner*,' he said, his face widening into a grin at Olivia's expression as she drooled over the prospect of such a feast. 'I will admit that I am every bit as hungry as you, so let us attack the food immediately!'

'Some more camembert, Olivia?' Raoul asked, some considerable time later.

'Oh heavens no! I've made such a pig of myself. . . .' She contemplated the empty plates and bowls in dismay. 'Did we really eat all that?'

'I'm afraid we did, *ma petite*,' he laughed. 'It is lucky that you have such a slim figure, is it not?'

'It won't be slim for very much longer if I go on like this,' she sighed, feeling sleepy and replete as Raoul poured her another glass of wine. 'That's your wine, isn't it?' she said, nodding to the bottle which displayed a cream label with the words CHATEAU CHEVAL NOIR above a drawing of a turreted castle, in front of which a black horse was rearing up on its hind legs.

'I—I thought red wine was produced in Bordeaux?'

'*Mon Dieu!*' Raoul sighed dramatically, burying his face in his hands in mock horror. ' "Red wine" indeed! Let me tell you my dear girl, that what I produce is claret. *Premier Grand Cru Classe* Claret—the finest, most precious drink in the world! The wines produced by my vineyard only begin to reach the peak of their perfection when they are thirty years old. To give you some idea of the time involved in maturing the wine, I can truthfully assure you that your grandchildren will be drinking this year's product—always providing it is a good vintage, of course.'

'But that's not red . . . I mean claret.' Olivia realised that the amount of wine she had drunk must be catching up with her faster than she had thought. Surely the bottle contained white wine?

Raoul laughed at Olivia's owlish expression as she squinted at the bottle of wine. 'Ah, yes, you are right—I was merely giving you an early lesson in winemaking. What you see here,' he held his glass up to the light, 'is a small experiment for which I have great hopes. Some of my land is not suitable for the various types of red grapes which go to form the claret, so I planted some white Sauvignon grape vines a few years ago. Last year was the first year that we produced any quantity. It is good, I think.'

'I honestly don't know a thing about wine,' she confessed. 'But it's lovely and fresh, and sort of—sort of strong as well. . . .'

'Bravo, Olivia! That is a very good description indeed. You clearly have a good nose and we will make a connoisseur of you yet!'

'I doubt that,' she grinned back. 'Do you do all the work by yourself?'

'No, I have a *regisseur*—a manager—and he has two full-time assistants as well as those who work in the *chai*—the wine store, and the bottling plant. Don't worry,' he smiled as she shook her head in confusion. 'I will show it all to you, and explain everything when we reach the château. It will be much easier for you to understand when you can see it all in action.'

'Does Henri work for you? You mentioned something about him and his mother living in a wing of your château?'

'Henri is young, of course, only twenty-two years of

age. He is at present studying at the Institut d'Oenologie at Bordeaux under Professor Emile Peynaud, possibly the world's greatest authority on wine. Unfortunately, poor Henri, unlike you my dear Olivia, does not possess a "nose" for wine. I think perhaps it was his mother, my sister Hélène, who persuaded him to try and become a winemaker, but I am doubtful about his prospects.'

'What does he really want to do?' she asked, idly watching a yellow butterfly alight on a nearby patch of clover.

'God knows! However, that extraordinary young girl Bridget will push him into something—I have no doubt about that! I find it hard to believe that she is really your cousin, you are so very different!' he laughed.

'Oh Lord, what's Bridget done now?' she wondered, realising too late that she had murmured the words aloud.

'What has she done? Hah! What has she *not* done would be a better question, *ma petite.*'

Olivia wished he wouldn't keep calling her that, but she didn't like to object since he was bound to ask why she minded. It must be the hot summer's day and the wine she had consumed, but she was feeling very peculiar. Sort of breathless and—well, oddly affected by his soft accent. . . . You've got to pull yourself together! she told herself desperately, shocked by her frank longing to rest her head on his broad shoulder, to feel his strong arms about her body. With a considerable effort she sat upright, trying to concentrate on what Raoul was saying.

'. . . Bridget seems to have taken hold of practically everyone at the château. One moment we were all living in peaceful seclusion—or relatively peaceful, anyway—and the next . . . *boom*!'

'It—it can't be that bad, surely?'

'No, I exaggerate, of course,' he gave a dry laugh. 'But not all that much. First of all, poor Henri is not allowed to take any days off from his course, not since the time she found him sneaking out of the cinema in the mid-afternoon. He returned home that day, with his tail well and truly between his legs! Then, there is my sister Hélène. She is very much older than myself, of course, and much given to whining and moaning.'

'Why—what's wrong with her?'

Raoul raised his arms to heaven in exasperation. 'Nothing! She just likes to feel sorry for herself because she is a widow, which I agree is sad. However, by the time she has moaned on for hours, one loses one's patience. Bridget's arrival has therefore caused a new excitement and interest in her life. The advent of a baby has also given her something positive to think about!'

'A—a baby? Do you mean that—that Bridget's going to have a baby?' Olivia sat bolt upright, looking at him with dazed eyes.

'*Mais oui*. Did she not tell you?' He raised a dark eyebrow in surprise.

'No—not a word! No wonder—no wonder she was so keen for me to come out for the wedding. . . .'

'Ah, well. *C'est la vie*, I suppose,' Raoul murmured, looking remarkably unconcerned, she thought, as he continued with the saga of Bridget's dramatic intervention in the lives of the de Varennes family.

'Even my Aunt Amalie has not remained immune! I must tell you, Olivia, that my aunt, who lives much of the year in her apartment in Paris, is very much of the old school. Normally very stiff, very correct, and always dressed in black, even if the black dresses are by the top couturiers, you understand. However, and only God knows how Bridget did it, she persuaded my aunt that she still had some life to live, and every day was precious. She took Aunt Amalie off to the Kenzo Boutique in Bordeaux, and the next time I saw my aunt, who is not a day under sixty, she was wearing a brilliant scarlet mini-dress, sipping what she referred to as a "bullshot" cocktail, and entertaining some equally ancient old men to a tea dance in the main *salon* of the château!'

'No—I don't believe it!' Olivia was giggling helplessly by the time Raoul had finished his tale of woe, laughing as much at his indignation, as at the picture he had conjured up.

'It is no exaggeration, I assure you,' he grinned. 'Only my younger sister, Nicole, has remained immune so far, but who knows what will happen next?' he added darkly.

'What does your wife think about all this?' Olivia murmured without conscious thought, wiping the laughter from her eyes on one of the linen napkins.

There was a long silence. With startled eyes she watched his face creasing into deep lines of pain. 'I have no wife,' he replied harshly, a muscle beating fiercely in his clenched jaw.

'But—but you said so, last night. I distinctly remember you saying. . . .'

'I said that I had been married,' Raoul interrupted curtly. 'In fact, my wife is dead.'

Olivia felt as if she had been hit by a hard blow to the solar plexus. The pain and anguish in his voice was terrible to hear, and her warm heart knew only an overriding impulse to comfort him in his deep unhappiness.

'I—I'm so very sorry, Raoul,' she murmured breathlessly. 'As—as you know, Lucille and I were hardly friendly, but I never. . . .'

'What on earth has Lucille to do with the matter?' he demanded coldly.

'But—but surely you married her? I mean, I assumed that . . .' her voice trailed away beneath his blank look of incomprehension.

'I have no idea of what you are talking about. My wife's name was Estelle.'

Her dazed mind whirling, Olivia stared blindly down at the table as her weary brain tried to make some sense of Raoul's words. Within the space of the last twenty-four hours, it seemed as if she had been the victim of one violent shock after another. First there had been Raoul's sudden reappearance in her life, then she had discovered that he was married, only to be told now, that not only was his poor wife dead, but she hadn't been Lucille after all! Well, that's two of us he threw over! she found herself thinking, and then felt guilty at allowing such an unkind thought to enter her mind, especially in the face of his obvious sorrow.

She looked up to meet his grief-stricken blue eyes gazing at her intently. Oh God! He really did love his Estelle, she told herself, certain that she had never felt quite so wretched as she did at this moment, when she must forget her own agony and concentrate solely on words of consolation to help ease his suffering.

'Roaul, I. . . .' She placed a tentative hand on his arm. 'I'm really very, very sorry to hear about your wife. It—it must have been so—so sad for you. Were you married long?' she asked softly.

'No. Only for just over a year,' he retorted bleakly, getting up from the table and walking over the grass to stand looking out at the river. 'And I do not need sympathy, Olivia. Certainly not from you, of all people,' he added harshly.

She sat staring at the back of his tall figure, before she turned and began to pack away the plates and dishes with shaking hands. Swamped by inexplicable feelings of depression and misery, her eyes almost blinded by the tears which were threatening to fall at any moment, she trembled nervously as she felt his arm go about her hunched shoulders.

'Come, you are tired,' he said evenly, holding up a rug and cushions he had obviously taken from the car. 'Why not rest for a while, and maybe sleep, hmm? I am going for a walk but I will not be very far away, and you need not fear that you will be disturbed.'

Not waiting for a reply, he led her to a patch of dappled shade beneath one of the trees by the river bank, spreading out the rug and throwing down the cushions. 'Sleep well, Olivia,' he said softly, before turning abruptly to walk away.

I'll never go to sleep, she thought, not being able to resist lying down on the soft mohair rug and resting her head on a cushion. Gradually, her senses became lulled by the tranquility of the rustling trees, the cooing of pigeons and the soft, murmuring drone of bees. . . .

Olivia came slowly back to consciousness. She really had fallen asleep after all, she thought bemusedly, blinking her eyes rapidly against a shaft of sunlight which slanted down through the trees above. As her vision cleared, she found herself staring into the glinting, steely eyes of Raoul, who was sitting about three feet away from her recumbent figure. His intense gaze seemed to carry some message, but even as her drowsy mind struggled to decipher it, his heavy eyelids descended to hide all expression in his face.

'You have had a good sleep?' he asked quietly.

'Yes, I—er——' she cleared her throat nervously, trying to tear her eyes away from the strong brown column of his throat, and the long legs encased in narrow fitting trousers which clung to the taut muscles of his thighs.

'I have been meaning to ask you about your old photographer friend, Ashley Warne. Do you still—er—see much of him?'

Olivia was startled from her distracted, wandering thoughts by the sardonic tone in his hard voice. Sitting up, she looked at him in confusion. 'I—I see him occasionally. Although most of his work keeps him in America these days, he does look me up whenever he's in London.'

'I just bet he does!' Raoul gave a snort of derisory laughter.

'He's an old friend of mine, so why on earth shouldn't he?' she demanded coldly.

'Why not indeed!' he drawled with a mocking cynicism that left her feeling flustered and perplexed. Why was Raoul suddenly so concerned about Ashley, for heaven's sake? Rising to her feet, she bent down to pick up the cushions.

'If you wish to wash your face and hands, the water in the river is quite clean,' he said in a cold voice.

'Yes, I—I'd like that,' she murmured, handing him the rug and walking down to the river bank. Intent on not getting her feet wet, she moved along the edge until she found a small cliff-shaped piece of earth jutting out into the river. Kneeling down, she leaned over to scoop up some water. Almost in slow motion, she felt the small spur of earth give way under her weight, a loud cry issuing from her throat as she tumbled head first into the river.

Alerted by her cry of alarm, Raoul raced across the

grass and dived into the river, discovering only seconds after she had done so, that the water was only three feet deep!

Olivia struggled to her feet, throwing back the heavy weight of wet hair from her face, to meet Raoul's look of fury as he stood up in water which only came to just over his knees.

'Oh God! I'm—I'm sorry,' she gasped, beginning to shake with laughter at both her own folly, and his expression of outrage as he contemplated his wet clothes. Once she had started laughing, she found that however hard she tried, she couldn't stop. The hysterical tones echoed loudly in the still air, until abruptly silenced as Raoul stepped forward to slap her face. Reeling back from his blow, she looked at him in dazed shock, her eyes large green pools of misery above chalky white cheeks which bore the red imprint of his hand.

'Oh, mon Dieu! Ma belle Olivia!' he groaned, drawing her wet, shaking figure slowly towards him. 'Je suis désolé . . . it was necessary, you were becoming hysterical, you understand?' he murmured as with his handkerchief he tried to dry her face, before stripping off his own wet shirt.

'It's my fault,' she whispered. 'You—you were quite right, I . . .' she found she couldn't continue, nor was she able to look away from the dark, silky hair on his chest, only inches away from her eyes. The blood seemed to be pounding in her head, her heart racing like a metronome out of control as she viewed the broad-shouldered torso she remembered so well. Raising her face, her senses spun giddily as she saw him looking down at her breasts thrusting against the thin, wet material of her blouse, before his glance moved upwards to gaze into her eyes, the intense gleam from beneath the heavy lids sending a red hot flame racing through her veins.

'Olivia,' he whispered huskily, drawing her trembling figure into his arms, gently and lightly kissing her forehead. *'Olivia!'* A deep groan broke from the depths of his throat as he crushed her body ruthlessly to his hard, bare chest, his mouth descending to close over her trembling lips in a kiss of fierce, urgent possession.

Just for a moment she abandoned herself to the overpowering intoxication of his embrace, her lips parting beneath his as he ravaged the inner sweetness of her mouth. And then, as the warning sirens wailed at the back of her mind, and she tried to withdraw from his embrace, she found that she couldn't; one of his hands having risen to hold her head firmly and immovably beneath his.

Her body seemed determined to ignore the danger signals flashing through her brain, instinctively melting against him as her arms wound themselves about his neck. There was no resistance from her as his hands moving caressingly over the softness of her body, her senses drugged and seduced into quivering acquiescence as his mouth moved down over her throat and neck, searching for the firm, warm swell of her breasts.

One moment she seemed to be drowning in ecstasy, the next she felt Raoul remove his lips, cursing violently under his breath as he pushed her roughly away. She stood blinking foolishly as the mists of her desire parted, and she could see that his eyes were blazing down at her with an anger she didn't understand.

'Raoul. . .?' she whispered, swaying wearily with confusion as she realised for the first time, that they had been embracing in the middle of a river.

'Never again—non, non, *non*!' he exploded with fury, seizing her by the arm and roughly dragging her over to the river bank. '*Mon Dieu!* What a fool I am!' he grated, leaping up on to the firm earth, and pulling her up beside him. His cold, contemptuous eyes travelled over her shaking, wet and dishevelled figure. 'I suggest that you immediately change into some clean clothes. You will find your suitcase in the boot of my car, which is unlocked,' he snarled. 'I will give you ten minutes before I return, and hopefully, *mademoiselle*, we can both forget that this sordid episode ever happened!'

CHAPTER FIVE

THE rest of the day's journey was completed in silence. A silence so totally inhibiting that Olivia sat hunched in her seat, her face averted as she stared miserably out of her side window, trying to avoid all contact with the dark, menacing figure by her side. He held the wheel with tightly clenched hands, driving with a repressed fury and intimidating force that left her pale and shaking, certain that they would crash at any minute. Stopping the car only once for petrol, the early evening shadows were lengthening across the countryside when Raoul drew up at a small hotel.

'They are expecting us,' he announced curtly as he switched off the engine. Venturing a brief glance at his profile, which was as cold and hard as ice, Olivia knew that she couldn't face another evening like the one they had spent last night at the Lion d'Or. She might have to live with the mortification and shame of her willing surrender to his lovemaking this afternoon, but there was no need for her to have to put up with his inexplicable fury and harsh, cold words—and what's more she wasn't going to!

Anger coming to her aid, she got out of the car, slamming the door as hard as she could before marching up the steps and into the friendly warmth of the hotel. Raoul joined her some moments later, his face as black as thunder.

'Just what do you think you are doing?' he snarled in an undertone as the proprietor came forward to meet them.

Turning her back on Raoul, she managed to sketch a brief smile as she asked the owner if he spoke English.

'Yes, certainly madam. What can I do for you?'

'This gentleman,' she jerked her head at Raoul, 'tells me that we have a reservation. In which case, I would be most grateful if I could go straight to my room. I am very tired and I will require no dinner.'

'Of course, of course—er—madam. . . .' The proprietor glanced quickly at the couple who were clearly not on speaking terms. Swiftly summoning a passing maid, he sent her upstairs with Olivia before turning to see to Raoul.

Sunk in the depths of despair and misery, she lay for a long time in the bath, trying in vain to think why Raoul should have been so angry at having made love to her that afternoon. In the end she gave up, realising that there probably was no answer, except that he was as totally unpredictable as he had always been. But far more dangerous, she warned herself, certainly as far as her present, fragile emotions were concerned. She hadn't seen him for almost five years, and yet it had been hardly any time at all before she'd been returning his kisses with fervour, moaning with pleasure at the feel of his hands on her body. . . . What on earth could have possessed her to have behaved in such a way? 'You must have been absolutely and totally out of your mind,' she told herself fiercely, as the salty tears rolled down her cheeks to splash into the cooling bathwater.

Very early before dawn the next morning, she was woken by the sound of her own crying—as had happened the previous night; but this time she sensed that she wasn't alone. As she struggled through to consciousness, her eyes wildly searching the darkness, she was certain that she had securely locked her door the previous evening. But—not the French window which opened out into a wide balcony, she realised, shaking with terror as she heard a light step crossing the floor from the direction of the window. She was opening her mouth to scream for help, when she felt warm arms going about her trembling figure, and a voice she recognised, urgently murmuring: 'Hush, hush *chérie.*' *It was Raoul!*

'W-what . . . w-what are you d-doing in here. . .?' she hiccuped through her sobs.

'Hush, *ma petite.* There is no need to weep,' he murmured, gently drying the tears from her face. 'I heard you crying—the bedroom walls are very thin,' he added in a whisper, placing her head on his shoulder and gently stroking her hair.

She couldn't speak, lying quiescent within his comforting embrace as her tears subsided, oblivious of everything except the warm musky scent of his body and the strength of his strong arms about her.

Raoul sighed. 'Come, you must now lie down and go to sleep, hmm?'

'I—I can't,' she muttered, sniffing unhappily and knowing only that she needed the security of his presence.

'But yes, you must,' he murmured, settling her down in the bed and pulling the sheet up over her scantily clad figure.

'Please—please don't leave me. . .' she begged, deeply ashamed of her weak longing for him, and yet not seeming to be able to do anything about it.

She heard him curse softly in French under his breath.

'Ah, Olivia. . . .' He sighed deeply again. 'Yes, if you wish. I will sit here until you sleep . . . fool that I am!'

She wasn't sure that she had heard his last words

correctly, as she contentedly closed her eyes and slowly drifted into a deep dreamless sleep.

Waking late in the morning to find that she had overslept, Olivia had difficulty in remembering exactly what had happened during the night. Her head felt muzzy, her mind still clouded and depressed by yesterday's events as she hurriedly dressed and packed her case. She didn't know how she was going to bring herself to face Raoul at breakfast, but not having had any dinner the previous evening, she felt famished— her stomach rumbling with hunger at the thought of hot rolls and coffee. Hesitantly making her way down the stairs, she was thankful to see that the dining room was almost empty, Raoul only making an appearance when it was time for them to start on their journey again.

Some hours later, waiting to board the ferry which crossed the mouth of the Gironde River from Royan to Le Verdon, Olivia took the opportunity to get out and stretch her legs. Looking back at Raoul's tall figure as he consulted an official about the ferry timetable, she gratefully filled her lungs with the fresh, salty air—so different from the taut, constrained atmosphere in the car this morning. Both of them, she noticed, had been very careful not to disturb what was clearly a fragile truce, only making brief, general references to the passing scenery and deliberately avoiding any references to what had passed between them.

It was early afternoon when Raoul and Olivia reached their destination. Driving down a long avenue of trees, surrounded on either side by black horses grazing on the rich, green grass of an extensive park, Olivia gasped aloud as she caught her first sight of the Château Cheval Noir. All but hidden by trees, the château slowly revealed itself as an exquisitely beautiful, early Renaissance building which seemed to float in the middle of a large, tranquil lake, the water reflecting back a vision more often to be found in fairytales than real life.

As the car passed through the wide entrance gates and they drove over a long, five-arched bridge which crossed the lake, Olivia looked down to see black swans gliding slowly along on the still water. Massive grey walls rose out of the lake, the round corner towers topped by steep conical roofs whose copper covering, parts turned green by age and the elements, gleamed brightly in the afternoon sun.

'It's simply lovely!' she breathed, grateful to Raoul for halting the car and allowing her to feast her eyes on the magnificent building.

'I am fortunate to be able to live in such a place,' he agreed quietly. 'However, I regret that we cannot stop here any longer. We have spent too much time on the journey, and there will be many matters requiring my attention.'

Olivia looked away, her cheeks flushing unhappily, despite his cool, even tone of voice, as she tried to suppress all memories of the previous day—and night. She was rescued from her distracted thoughts by the enthusiastic barking of a pair of golden retrievers as Raoul brought the Porsche to a halt in a large courtyard. The dogs bounded up to the car, their tails wagging furiously as they welcomed their master.

'Down! Down at once!' Raoul laughed as the animals leapt up excitedly, vying for his attention and trying to lick his face as he opened the car door. After patting them on their heads, he spoke a word of command in French and they immediately lay down, two pairs of anxious brown eyes following Raoul's tall figure as he came around to help Olivia alight.

'Gaston will see to the cases,' he said, issuing her before him as they mounted a wide flight of stone steps towards a massive pair of oak doors, set beneath a stone arch containing a large coat of arms.

Some moments after they had entered the large entrance hall, whose vaulted ceiling seemed to disappear far away above her head, Olivia stood silent as Raoul pulled a bell rope for the second time.

'Where is everyone?' he demanded, snapping his fingers in irritation, and telling her to wait as he disappeared through a Gothic arch at the far side of the hall. She could hear his voice impatiently calling for attention as she looked about her with interest. A large tapestry hanging over a gargantuan stone fireplace caught her professional eye, and she was still staring at the allegorical scenes woven so many centuries ago, when Raoul returned.

'I simply cannot understand it!' he snapped. 'Even the dining room looks like the *Marie Céleste*—all the plates full of half-eaten food and the wineglasses still on the table from lunch—it is disgraceful!'

Olivia opened her mouth to say that maybe everyone was busy, but quickly thought better of it as she noted Raoul's mouth drawn into a tight, angry line.

'*Allo, chéri—comment ça va?*' A voice floated down from above their heads. Olivia raised her eyes to see a petite, slim figure of a woman leaning over what looked remarkably like a French version of a minstrel's gallery.

'*Mon Dieu,* Tante!' Raoul thundered, before rattling off a stream of French at the woman, now slowly descending a spiral stone staircase in the corner of the vast hall.

Watching the woman step off the staircase and walk

across the ancient stone floor towards Raoul, Olivia saw that while she was no longer young, Raoul's aunt was making a valiant attempt to keep the years at bay. Her grey hair was cut short to curl loosely about her head, her body clothed in brilliant jade green trousers and matching silk shirt, festooned with rows of gold chains. Indeed, as Raoul perfunctorily introduced her, Olivia's overriding impression was of an attractive woman who, despite her years, possessed considerable sex appeal.

'I am delighted to meet you, Meez Harding,' Tante Amalie smiled broadly. 'Especially since I 'ave heard so much about you from dear Bridget. You are indeed as beautiful as she said you were!'

'For goodness sake, Tante!' Raoul interrupted sharply. 'I want to know what is going on? Where are Gaston and all the servants? I've never seen the house in such a state—it's disgusting!'

'Ah, *chéri*—what a disaster! We 'ave been visited by the plague!' his aunt declaimed in a horrific tone, dramatically raising her arms to heaven.

'Oh, my God!' Raoul groaned impatiently.

'But truly!' his aunt insisted. 'Poor Gaston and his wife, they 'ave the influenza. In summer—who can believe it? And now, alas, poor cook and also the *bonne* who 'elps her in the kitchen—they are saying that they do not feel well, either. Believe me, Meez Harding,' she added, turning to Olivia, 'it is indeed fortunate that you were not 'ere for luncheon—the food was so bad, it was not possible to eat it at all!' she shuddered in recollection of the meal, before floating over to check her make-up in a large mirror.

Raoul sighed heavily. But whether from news of the 'flu epidemic, or from his aunt's somewhat butterfly attitude as she gaily hummed a tune while studying her reflection, Olivia couldn't tell.

'Very well,' he said at last. 'I can see that there have been problems, but where is Nicole?'

'In the *salon*,' the aunt replied, coming over to take hold of his arm and casting him a smiling glance of cajolery from beneath her false eyelashes. 'Now, my dear boy, you are not to be angry with her—I absolutely forbid it. You must promise me—not one cross word!'

'Why on earth should I be angry with Nicole?' Raoul glared down at her sternly as he nevertheless allowed himself to be led away from the hall, Olivia trailing behind in their wake.

'It wasn't 'er fault, really. Well, not exactly, and she was engaged on an errand of mercy at the time. I can assure you about that.'

'Tante! I will cheerfully wring your neck one of these days!' he grated roughly. 'What has happened?'

'You will see. . . .' Tante Amalie refused to be drawn any further on the subject as she opened a door and allowed her nephew and Olivia to proceed her into a large, formal drawing room.

'*Mon Dieu*, Nicole!' Raoul exclaimed, hurrying forward to a woman of about thirty, who was resting on a sofa with both her legs in plaster.

'My poor niece—she 'ad a terrible car accident three days ago, and truly it was not 'er fault,' Tante Amalie murmured to Olivia as Raoul drew up a chair beside his sister and began to converse in French.

'Of course, the car is "written off", as you say in England, but only think what bad luck it was! Poor Nicole was simply going into the village, to fetch *le médecin*, when—vroom! The tyre blows out and she lands in a ditch. Do you not think it was wrong of the Good Lord to let such a thing happen? Especially when the child could have been in the car. I tell you, me, I was very cross and refused to say my prayers for two whole days!'

Olivia shook her head in confusion, watching with glazed eyes as Tante Amalie wandered over to a marble-topped table and began to pour liquid from various bottles into a silver cocktail shaker. Olivia realised that her previously formed views of orderly French family life were taking a beating, as she saw Raoul's aunt vigorously shake the mixture, before pouring it into some glasses.

'Of course, I understand that it is early in the evening,' the older woman confided, completely ignoring the sun blazing in through the *salon's* mullioned windows. 'But I really feel in need of some strong refreshment after that terrible luncheon. Will you not join me?'

'No, I—er—thank you, but I don't feel quite able to. . . .' Olivia could hear her voice trail lamely away, as she stared in fascinated horror at the particularly lurid, day-glo green colour of the proffered cocktail.

'Are you sure? This is absolutely my own recipe, you know. I call it the "Cheval Noir Screwdriver"! In any event it should help to keep away all those bad influenza germs, and it is particularly good for the 'ormones—or so I 'ave been told!' Tante Amalie's throaty chuckle accompanied by an outrageous wink, made her meaning only too clear.

What in the world am I doing here? It's a mad house! Olivia thought, swaying wearily as she felt the accumulated strain of the past days rapidly depleting her already sorely tried reserves of strength. Tearing her eyes away from the older woman, who had turned on a small radio and seemed to be practising some disco dance steps to the music, Olivia responded to Raoul's request that she should come over and be introduced to his sister.

Greeting Nicole, Olivia was relieved to find that at least one member of the family seemed to be fairly normal. She, in her turn, found she was being surveyed by calm, friendly grey eyes set above a mouth which was widely stretched into a welcoming smile.

'I regret that I was not able to greet you formally,' Nicole said, her plain face redeemed by a particularly sweet expression. 'However . . .' she glanced down at her legs set in plaster. 'As you can see, I'm afraid that I'm not mobile at the present time!'

'I—I was sorry to hear about your accident,' Olivia murmured, suddenly feeling tired to death, and wondering desperately just how long she could keep standing on legs that felt as weak as water.

'What on earth have you done to this lovely girl?' Nicole spoke sternly to her brother. 'She looks exhausted after your long journey and must rest before dinner.'

'Me, I do not intend to eat another excruciatingly bad meal in this house!' Tante Amalie's voice cut into the conversation as she swiftly tipped the second cocktail down her throat. 'I must go and telephone *mon cher Général* Dufour and insist that he takes me out for a decent dinner. *Au revoir mes enfants!*'

'For God's sake, Nicole—who is *Général* Dufour? One of Tante's new boyfriends?'

'I fear so,' Nicole grinned at the harassed expression on Raoul's face. 'Now, my dear brother, do please take poor Miss Harding to her room. The guest suite in the East wing has been prepared for her, as you asked that it should be. It was almost the last thing poor Gaston's wife did before she succumbed to the 'flu.' Nicole turned to Olivia. 'She is our housekeeper and I always thought I would be lost without her, and now indeed I find I am!'

'No, really—there's no need for you to bother. I was expecting to stay in a hotel in any case,' Olivia protested.

'Absolutely not! We wouldn't hear of such a thing, would we Raoul?' Nicole smiled up at her brother.

'Absolutely not!' He echoed dryly. 'Although as my aunt has pointed out, whether you will find either the accommodation or the food acceptable, is very doubtful!'

'I—I can't possibly impose on you all, especially at such a time. . . .'

'There is no imposition involved,' Raoul interrupted crisply, looking down at her pale face and weary figure. 'Nicole is quite right, you do look exhausted. Come, I will take you upstairs.'

There was clearly no point in arguing the matter any further, Olivia told herself as she allowed Raoul to lead her from the room. She would just spend a night here and then try and find somewhere else to stay tomorrow. Bordeaux wasn't too far away, and she'd still be able to see Bridget, who was apparently living somewhere in this huge building.

Raoul took her arm in an impersonal grip as she stumbled up the large curving flight of stone stairs, which led off a small hall behind the *salon*. They had just reached the landing when a tiny child came racing down the corridor.

'*Papa! Papa!*' the small girl cried, squealing with delight as Raoul bent down to pick her up and swing her around in his arms.

Olivia suddenly felt as if she had been turned to stone, cold and icy as the marble bannister beneath her trembling hand.

'I don't think you have met my daughter, Marie-Louise?' Raoul's voice, heavy with irony, seemed to come from somewhere far away as Olivia fought against the shock waves which filled her brain.

'You must say: *"Bonjour, mademoiselle"*, *ma chérie,*' Raoul instructed his daughter, his lips curving into a warm smile as he stroked her curly black hair.

The small child stepped forward and dropped an awkward curtsey. *'Bonjour, mademoiselle,'* she repeated obediently, smiling up into the tall English girl's strained, pale face. *'Elle est très jolie, Papa.'*

'Yes, Mademoiselle Harding is very pretty,' Raoul agreed blandly, looking past down the corridor as a plump middle-aged woman hurried forward. 'Ah, here is Annie come to claim you for tea.'

'Excusez-moi, Monsieur le Vicomte,' the nurse murmured taking the little girl's hand.

'Non, non, Papa!' the child clung to his legs.

'I will come and see you in a minute, I promise,' he smilingly reassured his daughter, who sighed and allowed herself to be led away.

'Your bedroom suite is along here,' Raoul said, leading the way down a long corridor away from the nursery, and ignoring Olivia's stunned, shocked figure as she trailed silently after him. They seemed to be walking for ever, she thought, realising that they were traversing the sides of the square, as shown by glances out of the passing windows on her left. The view of the inner courtyard was always the same, although seen from different angles.

'Here we are,' Raoul pronounced at last, opening a door by a small stone stairway and standing aside to allow her to enter.

Olivia found herself in an ante-room, containing a sofa and chairs grouped around a fireplace, with an ormolu desk and chair set between the two long windows, half-covered with watered silk festoon blinds.

'Here is your bathroom,' Raoul said, opening a door on one side of the room. 'And . . .' he crossed the floor, 'here is your bedroom. I hope that you will be comfortable, and I will see that your case is brought up immediately. Is there anything else you require?

'No—no thank you,' she whispered, staring down at a fine needlepoint rug and wishing with all her heart that he would just go away and leave her alone.

'*Ah, bon.* I will see you at dinner then,' he murmured, hesitating as he cast a swift, searching look at the bowed figure of the girl standing with her back to him in the middle of the room. A moment later she heard the door closing quietly behind him.

Like a sleepwalker, Olivia moved slowly over to stand gazing blindly out of the window at the lake and the cultivated fields beyond. Her mind was totally empty of everything except a deep, numbing pain which also seemed to have invaded her body. How long she stood there she had no idea, her trance-like state being broken by a knock and the entrance of a tall, young man who murmured something in French as he took her suitcase through into the bedroom.

'Thank you—er—*merci*,' she said haltingly as he smiled and left the suite.

Trailing through into the bedroom, which she saw was decorated in the same cream and gold colours and Second Empire style as the sitting room, she looked longingly at the large, wide bed. Swiftly stripping off her travel-stained clothes, she went through to have a quick shower, before returning to slip between the cool linen sheets of the bed, and within moments had fallen into a deep, exhausted sleep.

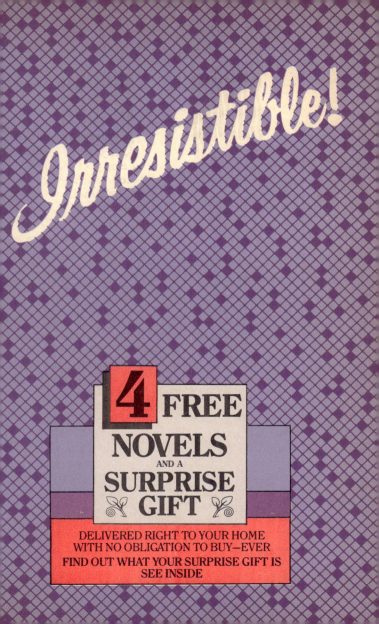

YOURS FREE
FOR KEEPS!

Use the edge of a coin to rub
off the box at right and
reveal your surprise gift ➡

DEAR READER:

We would like to send you
4 Harlequin Presents just like
the one you're reading plus
a surprise gift – all
ABSOLUTELY FREE.

If you like them, we'll send you 4 more books
each month to preview. Always before they're
available in stores. Always for less than the
regular retail price. Always with the right to
cancel and owe nothing.

In addition, you'll receive **FREE** . . .
• our monthly newsletter HEART TO HEART
• our magazine ROMANCE DIGEST
• fabulous bonus books and surprise gifts
• special-edition Harlequin Bestsellers to
  preview for ten days without obligation

So return the attached Card and start your
Harlequin honeymoon today.

Sincerely

Pamela Powers

Pamela Powers
for Harlequin

P.S. Remember, your 4 free novels and your
surprise gift are yours to keep whether
you buy any books or not.

4 EXCITING ROMANCE NOVELS PLUS A SURPRISE GIFT

FREE BOOKS/ SURPRISE GIFT

YES, please send me my four **FREE** Harlequin Presents® and my **FREE** surprise gift. Then send me four brand-new Harlequin Presents each month as soon as they come off the presses. Bill me at the low price of $1.75 each (for a total of $7.00—a saving of .80¢ off the retail price). There are no shipping, handling or other hidden costs. There is no minimum number of books I must purchase. I can always return a shipment and cancel at any time. Even if I never buy a book from Harlequin, the four free novels and the surprise gift are mine to keep forever.   **104 CIP AAGE**

NAME_____

ADDRESS_____ APT. NO._____

CITY_____

STATE_____ ZIP_____

Offer limited to one per household and not valid for present subscribers. Prices subject to change.

Mail to:
Harlequin Reader Service
2504 W. Southern Avenue,
Tempe, Arizona 85282

LIMITED TIME ONLY
Mail today and get a
SECOND MYSTERY GIFT

MAIL THIS CARD TODAY

You'll receive 4 Harlequin novels
plus a fabulous surprise gift
ABSOLUTELY FREE

BUSINESS REPLY CARD

First Class   Permit No. 70   Tempe, AZ

Postage will be paid by addressee

Harlequin Reader Service
2504 W. Southern Avenue
Tempe, Arizona 85282

NO POSTAGE
NECESSARY
IF MAILED
IN THE
UNITED STATES

Woken by a knock on her bedroom door, she sleepily glanced at her watch to see that she had slept for over three hours. A pretty young girl put her head around the door and then entered, bearing a tray. Olivia's French wasn't very good, but she understood the maid to say that Nicole had wished her to be woken with a cup of English tea.

Later, as she sipped the warm, soothing liquid, Olivia was touched by Nicole's thoughtfulness. Considering the state of the household 'below stairs', it was a more than kind gesture, and one she deeply appreciated in these alien surroundings. What an extraordinary person Aunt Amalie was, she told herself brightly. Definitely a perfect illustration of the old saying: mutton dressed as lamb. . . .

Olivia sighed heavily. It was no use. Trying to fill her mind with irrelevant matters such as seeing the funny side of Raoul's aunt, wasn't proving to be the slightest use in keeping her miserable thoughts at bay. As much as she didn't want to, she really had to face the fact that not only had Raoul married someone—only a month or so after he had jilted her—but he also had a child. Why did it hurt so much? Was it, because knowing someone was or had been married, was one thing, but seeing the actual result of his passionate and sensual lovemaking was—was quite another? The little girl she had met in the corridor was the outward, visible proof that he and his wife had created the child—together.

Lying here in bed, she couldn't prevent her thoughts returning to her past life, when she had been engaged to Raoul and had been so supremely happy. Raoul, who had taught her everything about the needs of her body—and his. Raoul, who had only to hold her in his arms, for her to become a yielding, willing slave to his desires. . . .

The memories suddenly became too painful, and she rolled over, burying her face in the pillows as she wept bitterly for what might have been, for her lost innocence and the cruel way he had chosen to discard her. Her slim frame trembled violently, racked by waves of overpowering jealousy. She seemed unable to stop torturing herself with the vivid images of Raoul and his wife together; the intimate moments when he must have held her passionately in his arms, and had given her the opportunity to bear his child.

The storm of tears ebbed slowly away, leaving Olivia pale and shaking with nervous exhaustion despite her recent sleep. She really ought to get out of bed and choose something to wear for dinner. . . .

'Hi, Olivia!' She looked up startled as her bedroom door was thrown open and her cousin Bridget stood on the threshold. 'It's really great to see you again and I'm absolutely thrilled you could make the wedding!'

Olivia's green eyes widened as she stared at her cousin. Surely her hair used to be dark brown? Bridget was now a strawberry blonde, her hair cut in a modern dishevelled style, while as for her clothes. . . ! Bridget can't possibly be pregnant, she thought, trying not to look at the girl's stomach as she viewed the slim figure poured into skin-tight, fluorescent pink jeans, topped by a low-cut, sleeveless T-shirt of the same colour, a wide gold lamé belt clasping her small waist. Oh God! Bridget hadn't changed one little bit in the past year—she was still dressing in her usual dashing style of outrageous, radical chic.

'Yes—er—it's good to see you, too,' Olivia murmured, sitting up in bed and wishing she had her sunglasses on—Bridget's outfit was hard on the eyes.

'I can't stay too long because I'm supposed to be cooking dinner!' Her cousin's long gold earrings tinkled loudly as she threw back her head and roared with laughter. 'As you know, my cooking rates a grade of minus zero, so be smart and bring your alka-seltzer downstairs with you!' She laughed again, Olivia wincing visibly at the sound of her cousin's raucous tones.

'Hey—are you all right?' Bridget asked, looking critically at the girl sitting up in bed. 'Your face is all red and blotchy—I hope you aren't coming down with what Tante Amalie calls "the plague"? I'm hopeless with anyone who is ill—about as much use as a sick headache!'

'No—er—I'm fine. It was just the long journey, I expect,' Olivia replied hurriedly. 'We got delayed by something wrong with Raoul's car, and—and everything took twice as long as I thought it would.'

'Really? I didn't think you were expected before this afternoon, but I expect I got the details wrong as usual.'

'Will—will your fiancé, Henri, and his mother be having dinner with us as well?'

Bridget shrugged. 'Not if they're sensible, they won't. They and you should have gone out with Tante Amalie—there's a game old girl! By the way, have you heard about my "happy event"?'

'Well, yes, Raoul did mention something. . . .'

'I bet old smoothy-chops did! Our Vicomte *really* doesn't approve of me at all. He nearly fainted when I turned up at a very smart party he was giving, wearing my fishnet jumpsuit. I told him to stop panicking and just be grateful it had pockets at all the strategic points! Anyway, the other men at the party thought I looked *sensational*! I sure as hell knocked spots off the other girls there, I can tell you! I had a fantastic time in Italy as well,' she said, going over to the dressing table to try some of her cousin's perfume.

Olivia found herself feeling unexpectedly sorry for Raoul. Living with Bridget was like living with an unexploded bomb—she was likely to erupt at any moment and guaranteed to cause the maximum damage. 'What happened to your job in Italy?' she asked.

'Oh, that,' Bridget shrugged. 'I was supposed to be an au pair for a family out there. It was OK for a while, but then the father of the kids started getting heavy—know what I mean?' She glanced at Olivia who was looking puzzled. 'Honestly! How can someone of your age be so dumb! You're two years older than me, and yet you manage to make me feel ancient.' She shook her head in bewilderment.

'You mean he—he. . . .'

'Yep. He fancied a bit on the side—me! Well, I wasn't keen, I mean, he was short and fat—ugh! Now, if he'd looked like our glamorous Vicomte, I'd have said "yes" like a shot! Believe me, in Italy, *macho* doesn't necessarily prove "mucho"—so I decided to leave. I'd got rather tired of the Italian men I'd met anyway. They all seemed to have two legs and eight hands!'

'Are—are you pleased about the baby?' Olivia asked, feeling stunned by her cousin's effervescent personality.

'Yeah—I suppose so.' Bridget sat down to try one of Olivia's lipsticks, leaning forward to critically survey the new colour on her lips. 'Henri's delighted anyway—so's his mother. Henri's really keen for us to get married. I don't love him of course, but when I found out I was pregnant, he was all for rushing me to the altar straight away!'

'Bridget! For heaven's sake! You can't marry someone unless you love them! It's bound to go wrong if you do.' Olivia looked at the girl with deep concern. 'Honestly, if you don't want to get married—then don't! I—I can help you out financially if you need any money for the baby.'

'Look, it's kind of you, but. . . .' Bridget swung around on the stool. 'I know I joke around a lot, but no kid of mine is to go through the sort of childhood I did, with no parents and that ghastly aunt and uncle always griping away, as if I was some terrible burden they had no choice but to shoulder. My child is going to have a father, and a grandmother, and an uncle who's got some money, and—and people who care . . . okay?' she added defiantly.

'Sorry, I—I didn't mean to interfere, Bridget. I know you had a rotten time as a child. . . .'

'Oh, what the hell,' she shrugged, giving Olivia a twisted smile. 'That was a long time ago. Heavens! I must get back down to the kitchen,' she cried jumping up quickly. 'I bet all the vegetables have boiled dry by now. I'd stay up here, if I was you—it's the best way to avoid poisoning! 'Bye.'

I wish I could stay here in the bedroom, Olivia told herself as she finished unpacking her clothes, trying to decide what to wear for dinner and dreading the thought of having to face Raoul once again. Why hadn't he mentioned his child when he had talked about his wife? It—well, it almost seemed as if he was being deliberately cruel for some reason. She was sure that he had been well aware of the fact that she didn't know of his marriage, almost deliberately shocking her with the news, that first evening in the hotel. And—and then there had been his passionate embrace after she had fallen into the river, which had been at *his* instigation, not hers. So why had he been so angry afterwards. . .?

The sound of a gong reverberating in the distance broke into Olivia's chaotic thoughts. She lifted her head, gazing at herself in the mirror with astonishment. . . . She had been so immersed in thinking about herself and Raoul, that she hadn't realised that all the while she'd been automatically dressing herself. Why on earth was she wearing this low-cut, figure hugging black jersey dress, whose simplicity of line called attention to her supple curves and the length of her long slim legs?

Glancing at her watch she saw that it was too late to change. Neither was there time, she thought hurriedly, as she felt her face blushing, to delve into the complicated psychology of why she had subconsciously chosen such a revealing dress. What with Bridget's cooking and having to face Raoul, she realised that she didn't need to be a clairvoyant to know that the evening ahead was going to be a total disaster.

CHAPTER SIX

'DAMN!' Olivia looked down at the small droplet of blood swelling up from the cut in her thumb. With a sigh of exasperation she put down the knife, and walked across the grey flagstones to where a tin of plasters rested on the large kitchen dresser. You're beginning to look like a walking ambulance case, she told herself with a wry grimace, looking down at the two burn marks on her arm and a plaster which was already covering a cut on her forefinger.

What had Ian Campbell said to her, back in London? That what she needed was a good holiday? Hah! Maybe he should try the so-called gracious life in a French château? Oh boy—would he be in for a surprise!

Olivia's lips twisted sardonically as she finished bandaging the cut on her thumb and turned to survey her surroundings. The ancient stone walls made the room look more like a dungeon than a kitchen. Thin shafts of early morning sunlight streaming in from the windows set up high near the ceiling, merely served to underline the prison-like impression. An ancient calor-gas cooker and an even older refrigerator, which throbbed and pounded as if at its last gasp, appeared lost in comparison to the size of the vast area. Only the enormous spread of the scrubbed wooden table in the centre of the room seemed made to scale. That and the old kitchen range, of course! Olivia hadn't been able to believe her eyes when she had first set sight on its mammoth bulk.

'For God's sake, it's practically out of the ark!' she had exclaimed on the evening of her arrival, viewing the heavy black monstrosity with startled eyes as she helped Raoul to unpack the meal he had ordered.

Bridget's cooking, never any good at the best of times, had plumbed new depths as she had tried to wrestle with the antiquated kitchen equipment. Having managed to burn all the toast for the chicken liver pâté, which had luckily been prepared by the cook before she took to her sick bed, Bridget had then served up her version of *Sole Bonne Femme*. Raoul had taken one horrified look at the pieces of fish swimming in a grey, watery sauce, and had swiftly risen from the table, politely requesting all those present to adjourn to the *salon* while he went to fetch a decent meal from the local restaurant.

Perhaps it was due to the amount of drink everyone consumed while they waited for their dinner, but the atmosphere had lightened considerably by the time Raoul arrived back with the food. Certainly Olivia had felt slightly tipsy and full of Dutch courage as she helped to carry one of the boxes down to the kitchen.

'This place is like living in the Middle Ages! How on earth do you expect anyone to work in here?' she had demanded incredulously, her stomach rumbling as she dished up the Duck in Orange sauce provided by the restaurant.

'Yes, well . . . .' Raoul had shrugged, giving her a brief smile. 'My great-uncle lived to a very ripe old age, and when I took over the estate, there was so much which had to be done. The vineyard was in a terrible condition; all the *cuves* were also in a very bad way, in fact one of them exploded during my first harvest and had to be replaced; the land required to be drained—believe me, the list was endless. So, I'm afraid the château has had to wait its turn. It hasn't been a question of money, you understand, but rather one of time and organisation.'

'Well, you'd better get yourself organised and spend some time and money on this place, tout-ever-so-suite!' she had said forcefully. 'I can't imagine anyone being sufficiently foolish enough to cook down here in this terrible place, if you don't.'

Famous last words! Olivia told herself derisively, returning to the large sink where a pile of carrots were still waiting to be scraped. But she really hadn't had any choice, had she? What else could she have done but take over the running of the château until the agency in Paris dispatched some temporary servants, as they had promised Raoul they would.

Tante Amalie had clearly never lifted a finger in her life, and Nicole was completely out of action. Hélène, Raoul's older sister, was as whining and ineffectual as he had said she would be, while no one—let alone Olivia—was prepared to suffer the vagaries of Bridget's cooking one moment longer than they had to!

The last three days hadn't all been on the minus side, of course. Used to running her own business, Olivia had first consulted Nicole, and then with the French girl's grateful thanks ringing in her ears, she had organised what was left of the depleted domestic staff into some sort of routine, which they had clearly lacked before. Luckily, the women who worked in the equally ancient laundry all came from the local village and seemed to have avoided 'the plague'. However, as each day passed, there seemed to be fewer and fewer helpers, only three maids now remained on their feet, and the last member of the kitchen staff had taken to her bed last night.

Still, considering the lack of assistants, she didn't

really feel she had done too badly, and even Tante had commented on the fresh bowls of flowers and the newly polished furniture. Furthermore, despite her grumbling, Olivia was quite enjoying reviving her Cordon Bleu culinary skills, not having been so severely tested since her cookery course at the age of seventeen. Every night she went up to bed with a battered copy she had found of *Le Grand Cuisinier Français*, and a dictionary, with which she attempted to translate some of the more obscure recipes. And, moreover, her newly assumed role of cook, house-keeper and chief bottle-washer did have one great advantage—it kept her out of Raoul's way. Apart from telling him of the day's menu, so he could select the appropriate wines from the domestic cellars next to the kitchen, and during mealtimes, she had hardly seen him. Although he, too, was undoubtedly busy, engaged in organising his preparations for the grape harvest, due to commence in a month's time. . . .

'Hi, skivvy! By the way, that was a really great meal last night,' said Bridget coming into the kitchen and going over to put a kettle on the old gas stove. 'I thought I'd make a pot of coffee—fancy a cup?'

'Too kind!' Olivia murmured ironically. 'And less of the "skivvy" business, if you don't mind. While I'm at it, why doesn't your future mother-in-law, Hélène, do her own cooking? Not that I'm complaining, of course. Oh dear me, no! But without the three of you at every meal, my job would be a lot easier!' she added bitterly, tossing a carrot to join others in a bowl of cold water.

'And miss your cooking? Don't be daft! Hélène and Henri haven't eaten so well for years, and certainly won't again—not if they have to rely on me!'

'But at least you've got a decent kitchen in your apartment over there,' Olivia gestured out of the window. 'Not an antediluvian edifice like—like this place.'

'Hang on—fair's fair! Hélène and I have been doing our "bit", you know. We've been running non-stop soup and toast to all the sick servants—up and down those stone stairs till I thought my legs would drop off! Incidentially, Gaston's wife looks awful, wheezing like an old pair of bellows.'

'Well, the doctor is coming again this morning, so I expect he'll give her something to make her feel better.'

'Ho! The doctor would be sure to find a reason to come and see Nicole, anyway. That accident of her's must have seemed like a Godsend! They're nuts about each other, you know.'

'Good for them,' Olivia murmured absentmindedly as she carried the prepared vegetables through into the larder. Coming back she had her first clear view of the outfit her cousin was wearing that morning. 'For God's sake! You can't wear that . . .!' Her startled eyes took in the fact that Bridget was wearing nothing beneath the bright yellow dungarees, the front apron only partially covering the ample curves of her breasts.

'Oh, don't be such a prude! Anyway, Henri says that he thinks I look dead sexy!' Bridget placed the coffee pot on the table and went over to fetch two cups from the dresser. 'You're right, this kitchen is frightful, isn't it? All it needs are thumb screws and a rack or two, and it would be a perfect setting for one of those horror movies! Still, I must say I quite fancy all those copper and brass pans hanging on the wall. Dead smart with the coat of arms engraved on them like that, aren't they?'

'Useless aristocratic rubbish!' Olivia retorted in crushing tones. 'All the bottoms need re-doing, you'd really get a stomach ache if I used any of them!'

Bridget laughed. 'Never mind, Livy, now you've done those blasted carrots, come over here and sit down. You need to relax and have a cup of coffee.'

'OK, I've just finished.' Olivia wiped her hands and went to join her at the table. 'I can't stop long, though. I have to take Tante up her breakfast tray in a few minutes.'

Bridget produced a packet of cigarettes. 'Oh, let the old girl wait. Here, try one of these coffin nails!'

'I gave up ages ago, I really shouldn't,' Olivia protested as she weakly accepted a light. 'It must be the strain of the last few days, that's all. But you definitely shouldn't be smoking, not when you're expecting a baby.'

'I know, I know, so don't nag! It's funny,' Bridget mused, 'I'd never thought about being a "mother" before I found myself pregnant, but now I'm quite looking forward to the baby. It would be nice to have a little girl like Marie-Louise, she's a cute kid.'

'Yes, she is, isn't she?' Olivia smiled. She had long ago recovered from her almost insane surge of jealousy over the child, and had become very fond of the precociously intelligent small girl.

Bridget sipped her coffee reflectively. 'The jolly old Vicomte and I might not always see eye to eye, but I've got to admit he really does love his daughter. Let's hope for her sake, that Madame Millot doesn't manage to pin him down.'

'Madame Millot?' Olivia looked at her cousin in surprise. 'Who's she?'

'Some old harpy who fancies Raoul. Her uncle owns a small vineyard on the edge of this estate. He's a widower and Madame Millot is his only relative. Tante is pushing Raoul to marry the woman and she's probably right—you know how practical the French are. If he's going to marry someone, why not get some more acres at one and the same time. . . . Hey! What's wrong with you, you're looking pea green!'

'Nothing, I—I'm just not used to French cigarettes, that's all,' Olivia assured her hurriedly. 'What—er—what's Madame Millot like?' she added as nonchalantly as she could.

'A rapacious divorcee and really poison!' her cousin said succinctly. 'I can't stand her and I don't think Marie-Louise is too keen, either. The woman's always sugary sweet, of course, but I guess kids know when someone's trying to put on an act. Mind you,' Bridget added, 'I've got to admit the woman's good looking, in a Lady Macbeth sort of way, but she's got some hot competition in Chantal—thank goodness!'

'Chantal?' Olivia looked at her cousin in confusion. 'I can't keep up with everyone in the château, let alone the locals. Who is Chantal, for heaven's sake?'

'She's a nice girl, you'd like her. Chantal and her brother, Alain, are the nearest people of Henri's and my age living locally, so we've seen quite a bit of them. Their dad owns a château vineyard, but not as grand as this one. We're a *premier cru*, you know,' she added with pride.

'That's the top wine classification, isn't it?'

'Yep. Out here, one's social rating amongst the Bordeaux establishment is strictly on the wine you produce. So even if old Raoul was just a plain mister and only had a few acres—the "first growth" wine he produces would still make him a *grand seigneur*.' She stubbed her cigarette out. 'Still, I guess he's got enough going for him not to need that—certainly Chantal thinks so. She's only eighteen and has a king-sized crush on the guy, which gives her an advantage over Madame Millot—randy old men like 'em young.'

'Raoul's not a randy old man!' Olivia burst out, and then fervently wished she hadn't, as Bridget looked at her with raised eyebrows.

'Ho! So that's the way the wind blows, does it?'

'No, of course it doesn't! Don't be so stupid, Bridget! Anyway, I can't sit here gossiping all day,' Olivia snapped crossly as she rose from the table. 'Poor Tante will have given me up for lost. Make yourself useful and see if you can get that nineteen-twenties toaster to work, while I make a fresh pot of coffee.'

'I'm not surprised you fancy the glamorous Vicomte—he can leave his shoes outside *my* door any night he pleases! But don't raise your hopes too high, Livy, Madame Millot has got her long, dark red nails well and truly hooked into him!'

'*Do you want another meal in this house . . .?*'

'OK, OK, I was only joking!' Bridget looked speculatively at her cousin, who was angrily banging some pans as she tried to light the gas stove. 'Turn the knob to the left,' she suggested quietly, her eyes taking in Olivia's flushed cheeks and nervously trembling hands. Bridget opened her mouth to say something, and then thought better of it, silently getting on with making the toast.

Knocking on Tante Amalie's door as she came to collect the empty tray an hour later, Olivia found the older woman dressed in a leotard, doing aerobic exercises accompanied by the taped instructions from a cassette recorder.

'*Ah bon!* Now I can stop,' Tante said, standing up and gasping for breath. 'This "keeping fit" is 'ard work, but dear Bridget says it is necessary.'

'Only if you enjoy it,' Olivia smiled. 'Your figure looks good enough to me. You really mustn't let my cousin bully you too much.'

'*Mais non!* I 'ave taken on a new lease of life since Bridget came to this château. As the dear girl said, I was gettin old before my time! It is a pity she and Raoul do not always see eye to eye, though.'

'Oh, I don't suppose he really minds her all that much,' Olivia remarked, picking up the empty tray. 'I expect she'll be much quieter when she has a baby to look after.'

'That is true,' Tante agreed, going over to sit down at her dressing table and sorting through her jewellery. 'I am fond of dear Bridget, of course,' she confided. 'But it is important that Raoul is not made unhappy. The dear boy looks after me very well, and I do not wish to annoy him . . . it would not be a good idea for me to do so, *vous comprenez*?'

'Do you mean that he—er—supports you?' asked Olivia, sitting down on the unmade bed.

'Exactly!' Tante beamed at Olivia for being so quick to understand the situation. 'Of course, he is a nice boy—very generous. He never, never reminds his old Tante that she lives on his charity—that is good, yes?'

'Yes—yes it is,' Olivia agreed slowly.

'*Ah bon!* Of course, in some ways, I feel responsible for him. His mother, my sister, she and her 'usband died when he was a young boy, and I 'elped to bring him up, you understand.' Tante Amalie paused, fiddling absentmindedly with her bottles of perfume. 'Me—I have a good memory. Yes, I thought your name sounded familiar, and then I remembered that Meez Olivia Harding was the name of Raoul's—er—his friend in *Londres* some years ago, hmm?'

Olivia could feel herself flushing beneath the shrewd, wise old eyes watching her in the mirror.

'Ah yes,' Tante continued in approving tones. 'How very wise it was of you to break off your engagement—

it would not have done, of course. He needed to marry someone—someone, let us say, of his own kind. Which of course he did, Estelle being the daughter of the Duc de Chambéry. What he should do now is to marry a woman like Madame Millot, who would be most suitable and be a mother to his child. Many Frenchmen, my dear, do marry foreigners, but I do not think that it is always a good idea.'

Olivia had opened her mouth to protest that it wasn't she who had jilted Raoul, but what was the point in raking up the whole thing all over again? 'I agree with you,' she answered firmly, getting up and walking over to the door.

'I knew you would. I realise that my nephew is still very attracted to you, but I am an old woman, my dear, and my advice comes from experience, believe me. So—now, tell me,' she added, changing the subject. 'What delicious dishes have you for us today?'

'Cold salmon trout in aspic for lunch, and escalopes of veal for dinner,' Olivia replied listlessly.

'What a wonderful girl you are!' Tante beamed happily at the thought of the gourmet meals in front of her.

But not wonderful enough, apparently, Olivia thought grimly as she slowly retraced her steps back down to the kitchen. That had been a fairly clear warning from Tante, who had not only remembered who she was, but had obviously caught the strained, electric atmosphere that sparked between herself and Raoul whenever they met. What was more, Tante was right, she told herself, suddenly feeling tired and depressed. Marie-Louise needed a mother, and however rich Raoul was, the addition of another vineyard would always prove useful to a man so concerned with his winemaking. Sighing heavily, she put the tray down on the kitchen table. After all, what Raoul did with his life was none of her business. It wasn't as if he meant anything to her anymore, was it? So why should she care who he married?

As she began to soften the aspic for the salmon trout, both of which she had prepared last night, Olivia was miserably aware that she did care—very much indeed.

'O-livia! O-livia . . .!' A small hand pulling impatiently at her skirt made Olivia sit up, blinking in the strong morning sunshine. What on earth was wrong with her these days? She'd only come out to the rose garden for a short break from her labours in the kitchen, and here she was dozing in the sun. She glanced down at her watch. Eleven o'clock in the morning, for heaven's sakes! Anyone would think she was an old lady, instead of a supposedly fit young woman of twenty-three! She wasn't sleeping well at night, of course, but that was no reason why. . . .

'Please tell me a story, Olivia?' Marie-Louise smiled hopefully up at her new English friend, who seemed to have an inexhaustible knowledge of all the best fairy stories. 'I like the ones about dragons best,' the child confided, climbing up on to Olivia's lap. 'Especially when they eat all the *jolie* ladies.'

'What a bloodthirsty little girl you are!' Olivia teased.

'*Mais non.* I am not little, I am a great, big girl. I am to be four years in *novembre*. Me, I am *grande*—big.'

'Four years old in November? Wow! That is very old indeed!' Olivia grinned down at Marie-Louise. 'Very well, for someone so ancient, I will try and think of a very, very old story. Let me see: Once upon a time there was a beautiful princess. Her name of course, was Marie-Louise. . . .'

The child laughed, nestling into her friend's arms until the end of the story. '. . . and then St George killed the bad dragon and everyone was safe, and lived happily ever after!'

'Oh, thank you, that was a very nice story!' Marie-Louise sighed with contentment before winding her small arms about Olivia's neck and giving her a kiss. 'Did St George marry the *belle* princess?'

'*Of course!* It is only in real life that hero's do not marry their princesses.' Both Olivia and the child looked around startled, to see Raoul lounging against a garden wall behind them.

How long has he been there? Olivia thought, blushing as she saw the gleam in his heavily lidded eyes as they swept over both her and the child in her arms. Marie-Louise slid off her lap and ran towards her father.

'Olivia tells such nice stories, *papa*,' she said, laughing as he caught her up in his arms.

'Very well, then, she must be rewarded. Do you think that maybe she would like to come out with us to Bordeaux, hmm?'

'Oh, yes, *papa*. Can we have lemonade and a *gâteau*?'

Raoul laughed. 'Very well, lemonade and a cream cake it shall be!'

'Am I going to be asked my views on the proposed excursion, to which it seems I am being invited?' Olivia asked with asperity as she stood up, brushing down her skirt.

'Absolutely not! If you are given a choice, you will only disappear back into the kitchen like Cinderella. I have experienced—er—considerable difficulty in even exchanging the time of day with you, my dear Olivia. I did not bring you down to this château for you to become a cook, delicious though your food is.'

'No, you brought me down for a wedding,' she reminded him sharply, her breathing seeming to be affected by the way his cool eyes rested on her figure.

'Ah—so I did,' he agreed blandly. 'But whose? That is an interesting question, *n'est-ce pas?*'

'Why, are you also thinking of getting married?' Olivia turned away to concentrate on carefully examining a full-blown rose.

'I might. Yes, I might very well be thinking of just such a thing. Do you feel it would be a good idea, hmm?'

'Why—why should I care one way or another?' She shrugged and gave a small, careless laugh, hoping he hadn't heard the shaky, shrill note only too evident to her own ears.

'Why indeed?' he murmured sardonically as Marie-Louise tugged at his hand.

'*Papa . . .!* The cream cakes. . . .'

'Well, you must ask Miss Harding very nicely, and then maybe she will condescend to take pity on us, and leave her delightful kitchen for a boring old trip into Bordeaux.'

'*Comment?*' Marie-Louise looked at her father in puzzlement.

'Stop teasing the poor child,' Olivia told him sternly, trying to stop herself from returning his wide, infectious grin. 'You know very well that I am hardly enamoured with that frightful kitchen, but what about the preparations for lunch? I'd like a break, but I don't see how. . . .'

'My dear Olivia,' he said, firmly taking her arm and leading her to the garage. 'Let my delightful family fend for themselves for once. It will do them all a power of good!'

'But I ought to leave instructions. . . .'

'*No!* I am quite sure you have left everything well

under control, and we will be back in plenty of time for you to do any last minute cooking that is required. Now, that is enough about food,' he added decisively. 'I am becoming bored by the subject.'

'Oh, all right.' She shrugged. It was clearly no use protesting any further and she couldn't deny that an escape from her culinary duties would be a welcome change.

Sitting beside Raoul in the Range Rover he used for travelling about his estate, she glanced sideways at his profile through lowered lashes. Beneath the tan, his face looked pale and strained. Maybe he was having trouble with his vines, she thought, feeling guilty at being so immersed in running the château that she had given little thought to any problems he might have.

Bordeaux, she discovered, was a delightful old town. Raoul left the vehicle in the underground car park next to the esplanade on the left bank of the river, taking her and the child over on to the terraces, to view the old port and its large eighteenth-century buildings. With Marie-Louise skipping along beside them, Raoul led Olivia along to view the Grand Theatre and the twelve large statues of goddesses in the collonade, before they walked slowly down an elegant pedestrian shopping area. She could see narrow old streets and squares leading off the main route through the town, all of which seemed to be beautifully preserved.

'Of course, there used to be as many English here as French, at least up to the end of the sixteenth century,' Raoul said as he led her and Marie-Louise to a table on the pavement outside a small cafe. 'It was Britain which established the Bordeaux wine trade, and even today you will generally find some members of the British wine fraternity having lunch with their French counterparts, in any restaurant you care to visit.'

Between being greeted by various passers-by,Raoul explained some of the arrangements he had to make for the grape harvest, and the number of grape pickers required.

'A hundred and fifty people?' Olivia looked at him amazed. 'Where on earth do they all come from?'

'Many come from the local villages, of course. Their families have worked in our vineyards for hundreds of years. But we do employ a considerable amount of casual labour, students and such, which is how Bridget came to meet Henri.'

'You—you don't really dislike her, do you?' Olivia queried, anxious about her cousin's future life on the estate.

'*Au contraire!* She seems to have made a man of Henri, which can only be a good thing, and if my aunt wishes to behave like a spring chicken, well,' he laughed, 'she is at least enjoying herself, *non*?'

'I'm so glad!' Olivia smiled at him in relief. 'I was just a little worried, I mean—well, it could have been awkward for Bridget and Henri living so close, and. . . .'

'Do not worry, my dear Olivia, there will be no problem. In truth, I find your cousin very amusing, but do not, I pray, ever tell her so! I suspect that she would far prefer to think that "old smoothy-chops, the Vicomte" should disapprove of her!'

Olivia tried to keep her face straight as Raoul accurately mimicked Bridget's casual, slangy tone of voice, but as she caught his wide grin, she dissolved into gales of helpless laughter.

'That is better. You should laugh more, my dear Olivia. Now—you must try one of these cakes, before my darling daughter eats them all. *Non chérie*, no more!' he said, turning to Marie-Louise, who had more cream on her face than in her mouth. 'You will grow too fat to fit into your bridesmaid's dress, and that would never do!'

'I can't understand how everyone can be so relaxed about a wedding which is taking place next week?' Olivia looked at him enquiringly. 'Surely there must be hundreds of things to arrange, but no one seems to be doing anything!'

'Well, *ma petite*, I must tell you that my sister Hélène, while extremely tiresome and always moaning, so much so that one would think she couldn't organise a tea party for only two people, is in fact extremely competent when she wants to be. Incidentally, the way she had been imposing on you is quite disgraceful, and I have told her so. I earnestly suggest that you do not put up with any more of her nonsense,' he told her sternly. 'However, the invitations have been sent out, the food has been ordered from a firm of caterers, and all is well under control It will, after all, be a fairly quiet wedding, you understand.'

'I'm pleased to hear about the caterers,' she grinned. 'I had visions of sweating down in that kitchen for days on end!'

'I am truly sorry that you have been forced to such a menial occupation, my dear Olivia,' he said taking her hand firmly in his and raising it to his lips.

Olivia blushed fiercely at the warm, caressing tone in his voice, snatching back her hand as soon as he released it. 'There's no need to worry, I'm—er—thinking of giving up interior design and taking up catering. I reckon if I can manage that stove, I can cook anything, anywhere!' She tried to force her nervously trembling lips into a smile, but the intense, questioning look in his eyes was making her heart pound loudly, and she glanced down quickly at her plate, her fingers tightly clenched together in her lap.

'I have finished, *papa*,' Marie-Lousie announced as she drained her glass of lemonade.

'I should think you have!' Raoul laughed. 'Come, it is time we went home, yes?'

They drove back to the château in a quiet, companionable silence. Crossing over the bridge, she heard Raoul mutter an oath under his breath as he drove swiftly past two cars parked in the courtyard and swung into a space behind the garage, next to the back door. Sternly ordering Olivia to stay where she was, he took Marie-Louise into the house.

Mystified, Olivia sat in the car as instructed, amazed as Raoul ran back down the steps, jumped into his seat and swiftly drove back the way they had come.

'What—what's going on?' she asked as they sped back over the bridge and through the large open gates. 'It looked as if you had visitors.'

'I have decided that we are going out to lunch,' he drawled blandly.

'But—but I can't possibly. . . .'

'Yes, you can. Tante, Bridget and Hélène are quite capable of serving their own food, you know.'

'But—for heaven's sake! There's a perfectly good meal just waiting to be eaten back there. What's got into you?'

Raoul shrugged. 'I might say that I am tired of your cooking, and wish for something different to eat, hmm?'

'You could, but just try it and you'll get a black eye!' Olivia fumed. 'Who in the hell do you think you are, to turn your nose up at my salmon trout in aspic, I'd like to know?'

Raoul threw back his head and roared with

laughter. '*Ma petite!* You seem to have become obsessed by food! And there is no need for you to sound so much like an outraged virgin!'

'How in the hell would I know what an—an outraged virgin sounds like? That's something you must hear very often, I shouldn't wonder!' she snapped angrily as Raoul brought the Range Rover to a halt outside a restaurant.

'*Mais enfin!* For heaven's sake, Olivia!' Raoul grated angrily, swiftly releasing their seat belts before his hard hands gripped her arms, jerking her towards him. For several moments he just held her there, imprisoned against him, and when she began to struggle, he firmly covered her mouth with his own.

His lips bruised hers, but as she tried to protest, her parted lips only succeeded in making his kiss even more intimate. A gradual, softening weakness invaded her body to take the place of aggression, as she found herself helplessly surrendering to his domination.

'*Alors—ma belle?*' Raoul murmured, raising his dark head and gazing down into her glazed eyes. 'I do not intend to have any more arguments from you, you understand? We are going to have lunch here, and we will have peace and quiet, hmm? Yes or no?' he demanded as she tried to gather her scattered wits. 'I can repeat the treatment if you wish?' he laughed softly. 'Indeed, it would give me much pleasure to do so!'

'No! I mean, yes, I w-won't. . . .' Olivia stuttered quickly as he prepared to gather her once more into his arms.

'What a pity!' Raoul laughed as he let her go. 'You may not believe me,' he added, coming around to open her door, 'but I can assure you that you will be far more comfortable in this restaurant, than in your kitchen, my dear cook!'

His warm smile robbed his last words of any sting, and as the delicious meal progressed, Olivia found to her great surprise that she was beginning to feel relaxed and at ease with her ex-fiancé. It was in great measure due to Raoul, she acknowledged. He was clearly determined to be friendly, and she found herself responding to his warm charm as he related humorous stories of the things that could—and often did—go wrong during the grape harvest.

'Will you at last agree that it was a good idea to have a break from your labours at the château?' he asked with a smile as they sat sipping their coffee at the end of the meal.

'Yes, I suppose I must!' she grinned. 'It was just the thought of Tante and Bridget making a mess of all the food. Goodness knows how the meal. . . .'

'*Je m'en fiche!* I don't give a damn about the food, Olivia!' Raoul retorted with suppressed savagery, Olivia's eyes widening in surprised alarm at his abrupt change of tone. 'You are not a fool—you know very well that I wished to be alone with you. We have much to talk about, you and I. *Enfin. . .?*'

'Oh Raoul, there's no—no point in talking about the past. . . .' Olivia couldn't say any more for a moment, a hard lump of unhappiness seeming to fill her throat. 'I—I'd like to go back to the château, please,' she muttered at last, refusing to meet the hard glint in his steely blue eyes.

Raoul snorted with exasperation. 'Go and sit in the car while I settle our bill,' he directed as she flinched at his cold, icy voice, so sharply at variance with their pleasant conversation of the past two hours.

The short journey back was conducted in silence. As they drove into the courtyard, Olivia noticed that the two cars were still parked by the front door.

'*Bon Dieu!*' Raoul swore briefly under his breath as he turned to face her. 'I realise that I should have told you before now, but I thought there was no need—no need to explain. . . .'

'Raoul, *chéri!*' They looked up to see Tante Amalie waving gaily from the open front door. '*Oh hell!*' Raoul ground out as he opened his door.

'Such a lovely surprise!' Tante beckoned behind her. 'Just look who's come to see us!'

Walking slowly into the château behind Raoul, it took Olivia some moments for her eyes to adjust to the light in the hall after the bright sunshine outside.

'Come along girls, here he is at last! Where on earth have you been, you naughty boy,' Tante scolded Raoul playfully. 'Here is lovely Chantal and dear Lucille, who are both just dying to see you!'

Standing alone in the shadows by the door, Olivia felt her legs nearly give way from shock as she saw the French girl she hadn't set eyes on for five years. *Lucille!* What on earth was she doing here? Olivia's mind whirled as Raoul coolly greeted the two women, one tall and dark, the other a pretty, young girl with blonde hair.

'And where is dear Olivia?' Tante asked. 'Ah, there you are. Come and meet dear Madame Lucille Millot and Mademoiselle Chantal Brincourt. This is Miss Harding who has been *such* a Godsend to us all.'

Olivia stared at Lucille, whose face was clearly reflecting the shock in her own. Trying to sketch a smile as the blonde girl gave her a nod, Olivia walked slowly forward.

'Dear Olivia,' Tante prattled on, oblivious to the emotional currents eddying about the hall. 'These poor girls were so sorry not to see Raoul for luncheon, so I've asked them to come again tomorrow—when we can *all* enjoy their company. I have also telephoned lots of friends to come and have drinks first; won't it be fun!'

It sounded very much as if Tante had been at the cocktail shaker again, both before *and* after lunch, Olivia found herself thinking. Her mind seemed, in some quite extraordinary way, to be continuing to function calmly and dispassionately despite the tense, dire situation in which she found herself.

'I must say that we thoroughly enjoyed the absolutely delicious lunch you left for us,' Tante continued blithely. 'The salmon was *formidable*, and as for that wonderful pudding—*fantastique*! All those lovely different fruits set in a creamy rum custard. Lucille was particularly impressed, weren't you dear?' She smiled up at the tall, dark woman who was staring at Olivia, white-faced with shock. 'Lucille wanted to know what it was called?'

'Did she?' Olivia never knew afterwards how she managed to walk so calmly past the knot of people in the hall, turning to face them as she prepared to mount the stairs to her room. Her lips twisted into a bitter smile, her eyes locking together with those of Raoul who was staring so intently at her from across the hall. 'Well, Madame Millot may be interested to know that it is a recipe I found in an old Spanish cookery book, some years ago. Not inappropriately— as I am sure Monsieur le Vicomte will agree—it is called: "Cold Love"!'

CHAPTER SEVEN

OLIVIA was still sitting hunched miserably on a window-seat, her brain numb from the shock of seeing Lucille again, as she stared blindly down at the lake, when Bridget bounced into her sitting room an hour later.

'Well, you really did it, kid! Talk about a grand exit—*wow!* I hope you realise that you left everyone absolutely pole-axed in the hall after you'd gone, and it's taken Tante and me all this time to calm down Raoul's two girlfriends, before sending them merrily on their way. What on earth was it all about?'

Olivia shrugged helplessly, her large green eyes filling with tears as she turned back to gaze sightlessly out at the distant vista of parkland and fields of terraced vines.

'Oh, come on, Livy! It doesn't take the mind of a genius to see that something's up, and all due, apparently, to the fact that both you and Raoul were conspicuous by your absence at lunch. My God, what a terrible meal that was! Not the food, of course, that was as delicious as ever; but the atmosphere was so thick you could have cut it with a knife!' Bridget gave her cousin a wry grin.

'First of all, those two women arrived at practically the same time, and if looks could kill, they'd both be lying dead in the *salon*! Tante and I kept putting off lunch in the hope that either you or Raoul would turn up—preferably Raoul as far as *les girls* were concerned, of course. Then, when it was quite clear that neither of you were going to put in an appearance, we staggered into the dining room. "Staggered", by the way, is the correct word for poor Tante, who had hit the bottle by then—and I for one don't blame her! Honestly, it was just like sitting at a tennis match—or maybe a fight between two alley cats would be a more accurate description! Anyway, my head became dizzy from jerking back and forth as Chantal and Madame Millot tried to score vicious points off one another. Believe me, they *really* don't like each other! The whole meal was absolutely horrendous—and where, may I ask, were you and Raoul?'

'We—er—he took me out to lunch. . . .' Olivia muttered listlessly.

'Lucky old you!' Bridget's voice dripped with sarcasm. 'Well, let me tell you that while you may have been enjoying yourselves, in the meantime, back here at the dear old château, things were beginning to get really nasty. When Chantal passed Madame Millot the salad bowl, murmuring the French equivalent of "age before beauty", even I could see the storm-cones being hoisted. True enough, when the merry divorcee, despite being puce in the face, managed a sickly smile as she asked Chantal how many more years she had at school—battle was fairly joined. All I can say is that I fervently hope I *never* have to sit through a meal like that again!'

'I'm sorry . . . I meant to be there. I. . . .'

'What do you mean you *meant* to be there?' Bridget demanded. 'What kept you from joining the happy family lunch?'

'I—I honestly don't know.' Olivia ran a distracted hand through the heavy weight of her chestnut hair. 'Raoul drove Marie-Louise and me to Bordeaux, just for a break, and when we got back at lunchtime, he took her into the house and immediately returned to drive off again. I did ask him why, but he—he didn't explain. . . .' Her voice trailed away as she went over the scene again in her mind. 'The cars!' she suddenly exclaimed.

'The what?' Bridget looked at her in puzzlement.

'It must have been their cars, which were outside in the courtyard. Raoul obviously knew all the time that Lucille and that girl—er—Chantal were here. . . .'

'And even the dear Vicomte figured he couldn't cope with three women at once—and so he scarpered!' Bridget threw back her head and roared with laughter. 'He may be a rat, but you've got to admit he's quick on his feet. Poor old Raoul must have hoped that they would have disappeared by the time he and you came back from your little lunch party, but he obviously didn't reckon on his girlfriends' staying power. Believe me, there was no way Madame Millot was going to leave before Chantal, or vice versa. They just sat and glowered at each other until you and Raoul turned up.'

Olivia shrugged unhappily. 'Anyway, all this has nothing to do with me. . . .'

'Hang on a moment!' Bridget interjected sharply. 'What do you mean it's got nothing to do with you? After your dramatic departure from the hall, you could have heard a pin drop. Chantal eventually tried to say something to Raoul, and practically got her head bitten off for her pains, while Madame Millot just stood trembling like a victim of shell-shock! God knows, I can't stand the woman, but even I felt sorry for her, she looked as if she was going to have a heart attack at any minute. Not to mention poor old Tante, who was busy trying to pour conversational oil on what even she could see were troubled waters.

Although she soon found herself out of her depth—we all were, for heaven's sakes!'

'I simply don't know what you're talking about. I don't see why . . .'

'. . . because Raoul was in a towering rage—that's why! I've never seen anything like it. He cursed us all, up hill and down dale, before stamping off to barricade himself in his study; and we know he's there because we could follow his progress through the château by the sound of the doors being violently slammed in his wake!' Bridget laughed harshly as she paused to light a cigarette.

'Like I said,' she continued in the face of Olivia's silence, 'Tante and I have been soothing down ruffled feathers for the last hour. It was only by lying through our teeth, and saying that Raoul had bad problems with his vines, that we managed to pacify his two girlfriends. Tante has now retired to her bedroom with a large bottle of brandy clutched firmly to her bosom, and I'm up here to find out the score. It's as clear as daylight that you and Raoul have got a "thing" going between you—and OK, that's your business. But it is also obvious that you and Madame Millot have met before; and so I want to know what's going on?'

Olivia shook her head distractedly. 'It's—it's a long, boring story and it all happened ages ago. I—I honestly don't want to go into it all—there's no point.'

'You may not want to, Livy,' Bridget spoke firmly. 'But I think you've got to. I honestly don't want to pry, but Tante has been mad enough to ask those two women back to lunch tomorrow—plus half the neighbourhood. You really can't expect Tante and me to go through another ghastly episode like today—not without knowing why. Do be reasonable!'

With a deep sigh, Olivia realised that Bridget was right, and that she couldn't evade the issue any longer. She rose from the window-seat and went over to sit down on a chair by her cousin. Haltingly at first, she began to relate the bare facts of her broken engagement and the subsequent shock of Raoul's reappearance in her life. 'So you see,' she concluded, 'I'm only staying on here because of your wedding. I'd—well, I'd have left days ago if it hadn't been for that. But I never guessed that Madame Millot was Lucille! I hadn't the faintest suspicion that she was still around—not once I discovered she didn't marry Raoul after all.'

'Wow! Gosh, Livy, I'm really sorry to have been the cause of all this trauma.' Bridget paused, and looked at her cousin with a frown. 'I can see that Madame Millot—Lucille—was pure poison from the word go, but why didn't she and Raoul get married after he chucked you? She's obviously mad keen to nail him down now.'

'I've absolutely no idea,' Olivia shrugged helplessly. 'Anyway, he married his late wife very soon afterwards. That's all I know.'

'Raoul's turned out to be a really first-class rat, hasn't he?' Bridget got to her feet and walked over to the door. 'You know, it's odd,' she added slowly, turning to face the other girl. 'But my chief feeling about his behaviour towards you, is one of total surprise. So, OK, I know I tease Raoul a lot, and I've even called him "the randy Vicomte", but that was honestly only meant as a joke. I never thought he was really that sort of a man. It's not that I don't believe what you say,' she assured Olivia. 'But well, it just seems so unlike him, somehow. . . .'

'*Quelle surprise!*' Olivia muttered grimly.

'Well, I must admit I was surprised to find you so keen on the guy, but I never realised that you were in love with him.'

'I'm not!' Olivia protested angrily.

Bridget lifted a quizzical eyebrow as she opened the door. 'Oh yeah? Who are you trying to fool, Olivia—yourself, or Raoul?'

The dew was still sparkling on the grass of the wide green lawn as Olivia walked slowly down to the edge of the lake, shivering slightly in the fresh morning air, despite the warming rays of the sun which glinted off the still water.

Sinking down on to a small wooden bench, she absorbed the magnificent view laid out before her. It was good to be out of the château and all the drama of yesterday's events. Deaf to the pleas of both Tante and Bridget, she had resolutely refused to leave her room, mostly, she acknowledged, for fear of running into Raoul. Telling Bridget that it was Hélène's turn to cook dinner, and that Raoul's sister could burn the veal escalopes for all she cared, Olivia had nevertheless promised that she would cook lunch for the party today. Really, she hadn't behaved at all well, she mused unhappily, remembering how she had grumbled at having to write out a menu and give her cousin a shopping list of all the things she was going to need.

Which was why she was out here in the garden, Olivia grimly reminded herself. A considerable amount of work lay in front of her, and she was supposed to be picking herbs in the walled kitchen garden, not mooning down here by the lake. But the beauty of the still scene held her in its thral as Bridget's words beat a continuous rhythm through her tired brain—as they had all the previous evening and night.

Who was she trying to fool? During the time she had remained locked in her room yesterday, she had been forced to acknowledge that as far as she was concerned, her feelings for Raoul were the same as they had always been. Despite his behaviour towards her in the past, and the intervening years during which she had thought she had recovered, nothing it seemed could alter the love she still had for the man who had betrayed her. How could she be so stupid as to be still in love with someone who behaved so badly? A question she asked herself incredulously, for what seemed the hundredth time, and to which she could find no solution.

With a deep, unhappy sigh she leaned back on the bench, shutting her eyes against the early morning sun. What a can of worms this trip to Bridget's wedding was turning out to be! Here she was, aching and trembling for someone who didn't give a snap of his fingers for her. Kissing her in the river, after their picnic, had meant less than nothing to him—he was just keeping himself in practice, she thought bitterly. It was obvious, now she thought about it, that his anger with himself that day was due to the fact that he'd suddenly remembered one of his other girlfriends, like Lucille, or Chantal or . . . whoever. I bet he's got women around here just standing in line for him—the swine!

Come on—this really won't do! she told herself roughly. Sitting here and moaning about Raoul wasn't going to achieve anything, was it? It was a waste of time torturing herself about Raoul when she still had to pick those damn herbs, and get on with the preparations for Tante's lunch party.

Trailing slowly back into the château, her mind was still so much on her unsolvable problems that she forgot to switch on the light as she descended the curving stone steps down to the kitchen. The smooth leather soles of her sandals slipped on the hard stone, and with a strangled yell she threw out her arms to try and save herself; the bunches of rosemary, tarragon and parsley flying through the air as she tumbled forward onto the hard flagstones of the dark corridor.

Olivia knelt, winded for a moment, before she felt strong hands about her waist, and Raoul's voice asking if she was all right as he helped her to rise.

'Yes—I—ouch!' she gasped as she stood upright. 'I—I think I've grazed my knee.'

'Come into the kitchen and we will be able to see the damage,' he said, putting a firm arm about her waist and holding her body close to his tall figure.

She looked wildly about the dark passage. 'I—I've dropped the herbs! I must get them . . .'

'For God's sake, Olivia! Must you always be so preoccupied by what is totally irrelevant? First it was cooking and now, it seems, it is herbs—*bon Dieu!*'

'You'd be the first to complain if you didn't get fed properly,' she retorted nervously as with his support she hobbled into the kitchen. 'I can't see you putting up with Bridget's cooking!'

'Very true,' he agreed dryly, swiftly lifting her up to sit on the kitchen table. 'Now, let me see your leg.'

'I'm—I'm sure it's nothing,' she protested breathlessly, disturbed as always by his close proximity.

Ignoring her words, Raoul pushed up the full skirt of her cotton dress. 'While I agree that you are not likely to lose your leg, you have a bad graze on your knee,' he told her. 'So be a good girl and sit quietly while I get a cloth and a bowl of water, hmm?'

Watching silently as he bathed her cut knee, Olivia gritted her teeth against the stinging pain and concentrated on trying to ignore the soft warmth of his hands on her bare leg.

'There,' he said, putting down the wet cloth. 'The scratches are now quite clean and I do not think you will need a bandage. Moreover, I must congratulate you on not having mentioned cooking—or herbs!—for the last ten minutes,' he added, staring down at her with eyes that gleamed with unconcealed mockery.

'Very funny!' she snapped, nervously pushing down the skirt of her dress. 'Those stairs are a death-trap you know? It's not the first time that I've slipped, although I haven't hurt myself like this before. And—and while I'm on the subject,' she demanded breathlessly, 'what are you doing down here at this time of the morning, anyway?'

'It may well seem odd to you, Olivia,' he drawled sardonically. 'But I do actually happen to own this château! And if I wish to make myself a cup of coffee, I really don't think that I should have to ask your permission. Or do you feel that I should, hmm?' he queried softly, his voice heavy with silky menace.

'No—no, of course, I. . . .' She hung her head, aware that her cheeks were flaming with embarrassment as his words struck home.

'My family and I are, of course, very grateful to you for all you have done during this trying time,' he said smoothly, putting a hand beneath her chin and tilting her blushing face up towards him. 'However, I do ask myself why, considering the past—er—circumstances, you are so very anxious to avoid my company? Can it be that you feel some guilt at last, hmm?'

'Guilt!' Her green eyes flashed with anger. 'You've got a nerve! Why in the hell should I feel guilty about you—you of all people? You're the one who should be ashamed of himself; but not you—oh no!' She gave a shrill laugh as she tried to jerk her chin away from his hand. '*You rat!* I can see that you're not known as the "randy Vicomte" for nothing. . .!'

'*Quelle insolence!* How dare you say such things!' he snarled, his face darkening with sudden fury as he pulled her roughly off the table.

'I can say what I damn well like, and—and anyway, your past record speaks for itself!' she lashed back, trying in vain to squirm out from beneath his firm grip.

'*Ah non, ma belle!*' he whispered savagely, his arms tightening like bands of steel about her struggling figure. 'You do not escape me so easily. We have much to talk over, you and I!'

'I've got nothing—nothing to say to you,' she panted. 'I—I hate you—and despise you, I. . . . No, no . . .!' she gasped, her vision filled by the dark head descending inexorably towards her.

Holding her head still beneath him, and ignoring the wildly gesticulating protest of her hands, he covered her lips with his in a firm, determined kiss that demanded a response. The burning heat of his mouth possessed hers with a masterly, knowing expertise that weakened her resistance. There was an urgency and a hunger in his kiss, and an overwhelming, deepening passion that tormented her senses and set the blood surging wildly through her veins. No one but Raoul had ever kissed her like this, so sensually and erotically, demanding that she acknowledge her awareness of her body's needs, and of his. As his kiss deepened, his lips becoming even more demanding and possessive, she moaned softly, knowing a wanton desire to surrender completely. . . .

Slowly and reluctantly, Raoul raised his dark head. 'Is that how you hate and despise me, Olivia?' he taunted softly, his breathing as rough and ragged as her own.

She could feel a tide of deep crimson cover her face. Twisting free of his embrace, she stumbled over to lean against the wide porcelain sink as she endeavoured to collect her shattered senses.

'Well? Can you deny your response to me?' he demanded, his voice sounding oddly thick and husky as it echoed around the large room.

'You—you seem to think that you've only got to put your arms around me, for that to somehow solve everything. Well, it doesn't!' she retorted bleakly, trying to control the weak trembling in her legs. 'Yes, I'll admit that you can get me to respond to you, even after all this time, but I'll—I'll never forget what you did to me—*never!*'

'I? What I did to you . . .? *Toi—toi que j'ai tant aimée? C'est une blague!*'

'It's no good sprouting all that French rubbish at me—I don't understand a word you're saying!' she ground out angrily. 'Why don't you just get the hell out of here, and leave me alone!'

'I said you were talking nonsense—and do not tell me of hell! You made very sure that I should be well acquainted with it, *espèce de sorcière*—you hell-cat! About hell—that to my cost, I know!' Raoul shouted angrily, his command of English breaking down as his tall, dark figure shook with fury.

'Call me a hell-cat, would you?' Olivia couldn't remember when she'd been so angry as she was at this minute. 'Get out!' she hissed through clenched teeth. 'Go away and play games with your beloved Lucille— or Chantal or whoever else you fancy at the moment, but leave me alone!' When he just stood staring blindly at her, her tortured feelings finally boiled over.

Almost without realising what she was doing, she put out a hand towards a bowl, seized a lemon and threw it at him with all her strength. 'I told you to get out!' she panted, as another lemon followed the first, missing his tall, angry figure and sailing on across the room towards the door.

'*Mademoiselle* . . .!' The warning cry from Henri, ducking his head to avoid the lemon, stayed her hand as she was about to throw a third. Olivia's eyes widened in horror as she saw that Bridget's fiancé was carrying Nicole's thin figure in his arms, as he stood looking bewildered in the kitchen doorway.

'I thought that I would come down and give you a hand with the food, Olivia,' Nicole smiled, her grey eyes gleaming with amusement as she took in the scene before her. 'Yes, just put me down in that chair,' she told Henri, who stepped forward gingerly as if he feared another bombardment from Olivia.

'I hope that I—er—haven't come at an awkward time?' Nicole murmured, her mouth twitching as she viewed the two rigid figures determinedly not looking at each other.

'Not at all, my dear sister. Your arrival was most opportune!' Raoul grated angrily before he spun on his heel and strode out of the room, slamming the door loudly behind him.

'I—er—I. . . .' Olivia shook her head in confusion, miserably aware of the deep blush which was reddening her cheeks. What on earth could she possibly say?

While she was still standing irresolutely by the sink, Nicole waved Henri away with a friendly dismissal, before turning her attention to Olivia. 'I can't, of course, do very much, but maybe you have some vegetables that need chopping? What are you planning for today's lunch?'

'Oh, my God!' Olivia's face blanched. 'The ducks! I'd completely forgotten. . . .' She hurried quickly over to the large gas stove and threw open the oven door. Moments later she sagged with relief as she saw that they had been well protected by their foil covering.

'Cold duck will be delicious,' Nicole said approvingly, her nose wrinkling as she savoured the aroma coming from the pan.

'Bridget could only get three, so it's a case of FHB, I'm afraid.'

'*Comment?* What is this FHB?' Nicole looked at her in confusion.

'Sorry! It's a shortened form of Family Hold Back; much used in England when there might not be enough food to feed all the guests.'

'Ah yes, we have something similar here in France,' Nicole laughed. 'So, now what can I do?' she added.

'Well . . .' Olivia paused. 'I'm going to serve cold leek soup—Crème Vichyssoise, first of all, and with the duck I thought I'd offer a lemon compote to offset the fatty taste. Maybe you could chop up the leeks for me, and pare the rinds off the lemons . . .' her voice trailed away as the scene with Raoul sprang back vividly into her mind.

'Ah, the lemons! All is now clear. My brother would not help you with the cooking, and what else could a woman of spirit do, but throw fruit at him? It is very understandable!'

'No, it wasn't like that. . . .' Olivia protested, before she caught Nicole's wide grin and realised the French girl was only teasing her.

'Oh—my brother's face!' Nicole's thin body shook with laughter. 'I do not think he has ever had lemons thrown at him before—*mon Dieu!*' She pulled out a handkerchief to wipe away her tears of mirth.

'Yes, well. . . .' Olivia was unable to prevent herself from grinning in response to the other girl's laughter. 'I shouldn't have lost my temper, but we were both very angry with each other, I'm afraid.'

'Do not apologise, my dear Olivia. For far too long Raoul has been so apathetic, that I have been worried. Always polite, of course, but only half alive, you understand? Now, suddenly, we have storms and rages from him—it is better, I think.'

'Well, it was only natural for him to be depressed after his wife's death,' Olivia muttered, gathering up the lemons from where they had rolled over the floor.

'Yes, of course that was very sad, very tragic,' Nicole agreed as she began to chop the leeks. 'Poor Estelle, Raoul should never have married her, of course. It was a great mistake.'

'Raoul's marriage was a mistake?' Olivia looked at her in astonishment, before hurriedly turning away to prepare the sugar syrup for the lemons. 'I—I thought he had been very happy. He certainly seemed most upset when he told me that his wife had died.'

Nicole looked thoughtfully at the back of the tall English girl who was distractedly spooning sugar into a kettle. 'Do you not use a saucepan?' she queried in a neutral voice.

'What? Oh my God—I must be going to pieces!' Olivia laughed ruefully as she washed out the kettle and measured the correct amount of sugar into a saucepan.

Nicole hid a smile as she bent forward to concentrate on her chopping. 'Raoul was not well when he returned to live in France, and he met and married Estelle, all in one month. I do not believe that to be a good foundation for a marriage.'

'Well, maybe he was very much in love?' Olivia

muttered, briskly stirring the syrup. 'Often such marriages work very well.'

'Alas, Raoul's did not. Estelle was Tante's choice of bride, and although she was very suitable and obviously adored my brother, he for his part was remarkably unenthusiastic.' Nicole sighed as she remembered the events of so many years ago. 'But, well, they got married and so that was that. But Estelle was never well during her pregnancy, and when Marie-Louise was born, Raoul asked me to come here and live with them. I have looked after the little girl ever since.'

'Didn't you want a life of your own?' queried Olivia, remembering Bridget's remarks about Nicole and the local doctor.

'Yes, sometimes, of course I wish that my life had been different.' Nicole pushed away the cut up leeks and began to attack the lemons. 'Ah well, what cannot be. . . .'

'But, why couldn't Raoul's wife look after her own baby?' Olivia came over to sit down and assist Nicole to cut the lemon rind into small slivers.

'We only learnt, when it was far too late, that Estelle had a past history of depressive illness. After the baby was born, she fell into a deep post-natal depression from which, it seemed, nothing could rouse her, and she killed herself here in the chateau only two months later.'

'*Oh no!*' Olivia gasped. 'No wonder Raoul was so desperately unhappy. . . .'

'Yes, it was truly awful. We had all gone out for the day to lunch with friends. Estelle wouldn't come, and when we returned, we found that she had taken an overdose of pills.' Nicole sighed heavily. 'It is a long time ago now, of course, but what a terrible tragedy, such a waste of a pretty girl.'

'Poor Raoul. I—I had no idea. . . .' Olivia looked down quickly as her eyes filled with tears.

'Yes, it was very bad for him, and made far worse by the fact that he blamed himself for her depression. He told me that he should never have married someone he did not love. The doctor explained that it was not his fault that Estelle had taken her own life, but he has felt guilty for such a long time. You can understand, therefore, why Tante and I are anxious that he should be happily married at last, and also provide a loving mother for his child.'

'Tante has made her views on that subject quite clear!' Olivia was stung by her tortured feelings into retorting more sharply than she intended.

'My dear girl,' Nicole put a gentle hand on Olivia's arm. 'My aunt is getting old, and maybe she sees only what she wants to see, hmm? She has told me that it was you whom Raoul wished to marry, when he was living in London. And it is very clear, certainly to my eyes,' Nicole smiled gently, 'that you both still have much love for each other. You see, I know my brother very well indeed, and I am aware of what he feels in his heart.'

'You must be the only one who is!' Olivia muttered grimly, and then immediately felt ashamed. Nicole was only trying to be kind, after all. She couldn't possibly have any idea of Raoul's real character. 'I'm sorry,' she gave the French girl a brief, apologetic smile. 'But, well, it's a long, complicated story, and. . . .'

'*Ah non*, Olivia,' Nicole interjected. 'Believe me, I have no wish to pry into your business, but I felt it was important that you knew of the background to all that has happened in the last five years. I am sure you had a good reason for breaking off your engagement, but I love my brother and wish him to be happy. He has had to bear so much misery in his life. I think you care about that, yes?' she added softly.

'Yes, of course I'm very sorry to hear about Raoul's problems in the past, very sorry indeed,' Olivia assured her. 'And—and I mean it when I say that I hope he will find true happiness in the future—but honestly, Nicole, it won't be with me!'

'Ah, surely you could. . . .'

'For heaven's sake!' Olivia protested, shaking her head in exasperation. 'I can't think why you and Tante seem to be so convinced that it was I who broke off the engagement. I can promise you, I didn't! It was Raoul—and Lucille—who did that. If you really want to know the truth, why don't you ask them? I'm sure *dear* Madame Millot will be more than happy to give you chapter and verse on the whole sordid episode!' she ground out bitterly as she rose, going over to check the progress of the soup on the stove, and striving to calm down her agitated emotions.

'I am very sorry, I had no wish to upset you, Olivia,' Nicole murmured, looking at the English girl with a puzzled frown. 'But my brother said . . . I always understood that. . . .'

'Yes, well, as Raoul pointed out when he picked me up in London a few days ago, it was just a small romance—a youthful indiscretion that happened a long time ago,' Olivia muttered, blowing her nose firmly before turning to give Nicole a shaky smile. 'The plain fact is that five years ago Raoul obviously decided that he didn't want to marry me, and I haven't seen or heard anything of him from that day until he walked into my shop to bring me here to France for Bridget's wedding. So, you see, it's just a very boring, silly little story—something that must

have happened to lots of other girls.' She glanced
down at her watch.

'Goodness me! Look at the time, I—I mustn't forget
to put out the cocktail canapés upstairs before the
guests arrive. I'll be back in a minute,' she assured
Nicole, as she hurried towards the larder to collect the
small savouries she had made earlier in the morning.

Olivia was placing the dishes strategically out in the
salon, when her ears were assailed by what seemed to
be a furious row in an adjacent room, between Raoul
and Tante Amalie. Not being able to understand a
word of the rapid French, Olivia merely shrugged and
got on with her job, before standing in the doorway to
check that all was in order.

'It looks great, kid!' a voice whispered from behind
her shoulder, causing her to jump in surprise.

'Bridget! For heaven's sake—don't ever give me a
fright like that again! What are you doing here
anyway? Shouldn't you be changing for the party?' she
added looking at her cousin's jeans.

'Oh, there's lots of time,' Bridget replied airily. 'I
was just eavesdropping on the row in there. Raoul's
going full blast, isn't he?' she grinned.

Olivia shrugged. 'They might be talking double-
dutch for all I know—or care.'

'Raoul's giving Tante hell for organising this drinks
and lunch party. He said she had no right to treat you
like a convenient servant, and he definitely doesn't
want her to keep on shoving Lucille and Chantal down
his throat—thank you very much!' Bridget laughed.
'It's a real humdinger—poor old Tante doesn't know
whether she's standing on her head or her heels!'

'Eavesdroppers never hear any good about themselves,' Olivia snapped as she turned to go back to the
kitchen. 'So just watch out! I expect he'll start

telling his aunt what an appalling girl you are, any minute!'

'What's got into you?' Bridget called indignantly after her cousin's swiftly disappearing figure. 'For heaven's sake! I thought you'd be pleased to know that Raoul's giving Lucille and Chantal the thumbs down?'

'I'm sorry to have deserted you,' Olivia smiled briefly at Nicole as she came back into the kitchen. 'Do you want me to arrange for someone to take you upstairs? I think the guests will be arriving very soon.'

'No, I am quite content to stay here for a bit,' Nicole answered. 'Henri has just looked in and will return later. In the meantime, I had him fetch a bottle of wine from the cellars for us. I see no reason why the poor cook shouldn't put her feet up for a moment!'

'That's a great idea,' Olivia agreed wearily, going over to the dresser and coming back with two glasses. 'By the way, I hope this isn't Raoul's best wine. I don't suppose he'd be pleased for those "below stairs" to be swilling the good claret!'

'Wine is to be drunk,' Nicole announced firmly, raising a glass. '*A votre santé!* Here's to the lunch, which I am sure will be delicious.'

Determined to keep off the dangerous subject of herself and Raoul, Olivia asked Nicole to tell her about the chequered history of the château, from its origins as a fortified castle through to the present day. They had been chatting for some time, before she heard a knock on the kitchen door, and a handsome blond stranger entered the room.

'*Bonjour,* Nicole,' he said, coming over to give her a kiss on the cheek.

'Ah, Alain. *Permettez-moi de vous présenter,* Mademoiselle Harding. Olivia, I don't think you have met Chantal's brother, Alain. . . .' Nicole said, smiling up at the tall, broad-shouldered man.

'Ah, *enchanté*, Mademoiselle,' he replied, bending down to raise Olivia's hand to his lips. 'You have rescued the family from famine, I hear,' he laughed.

'What are you doing down here, Alain?' Nicole demanded. 'As Olivia has so rightly told me, this is the servant's domain!'

Alain laughed. 'The servant's seem to be doing very well, especially if they are drinking Château Cheval Noir 1961! If you are prepared to offer me a glass I don't mind slumming for a while!'

'Oh lord!' Olivia looked at Nicole with worried eyes. 'I knew that it must be some of Raoul's good wine, it's been slipping down my throat like silk.'

'Don't worry about Raoul!' Alain smiled as he returned with a glass. 'He's far too busy trying to keep Lucille and my sister apart—the silly girls are behaving like two dogs quarrelling over a bone! Now, if he was a sensible man, he would be down here with you two beautiful ladies.'

'I should watch out for Alain, if I were you,' Nicole mockingly warned Olivia. 'He is a practised flirt, and quite notorious in the neighbourhood!'

'How can you say such a thing?' Alain groaned dramatically. 'Come, Miss Harding, ignore Nicole, she is only jealous! Let me pour you some more of this really excellent wine.'

'Oh no, I must get on with preparing the lunch. I— I didn't know that the guests had arrived.' Olivia rose to her feet, realising as she clutched the back of her chair that she had eaten no breakfast, and that the two glasses of wine she had consumed on an empty stomach, were rapidly going to her head.

'Whoops!' Alain laughed, catching her swaying

figure in his arms. 'I can see that it was definitely worth coming downstairs to meet the cook!'

'Forgive me for interrupting this little *tête-à-tête*, but it is *my sister* who requires your assistance up the stairs, Alain!' Raoul's cold, hard sardonic voice cut into the friendly atmosphere in the kitchen. Olivia turned her startled eyes to see his tall figure standing rigid with anger in the doorway, his face a blank mask of haughty disdain.

'Don't be such a dog in the manger, Raoul!' Alain laughed, his arms remaining firmly about Olivia's trembling figure. 'If you keep such a beautiful girl hidden in the cellars, you must expect her to be rescued by a Prince Charming! That's me by the way!' he added, with a singular lack of modesty as he smiled down into Olivia's apprehensive green eyes. 'Never mind, *ma mignonne*, I will go, only to return and whisk you away from this evil magician. . . .'

'*Alain!*' Even from where she stood, Olivia was clearly able to see the flash of dark anger in Raoul's steely eyes.

'OK, OK,' Alain murmured placatingly, releasing Olivia and going over to lift Nicole from her chair as if she was as light as a feather. 'Come, Nicole, let us leave this disagreeable brother of yours.'

'Yes, let's,' she agreed, ignoring Raoul, and surprising Olivia by giving her a friendly wink as Alain carried her out of the room.

Olivia stared down at the table, the silence seeming to lengthen unbearably as she felt Raoul's hooded eyes boring into her nervous figure.

'Would I be expecting too much, if I asked you to keep your hands off Alain?' he enquired with hard, bitter irony. 'Can you not be content with having wrecked my life, without also adding his scalp to your collection?'

Olivia's head jerked up, her green eyes widening in shocked bewilderment. 'I—I wrecked your life?' she managed to gasp incredulously. 'Are you out of your mind? How dare you accuse me of—of such a thing!'

'What else would you call it? And here am I, poor fool that I am, still wanting you despite all that has happened. *Mon Dieu!* I am indeed an *imbécile*, as you say.'

Olivia caught her breath. 'Raoul. . . .'

'I know—I know! You hate and despise me, hmm?' he retorted savagely. 'But believe me, *ma belle*, not half as much as I hate and despise myself!'

CHAPTER EIGHT

'ALAIN . . .!'

The handsome Frenchman raised an arm, waving in reply to someone across the restaurant, before turning back to Olivia. 'Would you excuse me if I leave you for a moment to have a word with my friend, Louis? I tried to telephone him this morning about a business matter, but unfortunately he was not in his office.'

'Yes, of course.' Olivia gave Alain a tired smile as he rose and threaded his way across the room, past the other couples dining in the elegant Louis-Quinze surroundings of the Dubern Restaurant in Bordeaux.

With a deep sigh, she looked down at her plate. She should never have ordered the *entrecôte à la bordelaise*, which had been so warmly recommended by Alain. Her appetite had completely deserted her at lunch, and despite the length of time she had spent at the hospital waiting for news of Bridget, she still didn't feel able to face the thought of any food—however delicious—all these hours later.

As she had feared, the lunch party at the château had proved to be one of the most hideously tense and ghastly meals that she could ever remember. The traumatic events of the morning, culminating in Raoul's bitter parting words as he slammed the kitchen door behind him, had left her feeling so shaken that she was unable to move for some time. When, at last, she managed to force her trembling limbs to continue preparing the food for lunch, she felt so totally exhausted, that it was as if she had

146

been pulled several times through an old-fashioned mangle.

She honestly didn't know what had shaken her most—Raoul's quite amazing accusation that she had wrecked his life, or her own submissive, weak surrender when he had kissed her after her fall down the steps. And then there had been Nicole's story about Raoul's married life. It was desperately sad about his poor wife, of course. Olivia remembered one of her friends who periodically suffered from deep depressions, and she knew just how devastating they could be, not only for the person concerned, but also for all the family.

It seemed that Nicole had been prompted to talk about Estelle by a completely mistaken belief that it was Olivia who had jilted Raoul—a fallacy equally shared by Tante Amalie. They had both been so certain of their version of events, and from whom could they have heard the story, other than from Raoul? *The one person who knew the real truth!*

Olivia's head was aching by the time she went upstairs to lay the table for lunch, passing the bright chatter from the *salon* and the noise of more guests arriving in the hall, as she slipped into the dining room. If only she could have some peace and quiet to think matters out. A period of calm reflection in which to solve the puzzle as to why Raoul should be playing the part that was, in fact, her role—that of the discarded lover. She sighed with resignation as she realised that it was a question which at the moment her tired brain seemed completely unable to cope with.

'Pst!'

Bridget's head peered around the door. Olivia winced as Bridget entered the room and she was able to view the full glory of her cousin's appearance. 'What on earth do you think you're wearing?' she demanded.

'For heaven's sakes, Livy, don't be such an old prune!' Bridget looked down at her sleeveless cotton jumpsuit, printed in army camouflage colours of green, brown and black. A heavy gun belt, with what looked like real cartridges was slung around her slim hips, and besides several heavily studded bracelets, she was wearing a spiky choker around her neck that looked remarkably like a knuckleduster.

'Old prune? Thanks . . .!'

'Well, you're getting jolly stuffy in your old age—it must be Raoul's evil influence! That was just a joke, Livy,' she added hurriedly as her cousin's eyes flashed with anger. 'Anyway, I think that I'm looking absolutely "brill", and perfectly dressed for the occasion. I mean, even I can see that today's lunch is going to be every bit as awful as yesterday, so I decided that my urban guerrilla outfit would be perfect! Us Hardings must stick together, you know.'

'Idiot!' Olivia gave her a wry smile, inwardly touched by Bridget's sense of family loyalty, however misplaced it might be.

'I just thought I'd pop in and see if you needed any help, but it looks as if you've got it all under control. Hey! That's the Sèvres china given to one of Raoul's ancestors by Madame de Pompadour, isn't it?' Bridget exclaimed, going over to look down at the place settings on the large mahogany table. 'I adore that deep green colour; I think it's dead smart, the way it exactly matches the green silk on the walls of this room, don't you?'

'What? Oh Lord—I didn't realise—I didn't know it was that valuable. . . .' Olivia looked down in dismay, which turned to consternation as she turned over a plate and saw the famous mark of the crossed L's, painted in dark blue enamel. 'Oh God!' she moaned. 'It's far too good to use just for lunch. Both Tante and Raoul will have a fit!'

'Don't worry. At least it will give Raoul something else to think about!' Bridget giggled. 'Poor old Tante's idea of a fun party has really landed him in the soup. While you've been sulking in the kitchen, Lucille and Chantal have arrived and are both sticking to him like glue, eyeing each other through a thick green haze of jealousy!'

'I expect he's playing one off against the other—and loving every minute!' Olivia muttered bitterly, ignoring the reference to herself. 'By the way, is the doctor here?'

Bridget nodded. 'When I left the *salon*, Tante had backed the poor man into a corner, and was demanding an innoculation against "ze plague".'

'Well, ask him to stay for lunch, would you? After laying places for all the family, besides Tante's General and her two other boyfriends—not forgetting *dear* Lucille and Chantal, of course—I found the numbers came to thirteen. So just in case anyone is superstitious, we'd better add another guest; and I'm sure Nicole would like the doctor to be included.'

'Oh gee! What it is to have such a warm, romantic heart!' Bridget mocked, laughing as Olivia forgot her years and responded by sticking out her tongue. 'OK, I'll see to the doctor. Are you coming to have a drink?'

'You must be joking!' Olivia gave the dining room a final check. 'I'm going upstairs to change, and then I'll be in the kitchen. Let me know when everyone's ready to eat.'

Safely within the sanctuary of her bedroom suite,

Olivia took her time as she showered and dressed for the lunch party. Despite the aspirins she had swallowed, her head was still throbbing angrily, her mind and body filled with apprehensive dread of the forthcoming meal. She had managed to avoid a confrontation with Lucille yesterday, but she couldn't hide up here for ever, could she?

When it came to chosing what to wear, Olivia gave a small, rueful smile as she remembered Bridget's extraordinary outfit. She wasn't really so very different from her cousin after all, she realised, although in her case she decided to opt for the protective armour of cool elegance. Slipping into an apple-green, raw silk dress by Jean Muir, she was pleased to see, as it skimmed over her slim figure, that it looked as fashionable now as when she had bought it, some five years ago. Although her shop was doing well, she still couldn't afford to buy many expensive clothes like the ones she had purchased in her carefree days as a model.

Procrastination isn't going to solve a damn thing— and you can't stay up here brushing your hair all day! she exhorted herself, taking a deep breath to steady her nerves as she left her bedroom to return downstairs.

Reaching the head of the large stone staircase, she hesitated for a moment and then went along to the suite of rooms occupied by Marie-Louise. Putting her head around the door, she saw that the large sitting room was empty, save for the child's nurse, Annie, who was quietly knitting a small sweater.

'Oh no, mademoiselle,' Annie replied in answer to Olivia's query. 'The little girl has gone to spend the day with her friend, Solange. Solange's mama called to collect Marie-Louise some hours ago.'

'Never mind, I'll see her when she returns,' Olivia smiled and turned back along the corridor. She was just thinking how she missed the bright chatter of the little girl, when she rounded a corner—and walked straight into Raoul's arms.

'Where have you been?' he demanded curtly as she backed nervously away from his tall, broad-shouldered figure. 'I have been looking for you everywhere. Why are you not down in the *salon* with the guests?'

'I—I've only just finished in the kitchen, if you must know! Or does the master of the house strongly object if the cook has a shower, and changes her clothes?' she retorted with heavy sarcasm.

'How could I, when the result is so—er—pleasing?' he murmured softly.

He didn't move as he stood before her, but all at once the atmosphere of the dark corridor became highly charged with an unmistakable sexual tension. Her mouth was suddenly dry, the blood pounding in her veins as she was swept by an overpowering, crazy urge to run into his arms. An impulse which she swiftly and ruthlessly crushed without mercy.

'I must go and begin the final preparation for lunch. Incidentally, shouldn't you be downstairs entertaining your two girlfriends?' she asked coolly, marvelling at the fact that her voice sounded so calm and steady as she prepared to walk past him towards the stairs.

'Not so fast, *ma belle!*'

His rapid movement gave her no time to escape. One moment the width of the corridor was between them, the next she found herself imprisoned within his arms, her breasts crushed against his hard, firm chest. Instinctively, she tried to jerk away backwards, the force of her action bringing her spine into jarring contact with the wall behind. She was desperately twisting to try and free herself when she realised from the darkening gleam in his eyes and the sudden hardening of the thighs pressing her so closely to the wall, that her struggling body was exciting him.

'Please—please let me go, Raoul . . .' she demanded huskily.

'Ah, but perhaps I prefer to—er—entertain a girlfriend up here?' he drawled.

'I—I'm not your girlfriend!' she gasped as her shaking figure was filled with a familiar sick excitement. She stared mesmerised up at his mouth, aching and longing to feel the hard, sensual lips moving against her own. Her heart was beating so fast that her ears seemed filled with its drumming. God! What was happening to her? 'Leave me alone!' she whispered helplessly.

'Ah, but how can I, when your body melts and quivers against mine so invitingly?' he breathed thickly, lowering his mouth to brush and tantalise her trembling lips, his hands slipping over the silk dress as he sensually caressed her soft body.

He was right, she realised with despair. She couldn't seem to prevent herself from responding blindly to the demanding possession of his deepening kiss, the potent urgency of the hard frame pinning her to the wall. Her breathless pleas for him to stop became an inaudible moan beneath the melting sweetness, the soft seduction of his lips.

A shudder shook his tall figure, a deep groan breaking from his throat at the erotic provocation as her body moved sensually beneath him.

Totally absorbed by the white hot heat of their mutual desire it was some moments before they became aware that they were about to be disturbed.

'Coo-ee. . . O-liv-ia . . .! Where are you . . .?'

Bridget's voice sounded along the corridor. 'Tante's going mad trying to find some cointreau for a cocktail, and she says that you pinched it for the pudding that. . . . Oops! Sorry . . . !'

Olivia stood paralysed for a moment as Raoul stepped hurriedly back, blushing a deep crimson as her dazed eyes met the embarrassed, nervous grimace on her cousin's face.

'I m-must. . . the f-food. . .' Olivia stuttered helplessly, before taking to her heels and racing away along the corridor and down the stone staircase, as if the hounds of hell were at her heels.

Halfway through what seemed an interminable lunch, Olivia felt a damp nose being pushed into her hand, and gazed down into the friendly brown eyes of one of Raoul's retrievers. Very different from his master's expression, she thought miserably, stealing a glance down the table at the grim, taut lines of Raoul's face. His hard, glittering steely-blue eyes met hers for a heart-stopping moment, before they both quickly looked away.

Olivia raised her head to view the ornate clock on the dining-room mantlepiece. Half-past three! Would this meal never end? She turned to smile blindly at the doctor, who was sitting next to her and who was talking about the effect of the influenza epidemic on the local population. At least, that was what she thought he was saying. Unfortunately, his English was about as good as her French, which meant that neither could clearly understand each other. Not that it mattered that much: the noise of Tante's three elderly boyfriends competing for her attention was so deafening that she could hardly hear what the doctor was saying, Olivia thought wearily, as she signalled to a maid that the General's glass needed refilling.

Thankfully, two of the maids had recovered from the 'flu and were able to serve the guests, which meant that she only had to go downstairs to the kitchen at the beginning of each course, just to make sure that all the correct dishes were produced. However, even with the maid's help, she still felt totally exhausted. Her passionate encounter with Raoul upstairs, and the tense atmosphere at the table, seemed to be taking a dreadful toll of her emotional reserves. Her nervous trepidation was not solely due to the smouldering dislike and jealousy between Lucille and Chantal, she acknowledged, but also from a fearful dread of what Bridget was likely to say next.

Her cousin had obviously drawn her own conclusions from the embrace she had witnessed between Raoul and Olivia, and had clearly decided to champion her cause. While she knew she ought to be grateful for Bridget's support, Olivia soon found herself wishing that the girl could have found some other time and place for her display of family solidarity.

'Stuff and nonsense, Lucille!' Bridget was saying as she cut into an amusing, artful little speech by the French girl, full of *bons mots* and classical allusions. 'How can you possibly maintain that what a man looks for in a woman, is intelligence? I've never heard of anything so ridiculous! I'm sure that Raoul, for instance, would much prefer beauty to brains, wouldn't you?' she grinned evilly at his tanned, handsome face. 'After all, most men can *see* and *feel* much better than they can *think*!'

'I don't believe your fiancée appreciates us men, Henri!' Alain's laugh sounded somewhat too hearty as everyone at the table tried to hide a smile, careful not to look too closely at Lucille's flushed face.

'How would you know what Monsieur le Vicomte

would or would not like!' Lucille snapped angrily. 'A silly young girl like you!'

'A silly young girl like me, Madame, unlike those of riper years—such as possibly yourself?—has quite enough sense to know that there is nothing like a good dose of another woman, to make a man appreciate the virtues of an ex-fiancée . . .!'

Oh God! Bridget's done it now! Olivia thought, shaking with apprehension as Lucille became puce in the face as she struggled to control her temper.

'That is quite enough, Bridget!' The firm, sharp and commanding note in Raoul's voice silenced the girl far more effectively than any waspish reply Lucille might have made.

'Ha ha!' Tante's voice trilled nervously in the silence which had fallen on the table, only punctuated by Nicole who seemed to have been overcome by a fit of coughing which necessitated covering her mouth with a napkin. Olivia was worried for a moment, until she met Nicole's grey eyes brimming with tears of laughter. 'Yes,' Tante continued. 'That was the most delicious pudding that I can remember eating for a long time! What, my dear Raoul, would we all have done without dear Olivia?' She raised her glass to the English girl.

'What indeed!' Raoul commented dryly, before turning to Bridget. 'Please don't let us detain you if you are anxious to leave the table,' he informed her with silky menace.

'OK, Raoul, I get the message!' Bridget's laugh prompted a faint twitch of his lips despite the stern expression in his steely-blue eyes. 'I'll give Olivia a break and go and organise the coffee.'

Olivia sagged with heartfelt relief as her cousin left the dining room. One more of Bridget's outrageous remarks to Lucille, and she would have had to have left too. Always supposing that she could stand on her own two legs, she told herself, dismally aware that they were shaking so much that they felt more like jelly than bone and sinew.

Glancing down the table as the plates were removed, Olivia caught the speculative, almost triumphant gleam in Lucille's hot, dark eyes. That's odd, Olivia found herself musing. Only making her appearance as the guests were sitting down to lunch, she had been saved from having to say anything to the French girl, who had spent the first part of the meal glancing quickly and nervously back and forth between Raoul and Olivia. Now, despite the battering she had received from Bridget's verbal assaults, Lucille seemed far more relaxed and at ease. It was—it was almost as if a heavy load had been removed from the French girl's mind. . . . Olivia's thoughts were interrupted by Tante wondering aloud what had happened to the coffee.

'I'll go and see to it,' Olivia rose and slipped out of the dining room. Arriving down in the kitchen she saw that there was no sign of Bridget, and with a sigh of resignation she filled the kettle and set it on the stove, wishing that for once she could cheat and use instant coffee as she did in England. Waiting for the coffee grounds to settle, Olivia was surprised to see Alain walk into the kitchen.

'Apart from the food—which was sheer ambrosia, my dear Cinderella—that was a remarkably dreadful lunch, was it not? May I suggest that we leave this place immediately?'

'Well, I don't see how I can . . .' she murmured, wishing that she really could escape, even if only for an hour or two.

'There is absolutely no problem,' Alain said firmly. 'I will take the coffee tray up to the dining room, while you go and sit in my car. I will join you in the twinkling of an eye—and then we will drive off for a tour of the local vineyards. Bridget tells me that Raoul has kept you imprisoned in this deplorable kitchen, ever since you arrived in France. Disgraceful!'

'It—it isn't anyone's fault,' she protested. 'When the 'flu hit all the servants in the château. . . .'

'Yes, yes, I understand. But all the more reason for you to escape before Raoul, who is clearly an evil magician, turns you into a toad—like many of the people dining upstairs, hmm?'

'You are an idiot!' Olivia laughed, responding to his engaging smile. 'Yes, all right, I'll go and sit in your pumpkin,' she agreed, passing him the heavy silver tray.

Feeling ridiculously guilty, Olivia was tiptoeing past the dining room towards the hall, when she was halted by a low groan from the *salon*. Quickly entering the large room, she saw Bridget lying on one of the sofas, obviously in pain.

'For heaven's sake—what's the matter?' Olivia hurried over and knelt down beside her cousin.

'I—I slipped and fell down the steps to the kitchen, and—and, oh Livy, I feel really awful. I've got the most dreadful stomach cramps. . . .'

'Oh Lord! Those damn steps!' She looked down at Bridget's white face with concern. 'I don't know what to suggest. . . . Oh, yes, of course I do!' she clicked her teeth in annoyance. 'How stupid of me. I'll go and get the doctor.'

'Don't—don't let anyone know—not even Henri, please?' Bridget begged. 'I can't stand the thought of any fuss, and especially not from that awful Lucille woman. She'd only sit and gloat.'

'Don't worry,' Olivia assured her. 'I promise I'll get the doctor here without letting the others know. Just lie still and I'll be back in a moment.'

About to enter the dining room, she met Alain coming out. 'I'm sorry,' she said in a low voice. 'I'm afraid I can't come out for a drive. She doesn't want anyone to know about it, but Bridget has had a fall and isn't feeling well. I'm just going to try and winkle the doctor quietly out of the room.'

'I'll do that,' Alain said firmly. 'You go back and stay with your cousin.' Within a few minutes he reappeared with the doctor in tow, and while Bridget and the doctor talked quietly together, Alain and Olivia moved away to look out of the mullioned windows at the lake below. 'I do hope she hasn't broken a leg, or anything like that,' Olivia murmured. 'It's only a few days to her wedding.'

'Mademoiselle,' the doctor called and she hurried back to Bridget's side. 'I am afraid that this young lady may have a problem. It is the baby, you understand? So I think it is best that she goes straight into hospital for observation, and I will therefore go and call for an ambulance.'

'Oh no!' Bridget murmured, almost in tears. 'I can't possibly go off in a huge ambulance. . . .'

'Can I take her?' Alain asked the doctor. 'My car is at the door, and she can lie down on the back seat. It will be a quicker journey, and she will be in hospital much sooner than the time involved in calling up the medical services.'

'Yes, I see no reason why not. But drive carefully, yes?' the doctor warned.

'Please come with me, Livy,' Bridget's face was pale and strained as she looked up at her cousin. 'And . . . and please don't let the doctor tell anyone about this? I don't want to worry Henri, and I'm sure I'll be back here straight away. I—I feel much better already,' she lied bravely as her body was clearly racked by another spasm.

'I won't say anything,' the doctor promised. 'Although, I must warn you that I am not hopeful that we can save the child,' he murmured to Olivia as Alain carefully lifted Bridget and carried her from the room.

It seemed as though years had gone by as Olivia and Alain sat in the hospital waiting to hear the verdict on Bridget. Olivia had tried to persuade Alain to leave her, and return to his own home, but he steadfastly refused. 'I would not dream of leaving you alone here,' he said firmly. 'Besides, you or Bridget may well need me to translate what the doctors say.'

It wasn't until almost seven o'clock that a tall, distinguished-looking doctor with a goatee beard entered the room. He announced that Bridget was doing as well as could be expected, and she was now under sedation.

'They will not know until tomorrow if they can manage to save the baby,' Alain said, after rapidly questioning the doctor in French. 'He suggests that we leave and return in the morning.'

Walking out of the hospital, Olivia stumbled with weariness, and Alain insisted on taking her to a small bar and producing the French panacea for all ills—a cognac. 'I know what Bridget said, but we really ought to let Henri know,' Olivia sighed, feeling helpless at not being able to do something positive.

'Yes, I agree. I did, in fact, give the hospital Henri's phone number at his apartment in the château, and they have promised to contact him straight away.'

'I'm—I'm so grateful for all your help and support, Alain,' she murmured. 'There isn't anything else we can do, is there?' she added, looking at him with tired, worried eyes.

'No, alas. So, I suggest that you drink up and then we will go for a quiet meal. Let them cook their own dinner at the château—for once!'

Olivia had felt too tired to argue, and meekly acquiesced to Alain's suggestion. Although now, as she toyed with the food on her plate, she wished that she wasn't sitting here in the heat and noisy atmosphere of the restaurant. The longing to put her head down in a cool, dark room and go to sleep for a week, was becoming almost more than she could bear. . . .

'I am so sorry to have deserted you for so long, my dear Olivia,' Alain said as he returned to the table, looking down with concern at her tired, weary figure. 'Come,' he added, decisively. 'You are looking exhausted and I suggest that I take you back to the château, immediately, yes?'

Olivia was drooping with tiredness as she watched the red glow of Alain's rear lights disappearing back over the bridge. With a sigh, she pushed open the heavy oak doors and entered the dimly lit hall of the château. It seemed a long climb up to her suite, and she opened the door with a heartfelt sigh of relief, stiffening with shock as she saw the figure sitting in one of the armchairs.

'So—you have returned at last.' Raoul's voice was cold and hard. 'Would it be asking too much if I enquired where you have been?'

Olivia leaned back against the door, suddenly feeling weak as she looked over at the man she loved so much. The long legs stretched out before him were clothed in dark narrow-fitting trousers which clung to the taut muscles of his thighs. He had unbuttoned his thin white silk evening shirt as though he was too warm, exposing the tanned skin and dark hair on his chest; and from the slightly tousled state of his hair, it looked as if he had been running his hands roughly through its dark thickness. Her stomach muscles tensed in nervous protest as he continued to gaze at her, his blue eyes glinting from beneath the heavy eyelids.

'I—er—Alain and I took Bridget to the hospital. She fell down those kitchen steps, and while they don't know for certain yet, they think she may lose the baby,' she answered huskily, suddenly feeling acutely nervous as her senses responded to the dynamically masculine aura projected by the man sitting the other side of the room.

'Ah yes,' he lifted a glass, apparently only interested in studying the golden liquid, and for the first time she noticed the bottle of Remy Martin on the table beside him. 'It was four o'clock when you left this house. Oh yes,' he murmured sardonically. 'I very quickly persuaded the doctor to tell me what was happening in my own château—did you really think that he wouldn't? It is now eleven o'clock; a very long time to wait in the hospital, hmm?'

'I—I don't see why I should have to account to you for my movements!' she retorted wrathfully, anger beginning to take the place of her initial panic at finding him in her room.

'I despatched Henri to the hospital, but he only arrived just after you had left, at seven,' he informed her bluntly. 'I want to know where you have been since then.'

'If Alain wanted to take me out for a drink and a meal. . . .' She gritted her teeth in annoyance at having so easily told him what he wanted to know. 'Why don't you mind your own damn business!' she snapped.

'*Bon Dieu!*' he ground out angrily. 'I *am* minding my own business—the unfinished business which lies between you and me, Olivia.'

'The "business" as you call it, was well and truly finished between us five years ago, Raoul,' she replied bitterly, moving away from the door.

'Oh no, it was not!' He put down his glass and rose slowly to his feet. 'And I intend to have an explanation, *ma petite*, if it takes me all night to drag it from you!'

'What on earth are you talking about?' she shivered, suddenly feeling intimidated by his tall figure. 'Explanation . . .? From me . . .? That's rich!' she laughed wildly.

'So, you find it amusing, do you? *Espèce de garce!* What a bitch you are, Olivia!' he thundered, striding across the floor towards her.

Gasping with outrage, she nevertheless backed nervously away from his rigidly angry figure, her legs trembling as she turned and tried to run for the safety of her bedroom. She quickly realised she had made a mistake, since he seemed to have no compunction about following her. She retreated, becoming panicstricken as she felt the edge of the bed touching the back of her legs.

'Please—please go away,' she whispered urgently, before she gave a frightened cry as Raoul pushed her roughly down on the bed.

'I told you that I had no intention of leaving here until I receive a full explanation,' he snarled. 'I want to hear from your own soft lips, exactly why you deserted me five years ago. So, start talking, *ma belle!*' he demanded.

'You're crazy!' she protested, moaning in fright as Raoul sat down on the bed beside her, and roughly grasped her arms, his face white with rage and determination.

'I am what you have made me,' he grated fiercely. 'Look at me, Olivia! Are you proud of your handiwork? How you must have laughed all these years. . . .'

'Laugh?' she demanded incredulously. 'What have I had to laugh about?' She struggled violently, intent on getting off the bed and putting a safe distance between them. Maybe if she could reach the bathroom, she would be able to lock the door. . . . 'Let me go—let go of me!' she moaned, twisting and turning as she tried to escape his increasingly fierce grip. All to no avail. Swearing beneath his breath, Raoul pushed her back on the bed, imprisoning her body beneath the weight of his, waiting calmly until she was exhausted and had no more strength left to fight him.

'You see? It is pointless of you to resist, *ma belle*.' He bent his head close to her, his breath fanning her face, his lips moving softly as silk across her mouth. 'You would do well not to provoke me further!'

'I'll scream,' she whispered, trying to steal herself against the sensual touch of his lips, now feathering across her cheeks. 'I'll scream and—and scream. . . .'

'Go ahead,' he taunted, lifting his head. 'Who will hear you? There is no one in this wing of the château except yourself. We are quite alone, you and I. So, come, tell me why you ran away from me, hmm?'

'I—I didn't. It was you—you who cast me aside without a word. You know you did! I—I don't know why you are playing this—this c-cruel g-game. . . .' Her green eyes swam with tears as the hopelessness of her situation became more than she could bear.

'Almost . . . almost I could believe you,' he murmured, staring down intently into her eyes as the tears spilled over and ran down her cheeks. '*Ah, non, mon amour*, do not cry, my love,' he breathed huskily, covering her sad eyelids with soft kisses before moving down to possess her trembling lips.

'No—no Raoul!' she protested weakly as some minutes later he raised himself, rolling her sideways to swiftly release the zip of her dress.

'*Mais oui, ma belle Olivia*,' he murmured, his breathing quickening as he quickly removed her silk dress. '*Dieu*—how I want you! How I have longed to make love to you—these last days have been such a hell, such a torment!' he groaned.

She knew that she must stop him. She knew that she ought to firmly push him away. But when he released the catch of her bra exposing her breasts to his gaze, she could only gasp in sensual abandon as his hands cupped their full softness. His mouth moved caressingly over her creamy skin, a husky moan being torn from her throat as his lips found and captured a hard, rosy peak. No one but Raoul had ever made love to her, but he had taught her well the delights and desires of the flesh. With his hard, muscular thighs pressing her down into the soft mattress as he wrenched off his shirt, displaying the dark hair on his chest which tapered towards the waist of his tautly muscled body, she found her emotions impossible to control.

His mouth followed his hands as he removed her remaining clothes, trailing down the length of her quivering body. 'So beautiful, *amour de mon coeur*,' he breathed, the aching caress of his hands and lips on her body sending her senses spinning in a frenzy of delight. 'I must take you—*Mon Dieu*, I must!' His thick, hoarse cry seemed to come from far away as under the tantalising intimacy of his touch, she was once again the same willing slave to his desire as she had been all those years ago. Only then she had been shy and tentative. Now she was a grown woman, who had for too long been denied the consummate sweetness of surrending to the man she loved.

She hardly noticed when he swiftly tore off his clothes, knowing only her raging need, her hunger to return his caresses with all the erotic sensuality she had suppressed for so long. His mouth continued to plunder her body, his tongue setting her flesh on fire, hotly inciting the raging flame which was rapidly consuming her. As she gasped with delight, moaning helplessly beneath the mastery of his touch, Raoul gave a deep groan of satisfaction before his mouth covered hers and she surrendered to her overwhelming passion and the sensuous pleasure of his ultimate possession.

'Olivia . . .!' he gasped as her limbs enfolded him, her body welcoming his shuddering thrust. Some part of her dazed mind realised that he was striving to temper his own passionate need as he stretched her senses to the furthest peaks of pleasure.

And then, the time for all conscious thought was gone; their two bodies becoming one flesh in a pulsating climax that caused her to cry out with overwhelming joy and pleasure.

CHAPTER NINE

SOMETIME later in the night, Olivia woke from a dream of such horrific nightmare proportions that her mind could never afterwards recall anything but the overwhelming feelings of sheer terror.

Her body was burning hot, and yet her slim frame was racked by trembling shivers that made her teeth chatter uncontrollably. Moving her head, she gave a small cry of pain, as the background throbbing in her head intensified to become a pounding torture, obliterating every thought except that of gaining some relief. Pushing aside the bedclothes, her shaking figure stumbled through the suite to the bathroom. She almost fainted from the sharp, stabbing pain in her eyes as she switched on the bright fluorescent light in her search for some aspirins.

It was only when Olivia returned to the bedroom that recollection of the previous evening's lovemaking with Raoul filled her mind. But Raoul wasn't there. He had taken his pleasure and returned to his own room, she thought miserably as she gazed at the large empty bed. She swayed dizzily, not able to remember when she had last felt so dreadfully ill, and so desperately needing the comfort and reassurance of the man she loved.

Slipping back between the sheets, her body shivering in the grip of a violent fever, she gave way to a rasping storm of bitter, wretched tears, crying with heartbroken anguish and grief as she realised that, once again, she had been deserted by Raoul.

The night seemed endlessly long and lonely, the aspirins she had taken only partially relieving her raging fever. Although she knew she must have slipped into a fitful doze from time to time, she awoke to find the morning sun streaming into her bedroom, hardly aware of having slept at all. Her body was drenched in sweat, aching all over as she alternated between gasping from the raging heat and shivering violently beneath the freezing, icy bands of steel about her head.

She must have caught the 'flu virus which had swept its way through the château, she realised, groaning aloud in dismay as she realised that however ill she might be feeling, unless she forced herself to rise and go downstairs, no one in this huge place would have anything to eat. Not even the poor servants who had been so ill, she thought, wincing as she tried to lift her head. With Bridget away in hospital, her future mother-in-law, Hélène, could not be relied on to continue the 'soup and toast run' as her cousin had called it.

She had no alternative but to get up and see to everyone's breakfast, only how could she possibly face Raoul ever again? Especially after their passionate lovemaking last night. She could only dimly remember her weak, miserable tears at finding he had gone from her side; but what else could she have expected? The painful throbbing in her head intensified as she squirmed with embarrassment and self-disgust. 'The wages of sin', she told herself despairingly, was not death, as the Bible said, but having to live each day with the full realisation of just how foolish one had been. Due, she supposed, to her strict moral upbringing at her convent school, she had never been able to lightly contemplate falling into bed with a man—however much she loved him—knowing that she would have to live with feelings of shame afterwards. It had been different, of course, when she and Raoul had been engaged to be married; but she had no such excuse for her sexual abandonment last night. She remembered reading in some magazine the cynical statement: People don't call it sin nowadays—they call it self-expression. Well, she'd certainly indulged in self-expression last night, hadn't she?

Olivia moaned as she tried to sit up, her aching head feeling as if it was in the grip of an ever-tightening steel vice. How incredibly foolish, what incalculable folly to have surrendered to Raoul's momentary desire for her body. She was, she reminded herself miserably as the stray tears slipped down her cheeks, only one of a long line of his conquests. Both those women at lunch yesterday, would have been more than willing to have given 'their all' at the smallest twitch of his little finger. She had meant nothing to him, nothing more than a moment's gratification, and how she could possibly face him again, she had no idea.

The dismally depressing, self-accusatory thoughts ebbed and flowed through her head, which was now pounding like a sledgehammer. She must get up—she must! She had to go downstairs, even if she felt like death warmed up. Poor Tante, for instance, couldn't even boil an egg. . . .

It had taken Olivia an interminable time to ease her aching body into a simple cotton dress. When she had done so, she was still shivering so much, despite the warm summer day, that she wrapped herself in a woollen evening shawl. It didn't really make her feel any warmer, but the soft cashmere was soothingly soft against her burning flesh. Dizzily clinging to the ornately carved stone bannister, she forced her weak, trembling legs down the stairs, halted from descending to the kitchen by Tante's voice calling to her from the dining room.

'*Bonjour, chérie*. What a lovely morning!' Tante Amalie waved from the end of the table as Olivia stood in the doorway. 'I have wonderful news for you!'

'You mean—you mean Bridget didn't lose her baby after all?' Olivia queried hoarsely, closing her eyes for a moment against the brilliant sunshine spilling into the room.

'Ah yes, poor Bridget. *Mais non*, I have not heard how she is, poor girl.' Tante's sad grimace was swiftly followed by a beaming smile. 'No, the good news I was referring to, is that both our housekeeper and cook have risen from their beds, and are now downstairs working away in the kitchen. Isn't it wonderful!'

Doesn't that woman ever think of anything but food? Olivia thought, squinting down the table and noticing for the first time the heavy silver coffee pot and the mound of fresh croissants. 'I'm glad—I—excuse me, Tante, I don't—don't feel very well . . .' she gasped as the room began to revolve around her shivering figure. She put out a hand to steady herself against the door, but it unaccountably wasn't there, as her trembling body seemed to be falling through a whirling Catherine wheel of brilliant, prismatic colours, and down—down into a deep, dark well.

Vaguely, as if in the far distance, she could hear someone shrieking, and through the swirling mists of unconsciousness she was aware of chattering voices nearby. A sharply barked command produced an instant silence as strong arms lifted her prone figure. Not all her senses were in a state of traumatic suspension. She somehow knew, from the warm musky masculine scent, that Raoul's arms were encircling her body and she relaxed within the total security of his embrace as the dark void claimed her once again.

Drifting in and out of her semi-concious state, it must have been the well-remembered scent of Raoul's cologne which tiggered off a return of the dark memories of their past relationship. As she tossed and turned, burning one moment and freezing the next, it was as though she was watching a slow-motion video recording of their first meeting, their love affair and the final, hideously cruel ending. During all this time she was dimly aware of firm arms lifting her shoulders and making her drink glass after glass of cold lemonade, and of warm hands gently sponging the damp perspiration from her body.

When at last she regained full consciousness, her fluttering eyelids opened to see Raoul's handsome, tanned face bending over her. 'What—what are you doing here?' she whispered in confusion.

'Merely putting a cold cloth on your forehead,' he said with a quiet smile.

'I—I must have caught the 'flu,' she muttered, closing her eyes against the brilliant light in the room.

'I'm afraid so, *ma belle*. You have been very ill, and I have been most concerned these last three days. . . .'

'Three days!' She looked up at him aghast, seeing for the first time the deeply etched lines around his mouth and the dark shadows beneath his blue eyes. 'But who has been . . .? Did you . . .?' Her cheeks flamed as she slowly realised that it had been his hands that she had felt on her body.

Raoul smiled gently. 'Tante is too elderly for me to take the risk of her catching the germs from you, *chéri*. Poor Nicole is still *hors de combat* in her plaster casts, and all the nurses available to the good doctor are busily engaged on caring for others afflicted by the virus. It seems to have swept through this area very much like the plague Tante called it.'

'Yes, I—I see. . . .'

He looked down at the blushing cheeks and fluttering eyelashes of the girl lying in the bed. 'I did not feel you would welcome the attentions of strangers, such as Gaston's wife or the cook. *Voilà*, I fear that there was only myself left available to be a nurse,' he explained softly.

'Yes, I—er—thank you, Raoul. I am grateful,' she murmured, trying to avoid his eyes.

'Come,' he said firmly, slipping his arm beneath her shoulders and raising her up into a sitting position. 'You must drink some more of this lemonade.'

'I can't seem to remember anything, except that I've had the most awful dreams.'

'Yes, I know. You became delirious and I was very worried.'

'Delirious?' She looked at him in sudden alarm. 'Did I . . .? I didn't say—er—anything, did I?'

'Your secrets are quite safe with me,' he replied gently as he laid her back on the pillows. What secrets? she thought uneasily as he straightened the sheet and leant over to brush her cheek with his lips. To her utter consternation, she felt her eyes filling with weak tears.

'Ah, you must not cry, *chérie*,' Raoul chided softly. 'Go back to sleep now, and when you wake you will feel much better, I promise.'

Olivia lay on a *chaise-longue*, looking out through the open window at the black swans gliding by on the still blue waters of the lake. The fresh scent of lime trees in the park, across the stretch of water, wafted in and teased her nostrils as she lifted the cup of tea to her lips.

It was over a week now since she had surfaced from the mists of her delirious, unconscious state. With youthful resilience she was swiftly recovering her strength and beginning to chaff at Raoul's insistence that she be treated as an invalid, and lie here in the *salon*. Glancing down at the tray beside her, she smiled ruefully at the delicate cucumber sandwiches, the hot buttered toast and slices of plum cake. Nothing she said could seem to persuade Nicole that she was unused to such a Victorian repast; one that was seldom served in Britain nowadays.

'You are English and must therefore have your English tea,' Nicole had said firmly. 'Besides, I have strict instructions from my brother. He says that you have become far too thin and must eat to regain your strength.'

'I'm surprised that he didn't say that I looked scrawny,' Olivia had muttered dully, remembering the dismay with which she had regarded her pale, white face in the mirror that morning.

Rather unfeelingly, she thought, Nicole had merely laughed and told her to eat her tea. 'That will be more flowers for you, I expect,' the French girl added as she turned her new wheelchair and left the room to answer the heavy chime from the front door of the château.

Everyone had been so kind, Olivia thought, looking around at the glorious assortment of blooms which filled the many vases in the large room. She had noticed Raoul's grim expression whenever he saw the bunches of red roses which arrived daily from Alain. They looked wonderful, of course, but she much preferred the little posies of sweet, wild meadow flowers, picked by the small hands of Marie-Louise. She was missing the little girl, whisked off five days ago by Tante, who had declared that the château was clearly a charnel house; and that she and Marie-Louise would stay with friends down the coast at Biarritz, until the plague was over.

'No, no more flowers from the florist today,' Nicole announced, rolling her chair back into the room and putting a tired bunch of drooping delphiniums on Olivia's lap. 'Here, these are from Henri who I have just met in the hall. It looks as if he has picked them from our garden, I'm afraid,' she added with a wry smile.

'Poor Henri—and poor Bridget,' Olivia said sadly, remembering how she had cried when some days ago Raoul had told her that her cousin had lost her baby. The warm, loving comfort of his arms as he had tried to help soothe her sorrow, had made her cry even more. . . . She must stop thinking about Raoul like that, she admonished herself severely. Thankfully, he had never referred to the night they had made love. But having him carry her up and down to her room every day was bad enough, without the added torture of wishing and longing for what could never be.

'Poor Henri, indeed,' Nicole was saying. 'I don't know what is wrong with Bridget, but he tells me that she is refusing to leave the hospital, and wouldn't even see him when he called there today. Apparently, she is perfectly well now, and so he is very confused by her attitude.'

'I'd no idea—I. . . .' Olivia shrugged helplessly.

'My dear, there is nothing you can do. We must just leave the young people to sort themselves out, yes?' Nicole said firmly. 'This is a wonderful contraption,' she added, patting the arm of her wheelchair. 'It was a simply marvellous idea of yours, and I can't think why I never thought of it myself!'

'Probably because you preferred having your doctor to carry you about!' Olivia murmured with a sly grin.

'How silly you are!' Nicole's thin cheeks flushed as she fiddled nervously with her handkerchief.

Olivia recalled the expression on the doctor's face as he had looked with hungry longing at Nicole. 'Why—why don't you marry your doctor?' she asked in a soft, tentative voice. 'Even I can see that he loves you very much. Is it because you feel that you can't leave Marie-Louise? I'm sure Raoul would not expect you to sacrifice your life for his child.'

Nicole shrugged unhappily. 'No, he has said many times . . .' she sighed. 'You see, I—I am not young, Olivia. It is maybe foolish of me to think that he and I . . . René has never said anything—anything positive. . . .'

'Not young? You're only thirty, for heaven's sake! I'm certain your doctor is crazy about you. Don't—don't lose your chance of happiness, Nicole,' she added, unable to prevent the husky catch in her voice. 'Don't make a mess of your life, like I did. Just love him, and marry him, and—and live happily ever after,' she pleaded.

'Oh, Olivia!' Nicole raised her handkerchief and blew her nose fiercely. 'Why can't you and Raoul just talk to each other. I'm certain. . . .'

'That's—that's quite a different matter,' Olivia said flatly. 'Just make sure of your own happiness. What on earth . . .?' she exclaimed as the sound of raised voices, followed by a scream of rage could be clearly heard coming from the direction of the hall. A loud bang shook the room as the heavy oak front door was slammed violently shut, and they could dimly hear the roar of a car engine as it raced away from the courtyard.

'Heavens! Whatever's happening?' Olivia's green eyes widened as she looked enquiringly at Nicole, who seemed remarkably unperturbed.

'That, I imagine, was Madame Millot's departure,' the French girl said with dry satisfaction. 'It was she who I let in just now. She rudely insisted on having a word with Raoul. It would seem, would it not, that she got more than she bargained for! I do not think that we shall be seeing much of her again.' She glanced sideways through her eyelashes at the averted, pale face of the English girl who was gazing abstractedly out of the window.

I've got to leave here, immediately! Olivia was telling herself, recalling Raoul's words in the rose garden, the day he had taken her and Marie-Louise to Bordeaux. He had said he was thinking of getting married, and if Lucille had been dismissed—as Nicole had clearly indicated—then it could only mean that he had decided to marry Chantal. She was, after all, a lovely young girl who patently adored him, and who would be sweet and kind to his little daughter. Yes, Olivia told herself again, she must definitely leave this château as soon as possible. . . .

'Will you have some tea, Raoul?' Nicole turned as her brother entered the room.

'No, thank you. I have merely come to take Olivia upstairs. If she is insisting that she is well enough to join us for dinner tonight, then I am insisting that she has a rest first.' He looked over at the girl whose heavy fall of chestnut hair, catching and reflecting the brilliant rays of the sun as they streamed in through the open window, hid her face from his view as she stared down at her nervously twisting hands.

'I'm—I'm fine,' Olivia managed to say, at last. 'There's no need to continue pampering me in this way, especially since I'm so much better than I was. Besides,' she turned her head to smile brightly at Raoul and Nicole, 'I really must make arrangements to fly home, now that the air traffic controller's strike is over. I—I'd be grateful if I could have my passport, Raoul,' she added, 'and could you book me a flight, please?'

'Of course, if you wish,' he said in a calm, cool voice as he came over and bent down to lift her slim, light figure from the *chaise-longue*. As always, she had to struggle to control her errant emotions at the warm comfort of his encircling arms. Not helped, on this occasion, by the heavy weight of depression in her stomach as she registered his cool disinterest in the fact that she wished to leave the château.

Cradled in his strong arms as he carried her from the room, her eyes were filled by the handsome profile only inches away from her own face. She was suddenly swept by an insane desire to smooth back the lock of dark hair which had fallen over his forehead, to press her lips to the long length of his tanned cheek. . . . A small sigh escaped her lips and she quickly lowered her eyelashes as he turned his head.

'Are you feeling all right?' he asked softly.

'Yes,' she mumbled, tearing her eyes away from his and looking about her in bewilderment. 'This—this isn't the way to my room?'

'No,' he agreed. 'It is the way to my apartment. I rather thought that you wished to make immediate arrangements for your departure, hmm?'

'Yes, yes, of course,' she murmured, a lump of misery seeming to constrict her throat at his having so quickly seized the opportunity to be rid of her.

A moment later, they entered a suite of rooms she had never seen before. He carried her through a large sitting room and into what clearly was a study, lowering her down on to a large sofa by a fireplace before going over to an ornate desk and pulling open a drawer. 'Yes, here we are, one British passport in good condition,' he drawled smoothly, coming over to hand her the small blue book and seating himself at the other end of the sofa. 'Now, my dear Olivia, perhaps you would be good enough to tell me why you are so determined to leave us, hmm?'

'Well, there's—there's no point in my staying now, is there,' she shrugged unhappily.

'"Now"?' he seized on the word. 'Why *now* Olivia?'

'Well, I—I mean, now that Bridget is not getting married after all, at least not for a while . . .' her voice trailed away as she felt his intense gaze on her flushed face.

'I don't somehow feel that is what you really mean, hmm? You could have left days ago, in that case. It would not have been advisable, but you would have undoubtedly survived,' he mocked gently. 'So why have you suddenly decided to leave now?'

Olivia looked down at her nervously twisting hands. 'Well, you're going to get married. . . .'

'I am? Who says so?'

'You did, in the rose garden. You—you said that you were thinking of getting married.'

'What an excellent memory you have, *chérie!*' he murmured sardonically. 'An idle thought is not necessarily a firm proposal—but never mind that. You obviously believe that I am to marry, and I would, therefore, be delighted to know who you—er—have in mind for me?'

'Well, I . . .' she blinked rapidly, very close to tears. 'I—I thought Chantal. . . .'

'*Chantal?* Ah yes, what a good choice! A girl hardly out of the schoolroom and almost young enough to be my daughter. Thank you, *ma belle,* but no! Have you any other suggestions? I'd be fascinated to hear all your plans for my future happiness,' he ground out bitterly.

'I—I don't know. It's nothing to—to do with me,' she whispered shakily.

'Nothing to do with you? *Bon Dieu!*' he exploded, rising swiftly from the sofa and pacing angrily about the room. 'You, who have haunted my life—my every waking hour and my dreams—for the last five years. You say it is nothing to do with you? *May God give me patience!*'

Olivia flinched back against the cushions, suddenly frightened and confused by the tall, dark and furiously angry man, who was now gesticulating wildly as he swore violently under his breath. 'Raoul . . .' she whispered, before cowering back at the look he threw in her direction.

'I have loved—truly loved—but once in my life,' he thundered angrily. 'I fell desperately in love with you from the very first moment I saw you, and I have had no other love for any woman since then. The last five years have been torture to me, *and I will have it no more*! You think I am to marry? You are "dead right" as Bridget would say. You, *mademoiselle,* are going to marry me, if I have to take you bound and gagged to the altar! Do you understand me?' he demanded, shaking with fury.

'You—you want to marry me . . .?' Olivia gasped, dazed and uncertain whether she had heard him correctly.

'Want to marry you?' he repeated incredulously. '*Toi—toi que j'aime tant*—you whom I have loved so much! For God's sake! I do not just want to, I can assure you I am going to. There has been too much unhappiness and misery for us both. I intend that it shall now cease—*tu comprends?*' he shouted angrily.

Olivia could only stare at him, her senses whirling, spinning dizzily as she realised she had indeed heard him correctly. He—he did want to marry her!

'Well, *mademoiselle?*' he whispered savagely, impaling her with an unwavering stare from his steely-blue eyes. '*Well?*' his voice rose sharply.

'There—there is no need to shout at me,' she heard herself saying quietly, amazed that she could sound so normal, when her heart was pounding so loudly in her breast that she was sure he must be able to hear it.

Her soft voice seemed to calm his furious rage; his tall figure relaxing as he walked slowly back to sit down beside her on the sofa. 'I—I am sorry, *ma petite*, I . . .' he shrugged unhappily, running shaking hands through his dark hair. 'God knows, I did not mean to speak of such things to you, yet awhile. I realise that you are still not well. But, when you said you wished to leave, I became desperate!' He took her trembling hands in his. 'I have loved you so much and for so long, that maybe I am not entirely sane, hmm?'

'But—but it was you who broke off our engagement and—and. . . .'

'No! I did not,' he interrupted sharply. 'It has been difficult for me to sort out what is true and what is false, but now I know all—thanks to your influenza, my darling.'

'The 'flu?' she looked at him uncomprehendingly.

'When you were so delirious, you seemed to think that you were back in London, all those years ago. I—I sat and listened to you relating events of which I had no knowledge. You see, I thought that it was you who had deserted me! The final pieces of the jigsaw fell into place this morning, during my interview with Lucille,' his voice hardened cruelly. 'I will never forgive that woman—*never*!'

'I don't understand. . . .'

'My darling it is a long, long story. If only you or I had known the truth. . . .' His husky voice seemed to catch for a moment as he cradled her lovingly in his arms. 'I will explain all, but please, for God's sake, tell me with your own sweet lips that you do still love me?'

The raw hunger, the desperate need in his voice, broke through the incredulous miasma that filled Olivia's mind. Without conscious thought, she wound her arms about his neck, lifting her face to him in mute invitation. He gave a sudden, deep groan, finding her mouth with his own and possessing it with a blind urgency that swept aside all barriers.

'Yes, yes of course I love you,' she whispered softly as he raised his dark head to gaze lovingly down into her dazed green eyes. 'There has never been anyone else for me, no one but you, Raoul.'

'Five wasted years! And what a cruel deception was played against us both! I shudder to think how we could have been so nearly parted again, *ma chérie*,' he murmured, covering her lips in a long drugging kiss. When he released her they were both breathing heavily.

'Why—why did you desert me?' she asked quietly.

'I did not,' he assured her firmly. 'When I first saw you at the stables in Newmarket—*wham!*—in one blinding flash I found myself in love! God knows I tried to restrain myself as best I could, you were so very young and innocent. But I—I nearly became mad with a longing for your sweet body, to have you love me as I loved you. The terrible row you had with

Lucille gave me the opportunity to rush you into a marriage with me; long before you were ready for it, of course. However, I was powerless to resist the chance the gods had offered! I just snatched at you like a greedy child, not able to believe my luck. You see, I was in the thral of such a feverish desire for you—body and soul, that I could not even resist taking you before we were to be married.'

'I did—er—have something to do with that, too, you know!' Olivia smiled lovingly into his eyes.

'Oh, my darling, we were so happy, were we not? You were like a sweet, innocent rose bud flowering in my arms. I—I took your innocence, but I loved you so much, *ma chérie*. I loved you with all my heart.'

'But then you went to America, and. . . .'

'Yes,' he breathed against her hair. 'It was terrible being away from you, and I counted the days till my return. I had to spend a week in New York before I caught my flight to London, and on the last day I began to feel very ill. I tried to ignore it, completing my business before catching the aeroplane. Unfortunately, Lucille was on the same flight, returning from a modelling job in New York. When I collapsed with a high temperature, she told the stewardess she would look after me, and on arrival at London Airport, she did indeed arrange everything. I was semi-conscious by then, still on my feet, but only just. Feeling so ill, I could only be grateful when she said she would take me to my apartment and call for the doctor. I managed to remember that you would be waiting to hear from me, and she promised that she would call you immediately.'

'But—but she never did! I was so. . . .'

'Hush, *ma belle*, let me tell you all first, hmm? Then you will understand how it was. You see, I did not know at the time, but I had caught something called glandular fever, and for days I was ill, just as you have been with the influenza, *tu comprends*? Lucille said she had called for the doctor and she would stay with me until he arrived. When he did not arrive straight away, she moved her case into my spare room, and said that she would stay and nurse me, since I was clearly too ill to look after myself. I, for my part, felt as though I was dying, and merely acquiesced with her suggestion. When the fever left me, Lucille was still in the apartment, and she said that you had telephoned and excused yourself from coming to see me, since glandular fever was so contagious—which it is—and you were frightened of catching it.'

'For heaven's sake! What would I have cared, especially when you were so ill?' Olivia protested heatedly. 'How could you have believed her?'

Raoul sighed heavily. 'I did not, at first. But I had been in a fever for over a week, and then Lucille showed me the ring you had sent back, and showed me a newspaper picture from the gossip columns, which showed you and Ashley Warne dancing together at the Studio 54 nightclub in New York.' He kissed her gently. 'The newspaper said how you had flown out to be with the man you loved over Christmas. I—I broke down then. I was so weak from the fever, so depressed with the illness, that I just gave way to despair. Can you understand my darling?'

'Yes, yes I do see, but you know what trash gossip columns print. Ashley—well, Ashley isn't—um—well, he isn't interested in girls. I only went out to join him because I thought you had deserted me, and he needed my help for a modelling job. You—you can't have been jealous of Ashley, for heaven's sake! He's a lovely man, but well. . . .'

'No? Truly?'

'Really and truly!' she said firmly. 'My God! When I think of that bitch Lucille. . . .' Olivia sat bolt upright, her face flaming with anger. 'I'll—*I'll kill her!*'

Raoul laughed as he pulled her back into his arms. 'Oh no, my sweet. You come a poor second to me— but I do not think we will either of us ever see her again. Not after what I said to her today!'

'Do you mean to say, that you are going to let her get away with what she did to us?' Olivia growled angrily.

'Hush, my fierce little one! Poor Lucille is to be pitied, you know. The man she married four years ago deserted her for a young girl of eighteen, and her uncle has upped and married his housekeeper, so I am told, Therefore, poor Lucille now has no prospects of the vineyard, which she was dangling in front of my nose—as if I would marry someone for their land!'

'Tante thought you would.'

'I love my Tante Amalie, but I once allowed her to interfere in my life with disastrous consequences— never again!'

'You mean—your wife?' she asked softly.

'Poor, poor Estelle,' he groaned, clasping her tightly in his arms. 'I should never have married her, and I have paid for what I did. She, at least, has known the peace of the grave, while I . . .' his body shook. 'I have had to live in guilt and torment for so long.'

'Oh, my darling,' Olivia took his trembling figure in her arms, soothing him with soft words of endearment as she might have done a child, until he relaxed and they lay quietly together.

'I don't know what Lucille had hoped for, but when I recovered from my illness, I thanked her and returned to France. You must understand that this glandular fever takes a long time to go from the system, and is an illness that leaves the patient feeling low and depressed for a long time. On top of that I had your desertion, as I thought, and I no longer cared what happened. Tante produced Estelle, and we went out to dinner a few times, but I was not interested. And then,' he sighed, 'then I saw the posters!'

'Posters?' Olivia looked up at him in confusion.

'The Riccardi posters—they were all over France in the New Year. Everywhere I turned I saw your beautiful face—it was living hell! I would be driving along the auto-route, and there would be another poster—my mind filling with memories of your sweet cries of pleasure at my lovemaking . . . I was haunted by the vision of your loveliness everywhere I turned. I—I became desperate and even thought of taking my life—instead of which I allowed Tante to persuade me to take a wife. Estelle was a lovely young girl, and she seemed to want to marry me, so . . .' he shrugged unhappily. 'So we married.' Raoul broke off his narrative to get up and pace about the floor.

'You will rightly accuse me of betraying you by marrying another woman, my darling. But I thought I had lost you for ever. I—I, well, I will not say anything about my married life, except that to my shame and guilt, I found that Estelle could never replace you in my heart, and I quickly realised what a terrible thing I had done to a young girl who deserved better than to marry a man such as I. Luckily, she found she was pregnant when we returned from our honeymoon,' his face flushed with embarrassment. 'We—er—we were never intimate again.'

Olivia, listening as Raoul related the sad story of his marriage, was surprised that she did not feel torn apart by jealousy of a woman who had been married to the man she loved so deeply. Rather, she was filled with compassion for the two people, who had found themselves locked together in what was clearly a mutual hell. 'Raoul, please don't say any more if you don't want to,' she whispered. 'I—I do understand, and I don't blame you, really I don't.'

'That is generous of you,' he said, coming over to take her into his arms. 'The Good Lord knows that I have indeed been punished for what I did, and I will carry the scars to my grave. Poor Estelle was never well,' he continued. 'And, as you know, she took her own life. It was a tragedy.' He sighed.

'But, darling, you have Marie-Louise, who is such a lovely little girl.'

'Yes, I have indeed been blessed,' he agreed. 'Whenever I saw you together with her, I—well, my heart used to turn over,' he confessed, burying his face in the soft fragrance of her hair. 'To have you back in my life has been a miracle.'

'Well, I still can't get over the extraordinary coincidence. When you walked into the shop that day, I—I nearly died!'

'Ah, but one must help coincidences along!' Raoul grinned sheepishly. 'I—er—I must confess that I did my best!'

'What on earth do you mean?'

'Well, my darling, I must tell you that our grape harvest here in the Médoc, is later than some of the vineyards further south. Last year, when I was visiting a friend's château just before my harvest, they were celebrating the end of theirs. All the young people who had been picking the grapes were invited to a party, and I was introduced to a weird-looking young girl who said her name was Bridget Harding. On closer conversation, I discovered that she was indeed related to you, and so I gave her my card and told her that there would be a job for her in my vineyard, if she cared to come—which she did!'

'That was sneaky of you,' Olivia laughed.

'Ah, yes, I was indeed "sneaky" as you say. You may not be pleased with me when I tell you that after Estelle died, I had detectives give me regular reports of your life in London. . . .'

'Well! of all the nerve!'

'. . . yes, I thought you might not approve of my action! I have followed your progress with much interest, my darling; and your romance with Ian Campbell with increasing fury!' he growled.

'But I never. . . .'

'I damn well hope not! But I was getting desperate, you understand? You might well have decided to marry such a suitable man—why not? However, when Bridget decided to get married to Henri, I pointed out the social necessity of having a member of her family at her wedding, preferably someone of her own age. And no,' he laughed at her astonished expression, 'Henri managed to produce the baby without my help!'

'Oh, Raoul, we mustn't laugh,' she chided him sadly. 'Poor Bridget has lost her baby now. Apparently something is wrong, because she is insisting on staying in hospital. I'm worried about her.'

'You have no need to fret,' he smiled. 'What a family the Hardings are! I called to see Bridget today, and discovered just why she is so keen to stay in her hospital bed. I must tell you, my darling, that your cousin is madly in love with her surgeon! She tells me it is the "real thing" this time—we shall see! I must say the poor man is looking as if a bomb has hit him—

well, why shouldn't he experience the full glory of Bridget? Never—but never will I forget that lunch party—*my God!*'

'I won't either,' she assured him with feeling. 'But are you seriously telling me that you knew who you would be bringing to France?'

'I hope so, since I planned it all; with a little help from God, of course. The airport strike was a gift, was it not?'

'So *that's* why you didn't seem surprised to see me! What a swine you were on the journey, too!'

For a moment there was silence as Raoul lowered his head, brushing her lips delicately with his own. 'My sweet, lovely Olivia,' he murmured huskily. 'I was so confused. Your beautiful presence disturbed my senses until I could not think straight. I loved you, and yet I hated you for what I thought you had done to me. I wanted you to suffer, and instead I was the one in deep pain and torment. That night when you woke crying, and I held you in my arms until you slept, I nearly broke down. I had heard you crying the night before, too, and I could not understand why.'

'It was a tremendous strain, being with you for such a long journey,' she explained. 'If only the car hadn't gone wrong . . . Oh no! You didn't fix that too, did you?' His flushed cheeks told the true story. 'Honestly! I'll soon believe you arranged for everyone in this place to get the 'flu!'

'To have you confined in that damn kitchen—are you mad? You seemed obsessed with food, and I nearly killed Alain when I found him with his arms about you!'

'Well, how do you think I felt about Lucille and Chantal?' she demanded caustically.

'We have talked enough,' he said firmly, sweeping

her up in his arms and striding through into a large bedroom. 'Now.' he said, depositing her on the king-sized bed. 'Are we engaged to be married, or not?'

'No. I'm certainly not going to be engaged to you!'

'Ah, my darling, my heart's desire,' he groaned. 'Please say you will marry me? Could you not see, when we made love the other night, how much I adore you? How I worship your body?'

'Raoul, darling, I can't face another engagement,' she said breathlessly as he lowered himself beside her, parting the light robe she was wearing, and allowing his long tanned fingers to move caressingly over the thrusting peaks of her breasts beneath the thin silk nightdress. 'But—but yes, I will marry you, if you really want me to?'

'*Want?*' He laughed. 'Ah, my dearest, darling girl. We will see the *curé* tomorrow, yes?'

'We can't marry straight away, I mean, there's the shop ... and what my mother will say, I can't imagine ...!' she panted helplessly as he lowered his head to kiss the soft valley between her breasts.

'There is no problem,' he murmured, his lips caressing the warm swell of her breasts. 'I have your mother's full permission to wed you immediately.'

'*What?*' Olivia's green eyes widened. 'How ...? I mean, when ...?'

'But naturally I must have your mother's approval, yes? So I phoned her last night, and when I explained all, she gave me her blessing. She is, in fact, delighted—and sends much love to her daughter, whom I have faithfully promised I will cherish and adore,' he added thickly, his hands moving more urgently over her body.

'I can't think how you managed to get around her— she isn't keen on foreigners. Your famous charm, I suppose?' Olivia added with a smile as she gently brushed the hair from his brow.

'Of course! But I rather fancy that she liked the idea of her daughter being a Vicomtesse, as well!' He grinned.

'Mothers! How typical! But what—what about my shop, Raoul?'

'My darling, do what you wish.' He gave a sudden bark of laughter. 'It would seem that I have solved my redecoration problems in a rather drastic way—by marrying an interior decorator!'

'Actually,' she murmured, 'I've been dying to get my hands on this place. I'm really not mad on all that heavy Second Empire style—especially for this fairytale castle. I thought that maybe light, airy materials, and pretty Colefax and Fowler prints, with. . . .'

'Enough!' he growled. 'I have other matters on my mind at the moment!' His voice was thick and husky as he removed the last vestiges of silk from her trembling body.

'Raoul . . .!' she gasped. 'You mustn't! We can't! Nicole is expecting us at dinner. . . .'

'I hope she has the sense to invite her doctor to take our place,' he said, swiftly stripping off his clothes. 'But for now, *ma petite*, if you do not want a madman on your hands, talk to me no more of family, or business or—God forbid!—of food. . . . Just allow me to make love to you, my adorable one, hmm?'

As pleasure flooded through her body, she realised that it was clearly a waste of time to recall him to a sense of family duty; and with a small moan of contentment, she abandoned herself to the possession of the man she loved so much.

An epic novel of exotic rituals
and the lure of the Upper Amazon

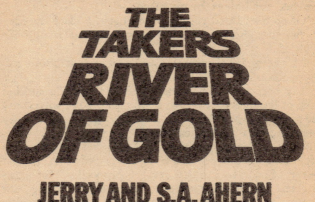

THE TAKERS RIVER OF GOLD

JERRY AND S.A. AHERN

THE TAKERS are the intrepid Josh Culhane and the seductive Mary Mulrooney. These two adventurers launch an incredible journey into the Brazilian rain forest. Far upriver, the jungle yields its deepest secret—the lost city of the Amazon warrior women!

THE TAKERS series is making publishing history. Awarded *The Romantic Times* first prize for High Adventure in 1984, the opening book in the series was hailed by *The Romantic Times* as "the next trend in romance writing and reading. Highly recommended!"

Jerry and S.A. Ahern have never been better!

TAK–3

Share the joys and sorrows
of real-life love with

Harlequin American Romance!™

GET THIS BOOK FREE as your introduction to **Harlequin American Romance** — an exciting series of romance novels written especially for the American woman of today.

Mail to:
Harlequin Reader Service

In the U.S.
2504 West Southern Ave.
Tempe, AZ 85282

In Canada
P.O. Box 2800, Postal Station A
5170 Yonge St., Willowdale, Ont. M2N 5T5

YES! I want to be one of the first to discover **Harlequin American Romance.** Send me FREE and without obligation *Twice in a Lifetime.* If you do not hear from me after I have examined my FREE book, please send me the 4 new **Harlequin American Romances** each month as soon as they come off the presses. I understand that I will be billed only $2.25 for each book (total $9.00). There are no shipping or handling charges. There is no minimum number of books that I have to purchase. In fact, I may cancel this arrangement at any time. *Twice in a Lifetime* is mine to keep as a FREE gift, even if I do not buy any additional books. 154 BPA NAZJ

Name _____ (please print)

Address _____ Apt. no. _____

City _____ State/Prov. _____ Zip/Postal Code _____

Signature (If under 18, parent or guardian must sign.)

AMR-SUB-1

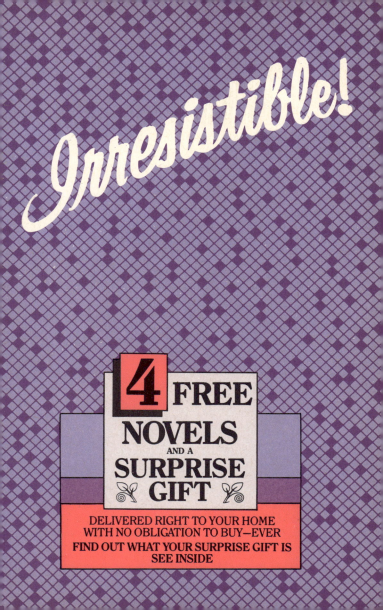

YOURS FREE FOR KEEPS!

Use the edge of a coin to rub off the box at right and reveal your surprise gift →

DEAR READER:

We would like to send you 4 Harlequin American Romances just like the one you're reading plus a surprise gift – all **ABSOLUTELY FREE.**

If you like them, we'll send you 4 more books each month to preview. Always before they're available in stores. Always for less than the regular retail price. Always with the right to cancel and owe nothing.

In addition, you'll receive **FREE**...
• our monthly newsletter HEART TO HEART
• our magazine ROMANCE DIGEST
• fabulous bonus books and surprise gifts
• special-edition Harlequin Bestsellers to preview for ten days without obligation

So return the attached Card and start your Harlequin honeymoon today.

Sincerely

Pamela Powers

Pamela Powers
for Harlequin

P.S. Remember, your 4 free novels and your surprise gift are yours to keep whether you buy any books or not.

4 EXCITING ROMANCE NOVELS PLUS A SURPRISE GIFT

FREE BOOKS/ SURPRISE GIFT

YES, please send me my four **FREE** Harlequin American Romances™ and my **FREE** surprise gift. Then send me four brand-new Harlequin American Romances each month as soon as they come off the presses. Bill me at the low price of $2.25 each (for a total of $9.00—a saving of $1.00 off the retail price). There are no shipping, handling or other hidden costs. There is no minimum number of books I must purchase. I can always return a shipment and cancel at any time. Even if I never buy a book from Harlequin, the four free novels and the surprise gift are mine to keep forever.   **154 CIA NA3T**

NAME_____

ADDRESS_____APT. NO._____

CITY_____

STATE_____ZIP_____

Offer limited to one per household and not valid for
present subscribers. Prices subject to change.

Mail to:

Harlequin Reader Service
2504 W. Southern Avenue,
Tempe, Arizona 85282

BUSINESS REPLY CARD

First Class   Permit No. 70   Tempe, AZ

Postage will be paid by addressee

Harlequin Reader Service
2504 W. Southern Avenue
Tempe, Arizona 85282

NO POSTAGE
NECESSARY
IF MAILED
IN THE
UNITED STATES

trusted with a classic. You're in danger of losing custody of your car if you don't take better care of it." His search brought him within a few feet of Lori.

Lori groaned and made a quick comparison to see which of them had the heavier bag. "Auto mechanics was one class I missed. Can we work on things one at a time, as my budget allows?"

Shade shook his head and grabbed at a morel before Lori could pick it. "At least three things aren't going to wait," he said seriously. "The brakes, a new battery, decent tires. I can get the batteries and tires for you wholesale." He straightened momentarily to ease a catch in his back. "I'll try to get to the brakes this weekend."

"You don't have to," Lori started to protest. She pretended to be concentrating on the search, but her eyes missed a couple of mushrooms poking up from the carpet of pine needles. "If you can just give me the name of a mechanic—"

"I could," Shade stopped her. He quickly claimed the mushrooms she'd missed and held them in front of her. "But you don't need that bill. This weekend. I'm holding you to that. In the meantime, I don't want you driving that car any more than you have to. It isn't safe."

Lori felt something cold click inside her. Those were Brett's words. He insisted on living his role as the male head of the house to the fullest. Their marriage was filled with one order after another. "I want you to stop by the store after work and pick up a few things." "Don't make any plans for the weekend; we have an invitation to a party." "Will you please buy yourself a dress? I'm sick of looking at jeans."

She wasn't married anymore. No man had the right

to give her orders. But she didn't tell Shade that. They were sharing what should be a delightful experience. Even Lori knew enough about the social graces—although Brett would probably argue that—to know that disagreements shouldn't be aired when there was a precious mood to be maintained. Lori gave Shade a noncommittal smile and turned the conversation to safer topics.

They scrambled around the clearing for a half hour, what they said to each other dictated by how close they were to each other at any given time. Lori gave the conversations only casual attention. She was busy absorbing her surroundings, touching base with her past, and whether she was willing to admit it or not, testing Shade's place in what had for years been her world. He fit in it completely.

She didn't expect to feel that, not after the way what he'd said had forced her to touch base with her marriage. But Shade seemed to have the same need she did to drink in pine scent, lift his eyes in the direction of bird calls, step carefully around the small, sharp pits in the earth left by deer hoofs. Lori noticed that he gave a pitch stain on his jeans no more than a casual glance and said nothing when a cloud of almost-invisible insects swirled briefly around his head.

He's comfortable here, she thought. *He belongs.*

"I'm afraid that's it for me," Shade said finally. To press home his point, he held aloft a bulging plastic sack. "What do you say we go home and clean these up."

Home. Lori didn't know which house he meant, but when she turned questioning eyes in his direction, the answer was in what he was and not any words he might say. Lori read the message in his eyes. He was challenging her, letting her know that there was a certain danger in going to his house. If she wasn't interested in testing the boundaries of their relationship, she should tell him to take her home now.

Lori didn't. She felt his warmth as he pulled her close to his side and acknowledged the chill that shot out in all directions from the spot where his lips met her neck. What they'd shared in the wilderness tonight had a profound effect on her. Shade had demonstrated his right to be here, with her. Dangerous or not, she wasn't ready to leave him.

He had to be feeling the same thing. When he brought her up next to his chest and sought her lips, she understood that he didn't want the evening to end, either. Lori surrendered to the emotion. She wanted— no, needed—to feel his lips on hers, needed his breath caressing her flesh. But that wasn't all. She needed more, much more than a kiss.

He didn't have to say it. Cleaning morels wasn't why they were leaving the clearing, getting into the Mustang, reentering civilization. What might happen once they were inside four walls would add a new dimension to their relationship. Lori didn't think about that dimension. Instead, she rested her head on his shoulder as he negotiated the car around chuckholes, her heart tripping over both itself and an ill-defined intensity igniting her nerve endings. As he turned to run his lips over her hair, she knew; he was feeling the same intensity.

When they reached the tree-lined residential street Shade lived on, Lori sat up. The area didn't satisfy her soul the way the house in the evergreens did, but she had to endorse his choice. The oak trees lining both sides of the street established the area as an older, well-cared-for neighborhood.

When Shade pulled into his driveway, Lori stepped out and looked back at the street. Two oaks stood sentry in front of Shade's house, blocking his front yard from prying eyes.

She let Shade lead her through the three-bedroom house with its quality but sparse furnishings. "Uninspired, isn't it?" Shade said after he'd shown her a bedroom with a single dresser and a deep blue coverlet draped over a rather lumpy looking bed. "I keep saying I'll give it more attention this winter."

"You don't belong here," Lori said without thinking. "Oh, it's a lovely neighborhood, but I don't feel your presence here the way I do at the other place."

"That's a little deeper than I want to get into tonight," Shade said as he steered her toward the kitchen so they could deposit their bounty in the sink. "You packed up and moved when you got divorced. I guess we all find different ways of putting down new roots after a divorce."

You're lost, aren't you, Lori thought as she watched Shade fill the sink with salty water to chase out any small insects in the mushrooms. *You need to be married.*

She shivered, drawing away from the revelation she'd just made. When he was married, Shade's life had direction. It was possible that he was actively looking for that direction again. Surely he didn't think she might be able to fill that bill. He had to realize how unfit, how unready, she was for such a role. All she wanted tonight was— She didn't finish the thought. "How did you find this place?" she asked in an effort to have something, anything, else to think about.

"I called a realtor. I told him how much space I needed, what I could afford. He took care of all the details."

"You mean you let him make that decision for you?" Shade was saying more about his state of mind following the divorce than he probably realized.

Shade shrugged. "I liked the neighborhood. The rest of it didn't matter that much."

"Oh." Shade had made Vicky sound like the lost one in their relationship. It wasn't until this moment that she fully understood how much Shade himself had been affected by the divorce. She wanted to give him something, anything, of herself to make things easier for him. "I—you made a good decision," she said with as much conviction as she could summon up. "It's a nice house."

"It's a house."

Almost before she knew she was going to do it, Lori reached out and laid her hand gently along the hard outline of Shade's jaw. She concentrated on the independent strands of hair taking off in all directions, the green eyes, like a deep, quiet pool in the middle of a river. They reminded her of swimming in the Yuba River with her father as a child and how she stayed close to him when they came to those deep pools because she couldn't shake the feeling that something could reach up from the bottom and touch her.

"What are you thinking about?" Shade asked. His hand covered hers, holding her palm against the hard bone and letting her feel his jaw working as he asked his question.

Lori laughed. They were on familiar ground now. "Have you ever gone swimming in a river in the middle of a forest? It's so cold you can't breathe but so clear and beautiful you don't ever want to swim in a swimming pool after that experience."

"No. I've never gone swimming in a river like that.

But I think I'd like to. I'd like to do it with you."

Sharing. Shade was talking about sharing experiences. "Black Bob had his favorite spots in California and Oregon and Washington. He didn't want to share them with anyone. Some of them were so remote we had to walk for miles to get there," she said, giving him a little more of herself.

"Do you think you could find them?"

"Oh, yes." Lori smiled. He was accepting what she was giving. It felt right. "I've probably been on every logging road in the western states. I might have a little trouble getting started, but I'd eventually find my way around."

"When can we go?"

Now he was taking the lead in the sharing that was taking place. She wasn't sure she was ready for that and tried to pull her hand away, but Shade wouldn't let her. "A river isn't anything like a swimming pool," she whispered, her words guiding her. "There are water snakes, and insects shed their skins on the rocks, and the footing is slippery."

"You liked it, didn't you?"

"I loved it." She felt her eyes come alive and didn't try to hide their sparkle.

"Then I want to do it. With you."

The rumble Shade's voice made on its way out of his chest stopped whatever thoughts Lori might have had. For an instant her mind flitted back to the night they first met, when she was aware of how deep the tones in his chest were. She'd been more interested in the sounds than the words then. That was happening again. Shade slowly pulled her hand away from his jaw and sandwiched it between his. Then he brought her hand to his lips and kissed the exposed tips.

"I want to do many things with you, Lori Black."

At his words Lori's legs went numb. In an effort to regain some sense of self-control, she tried to pull away, but something inside her needed the contact too much to allow her to try to escape. "I'd like that," she whispered, aware of how much of herself she was revealing but unable to stop. She was looking into emerald depths, caught in Shade's strength as surely as the wilderness had taken hold of a young girl's soul.

Shade took her in his arms, his massive hands covering the bulk of her back, pulling her hungry body toward his until she was no longer aware that she was in a dimly lit kitchen with mushrooms floating in a full sink. Lori lifted her face upward, wanting his lips on hers.

He obliged. Shade's lips were slightly parted, not in passion but in deep exploration. He'd waited so long for this! For as long as the kiss lasted, Shade believed that he was offering her more of himself than he had ever offered anyone before. Despite his need for her, he realized how much she was giving in return. Her arms went around his solid neck. He was aware of his strength, the powerful upper arms straining against the shirt fabric. He realized that his strength held no fear for her, and that knowledge affected him more than he thought it could. He'd never hurt her or push things faster or further than she was ready. Despite the machinery in the spare bedroom that kept those muscles in perfect tune, he had the necessary self-control not to take advantage of his strength. She was too precious to him for anything except complete physical equality.

Lori leaned forward until she was resting against him and parted her own lips in willing surrender. In the years since she'd placed a trusting hand in Black Bob's callused one, she'd never turned herself over to a man this way.

"Oh, God," Shade whispered. The sound rumbled in his chest and reached her breasts. "You feel so good, Lori. So good."

And I feel so safe here. Lori didn't speak. She wondered if she had lost the ability to work the necessary muscles in her throat, but the question didn't concern her enough to seek an answer. She boldly brought her tongue into play and tasted the soft insides of his lips. Muscles like iron; lips like a baby's cheek. Those simple contrasts said all she needed to know tonight about Shade Ryan.

With a groan Shade pulled away. He looked down at her with eyes that didn't seem to be focusing. He had to be sure. There could be no regrets. "I hope you know what you're doing," he whispered. "Because I'm not sure I do."

"I don't know anything," she admitted.

A fleeting smile touched Shade's lips. She was no more rational than he was. That was the emotional equality he was looking for to go with physical equality. He pulled one hand away from her back and brought it to her face. While he held her against him with his left, the middle finger on his right hand touched her lower lip so tentatively that he could feel the downy hairs. The knowledge made him hold his breath. He'd never known a woman's lip could be that sensitive.

Lori parted her lips and let Shade's finger find the entrance to her mouth. Now three fingers were tracing a slow, sensual pattern around her parted lips, a move that ignited nerve endings in her breasts and her belly.

Lori groaned in exquisite agony. She'd been married. Her husband had explored every inch of her. But Brett had never touched those nerves, never guessed the pleasure she was capable of feeling because a man's fingers were barely touching her lips.

When Shade removed his fingers, she thought she would cry out with wanting them back again, but before aching loss could wipe out pleasure, he was wrapping his fingers through the thick dark curls at the back of her head. He gently pulled her head back and bent over, consuming her lips with a mouth that was no longer interested in gentle exploration.

Lori, who had always fought for freedom, was securely in the grip of a man. His lips were pressed tightly against hers. One hand pressed against her back, giving her only minimum freedom. The other was grasping her hair so tightly that she knew there was no breaking free. But the strongest bonds came not from his strength but from two hungry mouths locked together. Lori gripped his powerful biceps in an effort to keep her balance, but her thoughts weren't on his total mastery over her.

What reasoning powers she still possessed were focused on the undeniable fact that there was a direct line from her lips to every nerve in her body. Lori strangled on a groan, spread her legs slightly and surrendered to the tidal wave that washed over her. Freedom was for later. Surrender, total surrender, was for this moment.

Chapter Seven

Lori lay on her back, knees drawn up slightly, arms exposed to the air. The cool sheets she'd slipped under a few minutes ago had absorbed her body heat, making her feel as if she were trapped in a sauna. She wanted to push the sheets away from her but lacked the strength to move. The window in Shade's bedroom was open, letting in the night air and sounds to reach her heated cheeks and ringing ears. She could hear the wind toying with the oak trees along Shade's street, the sounds of invisible crickets, the distant barking of a dog. They were familiar, comfortable sounds.

What her body was feeling was far from comfortable or familiar.

Lori drew in a deep breath and pulled the sheet away from her flesh. She wore nothing. Clean air touched the swell above her breasts and caused her nipples to respond. Not that they needed night air to respond. Shade was capable of doing that with a touch, a kiss.

He would be with her in a moment. She could hear him locking the front door, turning off the light in the kitchen. There hadn't been time for that a few minutes ago when he carried her into the bedroom and pulled down the sheet. There hadn't been time for ordinary things while he was slipping off her boots, unbuttoning her shirt, pulling her jeans off the trembling flesh of her hips. Now, wearing nothing save his jockey shorts, Shade was doing things she was incapable of thinking about.

Lori waited for the silent question. She should be asking herself what she was doing here, looking for some sign that said she'd changed her mind. It didn't come.

Instead, Shade came. She couldn't see him in the darkened room, she wasn't sure he'd made any sound. But she could sense his presence, smell him even. He was standing at the entrance to the room, his eyes seeking the still mound on his bed. Her mind's eye filled in the blanks. She pictured the elastic of his shorts clinging to his hipbones, the exquisite roll and ripple of muscle on his chest and upper arms, thick dark hairs matted over his taut thighs. The only thing her mind's eye didn't tell her was what he was thinking.

"I'm asking," he whispered. "Do you want to say no?"

"No. I won't tell you no."

When she sensed that he'd reached the bed, she lifted her hands and caught hold of his arms. He leaned slowly toward her, his breath on her exposed throat chasing away the night air. *I want you,* rang through her. *I want you!*

Shade sat gingerly on the edge of the bed, his hands telling him what his eyes couldn't. She hadn't moved since he placed her in the bed. She was here, waiting for him. For an instant Shade experienced something that might have been tears, but her fingers found his waist and chased away any thoughts other than what this night was for. There'd only been one woman in

Shade's life since his divorce, three dates ending with the woman's inviting him to come to her apartment. He couldn't even remember her name now, and that bothered him.

He couldn't imagine ever forgetting Lori Black. She was inside him as surely as her hands were on his exterior. He hadn't known it was possible to feel this way, to need this creature of the woods as desperately as he needed breath to live. Her possession of his thoughts, his physical sense, alarmed him even as he told himself that he surely wouldn't feel this possessed in the morning.

Gently, he pushed her to one side of the bed and lay down beside her. His hands were everywhere, cradling her breasts, rolling over the outline of her ribs, feathering the hairs low on her belly. He heard her sharp intake of breath and realized that possession, tonight, was a two-way street. She held his heart and body; he did the same for her.

Lori hadn't expected Shade to cover her body as quickly, as boldly, as he did. It gave her no time to prepare for each new assault on her senses. She'd been ready to feel his hands on her breasts. The lower exploration came before she was ready and carried her along in the sensation, as a twig is carried by a torrent of rushing water. She clung to him, grasping his biceps as if they could stem her headlong journey. Even as her fingers pressed into his muscle, she was reaching for his lips, sealing her to him, sealing her fate. There was only one way the night would end.

When Shade threw back the covering and rose on his elbow over her, she strained upward, pressing her breasts boldly against his chest. Their naked bodies touching from shoulders to toes wasn't enough. Lori needed the ultimate contact. She lay her head back on the pillow when his right hand found the hungry place that needed to be satisfied. Even then she needed his open mouth against hers; her tongue made an intimate assault as bold as the one his hand was making. She breathed sporadically, raggedly, through flared nostrils, sharing the air with him.

Her flesh and muscles and blood felt alive with her need. She could do nothing less than position herself for him, welcome him into her. He was over her now, his weight handled by his elbows, his hands somehow free to make contact with her hair and cheeks. But her thoughts weren't on his hands. He was offering her the most primitive pleasure she'd ever known. Lori's brain telescoped down until there was nothing except heat, intoxication, a need for fulfillment beyond any she'd ever had. She surrendered totally to what he was doing to her, knowing, somehow, of the surrender in him, as well.

The torrent of rushing water had become a raging river, taking everything she was or might be with it. Lori felt herself being lifted out of her body, reaching another plain, having the torrent lift her yet higher. She moved with Shade, her body mindlessly pacing itself to him. They were together in the current, traveling as one.

Then she was at the crest, suspended momentarily, shooting out and over. She heard herself sobbing something intelligible, but it didn't matter. The journey had been worth the destination. She understood, as she never had before, what it meant to be a woman.

Lori slept for three or four hours. The rest of the time she lay with her head resting on Shade's chest. She drank in the sound of his slumbering breath and recorded it to memory. There were no thoughts as to the morality of what they'd done. She'd needed Shade as she'd never needed a man before—might never need one again. In the morning she'd thank him for that.

Shade was the first one up. Lori became aware of the sounds of a shower running before she fully put the pieces together. She hadn't wanted to go back to sleep. She'd wanted to listen to him breathe. But she must have dozed off, and now he was gone from her and making himself ready to reenter the world that had seemed so far away last night. Lori slipped out of bed, slipped into the oversized shirt she'd worn last night and went into the kitchen to put on coffee. She was looking for the necessary ingredients when the aroma reached her. Shade had already thought of that.

She poured them each a cup and had started toward the bathroom with one when he appeared. "Your turn," he said softly. "I'm sorry. I have an early meeting."

"You're leaving?" She was aware of how naked she sounded, but there was no way she could hide what she was feeling.

"I'm afraid so." Like last night Shade was wearing only briefs, but this time his attire signified a retreating from her. "It was beautiful."

She didn't have to ask him what he was talking about. "It was," she whispered. "I could fix you some breakfast."

He shook his head. "It's a breakfast meeting." He came closer, took the steaming mug and pulled her close with his free arm. "We'll talk later," he said before kissing her.

After he'd left, Lori took a shower, made the bed

and then took her first true look at what he called home. The most outstanding room was the one next to his bedroom. It was a weight trainer's dream. There was a variety of equipment that looked like a cross between a medieval torture chamber and the latest in physical-fitness technology.

The living room contained a couch and matching chair, a coffee table, lamp and small TV. There was a beautiful hardwood table in the dining area, but it was covered with folders and files and other material Shade must have brought home from work. From the looks of the table, Shade probably never ate his meals there.

It wasn't until she was in her car heading toward the ranch that Lori shook off the residue of last night and concentrated fully on the day. They'd talk, he'd promised her. The promise sustained her and freed her to do what had to be done.

The other day she'd uncovered a cement fish pond built into the ground in front of the farmhouse. The pond had been so overgrown by vines that even Ruth had forgotten it existed. There were other, more pressing matters Lori could be concentrating on, but she decided to spend the day clearing around the pond, cleaning it out and having it filled. It would be something to show Shade, and maybe Ruth would feel like going to a pet store with her to pick out some hearty fish to stock it with.

Ruth was enthusiastic about Lori's project but begged off. "I'm sure I'll like anything you choose. I didn't get much sleep last night," the older woman explained.

Neither did I, Lori thought, but kept her thought to herself. Although she had hoped to get to town before the middle of the afternoon, she wound up having to drive into the city during the hottest time of the day. Despite the need to run several personal errands, she hurried back to the farm to deposit the fish before they expired. There was still a little clearing out that needed to be done around the pond, but at least it was filled with cool water and a half-dozen large, heavy-bodied goldfish were exploring their new home.

Lori thought about telling Ruth of her successful expedition, but because the drapes in Ruth's bedroom were drawn, Lori got in her car and drove home.

She'd just kicked off her shoes when the phone rang. "What do you have on hand to feed a hungry mechanic?" Shade asked without preliminary. "I'll be over in about a half hour."

Shade. He was coming here. Would there be any staying out of his arms if he walked in the door? "I'm not sure what I have," she stalled. "I didn't get to the store."

"You're hopeless," he groaned. "Look, I'm on my way to the auto-parts store. I'll grab some steaks or something, okay?"

"The auto-parts store?" Lori asked. She couldn't keep pace with his everyday conversation. "What for?"

"Can't you remember anything?" He lowered his voice for a moment. "If I didn't know better, I'd think you had your mind on something else. I told you I didn't want you driving your car any more than necessary until I've had time to go over it. I'm picking up spark plugs and a new battery. I think I'll have a mechanic look at the brakes before I do anything to them. I'm not sure what they need."

"A mechanic?" Lori protested. "I can't afford—"

"Don't tell me what you can afford," Shade interrupted. "Brakes aren't optional in a car. Don't worry. As long as you feed me, I'll do the work. I just want a second opinion before I tear your car apart." He said something about making sure the car was in the garage where he could work on it and then hung up.

Lori turned away from the phone, took a step toward the bedroom and wound up giving herself a hug. Shade was coming! She'd be seeing him in less than an hour! A glance at herself in the mirror told Lori that she had some work to do to erase the hot day from her face and body. She jumped into the shower, shivered under a cool spray and then quickly toweled off, remembering with a shiver that had nothing to do with being cold that Shade had seen her in a lot less than this. She slipped into jeans and a thin T-shirt and then grabbed her car keys. Lori eased her Mustang into the garage and pumped the brakes so that the car wouldn't roll into the far wall. It was then that she decided to see if any junk mail had made its way into the mailbox beside the road. There were two fliers from local businesses and a white envelope bearing the logo of Jordan Landscaping.

She'd read it later.

She went back inside and rummaged through the bathroom dresser for makeup. As she was putting on her lipstick, she felt the almost-physical presence of a vise reaching out to engulf her. Things had been moving terribly fast with Shade. Maybe it took seeing the envelope from her ex-husband to bring her up short.

What am I, she asked the image in the mirror. *You're acting like some animal in heat. Sure he has a zest for life and a fantastic house in the woods. That isn't enough reason to drop your guard and toy with more pain like the kind you put yourself and Brett through.* She'd thought she'd learned her lesson when the divorce became final. Now. Now she wasn't at all sure.

What you need is more time by yourself. That's what Black Bob always did.

Lori took a determined breath and turned off the bathroom light. It was sweet of Shade to offer to work on her car and bring dinner by, but she was going to have to talk to him about this, let him understand that she was going to put on the brakes, take some time to be by herself. To think. Surely, knowing what he did of her upbringing and unsuccessful marriage, he'd understand.

Unfortunately, when she opened the door to let Shade in, a serious conversation was thrown to the back of her mind by a kiss that lifted her onto her toes. "Umm, you look good enough to eat." Shade grinned as he released her. "I was hoping you'd meet me wearing nothing but a cheesecloth nightgown, but I guess I can live."

"A cheesecloth nightgown?" Lori cocked her head and relieved Shade of some of the packages he was gripping with one arm. She'd tell him what was on her mind—later. "I don't think they make them."

"They should. If that isn't an erotic thought, I don't know what is. Of course you could wrap yourself in one of those see-through curtains some people have in their kitchens. I'd like that just as well."

Lori blushed, responding despite herself to the image his words conjured up. "You're embarrassing me," she admitted.

"That's exactly what I had in mind." Shade deposited his packages on the kitchen table and started running his hands up and down her arms. "You're the best-looking thing I've seen all day. I spent six hours with a woman who had spent her life collecting dolls from all over the world. I've seen everything from French cancan dolls to vestal virgins, but none of them can hold a candle to you."

Lori's mind flitted briefly with what she tried to tell herself in the bathroom, but the thoughts evaporated before Shade's caress. "Ah, do you want dinner before you look at my car?" she stammered.

"What I want has nothing to do with food."

Lori glanced into Shade's eyes. He was ricocheting between joking and a seriousness that both alarmed and intrigued her. If she didn't stop him, she couldn't be sure how far the conversation would go. How far did she want it to go, she had to ask. "You're in a rare mood tonight," she pointed out, skirting the greater issue.

"Aren't I, though. Let's just say it's been a long day in the trenches and I'm eager to put all that behind me." Shade gripped her shoulders and pulled her to him for a kiss that went further and deeper than the one they shared at the door. He sensed a change in her from last night that bothered him. He didn't like this reserve, this holding back. But maybe he knew how to deal with that. He continued boldly. "All the time I was listening to that old lady talking about dolls as if they were her children, I was thinking about you. You're doing strange things to me."

Lori zeroed in on Shade's last sentence. He was no longer joking. "What kind of things?" she asked, frightened and yet knowing she had to hear the answer.

Shade stared down at her, his green eyes letting her partially but not all the way into his thoughts. "I can't explain them all," he started. "When Vicky and I got divorced, I told myself that was the last time I wanted to get into a complex relationship. I knew I needed time to reassess my thinking, try to figure out why I'd chosen a child bride to be a father figure to. I can't say I've done all the thinking I need to on that score, but I'm finding that all my thinking these days is about you."

"I'm flattered," Lori said in an attempt to lighten the conversation. The look in Shade's eyes told her she'd failed. "I've done a lot of thinking about you," she admitted.

"And what conclusions have you come to?"

"Not that fast." Lori pulled back, but not far enough away so he had to let go of her. "You're the one who started this deep conversation."

"So I did. Lori." He lowered himself onto a kitchen chair and pulled her onto his lap. "Have you ever wondered whether you were capable of a satisfactory relationship? Of course you have. Everyone does that. That's what I've been thinking about all day. Do you know what conclusion I've come to?"

"No. What?"

"That I'm tired of thinking. That I want to spend some time with you doing whatever we want to."

Lori trembled briefly. "One step at a time. Is that what you're saying?"

Shade nodded. "I guess I am. Does that make sense?"

It was Lori's turn to nod. She'd had the same thoughts just before he arrived. "Things were so simple last night. They aren't anymore."

Shade wrapped his arm around her waist, his fingers creeping upward until they were toying with her rib cage. He wasn't sure he wanted her to go on, but what she was thinking would have to come out sooner or later. "Does that bother you?"

Lori started to nod, but the gesture turned into a shake of the head instead. Shade's thumb had found the base of her bra. "I was a failure as a wife," she admitted, burying her face in the mass of curls on top of Shade's head. "I can't impose myself on anyone that way again."

"You wouldn't trust yourself in any kind of relationship? You think you'd be hurting the guy?" Shade's free hand covered Lori's breast while his other hand gripped her securely around the waist. "You don't think you have anything to offer a man?"

How could he hold her like this and ask that question? Shade wouldn't be touching her if he wasn't ready to dispute his words. Lori parted her lips and closed her teeth around a lock of hair. She pulled gently. "I don't like that kind of a question," she warned in mock seriousness.

"Ow! All right. I take that back." Shade's thumb and forefinger were swallowing inches of blouse fabric until the garment was bunched above Lori's bra. His thumb ducked under the taut white fabric and found firm, swollen flesh. "Besides," he whispered, "you have a lot to offer a man."

Lori's arms had been at her side, but now she wrapped them around Shade's head. It felt right to be burying her face in his hair while her arms encompassed his head. It was as if she had some control over him at the same time she was seeking safety and warmth from him. He was content to concentrate on her breasts, to wait until she could no longer pretend to be ignoring what he was doing to her.

Lori surrendered. She released Shade's hair and let her muscles relax, concentrating on nothing except what his fingers inside her bra were doing. There was a taste of the forbidden, of the dangerous, to what was happening, because he was caressing her in a lighted kitchen with her clothing on instead of naked in a darkened bedroom. Shade's hand left her waist and found the fastening at the back of her bra. She shivered once as her breasts were freed but didn't try to draw away. Instead, she continued to rest her face on Shade's head, her thoughts going no further than his hands. Shade was still holding her on his lap with his left hand, but his right one had gone from a teasing exploration of one breast to a bold capture of both mounds.

Lori squirmed on his lap, her senses screaming. She was being ignited in a way that went beyond her comprehension. What they were doing rode the boundary between play and sensual testing. That in itself was driving her frantic with wanting him.

"This is what I was thinking about when that woman kept yammering at me," Shade whispered. "I tried to concentrate on what she was saying, but my fingers were itching from the need to touch you."

"You sound sure of yourself." Her mouth, buried in his hair, made a muffled sound.

"I remember what happened last night."

"Oh."

"Does that surprise you?"

"Yes. No. I don't know," Lori admitted, although it was hard to think with Shade's hand over her breasts, the nipples nestled in his palm. "I thought you were sure of yourself."

"The only thing I'm sure of was that I wanted to make love with you last night. You agreed to it."

Lori struggled to open her eyes. "I agreed because—" *Because I wanted you so much it scared me.* "Things are happening right now," she pointed out with much more self-control than she felt. Surely he could sense her tensing thigh muscles on his lap.

"Yes. They are. Lori? Do you want dinner, or do you want to go into the bedroom?"

I want you to make love to me, she admitted, if only to herself. But he was asking her to set the boundaries of their relationship, to put on the brakes. Because she hadn't been able to dismiss her thoughts while in the bathroom, she spoke the words she wasn't sure she had the courage for. "I think we better eat."

Shade groaned and shoved her off his lap. He rose to his feet before she could think whether she wanted to turn toward or away from him. "I bought a couple of rib steaks," he was saying in a tone she'd never heard before. "Do you want me to start the barbecue?"

Lori tried to meet Shade's eyes, but it was obvious that he didn't trust himself to make that contact. He was rummaging through the package he'd brought in, his eyes as far as possible from her disheveled blouse.

"That—that would be fine." She could reach out and wrap her arms around him, burrow into the safe haven of his chest and feel his arms around her. "I'll make a salad." She pulled down on her blouse with fingers that hated their task.

Shade turned around. He was holding two steaks in his hands, but as soon as he saw what she was doing, he dropped them on the counter. What a liar he was turning into. He hadn't come here to work on her car or feed her. "Oh, hell." He took the step that brought them together and pulled her hands away from her task. "I don't give a damn about dinner."

"Neither do I."

Thank God! Until this instant he hadn't been sure how she'd react to seeing him. Her words were proof that she didn't regret last night. Shade swept her into his arms and held her tightly against his chest. He could feel her drawing in deeply for air and wondered if he was doing the same. "I'm not going to ask you again."

"I know. Shade, I want you."

Lori buried her head in Shade's chest as he carried her into the bedroom. She released her grip from around his neck only when he started to lower her onto the king-size bed. Lori lay back on the coverlet, knowing that Shade and Vicky had made love here but not caring. She was the woman with Shade Ryan tonight. He was unbuttoning his shirt for her and pulling off his belt for her.

She needed his help to rid herself of her clothes, but she needed no help when he joined her on the bed.

Lori remembered everything she'd learned about Shade last night, but now she was learning even more. The flesh on the small of his back was sensitive; if she wanted to take advantage of it, she could control him now that she knew that. Somehow her hands found the back of his thighs and tried to stretch her fingers over the width of muscle she found there. Her fingers rode lower and pressed against the sinew behind his knees. He was magnificent, magnificent and hers!

At the same time Lori was revealing things about herself that even she hadn't known until tonight. She loved the feel of a masculine finger brushing lightly over her earlobe. That same finger on the inside of her elbow was all it took to shoot electric sparks throughout her body. At his prompting, she lay inert on her back, hands uneasy by her side while he feathered her stomach and hipbones with his mouth and tongue. When she could no longer stand what his exploration was doing to her senses, she reached for him, digging her nails almost cruelly into his shoulder blades.

Shade waited until she was gripping him tightly and then straightened his back, bringing her off the bed with him. His hands found her backbone, the swell of her buttocks. He pressed against the flesh there, pushing her tightly against his body, cementing her body into his mind. His mouth reached for her hair, nipping and pulling gently as she'd done earlier. He wanted her, wanted to make love, but there was no urgency in his wanting. For maybe the first time in his adult life he realized that there was more to making love than the final act. There was the touching and the kissing and play that tuned them both into each other and blunted the definitions between their separate personalities.

"I can't get enough of you," he whispered, his hands back to exploring the velvet flesh around her naked waist. Her fingers dug into his shoulders, but he felt no pain. "I'm getting drunk on you."

Lori didn't answer, but that didn't bother Shade. He rather suspected that she was at a point beyond speech. As his hands worked their way around to the front of her waist, he learned what he needed to know from the ragged way she was breathing. There wouldn't be any stopping tonight. Tonight was everything he'd ever wanted a night to be.

"I'll work on your car tomorrow" were the last words he said.

Chapter Eight

Lori woke up first. She'd been sleeping on her side with her face away from Shade but her back resting securely against his strength. She stared out the bedroom window for several minutes, thinking of nothing except the slow shading from dark to light as the sun touched the evergreens. She could hear Shade's deep regular breathing behind her, a sound so right that it blended in with the sounds of the morning birds.

At length she became aware that the arm under her had fallen asleep and her fingers were in need of circulation. Lori eased herself out of bed and tiptoed to the window, rubbing her arm to return circulation to it. She was wearing nothing, which allowed the breeze coming in the open window to blow feathering kisses along her body.

Just before she stepped into the bathroom, Lori glanced back at Shade. His hair was flattened against his temple, and there was a crease mark on his cheek, little signs that made him unbelievably precious to her. If she hadn't been afraid that he would awaken, she would have gone over and kissed him.

Instead, Lori showered and dressed, trying to put her mind on her plans for the day. A man was coming to deposit a load of gravel on the road leading to the farm. Lori wanted to be there to make sure none of the gravel spilled onto the grounds.

She thought about Ruth and smiled. The older woman would approve of what had happened last night. Ruth was both a realist and a romantic. She liked Lori and Shade. She wanted to see them happy and made no bones about the fact that she thought they'd be happiest together.

Was it really as simple as that? She wondered if she and Shade could climb into the same bed every night and be happy. This morning—this morning she simply didn't know what her answer was. What she did know was that she'd never again be able to look at Shade without thinking of the gift, the knowledge, he'd given her.

She heard footsteps but didn't turn around until Shade spoke. "I'm starved, woman. Don't you ever feed people who come to your house?"

"It's your house in case you've forgotten," she pointed out. Shade had pulled on pants but was wearing nothing from the waist up. The crease mark on his cheek had faded, but there was another one across his chest.

"Minor detail," Shade pointed out. "You lured me here with talk of an ailing car, seduced me when all I wanted was something to eat, and now you won't even offer me a cup of coffee."

Lori studied Shade for a long minute before answering. "You're in a fine mood this morning. I don't know if I can keep up with you."

Shade frowned but didn't speak until he'd started the coffeepot perking. "I'm not sure I can, either," he said, sitting in the chair he'd used last night before they went into the bedroom. "I told myself I wasn't going to let that happen, that we'd have dinner, I'd work on your car, and maybe we'd talk. That didn't happen."

Lori leaned against the kitchen counter. Even when sitting down, his power overwhelmed her. "Do you regret what happened?"

"Isn't that what the man is supposed to ask the woman?" he asked in the same light tone he'd greeted her with a few minutes ago. "No. I don't regret what happened. And I don't think you do, either. But Lori, we both said things about not rushing into a relationship. I remember what it was like the first few weeks after Vicky and I separated. A divorce makes a person vulnerable. Wary and vulnerable all at the same time. I told myself I wasn't going to rush you into anything. I didn't keep my word, did I?"

"No, you didn't," Lori admitted. No matter what they might wind up saying to each other, this conversation was essential. "But Shade, it wasn't your doing. I was as willing to have it, both times, happen."

"I took advantage of what I knew you were going through. I know all about vulnerability firsthand."

"How do you know what I'm going through?" she asked. "Not everyone who goes through a divorce feels the same thing." For the first time today she thought about the letter from Brett waiting for her to open. She could almost sense him reaching out toward her, reminding her of everything that had gone wrong between them.

"Maybe. Maybe not." Shade glanced at the still-perking pot and then turned his alert eyes back on her. "But you're in the process of asking yourself questions about your ability to have a positive relationship with a man. You need time to ask yourself those questions."

How wise Shade was. "You're right," Lori whispered, finally admitting what had been tugging at the back of her mind since she woke up. "Brett told me that I wasn't cut out for sharing myself with someone else. I should have thought about that instead of—"

"Instead of letting your body get the upper hand."

Lori blushed and ducked her head. "Something like that."

"Don't be embarrassed," Shade pressed. "There's nothing wrong with what we did."

Wasn't there? Maybe not for Slade. She was the one who had been so sure a few short weeks ago that she wasn't cut out for personal relationships. She still didn't have the answer to that question. It was getting harder to focus on the necessary answer with Shade around, distracting her, arousing her. She wanted Shade physically. There was no denying that. But she didn't know if she was good for him.

"Maybe we have been rushing things," she said softly, reluctantly. "Maybe I am vulnerable."

Shade groaned. "I was afraid you'd agree with me. Look." He rose to his feet and stuck out his hand. "Why don't we shake on it? Whatever is happening between us is going to have to slow down for a while until you get your head together."

Lori stuck out her own hand and shook his soberly. She didn't want to make an agreement like this. She wanted to dive for the comfort of his arms. But that wouldn't be fair to either of them. What had Shade said? That she had to get her head together first?

Lori didn't touch Shade again before he left. For several minutes after she was left alone, she busied herself with everyday tasks, but she knew she was only putting off what had to be done. The letter from Brett was partially responsible for the mood she was in. The only way she could deal with her mood was to give it full rein.

When she opened the envelope, she discovered another small one inside the one from Brett. The short note was from her father.

"I'm sending this to Brett since I don't have your address," he wrote. "I guess he'll send it on to you. I've been working on an operation outside Seattle, but that's just about over. I was thinking I could get in touch with you and we could spend some time together."

The note wasn't signed, but that didn't surprise Lori. He hadn't said how he intended to get in touch with her, but knowing Black Bob, he'd simply call Brett when he was free and curtly ask how to contact his daughter. That was nice, Lori thought, blinking back tears that came from a childhood filled with warm memories. She'd like to see her father. She wondered what he'd think of Shade.

Reading the letter from Brett wasn't as easy. His bold script was impersonal and to the point as he explained that the letter from Black Bob had arrived the day before. "I guess I might as well tell you this now," Brett went on. "You'll find out, anyway. I'm getting married. I know; I told you I wasn't going to jump into anything. But she's right for me. I'm not like you. I never wanted to be a hermit. I need someone in my life."

"I'm not like you. I never wanted to be a hermit." Lori thought about these words a lot during the hours she spent at the farm that day. To outsiders she probably appeared to be a competent woman who knew her mind and stood her ground when the driver of the gravel truck wanted to turn around on a patch of ground carpeted with clover. But Lori begrudged the minutes she had to spend talking with the man. She wanted to work alone today, to redirect a vine climbing up the side of the well house so it wouldn't try to set down a root system in the rotting wooden roof. She wanted to listen to the birds and peacocks and wind whistling through the growing wheat. She wanted to feel the wind on her face and arms and hands and remember how much of her upbringing was tied up in sensations like that. She needed to get back in touch with what she was and how she felt when she asked Brett for a divorce. It wasn't what she wanted to do, but she knew she'd never resolve her inner conflict until she had. Brett knew her, maybe better than anyone else. He believed she was destined to spend her life alone.

Shade hadn't said anything about getting in touch with her, but she figured he'd call when she got back to the house. Her car was still ailing. If they could stick to the hands-off agreement they'd shaken on that morning, there was still a set of spark plugs on the kitchen counter. Having him here would put off the time of coming to grips with what she was.

Shade called a little before 7:00 P.M. His message was short and to the point. "I've been railroaded into attending a meeting of the county commissioners tonight. Something about their needing information on historic places that qualify for a tax freeze and how to go about getting a couple of other places considered for the freeze. This could go on half the night."

Lori sobbed inside but forced her voice to remain neutral. She said something about needing to spend time on setting up a pruning schedule for the fruit trees and wound up with a semicheerful good-bye. It wasn't fair! A man's voice shouldn't have the power to trigger memories of wild lovemaking.

Alone, she learned something else about his voice. The memory of it echoing inside her made it impossible for her to think about what Brett had said.

She slept poorly and went to the farm dragging the next morning. She would have liked to take Ruth walking to show her what she'd been doing, but Ruth put her off with vague comments about expecting a phone call from a cousin living in Wyoming. Lori spent the day identifying and photographing close-ups of several flowering bushes for future reference. She met with a member of the local horticultural society and gave the woman permission to cut slips of maiden pink for transplanting. Lori resented the intrusion into her thoughts, but Shade had told her that community relations were important in the right kind of publicity for the restoration project.

That evening she prepared a quick dinner and set about working on the pruning schedule she hadn't been able to concentrate on the night before. She actually lost herself in the work when the phone rang. Lori stumbled while hurrying from the dining room where her work was set up to the kitchen telephone, but the masculine voice she wanted to hear from wasn't on the other end of the line. "Lori Black?" a high-pitched woman's voice asked.

"Yes. Can I help you?" Lori asked, fighting down a wave of depression.

"Mrs. Black. I'm Vicky Ryan. Shade told me you were living in the house."

Vicky. Shade's ex-wife! "Where are you?" Lori asked before she could catch herself. "I'm sorry. That wasn't very polite. I just didn't expect to hear from you."

"I didn't expect to be back here so soon," the woman with the little-girl voice said. "Things came up, and I had to cut my tour short. I don't want to disturb you, but there are things I need from the house."

Lori wondered if Shade knew Vicky was back in town. Maybe that was why she hadn't seen him last night or heard from him today. "Of course," Lori said, grateful that certain responses were expected of her and she wouldn't have to grope her way through a relationship with Shade's ex-wife. "I just wish I'd known. I'll be out of here as soon as I can." Lori allowed herself a quick glance toward the kitchen window. She didn't want to leave here and find a place to stay down in the valley.

"Oh, no!" Vicky's words cut through Lori's thoughts. "I'm not going to kick you out. I don't want to live there. But, well, when do you think it would be convenient for me to pick up a few things?"

Lori blinked and concentrated. The conversation was ridiculous. Vicky Ryan shouldn't be asking for permission to come to her own house. "Right away," Lori said, and then cringed when Vicky agreed.

The two women hung up, and Lori returned to the material she'd spread out on the dining-room table. Should she clear any evidence that she'd made herself completely at home here? Instead of making that decision, Lori returned to the phone and tried to call Shade. All she got for her troubles was his recorded message telling her to leave her name and number. Lori hung up before hearing the beep giving her permission to speak.

She hurried into the bedroom and straightened the coverlet. Then she went into the bathroom and put away the hairbrush and toothpaste left behind that morning. She was hiding the last evidence of her dinner dishes when the doorbell rang.

Nothing about Vicky Ryan surprised Lori. Shade had done a good job of describing his ex-wife. The woman—a girl, really—was shorter than Lori, with youthful, flawless skin and hair too blond to give nature all the credit. She wore a ridiculous amount of makeup, which, to Lori's way of thinking, masked an innocent purity. Despite her tailored skirt and blazer and the expensive ruby ring on her right hand, Vicky was anything but a self-assured young woman. Her hands fluttered in front of her and she shifted her hips repeatedly as she tried to meet Lori's eyes. "I can't get over how brave you are," Vicky said as Lori was closing the door behind them. "I'd be scared to death to stay here alone."

Lori smiled and led the way into the living room. She would have liked Vicky to make the initiative, but obviously the younger woman didn't know what to do now that she was inside the house. "It doesn't bother me," Lori said. "I grew up in the woods, so I'm used to it."

Vicky perched delicately on the edge of a chair and waited for Lori to sit down.

"Shade thinks I'm such a child. I tried to stay here. I really did. But I hate living alone."

Lori took a minute to note the contrast between Vicky's almost-adolescent demeanor and her own comfort at wearing an old T-shirt and going around barefoot. "Not everyone is cut out for living alone," Lori acknowledged. *Just me,* she thought distractedly. *At least that's what my ex-husband says.*

"I wish Shade would see that. But then he thought I was crazy to go off on that tour through Europe. Nothing I do pleases him."

"Oh, I'm sure that's not true," Lori pressed, not sure why she should discuss the relationship between Vicky and Shade. "Besides, why should you try to please him?" Lori grinned. "We women are liberated. We can do whatever we want."

Vicky returned Lori's smile. "That's what my friend, the one who got me to go on the tour, kept telling me. Maybe that's why I cut my trip short. I want to get on with my life."

Lori nodded appreciatively. Vicky still sounded and looked like an insecure teenager, but what she'd said showed that the younger woman had been doing a lot of thinking. "What can I do to help you?" she asked. "What do you need? Where are you living?"

The smile left Vicky's face. "In a motel. At least I am until I can find a place to rent. I tried to call Shade when I flew in today to see if he'd find me a place, but I couldn't get a hold of him."

You don't want Shade to choose where you live, Lori thought, but she bit her tongue. She hadn't known Vicky long enough to say something like that. Lori told Vicky a little about her unsuccessful attempts to find housing in the valley, but she had the feeling Vicky wasn't really listening.

"How long have you known Shade?" Vicky asked.

Lori blinked. She had no idea how much Shade had told his ex-wife about the woman living in their house. She briefly sketched the professional relationship she had with Shade, winding up with the agreement to have her stay in the house until its future had been decided. "Of course if you want to stay here—" Lori started to say.

Vicky actually shuddered. "No, thank you! I know what I can and can't do, and staying here is something

I'll never be able to do. I looked at a condominium today, but I know what Shade will say. He thinks condos are the most ridiculous excuse for a home he's ever heard of."

"What does it matter what Shade thinks?" Lori asked. "It's your life."

Vicky wrapped her fingers around her upper arms and sank deeper in her chair. "Shade makes alimony payments. As long as it's his money—"

Lori blinked. She tried to put herself in the position of a divorced woman dependent on her ex-husband's money to survive, but it was almost beyond her comprehension. "Oh," she wound up saying. "Are you trying to find a job?"

To her surprise Vicky showed the first true animation she had since walking into the house. "I want to. In fact, I wanted to look for work when Shade and I first separated, but I was so confused, what with the business with the lawyer and everything. I really didn't do anything for several months. Then my friend insisted I go on this tour. That's one of the reasons I came back when I did. I want to get my life going. But—" Vicky dropped her head for a minute. "I don't have any real job skills. I was just out of high school when Shade and I married. I didn't want to be anything but a wife. That's what Shade wanted, too."

Shade had wanted a wife who had no existence beyond the house and him. That gave Lori a glimpse that she'd never had before of the man, but this wasn't the time to dwell on that. "What would you like to do?" she asked Vicky in what she hoped was a helpful tone.

"I don't know," Vicky moaned. "I took typing in high school, but that was so long ago, and I wasn't very good at it. I applied to a nursing school while I was married, but I couldn't keep up with some of the courses. Shade said I wasn't cut out for nursing.''

Lori frowned. Maybe Vicky would be a nurse now if her husband hadn't been so quick to let her drop out of school. Lori couldn't help but wonder what kind of a woman Vicky would be now if Shade hadn't always been there with a safety net stretched under her. ''Maybe you should look at nursing again?'' Lori suggested. ''You're a few years older now.''

''I don't know. Oh, it's so complicated,'' Vicky moaned again. ''That's why I couldn't enjoy the tour. I knew I had some big decisons to make. I had to be back here, not in Europe, to make those decisions. But I have to find a place to live before I can think about anything else.''

Lori couldn't argue with that logic. At least Vicky knew herself well enough to understand that she couldn't take on more than one major decision at a time. ''I don't know what's so wrong with a condominium if that's what you want,'' Lori said. ''Shade doesn't have to live in it, so what does he care?''

''You know how he is about this place. He can't understand why anyone would want to live with neighbors on the other side of the wall. But I need people around me. I like the idea of having people look out for each other.''

''And it makes you feel safer, doesn't it?'' Lori asked. It wouldn't be her life-style, but if Vicky was enough in tune with her feelings to believe she'd feel safe in a condominium, she should be allowed to do that. ''Is there some way you could try one out for a few weeks before making a decision?''

''I don't know.'' Vicky brightened. ''I hadn't thought about that.''

"All they can do is tell you no," Lori pointed out. "You'll never know unless you ask."

"You're right. Of course there's still Shade to contend with."

"He isn't going to stop making alimony payments, is he? He wouldn't cut you off if you weren't spending the money the way he thought you should?" Lori couldn't imagine Shade ever doing that.

"Oh, no." Vicky shook her head vigorously. "He didn't think much of my going on that tour, but he went ahead and paid for my share of the expenses, anyway."

"Well, then." Lori spread her arms and settled back in her chair. "Go for it. It's your life."

Vicky smiled briefly, tentatively. "Yes. It is my life. I just wish I didn't feel so unsure about it."

"Vicky, we all feel unsure at times," Lori admitted. "You're hardly alone there."

"Do you mean it? I mean, you're so independent and all. You have a responsible job, and you're not afraid to live up here by yourself. You don't know how much I envy you."

"Don't," Lori admonished, feeling a bit like Vicky's big sister. "I'm not nearly as together as you make me sound. I couldn't make a success of my marriage."

"But you found yourself a job, moved, all without anyone holding your hand. That's what I envy about you."

"I didn't have any choice," Lori admitted. "I'd decided my marriage was over. I couldn't very well continue to hang on to my husband's shirttail."

"That's what I've done." Vicky's voice was a sad whisper. "I'm not proud of myself. But it's so hard to know what to do. I've never had to make those kinds of decisions before.''

Lori leaned forward, acknowledging an urge to pat Vicky on the shoulder. "There's a first time for everything. We all have to do things we haven't done before.''

"I guess. It's just that it's harder for me than it is for most people. Look, I've taken up enough of your time. What I need is— If you don't mind, I'm going to need some silverware and dishes. Lord, I hate the motel I'm in. I have to find a place to live soon.''

Lori got to her feet and started toward the kitchen. "Look at a condominium. Listen to me," she said, turning back toward Vicky. "I'm giving you advice when that's the last thing you need. It's your decision.''

Vicky straightened her shoulders with an effort. "You're right. It is my decision. I guess all Shade can do is call me foolish.''

Lori found it hard to believe that Shade would ever call Vicky foolish, but since she hadn't been around to watch the interaction between them, she kept her opinion to herself. She tried to get Vicky to take more kitchen supplies than the fragile-looking woman wanted and then gave up. If Vicky didn't think she needed more than two pots, that was her business. She didn't need someone else butting in, telling her what to do. As Vicky was getting ready to leave, Lori wished her luck and asked Vicky to let her know when she'd found a place to live. She found herself meaning every word of it. She was interested in seeing if Vicky could put her life on course.

It wasn't until two days later that Lori learned Shade was the last to hear that Vicky was back in town. Lori had gone to the museum to meet with the financial director about some revisions of anticipated expenses for materials from a local grange. She was just finishing up when Shade walked in on the meeting.

"You should be happy, Frederick," Shade teased the financial director. "It isn't often people tell you they're going to spend less money than they thought they were going to. That isn't a trait you often see in a woman."

Frederick muttered something about needing to plug the figures into the computer and scurried out of the room. Lori waited until they were alone. "What do you have against women today?" she challenged. Her anger over her inability to come to grips with what she needed out of life made it easy for her to snap at the man who had complicated that life. "You're trying to stereotype us all."

"Am I? Then I apologize," Shade said, not sounding at all apologetic. "It's just that my ex-wife informed me this morning that she wants to sign a short-term lease for some damn fancy condominium. It'll cost less than her staying at a motel, so maybe I shouldn't argue."

Lori gathered her papers and stood up. She'd just gone through several days of not seeing this man, wondering how much he was responsible for the fact that being alive wasn't the same comfortable boring experience it had been before. "Why don't you let Vicky do what she has to? She's over the age of consent, you know."

"Look who is in a bad mood," Shade countered. "Are you holding it against me because I haven't been in touch with you?"

Lori shook her head. Yes, she'd missed Shade more than she wanted to admit, but she'd also appreciated the time to concentrate on her thoughts, her emotions.

"We were moving awfully fast. I think the past few days were necessary."

"Don't stand there in that see-through blouse and tell me that and expect me to agree," Shade said softly.

Lori glanced down. Her blouse was far from transparent, but the fabric was soft enough that it followed the outlines of her breasts. "I didn't do that on purpose."

"I know you didn't. It's just that my imagination starts working overtime whenever I see you. Vicky told me she's already seen you, picked up some things from the house. Why didn't you tell me?"

"That's between you and Vicky," Lori pointed out. "I'm not going to come running to you every time your ex-wife makes a move."

"Maybe you should," Shade said, his eyes narrowing. "That seems to be the only way I can keep track of what Vicky's up to."

"Shade, will you listen to yourself?" Lori warned. "That's your ex-wife you're talking about, not your daughter. Vicky's a free woman. She can come and go as she pleases."

"And spend my money as she pleases. I'm sorry." Shade placed his arm around Lori's shoulders. "I didn't mean to drop this on you. It's just that the habit of keeping tabs on my less than mature wife has been pretty deeply ingrained out of necessity. I know how irresponsible, how indecisive, she is. I'm always having to bail her out of one mishap or another."

"Maybe you should stop doing that," Lori said, forcing herself to concentrate on the topic despite the undeniable distraction of Shade's arm around her. "Let Vicky make her mistakes and learn from them."

"That's easier said than done, especially when you're

the one paying the bills. Vicky said you approved of this condominium business." Shade's voice held a note of disapproval.

"I told Vicky it was her decision and she'd never know what she thought of a condominium if she didn't give one a try."

"That's—forget it. I don't want to fight with you. Look, what else do you have to do today?"

Lori glanced up at the large wall clock above the desk. It was already after 4:00 P.M. "I was going to go out to the grange for some fertilizer and tools, but I'd have to rush making my choices. I don't want to have to do that."

"That's what I call a good decision." Shade grinned, the light in his eyes warming her heart. "I'll tell you what. If you can promise to behave yourself, I'll do some of that car work I promised the other night. I know I'm pretty irresistible, but I'm never going to get your car in shape if you insist on throwing yourself at me."

Lori eagerly joined in Shade's mood. They had been intense around each other. A casual, joking relationship was much safer. She frowned, pretending to be making a weighty decision. "I'll tell you what," she said slowly. "I've seen you work. I think your efforts are at least worth a hamburger. I might even throw in a salad if you don't track in any grease."

Shade gave her a quick squeeze. "Sounds like an honest wage for an honest day's work. Why don't you head on home? I'll finish up a few things here and join you."

Lori stopped at the grocery store for tomatoes and onions and hamburger buns. As a consequence, she'd only been at the house a few minutes before Shade showed up. He had a pair of coveralls in one hand. Apparently he was determined to accomplish his intended task this time. So be it, Lori acknowledged, willing herself not to let her eyes stay too long on his body. They'd skirted the edges of an argument earlier. Tonight they should move cautiously, tending to business and not bodily demands.

As Lori was pouring them a glass of wine, Shade asked her a few questions about her car, his features neutral, his hands never straying to her body. Then he went into the bedroom to change while Lori started looking through her mail. It wasn't until she had separated the bills from advertisements that she realized she'd been thinking about the envelope that came the other day.

"You're looking sober," Shade said as he rejoined her. "Bad news?"

"Not today." Lori spent the better part of a minute deciding what she should say next. Finally, she got up, reached for the envelope near the telephone and handed it to Shade. "My ex-husband is getting married," she said.

Shade glanced at both letters and then looked at her. "Does that bother you?"

"Not really," Lori admitted. He wasn't commenting on what Brett had said about her. "I just hope things work out for him. It seems as if he's moving awfully fast."

"Some people are like that. There's one good thing about a failed marriage. It usually tells people what they don't want the second time around."

If they're sure they're cut out for a second time around, Lori thought before pushing that tired thought to the back of her mind. "I'm glad he sent the letter from

Black Bob. He hopes we can get together. I'd like that,''
she said softly.

Shade leaned down and kissed Lori chastely on the
tip of her nose. "You know what I was thinking? The
museum makes extensive use of oral histories. Do you
think Black Bob would speak into a tape recorder, talk
about what it was like to work in the woods all his life,
the changes he's seen, that sort of thing?''

Lori responded to Shade's kiss by burrowing into the
warmth of his chest. "If you go slow with him. Dad's
kind of a rare breed. He doesn't like to talk much, but
he'll reminisce when he's in the right mood. He might
do it if he's convinced future generations will benefit
from what he says.''

"See if you can talk him into it when he comes here.
Now." Shade placed his wine on the counter and
wrapped his arms around Lori's shoulders. "I just want
to make something perfectly clear. I don't work cheap.
A quick dinner isn't adequate compensation for grease
under my fingernails and bruised knuckles. Do you get
what I'm driving at, woman?''

Lori admitted she did. She wrapped her arms around
Shade's waist and started to run a teasing finger up the
inside of his shirt, her nail running a light course along
his spine. Her body actually ached with the need to
make the contact deeper, but she refused to surrender.
There was nothing in Shade's voice to indicate he was
on the raw edge of passion.

Shade squirmed. "That tickles! Do it again. Ah." He
grinned down at her. "I think you can come up with
something.''

"Hmm." Lori pretended to be deep in thought. "I
guess I could darn your socks. Or don't women darn
socks anymore?

"Do you know how?"

"I haven't the vaguest idea. That wasn't one of the things I learned from Black Bob."

"Then I guess we'll have to come up with another form of compensation." Shade's hands had found the loose collar on Lori's lightweight sweater and was gently stretching the fabric, trying to reach the lace bra. "Can you think of anything?"

Lori stopped just short of surrender. "We said something about things going too fast," she pointed out.

"I don't have any idea what you're talking about. All I'm looking for is an alternative to your darning my socks. Lori." He pulled his hands out and gripped her shoulders, forcing her to look up into his eyes. "I've been doing some thinking about this sex business. People take it too damn serious, if you want my opinion. I remember a college roommate of mine who had a terrific success rate with the coeds because he convinced them that sex was the greatest form of recreation and exercise ever devised."

"You think our going to bed together is a form of recreation?" Lori asked, not nearly as shocked as she pretended to be.

"I think it's worth considering" was all Shade would say before picking up the necessary auto parts and going out to the garage.

For the next two hours Lori divided her time between the kitchen and garage, trying to be helpful, apologizing for having neglected her car for as long as she had. By the time she'd finally convinced Shade to quit, the car had been given a tune-up, but he was still muttering about the state of her brakes. "Those things belong in the museum," he said as he was washing up. "I'm going to give you the name of my mechanic. Go by the shop after work tomorrow and tell him to call me after he's decided what they need."

"Yes, sir," Lori agreed weakly. She wasn't used to accepting orders from a man without an argument, but in this situation at least, she had to admit she was out of her element. The brakes were obviously on their last legs, and she had no idea what they needed before they'd be reliable again. As she was placing food on the table, Lori admitted that this time, with Shade, she had no need to point out that she was capable of making her own decisions. It hadn't been that way with Brett.

They spoke little during dinner. Lori kept thinking about what Shade had said about sex being a fascinating form of recreation. It made sex sound like an alternative for physical fitness and not an expression of one's emotions, but when she studied the way Shade's eyelashes almost brushed his eyebrows as he looked up at her, she realized that sex with him wouldn't be nearly as detached an event as his comparison made it sound. No matter whether lovemaking was accomplished with deep sighs or casual vigor, she would still be sharing her body with a man who meant very, very much to her.

Shade leaned back in his chair, frowned at his grease-stained fingers and then smiled at her. "You wouldn't be interested in working off all those calories, would you?"

"Are you propositioning me?"

"Heck no. I just don't want you to go to bed with a full stomach. Don't you believe in exercise?"

The form of exercise Shade introduced her to in the king-size bed was certainly adequate for working off a late dinner, but even as Shade was demonstrating for her his version of warming-up exercises, Lori was unable to convince herself that their lovemaking was as lighthearted as they were trying to make it.

She tried. It was Lori's suggestion that finger exercises were a proper substitute for push-ups. She gave credit to her theory by pointing out that whenever she ran her fingers over his rib cage or lightly feathered the line of his hipbones, he jumped. Shade agreed. Didn't her body move restlessly on the fitted sheet as he explored the contours of her breasts?

"I think we should get a patent on this," Shade said between deep breaths aimed at self-control. "We've really stumbled on something. We could write a book and make a fortune off it."

"I suppose you'll want more than fifty percent. I'll probably have to hire a lawyer to get my fair share," Lori challenged. She threw a naked leg across Shade's in an attempt to coerce him into listening to reason. "Just because you had the idea first doesn't entitle you to more. After all, where would you be without a guinea pig to experiment on?"

"Some guinea pig!" Shade snorted, stopping her by placing a large hand over her mouth. "Don't talk unless you have something worthwhile to say. Our research might take all night."

It nearly did. When they were lying naked next to each other with a sheet thrown over them and her short curls were being crushed against Shade's chest, Lori made a confession. His arms and lips and powerful legs were enveloping more than her body. Her heart was involved.

And that frightened Lori. She didn't know how much of her separate self she was surrendering to this man.

Chapter Nine

Lori was standing under a black walnut tree that grew halfway between the farmhouse and the massive barn. She'd gone out to the barn to check on the barn owls and then had been distracted by an argumentative squirrel who was letting her know in no uncertain terms that the walnut tree was his and if she knew what was good for her she'd keep her hands off any of the forming walnuts. Lori laughed up at the squirrel, wondering if he could see her teeth as clearly as she could see his. "You're just a bossy old thing," she told the gray bushy-tailed creature. "You're never going to get a girlfriend if you carry on like that. Women don't take kindly to being scolded."

Lori turned at the sound of a car's tires crunching over the gravel drive and made out the black nondescript car Shade drove when on official museum business. She left the squirrel to his own devices and walked back toward the house. As Shade stepped out of the car, she tried to keep her eyes off his muscular thighs. She wondered if he felt as full, as satisfied, as she did this morning.

"Don't you ever do any work around here?" Shade called out. "I've been staring at paperwork since seven this morning. I decided to take a break and come out here to check on the work being done on the barn's foundation, and what do I find? You, staring up at a tree, hands in your back pockets.''

Lori shrugged, thinking that she liked him better in coveralls than the shirt and tie he was wearing today. The professional costume made him look official. "What are you going to do, fire me?" she challenged, grateful that he was continuing the same light mood that had defined their evening together.

"It's a thought. Have you seen Ruth today?"

Lori nodded, resolutely jamming her hands in the back pockets of her faded jeans. "Actually, I didn't see her, but I heard her in the kitchen. Why?"

"I have an idea. I've been concerned about that back porch. The wooden railing on the stairs is rotting. I wonder if she'd like the workmen to build her a new porch. It'd look just like the old one but be much more secure.''

"That's a good idea," Lori said enthusiastically. "She doesn't use that back entrance often, but I'd be afraid to have anyone lean on that railing.''

"I'm full of good ideas today." Shade winked. "Actually, I think my ideas last night were much more inventive. You're looking pretty spry considering what time you let me leave.''

"I *let* you leave?" Lori gasped in mock horror. "That's not how I remember it.''

"Really?" There was a smile in Shade's eyes as he asked.

I remember thinking that I had no existence beyond you, Lori thought, but she didn't have the courage to give voice to that thought. "I'm going to plead the Fifth Amendment on that one," she said instead. "Don't you have anything better to do than keep me from my work?" She leaned back against the walnut tree and spread her legs in an exaggerated lazy stance.

"I don't know what I'm going to do with you," Shade replied in mock exasperation. "Women these days have no respect for men. Damn hard to keep them in their place. What was it you needed from the grange, anyway?" he asked, turning the conversation quickly to business. He'd been so careful to keep the conversation, the relationship itself, in a light vein that it was beginning to be an effort. He wondered if she had any idea why he was doing that. "Aren't there enough things growing around here as it is?"

"They aren't all the right things," Lori pointed out, relieved to have the conversation take a safer track. "There used to be a lot of English ivy, but much of it was pushed out by blackberry vines. Now that the blackberries are going, I want to get the ivy reestablished."

Shade took a step toward the barn and then turned back around toward her. He wanted to talk to her about other things, things that would determine where they were heading, but there wasn't enough time now. Besides, he couldn't stop thinking about what he'd read in her ex-husband's letter. Mentioning what the man had said about her not needing anyone might mean entering territory he'd come to regret. It was easier to pretend that there weren't those dark spaces in their relationship, the possibility that she might suddenly pull away and leave him hurting. "That's why I hired you," he said simply. "I knew you'd have a plausible explanation for spending money." He turned away, feeling the weight of what still needed to be said.

Lori watched Shade pick his way through the tall

grasses leading toward the barn. He could have gone around to the road leading to the barn, but apparently he had little concern for the safety of his dark slacks. As Shade moved farther away from her, Lori's eyes recorded the picture of a man in modern dress being swallowed up by a setting that stretched back over a hundred years. He became a lonely figure, a man without time and form silhouetted against sky and wheat fields and a barn that had been housing farm animals long before the man was born.

The sight of Shade's solitary figure in the vastness of the farm's acreage made Lori think of her father. How many times had she looked into the depths of a forest and made out the one figure of Black Bob, a man completely at home in his surroundings?

That's what I look like here, Lori admitted. Many times since she'd gone to work for the historical society she'd been the only human in this junglelike environment. A woman like Vicky Ryan would have fled for her car or sought the safety of human companionship. But Lori didn't mind that she had only a hostile squirrel to talk to. Yes, she'd enjoyed the contact with Shade, but now that he was gone, she didn't feel lonely. In fact, she was being comforted by the gentle rustle of branches caught by the morning breeze. After all, that was the sound she'd grown up hearing.

Lori spent the next hour trimming an overbearing Babylonian willow. She took minute pleasure in slowly releasing some of the load on the sagging branches. As the breeze toyed with her hair, eradicating any efforts she'd made earlier at coaxing it into shape, she felt only pity for people who had to spend their days in offices tied to telephones and computers. Maybe that kind of work was what most people wanted. It simply wasn't what she could do and hold on to her sanity. Recycled air-conditioned air when she could catch the scent of honeysuckle brought to her by the breeze? Hardly!

Shade waved in her direction when he left the barn and headed toward the house, but he didn't stop to talk. Lori didn't mind. She was caught in the grip of her pensive mood and needed to hold on to it a little longer. How could anyone say it was quiet out here when her distant squirrel friend was continuing his monologue and the blue jays hidden somewhere near the holly were arguing loudly. Sounds had different meaning for different people, Lori decided. Human voices weren't the only forms of communication.

She had just tossed a branch onto her growing pile near the gravel road when Shade let out a shout that seared through her. "Lori! Ruth's hurt!"

Lori dropped her clippers and sprinted toward the house. She clambered up the front stairs and fairly threw the screen door out of her way as she followed the sound of Shade's urgent voice.

She found him in the living room kneeling over Ruth's twisted figure at the bottom of the stairs. "I think she fell down the stairs," Shade said without taking time to look at Lori. "She's cut her forehead."

Lori dropped to her knees next to Shade. Ruth's eyelids were fluttering convulsively, and she was making a faint moaning sound. The gash on her forehead was bleeding profusely, but Lori had seen enough logging injuries to know that a head wound usually looked worse than it was. Lori surged back to her feet and hurried into the kitchen where she found a dish towel to put over the cut. "Is she unconscious?" she asked when the towel was in place.

"No, but I think you better call an ambulance."

"No ambulance," Ruth groaned. "I'm not going to any hospital."

Lori let her breath out in a hiss of relief. At least Ruth could talk. "Where do you hurt?" she asked the still-limp woman.

"I'm fine." Ruth slapped ineffectively at Shade, who was trying to take her pulse. "Pull down my dress. I'm not going to expose myself."

"You look respectable," Shade reassured her as he gently straightened her limbs. "Very modest and proper. What happened?"

"I don't know what happened," Ruth snapped. Her eyes still weren't focusing properly, but Lori was relieved to see that she was able to move her arms and legs and she was carrying on a coherent, if spirited, conversation.

"Well, I do," Shade interjected. "You fell coming down those damn stairs. I told you that hand railing wasn't wide enough for a good grip. "You need to go to the hospital."

"I'm not going in any damn ambulance."

Lori glanced at Shade, too concerned to laugh when he rolled his eyes back in his head. "I'm afraid you're outnumbered, Ruth," she pointed out. "You don't want us to drag you to the hospital, do you?"

"I've never been in an ambulance in my life. I'm not going to start now."

Shade sighed. "Okay, forget the ambulance. What if we see if you can stand up and you can go in my car."

"I don't—"

"He's right," Lori interrupted. She didn't like the way Ruth's hands were trembling. "You need to have a doctor check you out. Do you think you passed out when you fell?"

"How should I know what happened?" Ruth snapped. "It all happened so fast."

Ruth started struggling to sit up. After fighting her for a few seconds, Shade gave up and supported her so she was able to get into a sitting position. Lori continued to hold the dish towel in place over the cut on Ruth's forehead. "There's no hurry," Lori pointed out. "We can take it slow and easy, but Shade's right. You need to have someone look you over."

Ruth started to turn away as if irritated by the cloth and then let out a startled gasp. She looked at Lori with anxious eyes. "Maybe you're right. My ribs don't feel so good."

It took a good ten minutes to get Ruth from the living-room floor into Shade's car. Once they had the older woman settled in the front passenger's seat with her head resting against the backrest, Lori slid into the back seat. She leaned forward, gently stroking Ruth's head as Shade eased the car down the gravel road and onto the highway.

"I feel like an idiot," Ruth said twice during the ride into town. Other than that, she said nothing, which did nothing to ease Lori's concern. She didn't think Ruth had fallen down many stairs, but any kind of fall had to be both painful and dangerous for a woman in her eighties. Lori knew that older people's bones were brittle and more likely to bruise or break.

They were in the emergency room two hours before they received the final diagnosis. Ruth had indeed bruised two ribs. They would have to be held in place with tight wraps until they could heal. Her cut forehead required three stitches; the doctor prescribed a painkiller for the bruises to Ruth's shoulder and side. "You're lucky you didn't break your hip," the doctor said as he was finishing up. "That happens a lot with people your age."

"Don't tell me about people my age!" Ruth snapped. Now that the painkiller had taken hold, she was no longer gripping Lori's hand. "Anyone can have an accident."

"I know." The doctor smiled indulgently. "But as we get older, we lose our ability to bounce back from injuries. I still say you're lucky. I don't want you tackling those stairs for several weeks. You're going to be shaky."

Ruth glared at the doctor. "What do you want me to do, pack myself off to a nursing home? That's the last thing I'd do. Shade? Are you going to get me out of here? This quack is probably charging me by the minute." When Ruth started to hoist herself off the examining table, Shade had no choice but to offer her his arm for support. He gave Lori a questioning glance over his shoulder as Ruth steered him out of the room.

Lori turned toward the doctor. "What do you suggest? Do you really think it's safe for her to go home?"

The doctor laughed. "Do you want to be the one to try to stop her? That's one stubborn lady. That's good. I'd much rather have a fighter than a quitter. But I don't like the idea of her being alone. Isn't there someone who could stay with her, a nurse or housekeeper, maybe?"

"I don't know," Lori admitted. "We talked about that before, and Ruth said no. Maybe this experience has changed her mind."

"I hope so," the doctor said as Lori turned to leave. "She might not get off so easy the next time she falls."

Not "if" but "when," the doctor implied. That was what continued to concern Lori on the ride back to the farm. Ruth was carrying on a spirited dialogue about how much hospitals cost and how much unnecessary equipment an emergency room contained, but Lori kept wondering if Ruth was talking to keep from having to face the fact that she'd narrowly escaped a dangerous fall.

It wasn't until they had Ruth settled on a couch in the living room and Lori was bringing in sandwiches for all of them that Shade brought up the subject of a housekeeper. "Think about it," he pressed. "You're always complaining that the spiders have the upper hand. Now you'll have someone around to keep them at bay."

"I like living alone," Ruth said in a weak, tired voice. "I don't want someone hovering around me."

"We're not talking about a nurse," Lori pointed out. "You're far from bedridden. But admit it. Wouldn't you feel a lot better if there was someone with you when you went up and down those stairs?"

Ruth frowned, obviously not ready to commit herself. "What if I don't like the person? I don't want some overbearing old nag telling me what I can and can't do."

"You can train her," Shade suggested, exchanging a look with Lori that said they were making ground. "I promise we won't saddle you with any war horse."

"I don't know." Ruth took a bite of her sandwich, her hand still trembling. "Who wants to live with an old woman like me?"

Shade leaned forward, grinning like a prowling timber wolf. "Is that an invitation? Say the word and I'll move in in a minute."

Ruth's eyes flashed, showing animation for the first time since her accident. "Who says you're man enough for me?"

Laughter rumbled up from Shade's chest. "That's the Ruth I'm used to hearing. What if I started asking around, send some women out for you to interview?"

Lori nodded to show that she seconded Shade's suggestion. "In the meantime, what if I spend the night here?" she offered.

"You have better things to do than waste time with me," Ruth started, but Lori held up her hand and shook her head.

"Do you think I could relax knowing you were here alone?" she asked.

"I think you better take Lori up on her suggestion," Shade interrupted. "Besides, I can testify that she doesn't snore. However, I do. Which of us is it going to be?"

Ruth was obviously delighted to hear that Shade knew whether Lori snored or not, but Lori was still upset when she walked out to the car with him after they'd finished lunch. "Why did you tell her that?" she asked. "Ruth has a vivid enough imagination without you feeding it."

Shade only shrugged. "It's true. You don't snore. What do you want me to do, lie?"

"I'd like you to be a little more discreet."

For response Shade ran his hand down Lori's thigh. "If you wanted discreet, you shouldn't have hooked up with me. I happen to take great pleasure in being with you, and I don't care who knows."

How could she be angry with that, Lori thought as she watched Shade drive away. Besides, it was next to impossible to pretend she didn't like being touched by Shade Ryan.

Lori helped Ruth settle down for a nap on the living-room couch. Although she didn't like the idea of painkillers, she had to admit that without them Ruth wouldn't be as comfortable as she was. Lori tried to go back outside to work, but she kept popping inside every few minutes to make sure Ruth was all right. A housekeeper wouldn't have to keep a constant eye on her, but it should be someone who was tuned in to the older woman and alert to what Ruth's limits and capabilities were.

Vicky.

Where had that thought come from, Lori asked. What made her think Vicky Ryan was what Ruth needed?

But the more she thought about it, the more she realized the idea had merit. Vicky didn't have many job qualifications, but surely she knew enough to keep the farmhouse clean and see to it that Ruth got nutritious meals. Vicky didn't like living alone. She liked having people around. True, Ruth was much older, but that might not be a disadvantage given Ruth's quick mind and interest in the world. Ruth had been an independent, liberated woman long before that had become today's woman's battle cry. There was a lot Vicky could learn about standing on her own two feet from the eighty-plus-year-old woman.

There was one major stumbling block to the idea. Shade probably wouldn't like it at all. He plainly didn't think Vicky could take care of herself, let alone look to someone else's needs. But they'd never know if Vicky wasn't given the opportunity.

In the end Lori decided to talk things over with Vicky before mentioning her idea to Shade. As she was preparing homemade soup for herself and Ruth, she told Ruth a little of what was on her mind.

"How old is this child?" was Ruth's first question.

"I'm not sure. In her early twenties. She hasn't had to shoulder much responsibility in her life, but I think she's ready to learn."

"When I was in my twenties, I'd already had three children," Ruth pointed out. "I don't know. Shade didn't talk much about his ex-wife, just enough to let me know he didn't think she could stand on her own two feet."

Lori tried a new approach. "Maybe that'll be your job. Vicky told me she wants to get her life in order. There's a lot you could show her in that respect."

"And she'd be there to make sure I don't fall on my face again. That's what you're trying to tell me, isn't it?"

Lori admitted that it was. "I could be getting ahead of myself. Maybe Vicky isn't at all interested in this, but if the doctor says you need a housekeeper, I think she could get paid for it."

"I don't know," Ruth said slowly. "It's something I'd have to think about. But not tonight. Those pills have put my head in a fog."

After dinner Lori changed the bed in the downstairs bedroom and then made up a cot for herself in the living room. Ruth tried to insist that Lori shouldn't have to sleep on a cot, but Lori had slept in less comfortable places while growing up and dismissed her concern. The two women watched TV and read the paper, but a little before nine Ruth admitted she'd had enough for one day.

Shade called just after Ruth had fallen asleep. He'd spent the afternoon talking to a couple of housekeeping services but was learning that finding a live-in housekeeper was easier said than done. "Do you think you could stay there another night or two until I get this straightened out?" he asked seriously. "I could come over to keep you company."

"Don't you dare!" Lori gasped. She wasn't going to let Shade know that given the right circumstances that was exactly what she would have wanted.

Lori hadn't thought about that since early in the day, but as she was getting ready for bed, she gave free rein to what had been on her mind earlier. Shade was taking over her life, her thoughts even. Was that what she wanted, or would she someday bolt and run the way she had with Brett, she had to ask.

It wasn't a question she could answer. Brett had never turned her on, not the way Shade could. Shade showed her what her body was capable of experiencing. She wanted—needed—that experience again. But the deeper question that needed answering was whether sexual satisfaction was an acceptable trade-off for privacy and independence. Those conditions were so deeply ingrained. What if she gave her heart to Shade and tried to ignore her other needs? Something might backfire.

Black Bob would have the answer to that. He knew his daughter, if anyone did. Unfortunately, Lori had no more idea of how to get in touch with him than she knew how to get in touch with her feelings.

Fortunately, running Vicky down wasn't as hard as she thought it would be. Lori had gone to Shade's house to pick up a few clothes the next morning. While she was there, Vicky called. "I'm still in the motel," Vicky started explaining almost before Lori had time to say hello. "Those condominiums are more expensive than I thought they'd be. I could afford one if I was working, but—"

"Have you been looking for work?" Lori asked,

sensing that the younger woman needed to feel that someone cared about her.

Vicky explained that she'd registered with an employment agency but didn't hold out much hope that she'd instantly become anyone's executive secretary. "They had me take a typing test," Vicky explained. "I hated it. I didn't realize typing was so boring."

"What are your feelings about doing housework?" Lori thought before allowing herself time to think about the timing of the question.

To her surprise, Vicky laughed. "That's one of the things I enjoy doing. I wasn't crazy about the house Shade moved me into, but I enjoyed taking care of it. I like things to look nice."

"Would you be interested in taking care of an old farmhouse and the woman who lives in it?"

When Vicky gasped, Lori hurried on to explain. She told Vicky she wasn't sure whether Vicky would be paid for her services, but there was more than enough room at the Kadin farm, and Ruth was at least willing to talk to her. "I think you'll like Ruth Kadin," Lori wound up. "But you have to watch her. I never know when she's serious or kidding. And her comments can get a little risqué at times."

"She isn't senile?"

"Ruth Kadin is about as far from senile as anyone can hope to get. She's not as sure on her feet as she used to be, and she won't be doing any driving for a while, but there's nothing wrong with her mind."

Lori expected Vicky to hesitate. After all, Shade had said that she was incapable of making up her mind. To her surprise, Vicky asked if she could come out to the farm that afternoon. "My lawyer said Shade was willing to pay alimony, so why don't I just sit back and enjoy it.

Right? But I don't like doing nothing. Everyone else is working. I want to be, too.''

Lori silently applauded Vicky's decision and set up an appointment for 4:00 P.M., when she thought Ruth would be up from her nap. She almost weakened and called Shade to tell him what was going on but stopped herself at the last minute. The three women didn't need Shade's approval.

Vicky was a few minutes late for the meeting, but since Lori had been working outside, she wasn't sure what time it was. Vicky watched Lori as she finished spreading sulfate of ammonia on the lawn and then gave Lori's arm a quick squeeze. "Do I look all right? I didn't know what to wear.''

Vicky was dressed in a blazer and skirt that stretched a little too tightly around her rounded hips, but Lori approved of her sensible low-heeled shoes. "You look fine. Don't be nervous. Ruth's a very earthy woman. She'll let you know in short order whether she likes you. She'll expect the same from you.''

"Oh, I couldn't do that," Vicky protested. "I've never been any good at saying things that might hurt people's feelings.''

"But it's something we all have to do at times if we don't want to get stepped on," Lori started, and then stopped. "Forget it. You don't need any advice.''

As Lori introduced the two women, she hoped her sudden nervousness didn't show. She'd never tried to set up a working arrangement between people before, and knowing she would have to get the conversational ball going made her long for solitude. She was rattling on about the work she was doing when the phone rang, allowing her a temporary escape.

It was Shade. "I know you're busy, but there's just

one thing," he said after she'd picked up the phone in the kitchen. "I'm about to lose my mind over this housekeeping thing." He sighed, exasperatedly. "I had no idea it was so hard to find someone who could stay nights. Also—"

"I thought you said there was just one thing," Lori interrupted.

"I lied.... I wish we could spend some time alone. Why do you think you keep cropping up in my mind no matter what I'm doing?"

Lori searched for a snappy comeback, but none came to mind. Instead, her mind insisted on focusing on what his unruly hair felt like caught between her fingertips. "I miss you," she said softly.

"Honest?"

"Honest. Shade, Ruth has company. I really should get back to them." Lori closed her eyes, surrendering to her thoughts. Even nicer than revelling in the texture of his hair was seeing him lying next to her in bed.

Shade promised to come by after work and let her go. For perhaps fifteen seconds after he hung up, Lori continued to hold the receiver in her hand as if something of him could flow through the line and reach her. The thought was more comforting than a load of firewood brought in on a winter night could ever be.

When she was finally able to shake herself free, Lori returned to the living room to find Vicky and Ruth engaged in a spirited conversation about the barn owls. "I didn't know there were any around here," Vicky admitted, looking at Lori with glowing eyes. "I think that's wonderful."

"Let me get my sea legs under me and we'll walk out and take a look at them. What do you think? When can you move in?"

Lori blinked. She didn't think Ruth would make up her mind about Vicky that quickly. She didn't know what Vicky was thinking.

The younger woman supplied the answer. She prefaced her statement by admitting that she left a lot to be desired as a cook but was willing to try her hand at painting walls and cleaning curtains if Ruth wanted her to. "I love this place," she chortled. "It's funny, but I don't think of the barn being isolated the way I do the house Shade and I lived in."

"That's because there's a lot of ghosts living in it," Ruth said in mock seriousness. "There's all kinds of relatives still rattling around here."

Vicky shook her head. "That's not it. I was so alone so much of the time when I was married. You're here. That gives the house life."

Lori gave herself an A for effort. There might be future problems in the arrangement, but there was no denying that a certain chemistry existed between Ruth and Vicky. Maybe Vicky saw the older woman as a sort of mother figure, but Lori hoped it went further than that. Ruth had a lifetime of learning to offer Vicky. And in turn the younger woman was able to fill the house with youth.

Vicky had left, and Lori was in the kitchen fixing dinner when Ruth limped in. "Do you want me to tell him, or do you? I know Vicky can't, at least, not yet."

Lori grimaced. "I'll tell him."

"Good." Ruth laughed. "I don't want that hunk mad at me. I know he won't stay steamed at you for long."

Don't be so sure, Lori thought. In fact, Shade had been at the farm for almost a half hour before she found a way to work her announcement into the conversation. Shade was sitting between the two women in the living room, holding Ruth's hand and giving her flirtatious glances while lightly running his free hand up and down Lori's thigh. "I did talk to one woman who said she'd come out here," he was saying. "But she looks like she needs more help than you do. I don't know how a scrawny thing like that can make a living doing physical work."

Lori took a deep breath, then met Ruth's eyes for a moment. "I almost forgot. You don't have to worry about that. Vicky is going to move in here tomorrow."

Shade's hand stopped in mid-stroke. "Vicky?" he breathed. "What the hell are you talking about?"

"Don't swear," Lori warned, feeling suddenly cold. She'd gone about telling him all wrong, but it was too late to back up. Quickly, she explained about the afternoon meeting and subsequent agreement between the interested parties. "It's on a trial basis right now. But I wouldn't be surprised if it works out."

Shade pushed himself off the couch and turned to face the two women. "Vicky? You've got to be kidding! She can't get herself out the door in the morning, let alone take care of someone else."

Lori matched his anger with a quick temper of her own. "Don't be so sure, Shade Ryan. Give Vicky a chance. I don't think you're giving her nearly enough credit."

"Credit!" he raged. "I was married to the woman, remember? I know what she is and isn't capable of."

"And of course she isn't capable of maturing. She was a child when you married her, so why should she be anything but a child for the rest of her life?" She didn't know why she was saying this; she didn't want to fight with Shade.

"You're making a big mistake." Shade turned toward Ruth. "I appreciate your efforts at finding my ex-wife a job, but you're going to be disappointed. She isn't the world's most dependable person."

"Why don't you let me be the judge of that?" Ruth pointed out, still looking at Shade from under her eyelashes in a parody of enticement. "It's something that has to be worked out between the people involved. I like her. She's a breath of fresh air."

"If you like living with a child."

To Lori's relief Ruth found a way of turning the conversation in a safer direction. Lori could still feel the tension in Shade's body, and there was no way she could misinterpret the fact that he was no longer touching her. But she'd been able to resolve Ruth's problem, and maybe, eventually, this would lead to Vicky's no longer being dependent on Shade. If he couldn't see that, then she wasn't sure she wanted him touching her, anyway.

She almost didn't accompany Shade when he walked out to his car. But it would have been the coward's way out to stay safely next to Ruth's side. Besides, his darkly glaring green eyes wouldn't allow her to ignore their challenge. Shade slid behind the wheel, closed the door and stared ahead for a moment. Finally, he turned on Lori. "That's meddling," he hissed. "Vicky is none of your concern. I don't want you getting involved in her life."

"You can't be serious." Lori gasped. "I didn't see any hands-off sign on her."

"I didn't know I had to paint one." Shade went on, his relentless eyes boring into her. "Do you have any idea how this makes me feel? There are two women in my life these days. One is part of my past. One—" He paused. "One I hope will be part of my future. I can't see anything healthy coming out of there being any interaction between the two of them."

"And you want me to pretend that Vicky doesn't exist? Shade, I don't have any animosity toward her. I didn't know either of you when you were married. That part of your life doesn't affect me. I happen to believe that what's happening is going to benefit everyone involved. I'll apologize if I'm wrong, but until then I'd appreciate it if you gave me credit for at least a little intelligence." There. There was no way Shade could doubt her convictions.

"What I can't understand," Shade went on, his eyes never leaving hers, "is why someone who grew up with practically no one to interact with has suddenly decided she's an expert in human relationships. Your marriage failed because you weren't cut out for a close relationship. Don't deny it, Lori," he continued when she tried to interrupt. "You're the one who told me that."

"And you're a marriage expert!" Lori shot back. Was Shde deliberately trying to hurt her? All right. Two could play that cruel game!

"I'm an expert when it comes to knowing what Vicky is and isn't capable of." Shade's voice became a whisper. "You're so eager to orchestrate a relationship between Vicky and Ruth that you've forgotten one crucial fact. Ruth could have been killed today. How are you going to feel when she has another accident and Vicky falls apart? Believe me, Vicky doesn't know the first thing about handling an emergency. You're playing with fire, and you can't even see it."

Lori grew cold inside, because there might be truth in what Shade was saying. But she wasn't going to knuckle under to him. He'd already said too much to hurt her. "What do you want me to do?" she asked in a voice that had grown cold. "Crawl back into the woods? Is that it? You think I'm some ignorant backwoods creature. You're probably right, you know," she went on, seeking a way to hurt him. "Why should I know anything about relationships? My divorce exposed me as a failure."

"I didn't say that."

"Didn't you?" she went on, too upset to gauge the direction her words were taking before they were out of her mouth. "I shouldn't inflict myself on people because I spent too much time alone while I was growing up. That's what you're trying to tell me!" Her head was pounding; her words swirled around her, making her desperate to escape both the words and the man responsible for making her say them.

"All right. I won't play with fire anymore." She turned around, tearing her eyes free from Shade's relentless ones. "In fact, I don't think anything I'd do would meet your exacting standards. I think our whole relationship is a mistake!"

"Lori!" Shade swung out of the car and reached out to grab her. "That's not what I was saying, and you know it! I was talking about Vicky and Ruth, not us."

"What's the difference?" Lori hissed as she tried to pull free. "I don't know a damn thing about relationships, about what makes people tick. I—I failed at my marriage. I should have learned my lesson." Lori pulled so fiercely that Shade would have hurt her had he held on. She stumbled toward the barn, praying Shade would realize she was in no condition to be around anyone.

She must have made her point. She heard the car

door slam again and a moment later heard his car slicing its angry way down the gravel drive.

Go on, Lori thought as she forced herself to concentrate on her footing. *Leave. I'm not what you want. I wasn't what Brett wanted. Maybe I've finally learned my lesson.*

Lori's mind continued to struggle against the emotions assaulting her as she hurried into the open-air barn and wrapped her arms around one of the support beams. She pressed her pounding head against the aged, splintered surface and let her bottled-up tears escape.

God! They'd said such horrible things to each other! Liking—love even—had suddenly twisted around and become something she couldn't handle. None of the arguments she and Brett had had affected her like this fight with Shade. It might have been because she had so much more of herself invested in this relationship.

And it might have been because she was terrified by something Shade said.

"You weren't cut out for a close relationship," he'd said. Yes. That was true. In fact, that was the one thing she and Brett had agreed on. She needed to keep a certain part of her personality free from the marriage relationship while Brett fought to absorb her entire being. She'd fled her marriage because she needed time to take a long, hard look at what had gone wrong.

And what had she learned, she asked herself. Not enough. The broadening chasm between her and Shade was proof of her inability to interact in a positive way with another human being. Shade meant more to her than even her unchecked tears revealed. But she wasn't good for him! She wouldn't be sobbing, and he wouldn't be driving with his foot shoving the pedal to the floorboard if their minds merged as perfectly as their bodies did.

"I'm sorry, Shade!" she sobbed aloud, although only the nesting barn owls could hear her. "I should have known. I don't know how to love a man. Not the right kind of love. I—I can't help it. I didn't have enough examples while I was growing up.

"Maybe I should have never left the woods."

Chapter Ten

The last thing Lori wanted to hear the evening following the argument with Shade was the phone ringing in the hilltop house. It had been hard enough pulling herself together and going back to carry on a semicivilized conversation with Ruth. She'd been grateful for work and even more grateful when Vicky showed up with her suitcases to take over the chore of being there for Ruth. Lori had worked almost until dark and then had driven home without being aware of having placed her hands on the steering wheel.

If Shade was calling to say anything more about Vicky's unreliability and her lack of judgment, she simply wasn't going to be able to listen to him. It was bad enough knowing what he thought of her now. What would be impossible to hide from him was the empty, frightened feeling that she'd lost something that had become terribly, terribly precious to her.

The voice at the other end of the line was masculine but from her past, not her splintered present. "You're almost as hard to track down as I am. I tried this number last night but didn't get any answer."

"Dad! Oh, my God, where are you?" Lori reached for the stool next to the kitchen phone and sat down heavily. "I didn't expect—I was hoping I'd hear from you."

"You know how it is," Black Bob went on, his voice gravelly from disuse. "I never know where I'm going to be. I wish I could have been around when you and Brett split up, but I probably couldn't have done anything to help."

You could have been there to hold on to, Lori thought, but didn't voice the thought. Black Bob prided himself on raising an independent daughter. It simply wouldn't have occurred to him that she wasn't as sure of her maturity as he was. "Are you near here?" she asked. "Brett forwarded your last letter to me."

"I'm right here in town, girl. I called Brett the other day. He gave me your address. The fact is, I'm between jobs and planning on going into the Cascades this weekend to check out a job I heard about. How would you like to spend the weekend with your old man, if you haven't forgotten how to fish, that is. We could do some of the things we used to."

Black Bob wanted her to spend the weekend fly-fishing in some of the Cascade streams. Lori hugged herself silently, blinking back tears. "I—I'd like that very much. I haven't done much fishing lately. I'm a little rusty."

"You'll remember quick. Look, I'm staying at the motel here next to the freeway. Noisiest damn thing you ever saw. You want to give me some direction so I can get to your place?"

"What if I meet you there, Dad," she suggested. "I'll throw a few things in a suitcase, and we can take off tonight. Remember how we used to drive into the mountains at night and I'd keep from falling asleep by looking for bears? Indulge me. I need to do that again."

"Are you okay?" Black Bob sounded confused. "I thought you'd grown past that kind of thing."

"Not tonight. Can't you humor me a little? I'll be there in less than an hour."

He still had a couple of arguments against Lori's spur-of-the-moment plans, but she brushed them aside. A house was a house, she told him. There wasn't anything here he'd want to see.

Probably not, Lori admitted as she was throwing jeans and sweatshirts into a suitcase. As long as the roof didn't leak and there were enough blankets for their beds, Black Bob figured things were pretty good. It wasn't that he didn't think his daughter didn't deserve better than a trailer with rusting walls, but Black Bob had never had a home to settle into and give his personal stamp, so he couldn't really know that it was what most people wanted out of life. He'd take one look at Shade's elaborate home with its broad expanse of windows and wonder if Lori was trying to make up for something she'd missed out on while growing up. Black Bob had done the best he could by his daughter.

Lori was ready to lock up when she made an impulsive move she didn't pretend to understand. She dialed Shade's number and spoke into the answering machine. "I'm taking Friday off," she said in clipped, impersonal tones. "My father's in town, and I need to spend some time with him. I'll make up the time next week."

She hung up. Was there anything else she should be saying, something about wanting to talk to Shade after she got back, she wondered. No. She hurt too much. It was time to draw back into herself, to take comfort in the solitude that had always been a part of her.

Lori was thinking about her father, wondering if

he'd missed having a woman in his life, as she negotiated the turns leading down the mountain. Funny,
they'd never talked about the deep ramifications of
Black Bob being a single parent. There must have been
times when he wanted someone to talk to, to hold next
to him. For the first time in her life she wondered if
Black Bob was as resourceful, independent and in control as the child living with him thought. Or, if she
mentioned the carved-out hollow in the pit of her
stomach, maybe he would understand what she was
talking about.

In the space of three seconds Lori was no longer
thinking. She was trying to survive. The Mustang was
traveling a little too fast to negotiate the right turn in
the road. Lori stabbed at the brakes, felt her foot slam
into the floorboard and pumped rapidly, trying to re-
store a flicker of life into the ancient brakes. This time
there was no response, no pressure to let her know that
the reluctant brakes had been coaxed back to life.

Lori gripped the steering wheel and hunched forward, steering her runaway car around the turn. Somehow she managed to negotiate the turn without going
over the edge, but before she could take a breath, the
road made an equally sharp turn to the left. This time
she had to keep the Mustang from straying over the
center line and crashing into the high dirt bank to the
left. Or should she, Lori thought wildly, her mind
speeding ahead to the turn beyond. By that time she
would be going far in excess of the speed limit. It would
take a miracle to keep the car on the road and away
from the steep drop-off.

The decision was made in the space of a single heartbeat. Lori gritted her teeth, said a silent apology to her
beloved car and turned the steering wheel toward the

dirt bank. The car hit the bank a glancing blow, grinding dirt and rocks into the left front fender. Lori was thrown out of her seat by the impact, but she refused to let go of the steering wheel. The car was still moving, tires crunching in the dirt shoulder. Again she pulled the steering wheel to the left, determined to use the bank to stop the car's forward motion.

This time her desperate tactic worked. She heard the left headlight shatter and accepted the harsh vibration that shook her body. She screamed involuntarily as the Mustang slammed to a stop.

Her body was thrown forward and to the left, her left knee striking the door. Lori barely noted the pain that seared through her knee and up her leg. The only thing she dared think about was holding on to the steering wheel, making sure the car wasn't going to escape again.

Because her heart was pounding crazily in her ears, it was close to a minute before she realized the engine had died. She was sitting inside a stationary car, surrounded by a silence that was just as jarring as the earlier sound of grinding metal and squealing tires.

Lori dropped her head to the steering wheel, her emotions going beyond tears. Her entire body was filled with adrenaline that escaped into her lungs and veins. She couldn't even tell if she was injured. At least the Mustang was jammed against the side of the mountain instead of careening over a cliff.

What now, Lori tried to ask herself. She couldn't open the left door because the car was jammed solidly against the bank. It was ridiculous to think the car was capable of moving again, but she was filled with an irrational need to get out of what had nearly been a death trap.

Lori slithered across the seat and reached blindly for the handle on the right front door. She's swung her body around and was starting to step out when she was brought to a halt by a repeat of the earlier pain that had seared her left leg. Lori grabbed her knee, gasping. Because she was wearing jeans, she couldn't see what the injury might be, but she could imagine flesh turning purple, a joint rapidly swelling.

"Damn!" she swore, mad at everything and everyone. Not only wasn't her car going anywhere, but now it looked as if she wasn't, either. It wasn't fair!

After gathering her courage, Lori made a tentative attempt to stand up. Her knee still throbbed enough to set her teeth on edge, but at least it didn't buckle under her. She tried to take a step. For her troubles she painfully learned that walking wasn't in the cards. "Damn!" she repeated, and clung to the car door, feeling rather like a bird with a broken wing—a very painful crippled wing.

It wasn't until she saw the headlights of an approaching car that she became aware that her mouth was twisted into a less than attractive grimace. The car was coming down the hill, sedately duplicating the journey she'd taken without brakes. The car pulled off the road onto the shoulder behind her Mustang, and an older couple got out. Lori tried to turn around to face them properly, but her knee refused to do her bidding. She was forced to cling to the open door, her left leg a useless appendage.

"Are you all right?" the woman asked. "My goodness, are you alone?"

"I'm afraid so," Lori admitted. She wasn't going to cry! "My brakes gave way. It was either hit the bank or risk going over the edge. How does my car look?"

"Forget your car," the man said as he stepped up next to Lori. "Are you hurt?"

"My knee has felt better," she admitted.

Five minutes later Lori was settled in the back of the couple's car, her suitcase beside her. She'd almost cried out as they helped her hobble over to their car, but the woman was a true mother hen, and the man took charge so easily that she was willing to put herself in their hands. They tried to convince her to let them take her to the hospital, but Lori couldn't stop thinking about Black Bob. She hadn't seen her father in over a year. Right now she wanted to be a little girl again, with her father making all the decisions. She gave the couple directions to the motel and assured them that she would call a tow truck to move her car.

Black Bob didn't even blink when her misadventure was revealed to him. "I never could get her to understand what cars need," he pointed out as he was swinging her into his arms and carrying her into his motel room. "Thanks for everything you've done, but we can handle things now," the big, dark bear of a man said to the middle-aged couple.

Wasn't that just like her father, Lori admitted as he was making arrangements to have a tow truck haul the Mustang to the garage Shade had told her about. Father and daughter had always done for themselves without outside help. The established order wasn't going to change now.

"You aren't going to be much account as far as fishing is concerned," he pointed out as he was rolling ice cubes from the ice machine into a white towel. "This wouldn't be some scheme so you wouldn't be shown up for the tenderfoot you've become?"

"You think I planned this?" Lori laughed, liking the

sound of her laughter. Black Bob had never coddled his daughter. Now that her adrenaline level was coming back to normal, she realized she didn't need coddling. "If that wasn't the dumbest thing—"

"You don't have anyone to blame but yourself," Black Bob pointed out. "Now how about sliding out of those jeans so we can see the damage."

With her father to lean against, Lori was able to stand long enough to unzip her jeans and ease the denim past her hips. When she saw her knee, her first reaction was to silently cuss Shade. If he hadn't lost his temper and refused to talk to her, the brakes might have been fixed by now.

But that wasn't the whole truth. Lori had breathed enough fire of her own. She couldn't really blame him for wanting to have nothing to do with her.

Pain shooting up her leg when she tried to bend her knee stopped that kind of thinking. Her knee more closely resembled a basketball than a joint. The entire area around the bone was a vibrant purple, with the potential for becoming even darker. It was so swollen that even if there hadn't been any pain, Lori knew she wouldn't be able to bend the joint.

"Well, now, I've seen prettier things in my life," Black Bob observed as he plunked a towel filled with ice on her knee. "Keep it there," he ordered when Lori winced. "You want to get the swelling down."

"Damn! What am I going to do?"

"You aren't going fishing, that's for sure," he pointed out practically. "I'll tell you what. We'll spend the night here and then go into the Cascades in the morning."

Lori nodded. Her father hadn't changed. A person didn't go to the hospital unless they were losing blood faster than it could be replaced. A banged-up knee meant a slight change of plans, not a cancellation. Despite her trepidation at the thought of trying to get any sleep tonight, Lori admitted she had no desire to argue with her father. She'd never once gone to the hospital in all the years she was growing up. In fact, her father had only gone once himself, and that was only because his foreman had insisted he needed stitches. Lori had only three days to spend with her father. They weren't going to be spent in an emergency room.

Father and daughter talked until far into the night. There were stretches of comfortable silence intermingled with the words while Lori studied her father, finding herself in him. He hadn't aged since she saw him last, not really. Gray flecks, now softened the solid thatch of black hair, and maybe his skin was a little drier, but his eyes still danced with the mystery of being alive. The only thing that wasn't right about the evening was that Lori kept wishing Shade was here, seeing the same things she was. Shade, she knew, would like Black Bob. Her father didn't fit any mold. He was an individual, a maverick. For some strange reason Shade had been attracted to a younger female version of that maverick.

But not anymore, Lori kept telling herself. Words, an argument, had put an end to that.

It wasn't until they were in Black Bob's battered old pickup the next morning that Lori told her father about Shade Ryan. "He's establishment, Dad," she explained. "He wears a suit and tie sometimes and has to court specialized organizations for the society's financial base. Yet he has another side to him that's very antiestablishment. He used to live in an isolated house with every modern convenience except curtains. He flirts outrageously with an old lady and has been a weight trainer for years. He loves barn owls and was fascinated when I told him about what you've done with your life."

"And you love him?"

Lori should have been ready for that question. Just the same, she wasn't ready to answer it directly. "I don't know," she tried. "I admit there are times when he's very important to my life, but after what happened with Brett, I'm not sure I'm ready for another relationship. What if Shade wants me to make nice talk with the women in the historical society's booster club? I can just see myself sitting there trying to hide the dirt under my fingernails and feeling like I'm going to scream if I can't get outside. I tried that once before and failed." Lori turned toward her father, moving her left leg gingerly. Some of the swelling had gone down, but she was a long way from doing any running on it. "I need more time by myself before I make any kind of a decision."

"Well, we're going to have that, all right," Black Bob pointed out. "I don't think this foreman I'm going to see has hired any crew yet. It's going to be damn quiet in the woods."

Lori touched her father's arm. "Why do you think I said yes to this weekend? You and I haven't done this for years. I've missed it."

After that the conversation left serious subjects. Lori told Black Bob about Ruth Kadin and what she'd learned about the farm's evolution through the years. She mentioned that she thought Black Bob and Ruth would find a common ground, but her father didn't seem much interested in meeting the elderly woman. "What do I know about farming?" he asked. "You know I've never been any good at small talk."

Lori didn't feel compelled to fill Black Bob's pickup with words. While she was growing up, there were whole days when she and her father hadn't said more than a half-dozen words to each other. The conversation last night and this morning was the longest sustained one father and daughter ever had.

In a way it was sad. Two people who'd spent so much time together should have more to say to each other, but that was the way Black Bob was—silent. Lori had always been comfortable with that, but marriage and getting to know Shade had changed her. She now accepted that people who spent time together spent a great deal of that time talking to, communicating with, each other. True, too much of her time with Brett had been wasted in arguments, in discovering how little they had in common.

It wasn't that way with Shade. From the day she met him, Lori had found things she wanted to talk to him about, to share. Even their disagreement about Vicky had been a form of communication. Their communication could have come about because everything was so right when they made love, but Lori doubted that. She'd never seen herself as a sexual creature, someone who could shut off her brain when some man asked her to go to bed with him. Sex with Brett had been acceptable because she admired his intellect. Sex with Shade—there simply weren't words to describe the total sense of fulfillment that permeated the act.

But something had gone wrong. Shade resented her interference in Vicky's life, because maybe he felt only he was capable of dealing with it. Had she been wrong to step in that way, she asked herself. But she'd felt so good about solving both Ruth's and Vicky's problems that maybe she'd missed something vital that Shade had been trying to communicate. That could have been the problem. She wasn't tuned in to Shade, after all.

Lori glanced over at Black Bob. She hadn't told her father why her marriage failed because she didn't think he would understand such things as different backgrounds, standards and beliefs that couldn't be changed. And, after all, she was Black Bob's daughter.

How much of you is in me, she asked her father's profile. *I believe you're happier alone than with someone. Maybe I'm the same way and just haven't accepted that yet. Maybe—maybe Shade knows that about me.*

Yes, Shade was willing to talk to her, joke with her, make love with her even, but maybe that was where the line had been drawn. She'd failed at her marriage. Wasn't that enough proof of her inability to interact with a man beyond a physical level?

Lori gave herself a mental shake. This searching and self-doubt was doing no earthly good. She only had her father for this weekend. She was determined to make the most of her short hours with him. There was the rest of her life to figure out where she was headed. "Do you really think you'll get the job?" she asked as a way of breaking the silence.

"Sure," Black Bob said confidently. "I probably know more about working in the woods than this character I'm going to see. You know what a guy told me last year? He was the owner of some big logging operation. He told me he'd hire me in a minute to oversee the operation. Offered me more money than I'd know what to do with."

"Why didn't you take the job?"

Black Bob turned toward his daughter as if she'd asked him why he didn't want to cut off his leg. "I'd have to boss men around, do the hiring and firing, take care of payrolls and deal with accountants and stuff. Are you kidding? All that time talking and on the phone and filling out forms? You know me, Lori. I don't like people that much."

Lori slid closer to her father, gritting her teeth against the pain in her knee. "You like me," she teased.

"That's because you're like me, kid. You and I, we think alike."

There it was again! There was no way Lori was going to escape a serious look at her life this weekend. Even as she was telling her father about the slide show she'd seen on historical logging and Shade's suggestion that Black Bob do an oral history for the historical society, Lori was thinking about how torn she was between being with her father and seeing Shade. But maybe it didn't matter, after all. Lori had gone off with her father without consulting with Shade first. If she'd done that with Brett, he would have ranted at her until she felt like the most disloyal wife alive. Could she blame Shade if he felt as if he'd been deserted, she asked herself. That was what Brett had always hit her with when she asked for time away from him.

It wasn't until they reached the logging operation that Lori was able to put her questions on hold. With the use of a wooden staff she was able to hobble painfully around the camp, poking into the corners of her memory. The sight of a mammoth caterpillar clinging to the side of a mountain took her back to her eighth year when Black Bob first let her sit on his lap while he ran one. The weather-scarred trailer the foreman was staying in wasn't any bigger than several her father had owned. Although inside it was an office and not a home for two people, even that was a familiar memory. Lori had been in a dozen trailers like this. The sight of an overflowing ashtray, a table cluttered with maps, order forms, forest-service permits, were more links with the past.

When Black Bob had shaken hands with the foreman and then offered to drive Lori over to a previous clearcut now filled with seedling pine trees, Lori touched base with another part of her growing up. She'd always had a fascination with growing things, especially new life poking its way through the ground fertilized with pine needles and rotting wood. She slipped out of the truck and made her gimpy way over to the new growth. She thought of the evening she and Shade had spent hunting mushrooms in a site almost identical to this one but refused to let the thought stay long enough to threaten her mood. "Remember how we used to come back to logging operations in the spring and make ourselves sick on morel mushrooms?" she asked.

"You miss it, don't you?"

Lori leaned closer to the ground, making out the difference between established growth in the seedlings and the pale growing tips of the struggling trees. She ran her fingers over the new growth, loving the velvet softness. "Yes, I miss it." Then, taking her thoughts a step further, she said, "But I love what I'm doing now. Dad, I'm having so much fun at the farm. I'm working with living things, out-of-doors. There are all kinds of chickens and peacocks and geese at the farm. They aren't the same as deer and bears and chipmunks, but I get the same pleasure from seeing farm animals as I did seeing mountain wildlife."

"Not me," Black Bob observed as he helped Lori back to the pickup. "I don't know the first thing about farms. All I know is felling trees and running heavy equipment.''

I've gone beyond your experience, haven't I, Lori thought, not knowing what to do with that revelation.

They spent the rest of the day taking the four-wheel-drive truck along logging roads and jeep trails. There were times when it was all Lori could do to keep from crying out when her father hit a particularly deep rut, but she wasn't going to put a stop to what was happening. This day was for a precious step back in time, a return to her childhood and the experiences that had shaped the woman she'd become.

They spent the night in a cheap, quiet motel in a little town at the base of the mountains, and in the morning Black Bob went looking for a trailer to replace the one he'd left in Washington. As Lori waited for her father to dicker with the salesman, she tried to remember how many different trailers they'd lived in over the years. Most of them were so ancient that they couldn't stand being hauled to more than one or two logging sites. The old was always being replaced by another, not newer but closer to the current logging operation. Not many other girls would have been content with that kind of housing, but she'd never rebelled. Old rusting trailers were simply how Black Bob and his daughter lived.

Lori wasn't much help when her father and the salesman hooked the trailer up to the back of his pickup. She sat in the passenger's seat, gingerly rubbing her aching and still-swollen knee. For the first time she wondered if her Mustang was at the auto-repair shop. Maybe the shop owner had gotten in touch with Shade. If that was true, maybe Shade was asking himself questions he couldn't possibly answer about what she was doing, whether she was all right.

Lori groaned and threw her head back on the truck seat. All Shade knew was that she'd left a message saying she'd gone off with her father for the weekend. He'd have no idea whether she'd wrecked her car before or after leaving the message, whether she'd been injured, where she was right now.

Maybe she owed Shade Ryan more. He'd given her so much more than a job. He'd given her a place to stay, his friendship, his body, her first taste of full womanhood. And what had she given him in return? A message on a recording machine.

Other women didn't do that to the men in their lives. Other women spent their weekends with their men and found ways to make up for whatever fights they might have had. Other women knew what had to be said and done to rectify whatever had gone wrong.

But Lori wasn't like the women who existed in her thoughts. She hadn't had enough of watching how men and women interacted. Oh, yes, Brett had tried to teach her with words and arguments and accusations. Time and time again he'd told her that a man wants to feel he comes first in his wife's life, that she puts her own selfish thoughts aside and does what he wants her to do to please him.

What was it Shade wanted from her, she couldn't help but ask. Maybe he deserved, expected, more than a message on a recording machine. Had she failed him too deeply to ever make up for it? Maybe it was possible that Shade understand that she didn't know how to deal with their argument and needed this weekend alone with her father to try to find out some things about herself.

Oh, Shade, I don't know, she moaned as Black Bob was paying the salesman. *I don't know if I'm doing any-*

thing right. I just know I have to do what feels right for me. I hope you can understand that!

Lori didn't find the answer to that question when Black Bob drove her home Sunday night, and she was no closer to an answer when she struggled out of bed Monday morning. Unfortunately, or maybe fortunately, her father had been in a hurry to get back to the mountains and hadn't taken time to come into Shade's house. Together they'd taken a look at the strange car parked in the driveway and read the note from the mechanic explaining that it was a loaner for her to use until the Mustang had been repaired. Lori stayed awake for an hour, worrying how she was going to pay for the repairs. She also wondered whether Shade was footing the bill for the loaner car. It was that thought that finally allowed her to fall asleep. He might be angry at her for meddling in Vicky's and Ruth's affairs and leaving for the weekend, but at least he was practical enough to realize she'd need a way to get to work.

If she was capable of working, Lori thought as she was trying to loosen her stiff knee under the shower. The orange-and-purple discoloration was in full bloom, making her grateful for a job that allowed her to work in pants. She was now able to walk around the house without a cane but wasn't sure how much her knee could handle on the uneven surface around the farm.

To her relief, the loaner was an automatic shift. She eased her left leg into the car and eased her way down the mountain, acknowledging the knot in the pit of her stomach as she passed the spot where she'd plowed into the bank. She thought about Black Bob going to work that morning in mountains much more remote than the ones around her. She'd kissed him as he was getting ready to leave the night before and received his promise that he'd get in touch with her soon about doing an oral history, but neither of them had said anything about what was going to happen with the two of them beyond that. That knowledge cast a shade over Lori's day, and yet she understood her father enough to know that he didn't make those kinds of commitments. He'd raised his daughter and given her love and affection. Now it was time for her to go it alone.

I love you, Dad, Lori thought as she reached the bottom of the mountain. *I also know how you feel about relationships.*

She might be a carbon copy of Black Bob. She could picture herself feeling love and responsiblity for a child but being ready to let go when that child became an adult. The memory of Shade's eyes searching hers stopped her. Letting go of that man wasn't something she wanted to think about.

Lori's first contact with human beings other than her father came when Vicky ran out to the car and insisted that she come in and join her and Ruth for coffee before going to work. "You wouldn't believe what a bear Shade's been." Vicky laughed as she brought coffee for the three of them onto the enclosed front porch. "He came by twice this weekend to make sure I wasn't burning the place down."

"Oh, no," Lori objected. "I'm sure he has more faith in you than that."

"I'm not sure what the burr under his saddle is. Something has turned him into a bear, all right," Ruth said. "I'll tell you one thing. He sure didn't like not having you around for three days."

Lori stared into her coffee. Given the fact of their argument the last time they saw each other, Lori would have thought Shade would be relieved to have her out of the way. "Did he say much about me?" she asked tentatively.

"Not much," Vicky supplied. "He was pretty mad at himself. Something about your accident being his fault and wishing he'd insisted on your brakes being fixed instead of other things."

Lori remembered a night that was supposed to be devoted to her car that had turned into a night of love-making. "Shade isn't my mechanic," she tried to explain. "It's my fault I neglected those brakes, not his."

"Tell him." Ruth shook her head. "That man sure knows how to nurse a guilt complex. He's probably going to jump all over you, but it's just because he's been so damned worried about you."

Worried. She couldn't remember anyone ever really worrying about her. Her father had always assumed that things were going to turn out all right, and Brett was much more concerned with getting her to fit the mold he was trying to carve. She'd never understood the guidelines that said men were supposed to be in charge of cars while women reigned in the kitchen. Lori concentrated on her coffee. She'd never been able to work out a viable marriage contract with Brett. Now, it seemed, she wasn't doing any better with a man who meant more to her than her ex-husband ever had.

Lori was in the greenhouse separating healthy plants from those that weren't going to survive and deciding how many glass panes in the greenhouse wall would have to be replaced when Shade's car pulled up the driveway and parked in front of the house. From her secluded location she could see him turn to look at the loaner car before going toward the farmhouse. Lori returned to her work, her body tense, tears seeking a way to break free. She didn't know if she could bear not having him near.

He didn't give her long to think about the answer. She still hadn't been able to force her mind and hands to return to business before he was pushing the greenhouse door open. Lori turned toward him, carefully bringing her injured leg around with her. Humidity from the greenhouse had already plastered her bangs against her forehead, and she could feel sweat on her upper lip. Lori reached her right hand to the wooden shelf holding some thirty plants in their clay pots, afraid to look down to see if it was shaking.

Shade reached out and absently ran his fingers along the branches of a jade tree. She was here! Safe. "It shouldn't cost much to have your car repaired," he said without introduction. That he was able to speak at all amazed him. His moods had swung in a thousand directions since he heard her voice on the recording machine, since seeing her car. "My mechanic friend has always wanted to work on an old Mustang."

"Thank you for the loaner. I'd be lost without it."

"Did you have a good weekend?"

"Yes. It was good to see my father again."

"Did you talk to him about the oral history?" Damn! This wasn't what he wanted to say at all. He needed to pull her close against him, assure his body that she was really here, after all. But the ghost of an argument still stood between them. He had to respect the rift that argument had created. "Do you think he'll be interested in the idea?"

"Yes. He's going to be in the Cascades for several months. I—I hope to see more of him than I have for several years."

"Maybe I can meet him someday." Shade was still

fingering the jade tree, but there was a tension in his fingers he knew he'd have to control if he wanted to avoid harming the tree. If only he could touch her! It might solve everything. But maybe it would only make things worse.

"Maybe," Lori said tentatively. "You have to understand my father. He doesn't like to be nailed down. He's always done what he wanted, when he wanted. I'm just happy he's going to be around for a little while."

"And you think you turned out like him." Shade's lips tightened, causing him to admit how wide the gulf between them was. "Black Bob's always on the move, isn't he?"

"What's wrong with that?" Lori snapped. She didn't want to argue with Shade. Anything but that! But the dark glowing lights deep in his jade eyes were scaring her. She hadn't admitted how much she'd missed him until now.

Shade let his hand drop heavily to his side. "Nothing. Absolutely nothing. Some people believe in putting down roots, developing ties. Others don't want anything to do with that. I did a lot of thinking about that while you were gone."

"You did?"

Shade turned away and gave her nothing but his back to stare at. "I didn't have that much else to think about. You didn't even bother to tell me about the accident."

"I—I'm sorry," she stammered. "But I hadn't seen my father for so long. I wanted—"

"You had better things to do than get in touch with me. Don't bother to explain. I understand. Like I said, commitment means different things to different people." He didn't understand his anger or his need to hurt her. All he could do was flow with the emotion, allow it the life it was demanding. If he said anything more— No.

Lori didn't try to stop him as Shade slammed the greenhouse door behind him. Her leg wouldn't allow her to run after him, and her heart was too deeply wounded to allow her to speak.

Ruth had said Shade was worried about her. It wasn't that at all. He didn't want anything to do with her.

Chapter Eleven

Two things went right in the next five days, but they had so little impact on what was happening to Lori's heart that she was able to take only minimal comfort from them. Three days after seeing Shade in the greenhouse, Ruth informed her that the doctor's statement to the effect that she needed housekeeping services had been accepted by the powers that be. Vicky would get paid for the work she was doing. Not only that; Ruth was finding that she fully enjoyed having the younger woman around. "Shade was right," Ruth admitted. "Vicky has a lot to learn. But she's eager, and I love having someone to boss around and talk to."

Thursday after work Lori stopped off at the repair shop to ask about the work that had been done on her Mustang. To her suprise she found that the car had been repainted after the dents were pounded out. "I used the original color, because that's what helps those old classics retain their value," the mechanic explained. "The left side needed a lot of work. It wouldn't have looked good if I'd only had part of it painted."

"It's going to cost an awful lot," Lori started before

the mechanic interrupted to tell her that she was only going to be charged for materials, not labor.

"If you don't mind, I'm going to display before-and-after pictures. I'll get enough publicity off those pictures that I should be paying you. The brake work will be completed tomorrow. You can have your car back then."

Lori nodded, a little apprehensive, because that would mean having to use her left leg to work the clutch. She hadn't given her knee near the attention she knew it needed, but with her heart in the state it was, her knee had to come second.

She hadn't seen or heard from Shade since Monday. Ruth had told her that he'd been out to the farm every evening, which made her wonder if he was trying to avoid her. She told herself he was checking up on his ex-wife, waiting for the time when he could tell Lori that her decision to throw Vicky and Ruth together was the work of a misfit who didn't know anything about successful relationships.

He was right, she admitted, when the tears she controlled all day sprang free at night. The only thing she knew about relationships between men and women was that women, this woman at least, had fallen in love and didn't know what to do with a heart that was more vulnerable and wounded than she dreamed possible.

It wasn't fair! Shade should have told her she was going to fall in love with him. He was the one who knew how to deal with old women and ex-wives and board members and volunteers and the hundreds of people who turned to the historical society. He was the one who dealt with humans day after day. He knew what made them tick, what went on inside them, not her.

Hadn't he offered her his friendship, his house, his body? He must have known how she was going to react. He must know that even now she was crying into the pillow he'd bought in the house he loved because that pillow and that house were filled with his presence.

I've got to get out of here. Lori sobbed as she searched for a cool spot in the hot bed. *I have to go on working for Shade, but that doesn't mean I have to live surrounded by him.*

What had he said? That commitment meant different things to different people? Yes, he'd been striking out at her when he said those words. But, she now believed, his words had even more application to him than her. He was committed enough to Ruth and Vicky to see them every night. She—she didn't even rate a phone call.

I'm not going to call you, she told the memory that lingered in the bedroom. *I'm not going to expose my heart to you and let you see how deeply it has been touched by you.* She didn't have much left; all she had was her pride. And an upbringing that didn't tell her enough about how men and women interacted.

After work Friday Lori exchanged her loaner car for her Mustang and drove up the mountain. She let herself into the house. Heat from the summer day was still trapped inside the house. Lori walked slowly to the sliding-glass door and opened it to welcome in pristine air scented with pine. She cocked her head, listening to the silence. She hadn't thought much about that silence in the past week; too much had been going on inside her head. But now silence wasn't what she wanted to surround herself with.

Lori turned on the stereo, choosing the records Shade had shared with her. She didn't really want to spend the weekend looking for another place to live; this place was where she wanted to come home to. But that wasn't her decision, not in the long run at least. Vicky was content where she was staying now. In fact, with Ruth's encouragement, she'd started looking at the possiblity of going back into nursing. Vicky might soon have the self-confidence to come back here to live. Or maybe by now Shade had decided that there was enough distance between him and his marriage that he could bring himself to move back.

There were things that had to be decided. Lori couldn't go on living in limbo. She turned the stereo up enough for the sounds to reach the bedroom and went in to change out of her work clothes. Finally, dressed in a robe that floated to the ground and covered her purple knee, she sat on the bed and dialed Shade's number.

When he said, "Hello," she had to take three deep breaths before finding the courage to speak. "I think we need to talk about the house," she managed. "I don't feel right staying here anymore."

"Do you want to tell me why?" he asked, giving her no easy way out.

"Can't you figure it out?" He didn't have to make this so hard for her. "Things—things have changed between us. I'm not sure you want me to stay here anymore."

"Wait a minute. You're getting ahead of me. I'm not going to discuss this on the phone." Before she could stop him, he'd informed her that he was on his way up and had hung up.

Lori dropped her hands to her lap, nervously crumpling the loose fabric of her robe. She tried to tell herself that this wasn't at all the way she wanted the conversation to turn out, but halfway through her pronouncement she stopped herself. That wasn't the truth. She'd had five lonely nights with no one but herself to talk to since saying good-bye to her father. No matter what was said between her and Shade tonight, she had to see what was in his eyes.

She'd slipped into sandals, done a little dusting and made sure there was something cool in the refrigerator when the doorbell rang. Lori walked to the door, feeling the strain of the day in her knee. To her surprise Shade was not wearing a suit and tie or slacks and knit shirt but a sweatshirt and a pair of jeans that had been softened by age and hugged the contours of his muscles with easy familiarity. The sleeves of his sweatshirt had been cut off just below the shoulder, making it acceptable for warm weather. He glanced at her comfortable attire and then touched his sweatshirt. "We feel the same way about Friday night," he pointed out noncommittally.

Lori stood aside to let him in. Her body felt rigid, her thoughts constricted. If only she wasn't thinking about other evenings they'd spent in this house, evenings when having him with her felt as comfortable as wearing this old robe.

"What did you want to see me about?" In the background the stereo was playing, but she was conscious only of the way her heart was pounding, how powerful the desire to touch him had become.

Instead of answering, Shade walked into the living room and stood at the deck door looking out at the mountain. It had very nearly killed him to stay away from her, but he'd felt he needed space in order to think. Now, he realized, he hadn't thought enough. He wanted to have back what they'd experienced before.

But maybe it was too late for that. He didn't look at her as he spoke. He didn't trust himself to. "You're playing the stereo. I wouldn't think you'd be interested in touching the memories that go with that music. Or maybe memories don't mean as much to you as—" He turned around. Damn! He didn't want to get into that! "Do you really want to move?"

No! "It isn't an easy decision to make," she said instead.

"Isn't it?" he challenged, because he was raw inside and afraid of letting her see that rawness. "If I remember, you make decisions easily."

"What are you talking about?" Lori knew she was gripping her loose robe so tightly that she was wrinkling it, but she couldn't help herself.

"You threw Vicky and Ruth together without bothering to consult me about it."

"Please, Shade, don't. If you came up here to discuss that—"

"No, I didn't," he interrupted. This wasn't going right. He tried again. "But for your information, I have to hand it to you. I didn't think it was going to work out as well as it seems to have. Of course, Vicky is still acting like she's launched on some new adventure. She isn't taking things very seriously."

Lori thought about Vicky's renewed interest in nursing and wondered if Shade simply wasn't able to see the changes in his ex-wife. Still, she was the one who didn't want Vicky to come between them any more than she had already. "You don't like it when women make decisons independent of you, do you?" she challenged as a way of getting around the tension gripping her.

"I'm not used to the women in my life making independent decisions. But you're an independent woman." He had to give her that much. He'd be lying if he didn't. "You don't really need a man."

Lori cringed but refused to let Shade see the pain he'd inflicted on her. "Do you want me to apologize? I wouldn't before, and I'm not going to now."

"I know that." Shade was still staring out at the deepening shadows. He'd wanted her to deny his statement, but she hadn't. Now he hurt too much to drop things. "I'm not going to apologize for what I said about you not needing a man. You made that very clear last weekend. I didn't mean enough to you to rate a phone call."

"I did call you," Lori pointed out, hating the hard, unrelenting line of his neck, hurting because the desire to kiss away that hard line was so strong.

Shade turned on her. His eyes flashed daggers of light capable of searing her soul. "A message on a recording machine! A wrecked car with no explanation. You didn't even care enough to tell me whether you'd been hurt or not. Didn't you think I deserved that?"

"Shade?" Lori dug her nails into her palms to keep from putting her hand between herself and his flashing eyes. "Everything happened so fast. My father—"

"I know. There's really been only one man in your life, hasn't there, Lori?" Damn! This wasn't how he wanted things to be between them. If only he could think without his heart getting in the way. "The only real need you've had for another human being was when you were a child needing a parent. Why should you think I might be worried about you? After all, all we shared were a few laughs, a few nights together."

"Please don't do this to me, Shade," Lori begged, collapsing onto a couch before her knee could give out on her. "Do you have to be this angry? All I wanted to do was talk about the house."

"Of course, the house." Shade dropped his own body in a nearby chair. He took a deep breath and spoke through lips that barely moved. "You said you don't feel right about living here anymore. I'm trying to understand why."

Was he, Lori asked herself. He was so used to being consulted on Vicky's every move that maybe he couldn't fathom a woman who made her own decisions.

Only she wasn't as strong as he thought she was. If she moved, she would be walking away from everything good that had happened between herself and Shade Ryan, and that might kill her. "I was only supposed to stay here a short while," she started, trying to work her way through her feelings as she formed the words. "It isn't as if this was a permanent arrangement."

"And what does Black Bob's daughter need with a permanent arrangement?" Shade asked with the same bitterness that had posessed him since he got her phone call. "You know, maybe having your father drop back into your life was best in the long run. It let you get back in touch with your true feelings. After all, a woman who spends weekends traipsing around the wilderness doesn't have much need for a permanent home. I'm just surprised you agreed to take the job at the farm. You're not the kind of woman to tie herself down very long." No. The last thing he wanted to hear was her agreeing with what he was saying.

This time Lori did raise her hand in a futile attempt to protect herself from the pain of Shade's words. "You really hate me, don't you?" she asked, terrified of the answer. "As far as you're concerned, nothing I do is right."

"What do you care what I think?" Shade pushed

himself heavily to his feet. He'd done it. Said fatal words that couldn't be taken back. "I was wrong, Lori. I thought I sensed something in you that obviously isn't there." He wanted to run out the door and hide from his words. But it was too late. The only thing left to do was to hurt her as much as he hurt. "You tried to tell me that you needed to be free, unencumbered. I'm not going to try to change you. I'm sorry if you feel you've been saddled with this house." He started toward the door, speaking over his shoulder. "Leave whenever you want to."

Lori didn't try to stop him as he stalked to the door and let himself out. She wasn't even aware of the effort it took for her to stand. Indeed, she was standing where Shade had stood a few minutes ago when he was staring out at the mountain without asking herself how she'd gotten there. What she felt at this moment, with the stereo sounds assaulting her, went beyond tears. Lori pushed open the sliding-glass door and stepped out onto the high deck. She looked down into the valley. How little effort it would take to climb onto the railing and hurtle herself into space. It wasn't a suicidal thought. Rather, given the other emotions she was being forced to weather, the question of whether it was possible for her to fly was much easier to concentrate on.

Her fingers clutched the wooden railing; she leaned forward, cocking her head in an attempt to hear comforting woodland sounds. All she heard was the sound of Shade's car starting toward the valley.

In her mind and heart, she followed him down the mountain.

"You look like hell," Vicky proclaimed the next day. "What'd you do, spend the night watching the old

black-and-white movies and drinking your way through
a bottle?"

Lori tore her eyes away from a map of the farm she'd
been staring at for a good ten minutes and faced the
younger woman, who had somehow managed to join
her by the fish pond without Lori's being aware of it. "I
don't drink, at least not like that" was the best Lori
could offer.

"Then you should. At least that way you'd have an
excuse for the way you look." Vicky thrust a mug of
coffee in Lori's hand. "I tried to talk to Shade a few
minutes ago. The man sounds like a throwback to Cro-
Magnon man. I wish the two of you would resolve your
differences so I don't have to look at and listen to two
miserable people."

Throughout the sleepless night that accounted for
the deep hollows her eyes turned into, Lori kept telling
herself she wanted to be alone, drive into the mountains and lose herself in wilderness. But this morning,
with Vicky offering what might be a sympathetic ear,
Lori changed her mind. "There's nothing left to resolve," she moaned. "Shade doesn't want anything to
do with me."

"Like fun he doesn't," Vicky snorted, her voice
sounding older, more settled, than it had when Lori
first met her. "The man acted like he was crawling out
of his skin while you were gone for those three days.
He went over and over what might have happened
when you had your accident until I wanted to tell him
to shut up. You know what he said? He said he was
afraid he'd lost you to your past. I didn't know what he
was talking about, but since he wasn't in any mood to
explain, I didn't ask."

Lori shook her head, regretting the movement, since

it sent stabbing pain through a head already filled to bursting. "You didn't hear him last night. He—he wouldn't have said what he did if he cared."

"Boy, you don't know Shade, do you? Listen to me." Vicky laughed. "I'm hardly what anyone would expect to be an expert on Shade Ryan, but I do know that he cared for me a great deal. Not the way he cares about you, but protective feelings just the same. He has this thing about getting close to people. It comes naturally to him. You know what I think? You don't fit any mold he's ever seen before."

Lori faced Shade's first wife. "What are you talking about?"

"I'm talking about the difference between you and me," Vicky pointed out. "I needed a father figure, a big brother, something. I'm not crazy about admitting that. I'm hoping it's a sign of maturity that I can see it now. Anyway, you're so different from me that it's a wonder we have as much to talk about as we do. Look at yourself," Vicky went on when Lori started to speak. "You're a professional. You have a career, confidence in yourself. You practically raised yourself. You don't need to cling to anyone's shirttail. Can you blame Shade for being confused? He married a clinging vine, and now he's in love with a totally independent woman."

"Shade doesn't love me."

"Like fun he doesn't! I don't know about you two." Vicky shook her head in mock exasperation. "I wish you would get married so you could go to a marriage counselor and get things straightened out."

Because she'd promised to take Ruth to the beauty parlor, Vicky wasn't able to stay and talk to Lori. As Lori watched the younger woman skip back toward the farm, she bit her lip, thinking about how much Vicky had changed already and how much potential for maturity was in her. She wondered if Shade would now admit that maybe Lori had known what she was doing when she suggested Vicky as Ruth's housekeeper.

Not that she was going to ask Shade that. Last night's attack on her emotions was all she could deal with for now and maybe for the rest of her life.

Lori had had arguments before in her life. There'd been too many of them in the months before she and Brett separated. But although those disagreements left her frustrated and sad, they didn't tear her to shreds the way Shade's words had.

Vicky was wrong. There was no way Shade could love her. He wouldn't have cast her aside, told her she could get along without him, if he had.

Lori made no effort to return her thoughts to the map she held in her hands. Instead, she stepped slowly away from the low-hanging willow tree hovering over the fish pond and walked to where she could stare out at the veil of trees and brush that obscured her view of the barn. There were tree roses climbing their way up a pair of oaks, a bank of rhododendron so thickly bunched that they had become a barrier, but Lori wasn't thinking about the work that lay ahead of her. Instead, she thought of a man who loved to sit in a darkened room listening to the stereo with the door open to let in the scent of pine.

There were so many good things about Shade. If he'd insisted on surrounding the two of them with other people, on being the social creature Brett had been, maybe Lori wouldn't have fallen in love with him. But Shade had a side to him she'd never seen in a man outside her father. Shade could be content without the phone ringing, the TV on, somewhere to go for dinner. He took pleasure in the simple things that added together to make the sum of life.

Damn you, Shade Ryan! Why didn't you tell me I wasn't what you wanted before I fell in love with you!

Lori reached out and drew one of the climbing roses to her, grateful for the thorn in her forefinger that provided relief from her thoughts. She had no idea how she was going to go on working here feeling the way she did about her boss. If she took self-preservation seriously, she would throw her belongings in her Mustang and head for the nearest road out of the county.

That's what she'd done when she left Brett.

But Lori had changed. Shade had changed her. She loved her job and Ruth and Vicky and what she was learning about friendships between women. She'd committed herself to a project, a living monument to the past. She couldn't walk away from the commitment and have much pride in herself.

Somehow, someway, she was going to have to make a wary peace with Shade, forge a working relationship they could both live with. Somehow she had to make her heart understand that.

Lori waved Ruth and Vicky off, feeling a little sad that she wasn't part of the expedition to a beauty parlor. But, she reminded herself, it was just as well. If she looked like hell the way Vicky said she did, the beauty-parlor staff probably wouldn't let her in the front door.

Resolutely, Lori forced herself back to the map clutched in her hand. She wanted to have the trenching for the underground sprinkler system done and covered up before she did much with the vines that carpeted the ground. She'd tentatively mapped out the location for the sprinkler heads. The workmen were due out tomorrow, and Lori had to make sure she was satisfied with the map she'd be turning over to them.

She was stepping off the route the system would take and watching the antics of a pair of courting peacocks, her mind resolutely off thoughts of Shade Ryan and last night, when a misstep took her beyond the firm path and into the vine growth. Lori took another half step. It was too late. The uneven surface, hidden by foliage, threw her off balance. She might have been able to catch herself if it hadn't been for her weak left knee. One moment Lori was reaching out for support. The next she was landing unceremoniously in the middle of the heavy ground cover. Lori made a half movement designed to push away the vines tickling her throat when the first wave of pain struck her.

Lori gasped, taken by surprise at the intensity of the agony slicing up her knee until it seemed as if her thigh, her belly even, was injured, as well.

"No!" she gasped, forgetting that only a pair of self-absorbed peacocks had seen her fall. "It can't be!"

But it was. The injury that had begun with an automobile accident had taken a new, more serious turn. Lori didn't dare move. Laced together with the pain was the undeniable sensation of muscles and tendons stretched beyond their limit. Lori had pulled a muscle or two in her life. She had a pretty good idea what had happened. What frightened her was the knowledge that everything that existed below the skin on her knee was no longer where it was supposed to be. How much damage had she done!

Lori had two hours to worry about that, to fight off pain and insects and thirst that grew as the day warmed. Her sporadic, tentative attempts to stand were rewarded by fresh stabs of pain that forced her to close her eyes and breathe heavily to keep from crying. The barn was so far away that none of the workmen could possibly hear her. Her knee beneath the layer of faded denim was swelling to the point where she was sure her jeans would have to be cut off. The pressure of fabric against sensitive flesh gave her more than the pain of torn ligaments to think about.

Her knee would have to be looked at. She raged at herself for thinking she knew enough about joint injuries to act as her own doctor. Growing up a hundred miles from a hospital definitely had its drawbacks, she finally admitted. It made people think they had to handle all injuries on their own instead of relying on medical science.

It was too late to worry about that. She would face the tongue-lashing of doctors and nurses when and if she could get up off the ground and into a hospital.

It was all Lori could do to keep from screaming when she finally saw Vicky's car pull into the driveway. But Lori was determined not to appear as a helpless, terrified woman. She might not have much left, but she did have her dignity.

She waited until Vicky had gotten out of the car and was holding the door open for a neatly coiffed Ruth. Then she called out in what she hoped was a controlled, self-possessed voice. "Vicky? Can you come here a minute?"

An hour later Lori was being wheeled into the county hospital emergency room with a thin-lipped Vicky holding her hand. Vicky had assessed the situation, run to the barn to summon a couple of workmen and then directed the action as the men lifted a white-faced Lori into the car seat Ruth had vacated. Ruth's look of concern as Lori was trying to get her leg into the confines of the car had kept her from crying out when pain reached the top of her head.

"I'm going to call Shade," Vicky said once Lori was settled on the examining table.

"Don't!" Lori turned anguished eyes toward her young friend. "Not yet, please. Let's see what the doctor has to say. I don't want to disturb Shade if it isn't serious."

"It's serious," Vicky pointed out. "Look at that knee. It's more than twice normal size."

While Lori dug into the sides of the examining table with taut fingers, the doctor slowly, carefully, examined her knee and the surrounding area. She relaxed a little as Xrays were taken but froze again when she saw the look on the tall, slender doctor's face. "Why didn't you keep this wrapped when you first injured it?" he asked sternly. "Didn't you realize how weak it was?"

Lori swallowed, feeling too much like a child being chastised for some misbehavior. "I've never taken injuries very seriously," she tried to explain. "I grew up where there was no medical treatment available. My dad always said that if you leave the body alone it takes care of itself."

"That's a pretty blanket statement," the doctor snorted. "Tell me something. If you got something embedded in your eye, would you leave it there?"

"Of course not," Lori countered, reacting negatively to the man's superior attitude. "I'm talking about day-to-day injuries. This isn't the first time I've had bruises."

"What you have is a complete tear of your knee ligaments. They were probably simply strained when you had your first accident. If you'd kept the knee wrapped, you wouldn't be in the mess you're in now."

"What—what are you going to have to do?" Lori hated the sound of the diagnosis. A ligament tear had to be more serious than a bruise.

The doctor ran his forefinger gently over Lori's misshapened knee. "Go in and repair it."

"Surgery?"

"Surgery," the doctor said with a note of finality that struck Lori like a bucket of ice water. "You don't want to be a cripple, do you? The ligaments need to be properly replaced. Following that, you're going to need extensive physical therapy. Mrs. Black, you're now in the position of a lot of professional athletes. Not enough knees heal themselves. The sooner we get to work, the sooner you'll be back on your feet."

When the doctor left to make arrangements to have her admitted, Lori shut her eyes tightly, fighting back anger, helplessness and a strange, overwhelming fear she didn't know how to handle. She'd never been to a hospital before in her life, let alone faced surgery. There wouldn't be anyone to hold her hand, to pat her on the head and tell her she was going to be okay. Lori had no experience in being helpless and vulnerable. As a result, she had no defense against the emotion.

She dropped her head as far forward as possible without moving her knee. It wasn't fair! Except for a few square inches of her body, she was a healthy young woman. How dare everything come to a stop simply because a joint in her leg wouldn't function the way it was supposed to! She reached out a tentative finger and brushed the purple flesh. Her Mustang had lost all reliability because the brakes wouldn't function. Now she was a helpless hospital patient because of her damn knee!

She didn't know how to deal with this. Lori, who had

never so much as had the flu in her life, didn't know the first thing about being a patient, about being dependent on any person or institution.

The plain, undeniable truth was that Lori was frightened, terrified. She hated and feared this strange sense of vulnerability, of being trapped where she was in this helpless body. If only she could swing her legs over the side of the bed, slip into her shoes and—

Where would she go? Shade hadn't said anything last night, but surely he didn't want her at his place anymore. She could go to the Kadin farm, but that was only wishful thinking. Lori Black couldn't move a step under her own steam.

Again she dropped her head forward and stopped fighting the tears that had built to overflowing. She was scared, plain and simple.

Lori felt a powerful hand on her shoulder. "I've never seen you cry."

Chapter Twelve

Lori didn't have to open her eyes to know who was speaking. His voice was as familiar as her own heartbeat. And as essential. No matter what happened with the rest of her life, that would never change. She longed to lean against Shade, absorb his strength and make it hers. God, did she need that!

But his words from last night still echoed inside her throbbing, frightened body. They had no commitment to each other.

Denying her heart, she fought against the tears that were still seeking release and faced her boss. It was impossible to raise her voice above a strangled whisper. "The doctor said I'm going to have to have surgery on my knee."

"Is that all?" Shade was breathing deeply, heavily. That should be some kind of a clue to his emotions, but Lori was too wrapped up in her own to try to fathom them.

"All?" Lori managed. "Maybe the idea of going under a knife doesn't bother you, but it's the last thing in the world I want."

"Why?"

Why? That was an insane question. "Because I'll be

stuck in this damn hospital! I can't leave. Can't go outside. I'll have to sit in bed waiting for people to bring everything to me. I won't even be able to go to the bathroom without help."

Lori flushed at what she was revealing, but the fear she was battling was too strong. There were things she had to get out of her system or risk losing her mind. Shade already knew more about what went on inside her than anyone else. "I've always been able to do what I want, go where I want. I've never felt helpless before. I hate being like this!" She waved her hand over her knee, careful not to jostle it.

Shade gripped her shoulders and forced her to look at him. His eyes held her with more strength than his arms ever could. "Where was it you wanted to go?"

Lori moaned as her knee resisted the pull on her body. She lifted her arms, trying to shake off Shade's grip. Since he couldn't be tender with her, she didn't want to be touched by him at all. The power in his eyes was more than she was capable of dealing with. "Into the mountains with Black Bob!" she said, grasping at the first thing that entered her mind, wondering if she could use words that would hurt him. "Dad's out there skidding logs, and I'm stuck here while some doctors get rich."

"So that's what has you so upset. I was a fool to think it might be anything else." Shade released her, his eyes saying nothing about being sorry that he'd hurt her. "You and I had a disagreement, and now you want to run off where you don't have to face me. I guess I should have expected it. I'm sorry this—" He jabbed a finger in the direction of her knee. "I'm sorry this has spoiled your plans."

As Shade continued to stare daggers at her, Lori became aware that from the waist down she wore nothing but underpants. Shade had seen her in less, but she didn't need to feel exposed on top of everything else. Maybe she should ask him to leave. She had to get a hold of herself. "My knee, the surgery, it's going to spoil a lot of things," Lori pointed out between clenched teeth, denying everything her heart wanted to say. "I'm not going to be able to do much work around the farm for a while. I think you better look for a replacement."

"I'll make that decision, thank you. Let's wait until we know what the doctor thinks."

Of course, Lori thought. The historical society wouldn't want to have to pay an employee who was a liability. "What did you come here for, anyway?" she asked. One word, one gesture, from him and she'd be burying her head in his chest. She had to guard against exposing herself that way. After all, he was the one who said that not all people were cut out for commitment. Obviously that was what he now believed about her. If that was the way he felt about her, she wasn't going to cling to him.

Shade didn't answer right away. "I'm here because Vicky told me to come." He laughed briefly. "That's the first time Vicky has ever given me an order. She's changing."

"What else did Vicky say?"

"She said that you were at the hospital and you needed me." Shade's clipped tones softened. For an insane second Lori believed he wanted to touch her cheek. "I told her you didn't need anyone, especially not me. But she told me to come, anyway."

Oh, Shade, I need you more than I've ever needed anyone in my life. I'm scared and helpless, and it isn't my father I need, after all. But she couldn't tell him that. She would have exposed her heart to a man who didn't want that heart.

"I hope I didn't upset her or Ruth too much," Lori managed around her thoughts.

Shade laughed that deep rich rumble that could warm her soul. "Those two war horses are doing just fine. You know, I've always admired Ruth's independence, her self-confidence. I think it's starting to rub off on Vicky. I have you to thank for that."

"Don't start on that, Shade," Lori warned, fearful of the direction this conversation might be taking them. "I'm in no mood for an argument."

"What argument?" Shade shrugged. His stance might be casual, but his green eyes were edging into black. "Listen to me. I'm going to make a confession. One that's overdue." He jammed his hands in his pockets and took a step backward. For a long minute he said nothing, and Lori, who didn't breathe during that time, concentrated on the slow way his features were drawing together. "I was wrong. Things are working out between those two, after all. It might not be a marriage made in heaven, but I can see that it's going to benefit both of them. Vicky doesn't bear much resemblance to the woman-child I married. You were right. Do you hear what I'm saying? You're right, and I'm wrong."

That's the only thing I'm right about, Lori admitted to herself. *I didn't know what was going to happen when I fell in love with you.* "You don't have to stay here any longer." Lori had to take a deep breath, because the words she had to say didn't want to come out. "You've done what Vicky told you to."

"Do you want me to leave?"

"You have better things to do than sit here and watch my knee turn black."

"You're wrong. This is the only thing I have to do today. It is going to crimp your style for a while, isn't it?" Shade observed, bending over for a closer look. "You're going to have to put your mountain-climbing plans on hold."

Lori didn't want to climb a mountain. She wanted to reach out for the man she loved, have him tell her he was staying here for as long as she needed him and there was nothing for her to be scared of. But that was the ultimate surrender.

There wasn't time for Lori to wonder why Shade couldn't see in her eyes what her heart was saying. There wasn't time for learning the reason behind his own darkened eyes. The swinging doors leading to the examining room opened, and a nurse, followed by a brawny young man in rumpled whites pushing a stretcher, entered the room. Shade stepped back to let the two near her.

Lori tried to concentrate as the nurse explained how she and the orderly were going to lift her onto the stretcher without disturbing her knee any more than necessary, but the thought of becoming a helpless exhibit being wheeled down a sterile white corridor to prepare for a surgeon's knife was almost more than she could handle. Her emotions were too close to that of a wild bird with a broken wing. If she thought her knee was capable of it, she would have jumped from the table and fled the hospital wearing nothing except a blouse and underpants.

But her knee was holding her prisoner within these white walls. There was no way she could stop the orderly from placing his arms under her armpits or kick away the nurse who was controlling the movement of her lower body.

Lori felt her mobile bed turning around, being backed out of the examining room. As the swinging doors opened to accommodate them, Lori surrendered. The look she gave Shade was one of total helplessness—fear that existed despite all reason. It didn't matter that he could read her naked emotions. Nothing mattered except not giving way to panic.

"Lori?" she heard him whisper, but it was too late. She was being swallowed up by the institution.

A while later she was settled in a small room, an elderly snoring woman in the other bed. She nodded, only half concentrating, as the doctor explained that her surgery had been scheduled for the first thing in the morning. In the meantime, the hospital staff was going to do everything it could to hold down the swelling. "I'll have a physical therapist talk to you, and I'll make sure you get a sleeping pill tonight," he said impersonally. Then he patted her shoulder and left.

Lori glanced over at her snoring roommate. How could anyone sleep here! She took several deep breaths accepting the fact that additional oxygen wasn't going to be enough to calm her. Somehow she was going to have to find a way to control her fear, or it would overwhelm her.

"Lori?"

This time Lori didn't try to stifle the sound that ripped its way up her throat. She saw Shade coming toward her, his eyes the rich jade shade she loved, his outstretched arms a lifesaving haven. Desperately, she reached out for the security he was offering her. Her animallike moan had told him everything she didn't have the words for. His arms were her one defense against fear.

His chest was the heaven-sent refuge Lori prayed it would be and more. She buried her hot face against his rib cage and moaned like a frightened animal as he started stroking her hair. Was the man really that strong, or did he feel that way only because she felt so helpless?

It didn't matter. What registered was that he was here, holding her firmly and yet gently. He wasn't asking her why she was crying or telling her she was shaking like a child. He wasn't saying accusing things about her not knowing how to take care of her injury or deserving what had happened. Instead, he was whispering things like "It's all right. I'm here."

He was here. That was all she had to know. The front of Shade's shirt was becoming soaked with hot tears. Lori's nose had started to run, and she was afraid she might awaken her snoring roommate. But it felt so good, so natural, to let him be her strength. Somehow he had the power in his body to hold back fear. It was hard to remember that she'd been terrified by white walls, a man in a white uniform. There were worse things in life than having to spend time in a hospital and submitting to an operation. She could no longer remember why it had been impossible for her to see that a few minutes ago. Finally, when she didn't have to gulp in order to breathe around her sobs, Shade helped her straighten and handed her a Kleenex. He continued to make contact with a broad hand in the small of her back. "Do you feel better?" he whispered.

"My head's splitting," Lori admitted, suddenly embarrassed because she'd revealed so much of her private self. There was no way he couldn't know what she'd gone through emotionally. "I—I've ruined your shirt. I'm sorry."

Shade ran his hand through her curls, touching her hot scalp. "You really hate it here, don't you?"

He wasn't laughing at her. Lori tried a steadying breath and something that resembled a tentative smile. She still sounded like a scared child. "I've never been in a hospital before. I—I feel so helpless, so trapped."

Shade frowned, his hand still in her hair. "I never thought about a hospital as being a trap. It is rather confining, isn't it?"

Lori nodded, her pounding head complaining. She didn't know if he would pull back if she reached for him again. Maybe, in a minute, she'd have the courage to answer his question. "I've never been confined like this before," she explained around the residue of tears. "I didn't know it was going to get to me like this."

"Would you rather be in the woods with Black Bob? Or alone?"

"I—I don't know if I could handle being alone right now," Lori whispered. She sagged slightly, and he quickly supported her by pulling her against his chest. "Not as long as my knee's in this shape," she whispered. His warmth was giving her the courage to speak from the heart. "Shade? Will you be here when they take me to surgery?"

"Do you want me to?"

"Yes."

"Then I'll be there. You know," he went on after a moment of silence, "I'm seeing a side of you I didn't know existed. I've done you a disservice by labeling you the original independent woman." He brushed his lips against the top of her head. "I always thought of you as rugged, determined to stand on your own two feet. I didn't expect what I saw today."

Lori wanted to pull away, to try to read what Shade's eyes were saying, but it was much safer staying where she was with him supporting her. He was going to help her get through the surgery. If she didn't move, would he hold her through the night? "I—I left you a message, and I wasn't alone. I was with my father."

"That wasn't the only time," Shade pointed out, his voice sounding strangely wary. "Remember? There was another weekend when you went off exploring the county. You didn't want anyone with you then."

"No," Lori said honestly, "I didn't. Shade, it was like that a lot of my life. I'm used to doing things on my own. And you didn't mean to me then what you do now."

"Because you don't need anyone else."

"No. You're wrong." Lori said the words so softly that she couldn't be sure Shade would realize how much she was revealing. But even if she couldn't speak above a whisper, she had to try to explain. Somehow, she sensed, what she said would shape their future. He had followed her into the room, helped her release her tears. There was at least that much between them. "Maybe I thought that way once. I know I came to cherish my privacy when Brett wanted to spend every waking moment possessing me. But—Shade? It's different with you."

"How different?"

This time she pulled back enough to look into his eyes. He wasn't asking a casual question or expecting a casual answer. Good. She couldn't be anything but totally honest with him no matter what the outcome. "I feel different around you," she admitted, aware that

she was revealing something about herself she hadn't
known existed before meeting this very special man. "I
can't say there won't be times when I want to be by
myself. Everyone needs their own space sometimes.
I'd never ask you to account for all of your time. But—
don't make fun of me—I want to tell you things, share
things I've never felt a need to share before."

"Like what?"

"Like not having to pretend that I'm not scared."
Lori wanted to go on, but the sudden constriction in
her throat wouldn't let her.

"I appreciate that," Shade whispered. He placed his
hands on both sides of her neck, a gesture that was
both supporting and comforting. And yet words and a
touch didn't tell her what was in his heart. "Lori? I'm
sorry I got so angry with you the other day."

"Why did you?"

"What is this?" Shade asked, and Lori felt the hesi-
tancy behind his words. "Confession time? All right.
I'll tell you what I was thinking. It scared me when I
realized you'd been in an accident. It scared me because I don't want anything bad ever happening to you.
I wanted to bundle you up in bed and bring you chicken
soup and have you ask me to take care of whatever
your car needed. But you didn't need me for that. I
believed that." Shade ran a hand quickly through his
hair and then pressed it against her neck again. "You
didn't need me for a damn thing."

"Shade. That isn't true!" Lori gasped, but he wouldn't
let her continue.

"That's what stuck in my mind," he pressed. "That's
what I convinced myself I had to admit. Look at the evidence. Your father is a loner. You admitted you were like
him. Do you remember what I said when we were in the

greenhouse? I said Black Bob was always on the move and you were like him. I didn't want to say that. God, that was the last thing I wanted to think! But can you blame me? I had all the evidence I needed.''

"What evidence?" Lori interrupted. "You didn't give me much chance to talk."

"You did enough talking when you had me up to the house a few days later. You told me you didn't want to live here anymore."

Lori gasped. It was incredible that they could have interpreted the same conversation so differently. "I said I didn't feel right about living there. There's a difference."

"That's not the impression I got from talking to you." Shade knotted his brow as if wrestling with thoughts he didn't quite understand. "You reminded me that your living there wasn't supposed to be a permanent arrangement. You weren't interested in tying yourself down."

Had she said that? Lori was sure she hadn't. Shade had heard certain things, but they weren't necessarily what she was trying to tell him. "I—you were angry at me. I thought you didn't want me there. I was trying to tell you that I understood."

Shade's body tensed. "I didn't want you there? Where did you get that idea?"

"You—you told me to leave whenever I wanted to. You—you said I shouldn't feel saddled with the house."

To her surprise Shade increased his grip on her instead of letting go. "I said that because I wasn't going to try to force you into something you didn't want. I promised myself I'd never tie you down. Do you think I wanted you to move out? That's the last thing I'd ever want." Shade's eyes darkened as they had in the examining room. "I couldn't stand living there after Vicky and I split up. But after you moved in, I wanted to come back. You made the difference. You turned a house into a home for me. But—I believed you didn't feel the same way I did. Lori? The last thing I'd ever do is try to force you to do something. That's one lesson I learned from my marriage. I tried to mold Vicky." He shook his head as if trying to clear his thoughts. "It wasn't right for her. Brett tried to make you into what he wanted. You bolted." Shade's right hand moved from her neck to her chin, forcing her head back so she had nowhere to look except into his probing eyes.

"It tore me apart not to hold on to you, but I knew I'd only make things worse by trying."

"Shade?" It was almost impossible to speak with his lips so close. Her previous fear of her surroundings had turned into a fear of what he would say next. "What if I want you to hold on to me? What if I tell you I'm not like my father?"

Suddenly, she saw it. Something vulnerable was being exposed in Shade's eyes. That was what had been behind their mysterious darkening. His heart was as vulnerable as hers. "Do you mean that?" she heard him whisper.

"With all my heart. I learned something about Black Bob last weekend that I didn't know before. I was a part of his life when I depended on him, but now that I'm an adult, he doesn't feel a need to include me anymore. That's how he is." She was silent for a moment and then finished what had to be said. "I'm not like that. I could never be like that with—you. I love you too much."

"And I love you." Shade's breath caught against

Lori's eyelashes and dried the moisture her words had put there.

It cost Lori to lift her torso toward Shade's mouth, but the reward was worth the effort. In truth, it would have taken far greater pain than she was feeling to stop her. She parted her lips slightly as they met, but the kiss they shared in the hospital room was gentle, not passionate. There had been and would again be times when Lori wanted Shade's body more than anything else in life. Right now she needed his understanding, his love. Nothing more and nothing less.

Her kiss revealed everything she was ready to have exposed. She wanted to commit herself and have that commitment returned. His lips bore the proof she needed that love was a shared emotion.

SHADE WALKED BACK into the hospital room the next morning as Lori was being prepped for surgery. She clutched his hand tightly, her wide, staring eyes telling him that she still hadn't mastered her fear of being confined. Shade stepped back to allow a nurse to take Lori's pulse and temperature; then he took her hand again.

"You look like a sheep being led to the slaughter," he said as he smiled and bent to kiss her lightly on the forehead. He could sense that she needed to hear him speak. "Vicky and Ruth send you their best. They're going to be here right after the surgery. Vicky wanted you to know that if you needed a nurse she was volunteering. I told her that was my department."

"I'm going to be a cripple for a couple of weeks," Lori whispered, her eyes on the hovering nurse.

Briefly, Shade explained that he'd spent last night juggling his schedule so he could have the next two weeks off. Soon they'd work out a relationship that gave each of them an equal partnership. Right now, however, he sensed that she needed him to take charge. "I'll let you have your precious independence back when you're walking on your own two legs again," he promised. "Until then I'm the boss."

He waited for the reaction of the woman he loved. At length, a slight smile touched her tight lips. "Yes, boss," she whispered.

Shade helped Lori tuck her hair into the floppy white cap the nurse handed him and supported her shoulders as she was moved from her bed to the stretcher that would take her into the operating room. At that moment Lori reminded him of a baby wrapped in blankets in a hospital nursery, but he also knew that the child would soon become a woman again. A woman he wanted to share the rest of his life with.

"I'm going to be moving back into the house after we get this old war injury operated on," he promised her. "The doctor said you could probably come home the day after tomorrow."

"Home? Your house?"

Shade leaned forward, pushing the nurse aside with his bulk. The operating staff could wait a minute. There was something he had to say first. "Our house, Lori Black. Vicky wants me, us, to have it. By the way, when do you think you'd like to change that to Ryan?"

"Lori Ryan?" the woman Shade loved said. "Do you mean it?"

"Of course I mean it. Do I have to spell out everything for you?" Shade took a deep breath and decided to let everything out. "I'm willing to give you free rein in a lot of things, but I expect you to make an honest man out of me."

This time Lori's smile lasted longer, went deeper. "How about as soon as I can walk down an aisle?"

"That can be arranged. I'll talk to your boss, see if he'll let you have the time off."

The last of the tension in Lori's face evaporated. "That shouldn't be a problem. He's a good boss."

"He'll make an even better husband." As the nurse prepared to move Lori out of the room, Shade stepped aside. "Sorry, it's time for you to go. Behave yourself. I'll be waiting here when you get back."

Shade continued to stare at the door long after Lori had left, wondering if, even with the drugs, she knew how much of him she was taking along with her. Mentally, he was going with her, loaning her his strength, knowing he'd never get back all of his heart. That was all right—very much all right. Hearts were for sharing.

He could feel part of her heart lingering in the room with him.

That was the way Shade wanted it to be between them. They would always remain separate individuals. A healthy, loving marriage had to be that way. But although their interests might take them down different paths, there could always be that sharing of hearts. He would have a part of her with him while he was at the museum and she was out at the Kadin farm. She would keep a portion of his heart tucked in her pocket while she peered into a darkened barn looking for nesting owls.

At night their hearts would be joined back together, refashioned into a whole. In bed, with the window open to let in the pine-scented air they both loved, there would be a single beat.

Shade sighed, flexed his muscles and went out into the hallway to wait for Lori to be returned to him. Even as he was settling his body into an uncomfortable chair, his mind was going back—back to the early days when he was only half aware of the hold the woman was gaining on his heart. How close they'd come to not knowing the strength of that hold! If it hadn't been for Vicky's insisting that he come to see her yesterday—

No! Vicky didn't deserve credit for that. Even before his ex-wife had said anything, Shade had known that nothing could keep him from coming to see Lori.

Thank God for that. Soon, very soon, he'd be able to tell her that not once had he thought of giving her up.

Shade sent out his silent message. *I'm waiting, my love. Can you hear my heart talking to you? I'm waiting for you.*

Discover the new and unique

Harlequin Gothic and Regency Romance Specials!

Gothic Romance

DOUBLE MASQUERADE
Dulcie Hollyock

LEGACY OF RAVEN'S RISE
Helen B. Hicks

THE FOURTH LETTER
Alison Quinn

Regency Romance

TO CATCH AN EARL
Rosina Pyatt

TRAITOR'S HEIR
Jasmine Cresswell

MAN ABOUT TOWN
Toni Marsh Bruyere

A new and exciting world of romance reading

Harlequin Gothic and Regency Romance Specials!

You're invited to accept
4 books and a surprise gift *Free!*

Acceptance Card

Mail to: **Harlequin Reader Service®**

In the U.S.
2504 West Southern Ave.
Tempe, AZ 85282

In Canada
P.O. Box 2800, Postal Station A
5170 Yonge Street
Willowdale, Ontario M2N 6J3

YES! Please send me 4 free Harlequin American Romance® novels and my free surprise gift. Then send me 4 brand new novels as they come off the presses. Bill me at the low price of $2.25 each —an 11% saving off the retail price. There are no shipping, handling or other hidden costs. There is no minimum number of books I must purchase. I can always return a shipment and cancel at any time. Even if I never buy another book from Harlequin, the 4 free novels and the surprise gift are mine to keep forever.

154 BPA-BPGE

Name	(PLEASE PRINT)	
Address		Apt. No.
City	State/Prov.	Zip/Postal Code

This offer is limited to one order per household and not valid to present subscribers. Price is subject to change.   ACAR-SUB-1